"It's okay, Jacqueline. It's all over now."

Her face turned his way. It seemed like a tragic mask to Manley, lips turned downward in agony, eyes dulled with grief. But there was something else in her expression— terror, accompanied by an animal fear so intense he could almost smell it.

Abruptly, Jacqueline ripped her hand away from him and leaped to her feet. In a flash, she was beyond and into the hall, frantically running back to the kitchen.

"Jacqueline!"

He hurried after her and was soon staring in awe at the sight of Jacqueline rolling on the floor, clutching whatever food she could get her hands on. The kitchen was a mess, a battle zone. Shreds of fruit and vegetables littered the room; raw meats were piled in uneven rows and columns like ghastly marchers in a butcher's parade. In the center of it all, Jacqueline writhed on the floor, rapidly stuffing candy into her mouth without even removing the wrapping . . .

THE
OBSESSION

Avenue, New York,

PRINTED IN THE UNITED STATES OF AMERICA

O   0 9 8 7 6 5 4 3 2 1

Bantam Books by David Shobin

THE OBSESSION
THE SEEDING
THE UNBORN

BANTAM BOOKS
TORONTO • NEW YORK • LONDON • SYDNEY • AUCKLAND

THE OBSESSION

David Shobin

THE OBSESSION

A Bantam Book / March 1985

ISBN 0-553-24537-6

Published simultaneously in the United States and Canada

Bantam Books are published by Bantam Books, Inc. Its trademark,
consisting of the words "Bantam Books" and the portrayal of a
rooster, is Registered in U.S. Patent and Trademark Office and in
other countries. Marca Registrada. Bantam Books, Inc., 666 Fifth
~~~ ~~~ ~~~, New York 10103.

*To my parents
who fattened me with their love.*

PART ONE

February and March

Chapter One

"And I would have done it all over again. . . . If only we'd had more time!"

The grief-stricken young nurse, alone in her apartment at last, sat on her bed, holding the man's photo on her lap. She made no attempt to still the trembling of her hands or to stifle the quivering of her lips. "I promised myself I'd be brave. I thought I'd prepared myself for the pain! But now that he's gone, it all seems so . . . futile."

Suddenly, she clutched the picture to her breast and rocked slowly back and forth with it as she sobbed in agony.

Finally her tears ceased. The photo slid from her numb fingers. The expression on her face was a curious mixture of defeat and determination. Her eyes were muted, dull. It was as if nothing mattered any more. It was all behind her now. She turned to the night table and picked up the vial of pills, eyeing the date on the label. The prescription was nearly two years old. She doubted that was important; she would make up in quantity whatever she lacked in quality. She emptied the vial's contents into her palm. Out of the original fifty, forty-five of the red capsules remained.

"God . . . my doctor would kill me if he knew what I'm about to do."

The ludicrousness of the statement struck her. She threw her head back and roared—an exultant, strangely jubilant laugh. Then she widened her lips and poured the pills onto her tongue. She reached for the glass of water nearby, filled her mouth, and surprised herself by downing all the pills in one generous swallow.

"Not bad for a beginner."

She fell silent, lost in her thoughts. She got out of bed and slowly slipped out of her nurse's uniform, hanging it carefully in her closet.

"An 'A' for neatness." She laughed. "You always were compulsive."

Satisfied that her clothing was tidy, she sat before her vanity, clad only in her slip. She began to brush her long, glistening hair, taking a full five minutes, just as she had always done before she went to sleep. Finally, another abbreviated laugh—tipsy now, as the medication began to take effect. She somewhat clumsily returned to the bed, where she stretched out on her back. Her fingers strayed to the picture frame and rested there.

She was looking up at the ceiling. She found herself blinking, eyes bleary and filled with tears, until her lids simply became too heavy. She was floating.

"Good night, Allison," she told herself.

And then she closed her eyes forever.

"Fade . . . fade . . . cut!" Alan Hammill rose to his feet and clapped. "Splendid, Jackie. Splendid!"

The actress opened her eyes and swung her long legs over the side of the bed. The bright stage lights dimmed. There was a smattering of applause from around the set. The actress wrinkled her forehead and then gently rapped her knuckles against her chest. She coaxed forth a genteel burp.

"You sure those capsules were dummies, Alan?" she asked. "Or am I?"

"Pure gelatin. Unadulterated."

"More than I can say for my stomach."

She rubbed her abdomen and rose to don the bathrobe given her by the wardrobe clerk. The director approached and gently grasped her wrist, a gesture of appreciation.

"How did it feel?"

She threw him a curious look. "Swallowing a handful of pills? Or are you referring to dying?"

4

"Let's not be obtuse, darling. The scene. From my angle it looked super."

"Are you serious?"

"As always. But you're the actress. How did it feel?"

"Shambles. Complete shambles." In truth, she wasn't certain; yet something was bothering her. "I hope it convinced the viewers. I'm not sure it convinced me."

His jaw dropped in surprise. "You're joking."

She began to walk toward her dressing room. But after several paces she hesitated and turned back to him. The lines in her face softened, emerging as a smile.

"Yes, perhaps I am."

"Ah, Jack-O. . . . Now that school's out, pin the tail on the director, hmm? I might have known!"

What started as an expression of chagrin changed into a smile that slowly widened until he was beaming. He joined in the applause that accompanied her to her dressing room. Then Alan Hammill just stared at her shadow, hands clasped together, lost in thought.

She was marvelous, irreplaceable. True, he'd given his blessing when she asked to leave the show, but now. . . . Rocks in his head that day, Christ.

Her dressing room was emblazoned with a gaudy star, beneath which the name Jacqueline Ramsey was printed in large italic letters. She walked in and shut the door, annoyed at herself. Why hadn't she stopped to speak with those who were applauding her? It was going to be hard to leave them and the show. They had always been marvelous to her, from the director on down. She had never behaved like that before, and certainly not to Alan, who was an absolute dear.

Rather than dwell on it, she sat in front of her mirror and once again ran a brush through her shining hair, this time trying to remove residual flecks of sticky lacquer and to smooth out the curls and waves the hairdresser had molded earlier that morning. Then she saturated cotton balls with moisturizer and applied them to the artificial coloring on her cheeks.

She discarded the cotton and gazed at herself in the mirror, still perplexed. She had never been cavalier when

5

it came to compliments, generally accepting them with sincerity—at the very least, acknowledging them. Yet in the scene just completed—her last on the show—she had virtually disregarded every bit of flattery and applause directed her way.

Was being blasé her way of coping with the sadness and difficulty of saying farewell?

Jacqueline clucked her tongue, sniffing in amusement at her lame attempt at self-analysis. Honestly, now—that was something she really ought to save for Rick Manley. If anything, she thought, what was making her uptight was more likely his absence. He had just left, and she was missing him already. Damn those psychiatric conventions. She got up and sighed.

"Yah, ve vill have to discuss my furshtoonkin emotions ven you return, Dr. Manley."

She hesitated, then bit her lip. The explanation just didn't fit. Naturally she missed him, but. . . . She slumped into a nearby recliner, her robe falling open to expose a curve of slender thigh when she crossed one knee over the other. Absentmindedly, she drummed her fingers on the seat's armrest. Catching sight of what her hand was doing, she immediately balled it into a tight fist.

"For the love of God, already."

She leaned back and for the next few minutes ruminated without satisfaction. Honestly, now—what was wrong with her lately?

PMS, her internist had said. Just cut down on the salt, Miss Ramsey, stay away from caffeine, and here—try these samples. A few of these pills and you'll feel on top of the world. Give the office a call and I'll phone in a script to your pharmacy.

But she wasn't premenstrual; she *knew* that. And she'd be damned if she'd start pill popping without one hell of a good reason. And the more she thought about it, the more she concluded that it wasn't simply Rick's absence, either. She'd been feeling unaccountably tense for well over a week now—since days before he left.

It was a tenseness for which she had no explanation. On the contrary, considering everything that had been happening to her, she should have been feeling better than ever. Her relationship with Rick was more harmonious than she'd dared anticipate, given the diversity of their interests; her demise on *Hospice* promised to garner the highest ratings ever on what was already the most talked about soap opera on daytime TV; and her upcoming Broadway production was falling into place with no snags whatsoever. And if that weren't enough, she had just recently returned from one of her semiannual jaunts to the Spa at San Sebastian, an exclusive clinic whose treatments ordinarily left her feeling on top of the world. Thank God for that. If it hadn't been for the Spa. . . . It didn't take long to reply to her own conjecture.

"A big fat cipher, folks," she concluded in a low voice. "And you can underline the 'fat.' So, loyal soap fans, where does Jacqueline Ramsey go from here?" She paused long enough to sit up straight. "Enter the Great White Way."

She got up sluggishly, plucked a pin from her hair, and tossed it onto the vanity, where it caromed off the mirror. She turned to appraise her full-length reflection. "What do you think, Mother?" She slowly eyed herself from head to toe; then, more softly, "Am I thin enough for you yet? What'll it take to make you proud of me?" Her tone was jaundiced by an inflection of sarcasm. "Is a hot soap the ticket? No? Then how about a simply smashing Broadway debut?"

Jacqueline continued to concentrate on her reflected image, not so much fuming as glaring at it, until her obvious annoyance upset her still more. She whirled about. "Oh glom up, you petunia." She threw off the robe and marched to her wardrobe. "Dammit, Rick. I hate it when you're away." She pulled her jeans from a hanger. "Of all the times to go down the river and milk the fish."

Moments later she was dressed, encircling her neck with a scarf thick enough to keep a still frigid March at bay. Both the wool and thoughts of Manley served to warm her, to lessen her peculiar tension. Leaving her dressing room, she once again encountered stagehands as she was departing the studio. This time she behaved more like her

7

old self—the pleasant, appreciative Jacqueline Ramsey everyone knew so well. They coupled their disappointment about her leaving the show with wishes for continued success on the stage. Knew it all along, they said. Had to happen.

Outside it was brutally cold. She looked about for her driver until it struck her that she had no ride that night. She'd forgotten; her eyes rolled upward in disappointment. Of all the days for her limo to have a coronary—Christ!

Jacqueline stamped her feet to keep them warm. She searched the street for a cab, her breath trailing away in a frosty vapor. Nothing. Useless at rush hour, she thought. Dummy.

Fortunately, the studio wasn't far from a subway entrance. Jacqueline sifted through her handbag for the overly large sunglasses worn by those wishing to remain anonymous. Then she set off down the street, treading with military precision. She held her head high, and a smile deflected her lips as she thought about the present from Manley waiting for her at home. The day before he left he'd somehow conquered the cold to bring her a gift of a miniature mock orange. He had kept it under his overcoat to protect it from the wintry chill. She had kissed him with fervor and immediately set about administering to her newest charge.

Jacqueline's apartment was lush with plants of all kinds. She doted on them—softly cooing to them, gently tilling their potted soil with her manicured nail, and endlessly misting their foliage. Manley could never understand the extent of her devotion, given the incessant demands on her time. Nor could she understand how he, a doctor, was not more interested in the hobby than he was. After all, she had pointed out, horticulture and medicine had a lot in common. Plants responded to the same things people did: adequate nutrition, treatment of disease, clean air and water. But unlike people, they never complained if hurt, promptly paid their bills in blossoms and fruit, and didn't sue for malpractice. Furthermore, she was convinced, she could predict a young doctor's eventual specialty from the way he related to his plants.

8

"Orthopedists would stake the stems to make them grow straight," she contended.

"And surgeons?"

"Whittle away at bonsai and trim off surplus growth."

"Obstetricians?"

"Endlessly take cuttings to regenerate new clones."

"How about pathologists?"

She turned to him, raising one eyebrow in inquiry.

"What does a pathologist do?"

"Autopsies."

"Leave all the dead flowers, then. To wither and drop off."

He thought her lighthearted insights astute. He would have loved to continue their banter, but he had to prepare for his trip. Still, he had to ask one more question: that which pertained to him.

"What of psychiatrists?"

"Easiest of the lot," she replied. "They would simply stare at the leaves and listen."

"What if the leaves talked back?"

"They do talk back, silly," she said, kissing his passing cheek as he started for the bedroom to pack his baggage. "You're just too busy to hear them."

As she left the subway, Jacqueline was still smiling as she recalled their interchange. Arriving home, she was struck by how quiet her empty apartment was. She hung up her coat and scarf and apprehensively nibbled her underlip, starting to experience again the same edginess she'd felt earlier. She pressed her palms to her face—a peekaboo gesture—as if by hiding she might wipe away unwanted emotion. Nonsense, she concluded, immediately uncovering her face. There was nothing wrong at all. Except maybe loneliness.

She crossed into the kitchen and turned on its light, pursing her lips into a pout. This was getting ridiculous. The few months she'd known Rick were far too short a time to make her feel so hopelessly dependent. She pulled open the refrigerator door, glanced inside, and just as quickly closed it. She wasn't really hungry. She pivoted to the nearby wall phone and lifted its receiver, tilting her head to one side in contemplation. Sheila Hastings? she wondered. No, today was Friday; Sheila had acting class. She narrowed her eyes in concentration. Suzanne, she decided: maybe Suzanne Fontaine. After all, they'd started out in acting together. She could still see them on the Hollywood movie set. The take done, and as the film crew was reloading the camera, two preadolescent girls walked to the studio confectionary. Theirs was an awkward ambling, an uncoordinated swaying of hips, a gait later to be refined into smoother, more graceful strides. They spoke gibberish. Yet somehow it didn't seem to matter what they talked about; for although they were stars, they were school-age girls nonetheless, and as such entitled to the same endless, giggly prattle as their nonacting peers.

Jacqueline thumbed through her phone directory until she found the number. It was only four p.m. California time. Suzanne was a night owl who never emerged before eight; she had to be home. Jacqueline hurriedly dialed the number and waited. Twelve rings later, she hung up in disappointment and confusion.

Her lips flattened into a humorless smile. "Foiled again." Her mind sought refuge in subtlety, but she could no longer find it. "Hopeless," she intoned. "Utterly hopeless."

That left only her work, though it was that at which Jacqueline excelled. The script for her new play was in her bedroom, its pages still unmarked. She beelined across the carpet and was soon leafing through the looseleaf-bound first act.

Jacqueline scanned the script and soon developed the proper mind-set. The play called for an unusually early love scene. Somewhat capriciously, Jacqueline decided that she wanted to dress the part.

She slipped into a frilly night dress and plucked at its lacy pleats, surprised at the way they seemed to cling. She glided back to the living room. Script in hand, she stood at attention before her plants. Then she bowed to the floral assemblage with a radiant smile, giving them a knowing wink before she began her lines. Now serious, she led off the scene with a sweeping theatrical gesture of her arm, as if going through a doorway.

10

"I hope I'm not disturbing you. May I come in?" she said, effecting a facial expression that was at once both sunny yet timid. Then she paused, counting out the time for the silent reply. "I would have called," she went on, "but I know you despise that. I forced myself to be bold. Courage and a stiff upper lip and all that, like in those sherry commercials that never quite convince me. So here I am." She gazed longingly at her plants, hearing unspoken words in her mind. At precisely the right moment, she began walking slowly forward, fixing her sanguine stare on an African violet that was to be the recipient of her dramatic affections. "Darling, I—"

She abruptly stopped speaking, something the script did not call for. Her stage face was replaced by a look of concern as she peered at the plant's lavender flowers. When she touched its foliage, a faint cloud of fine dust rose into the air. She immediately concluded that the plant was infected by a malady known as gray mold.

Jacqueline was unnerved. Through her skill or luck, her plants had suffered neither pests nor disease. To her way of thinking, such afflictions were a reflection of indifference on the part of the gardener. Certainly she could not be accused of that: she purchased only the finest stock, inspected her charges regularly, kept their environment clean and well ventilated, and neither overwatered nor overfed them.

Quickly she removed the plant from the others. She carried it to the kitchen, holding it at arm's length as if it were carrion. She had no idea whom to approach for advice on treating it, or if she should even try. Suddenly, it all became too much for her: she unceremoniously dropped the plant in the garbage, flowerpot and all.

Still shaken, she whirled with a prowler's apprehension to stare through the window at the city's nighttime panorama. Yet its bustling familiarity did not calm her as she had hoped. For several moments she nibbled on her lower lip, watching a parade of distant taxis and unconsciously stretching the pleats of her nightgown where her breast met her arm.

"What is *wrong* with this thing?" She turned to peer at

11

the thin material as she grew aware of its uncomfortable snugness. "They should have realized that hot water would shrink it."

Suddenly, Jacqueline looked up, pale as hovering mist. An inadmissible thought occurred to her. She fled from the kitchen and retreated to her unlit bedroom, as if she could outrace the notion by mere speed of foot. There, she struggled out of her night dress, yanking its hem up and over her head in one uncoordinated movement. The silky fabric slipped from her stiff fingers and fell to the floor. Naked, Jacqueline just stood there, shaken and trembling, staring into the dark.

Chapter Two

"Well, then. Can you begin on Monday, February 4? I know it's short notice, but the position became vacant rather unexpectedly."

"Yes, Miss Howell," the young woman replied without hesitation. "What time should I arrive?"

"The Spa's morning nutritionist finishes work at two, so if you get here at one-thirty, you'll have an opportunity to go over the patients beforehand."

"I'd like that."

"Very good." The head nurse indicated her satisfaction by placing her palms on the desktop. Her lips widened into a tight, restrained smile as she arose from behind the desk. "Come. I'll show you around."

They left the small office and proceeded into the empty corridor beyond. Yet after several steps, the older woman's pace slowed and then stopped entirely.

"Before I forget, Miss Kessler—"

"You can call me Sally."

"Outside of the Spa, perhaps. But Dr. Hume accepts nothing less than absolute decorum at San Sebastian, and he prefers that members of the staff address one another by their surnames. It's very proper, don't you think?"

"We weren't into surnames at U.C.L.A.," Sally Kessler replied good-naturedly.

"No doubt. However, etiquette is essential here, especially in regard to our patients—whom we refer to as guests." Again, the thin smile. "I hope that won't prove a problem for you."

13

Sally knew there could be only one reply. "It won't, Miss Howell."

"Good. Now, concerning where you park: after entering the main gate, immediately bear left onto the small service road. Follow it to the staff parking lot, which is roughly two hundred yards behind the main building. It's surrounded by a superbly dense privet hedge. You can't miss it. Under no circumstances should you park the way you did today, in front of the building. That simply won't do."

"I get the point," she nodded. "Once I'm in the lot—is there a path that leads to the building?"

"No. There's a tunnel." Miss Howell resumed walking.

"A tunnel?"

"I realize that sounds odd, but Dr. Hume is concerned about our guests' privacy. He's really quite devoted to their comfort. He suggests that they not mingle with the staff. Not even see them, if possible. Unless of course in relation to a staff member's function. In fact he constructed all of San Sebastian with an eye toward privacy. Our guests often comment that they see so few personnel, they think the Spa abandoned. Yet it functions perfectly."

"How is that possible?"

"Strict scheduling, for one thing. It's all in the timing. Dr. Hume has a genius for that. Guest activities are so rigidly supervised that they literally have no time to wander. And then there's the building's architecture. Nothing short of unique, if you ask me. San Sebastian is a building within a building. For instance, this corridor," she said, gesturing broadly with her hand, "is used by staff only. To my knowledge no guest has ever entered it. Similarly, the guests have their own rooms and hallways, which are off limits to us."

"Secret chambers, hidden passageways?"

"Goodness, no!" the older woman scoffed. She hesitated before continuing. "And yet I must admit there are some areas which even I have never seen."

"Which are they?"

Miss Howell smiled to herself. "I like to think of them as the 'star chambers'—rooms reserved for Dr. Hume's most exclusive clients. They take up a separate wing. Dr. Hume personally supervises every aspect of their care. With the help of Vincent."

"Who's Vincent?"

"I'll introduce you soon. Oh, don't misunderstand me; there aren't many such rooms. Three, maybe four at the most. Here, follow me."

Miss Howell turned a corner and drew to a stop before a wall of floor-to-ceiling glass. Peering through it, Sally Kessler saw that she was looking down into a large exercise room one floor below, inside which three obviously overweight women were furiously pedaling on gleaming exercise bicycles, evenly lined up side by side. In a far corner, another woman was being instructed in the use of pulleys. Her supervisor was a stocky, powerfully built man who appeared to be in his forties. When he backed away from the apparatus, he did so with a limp.

"One-way mirror," said Miss Howell, lightly tapping the pane with satisfaction. "We can't be seen."

"Who's he?" Sally Kessler pointed.

"That is Vincent."

"I might have guessed."

"Beg your pardon?" said Miss Howell, looking at Kessler askance.

"Oh, nothing. What does he do?"

"His official title is chief orderly. He is also the exercise and weight-training instructor. Doubtless you can see why."

Sally stared at the man's biceps. "I get the general idea."

"You might call Vincent Dr. Hume's right-hand man, something of a jack of all trades. He also does various errands for Dr. Hume. Drives the guests to the airport or some such. A bit on the silent side, but really a dear man if you get to know him. He's the only person who's been here longer than I have."

"What happened to his leg?"

"He won't discuss it, so no one is certain. But rumor has it that it resulted from a gunshot wound."

"In the leg?"

Miss Howell tapped her skull. "To the head. Nasty scar behind his ear. I suppose that would make him a veteran, wouldn't it?"

Sally shrugged in uncertainty.

"Vincent vaguely hints that he would have died if it weren't for Dr. Hume. His implication is that he's lucky to be a cripple. Whatever the truth may be, Vincent is devoted to Dr. Hume." Her smile had a hint of pride. "Absolutely devoted."

Proceeding on, they rounded a corner and descended a narrow staircase that led to the ground floor. Miss Howell walked past the exercise area until she came to a round, porthole-sized pane of glass, through which she peered with caution.

"Empty," she announced, opening the door halfway to reveal the room beyond it.

Sally Kessler poked her head through the doorway and inspected the spacious, carpet-lined apartment of what appeared to be masseur's chambers. Unlike most of the Spa's interior—constructed of gleaming white marble spanned by massive stainless-steel joists—the walls of the massage room were paneled in the finest cedar. In its center was a single masseur's table of highly polished teak, while the room's corners housed hospital-sized whirlpool tubs—fashioned not from the customary steel, but from the most ornate onyx. The tub's legs were sculpted to resemble lion's paws, and its spigots arched with the graceful curvature of a swan's neck, all glinting of gold.

"There are separate doors at the rear for the steam bath and sauna," Miss Howell explained. "The type of massage is individualized to the needs of the patient and ranges from traditional Swedish style to deep myofascial therapy. All of the whirlpool treatments are based on the curative properties of seawater. Dr. Hume's research has shown that it is the most physiologic immersion possible. Marvelously beneficial."

"Where are all the patients?"

Miss Howell consulted her watch.

"Some may now be at lunch. Others are no doubt resting. We stagger their activities to avoid overlap and to give each guest the most personal attention possible. We accommodate no more than a dozen patients at any one time."

Sally's eyebrows arched. "That's all? How does the place make ends meet?"

Miss Howell bequeathed her most indulgent look.

"You needn't concern yourself about its solvency. San Sebastian is the most exclusive facility of its kind."

She made an abrupt about-face and continued through the immaculate white and silver corridors until they came to a sort of rotunda, in the center of which was a round formica table. Seated beside it was a woman dressed in a traditional nurse's uniform, sans cap. She finished making an entry in a chart and looked up as the two women approached.

"Good day, Miss Howell."

"Everything under control, Miss Phillips?"

"Yes, ma'am."

"Good. I'd like you to meet Miss Kessler," she said, turning her head and indicating with a nod. "She is replacing Miss Neal as evening-shift nutritionist. I've explained how we work as a team, and I assured her that all members of the staff will be happy to offer assistance during her transition. Wouldn't you agree?"

"Certainly, Miss Howell."

"Is Miss Fontaine resting comfortably?"

"Yes, until three p.m."

"Excellent." She turned to Kessler. "Right this way."

Soon they arrived at the dietician's office, a spartan cubbyhole of a room. There Sally was introduced to Miss MacMurray, the morning nutritionist. Unlike the two older women Kessler had thus far met, MacMurray appeared to be in her late twenties, little older than Sally herself. Sally felt an immediate sense of relief.

"When you finish reviewing nutritional policies," said the head nurse, "please show Miss Kessler back to my office."

"Yes, Miss Howell."

Miss Howell had scarcely begun her departure when she turned around again.

"Before I forget, Miss Kessler. Your outfit," she said, gesturing to the stylish white pants suit. "You do have an ordinary white uniform, don't you?"

17

"Yes, but—"

"See to it that you wear it on Monday. Dr. Hume prefers that the staff dress appropriately."

Then she turned and left, leaving a contrite Sally Kessler to fidget in silent discomfort. As the footsteps receded, MacMurray winked and waved her hand reassuringly.

"Don't worry," she whispered. "It looks great."

"And here I had it specially fitted."

"Don't take it personally. She's like that with everyone."

"I was beginning to wonder."

"Coffee?"

Sally was surprised; Howell had told her that coffee breaks weren't permitted during working hours. "I thought that—"

"I know, I know," said MacMurray, putting her finger to her lips to indicate quiet as she tiptoed to her door and closed it. Hurrying back to her desk, she removed a small hotplate from the lowermost drawer and placed a coffeepot atop it. "I have instant or tea. Or are you decaf?"

Sally relaxed and sighed, her sense of uneasiness allayed.

"Tea, thanks. Is it really that strict around here?"

"Tight as the proverbial drum." She plugged the hotplate's cord into a socket. "And before you ask, it's Alice." She extended her arm in greeting.

Sally took her hand and gratefully reintroduced herself. "You'll leave me a list of whom to salute?"

"Sure," Alice grinned. "It's a snap. Not many employees here."

"So I noticed. The place looks empty."

"Small staff, few patients." She held up a thumb and forefinger and rubbed them together. "But all with heaps of money."

"Dr. Hume must do pretty well for himself."

"You'd better believe it. Did you meet him?"

"Not yet. Anything like Miss Howell?"

"God, no. And don't jump to conclusions before you do. The man may have some quirks when it comes to how the place is run, but I'll tell you one thing: he certainly gets results."

"With the patients?"

18

MacMurray nodded. "Right. To them he's a miracle worker." She slowly shook her head. "Honestly, I'm not sure how he does it. I mean, I *know* the basics of the two-week treatment, but I'm always amazed how much they actually lose. Maybe it's his personality."

"He scares the pounds off?"

MacMurray duly grinned. "Just the opposite. More likely charms them away like a piper. For a doctor, he has a fantastic personality. At least compared to the other doctors I've known. And not bad looking, either. Sort of a Rossano Brazzi with straight hair."

"Who?"

"Terrif—you *are* young." The water began to boil as MacMurray selected a handful of charts and checked her watch. "Don't have much time now. But let's try to go over some of this stuff so we won't have that much to do when you start next week."

The following Monday, after encountering an unexpected midday traffic jam, Sally arrived at the Spa at two p.m. sharp. Alice MacMurray regretted that she had an urgent appointment to keep; after promising to review the charts with Sally the next day, she gave her a cheerful thumbs-up sign and hastily departed. Sally sighed and slowly sat down at the desk, loosing an utterance that rang more of lament than enthusiasm: "Here goes, coach."

There were sixteen charts in the rack, although the last three were empty. Each of the filled charts corresponded to an individual patient. Twelve were in ordinary hospital folders, but the thirteenth—like the three empties behind it—was contained in a lightweight metal housing Sally guessed was aluminum but later discovered to be platinum. She gave it a dubious stare.

"Star chambers my arse," she murmured. She decided to save the thirteenth for last.

Just follow Dr. Hume's written orders, Alice had said. Okay, Sally thought, forcing an indifferent shrug. If these are the cards they deal me, these are the cards I'll play.

After their introduction several days before, MacMurray had explained how astonishingly simple their job was. The individual dietary orders signed by Dr. Hume listed the number of calories each patient was to consume, further dividing that amount into percentages of fat, protein, and carbohydrate. All the nutritionist had to do was make selections from the fare the chef prepared daily, matching entree content and size of portion to the caloric regimen allotted.

There was need for neither the creative dietary planning nor the individualized patient instruction Kessler had had to master as a prerequisite for her degree. Undemanding though her task was, the job paid remarkably well—twice what someone with her lack of experience would ordinarily command.

She had slowly worked her way through the first dozen charts, performing what amounted to the most fundamental of meal calculations, and growing increasingly bored in the process. That done, she opened the thirteenth metal folder.

Like most medical charts, the first page was a face sheet containing demographic data that pertained to the patient. Unlike the twelve previous patient names—all of which were unfamiliar—the thirteenth made Sally's eyes widen in fascination.

Could it be? she wondered. Could Suzanne Fontaine— the vocalist idolized by Kessler, not to mention half of America—actually be a patient at the Spa? Here, now— indirectly under her dietary care? She scanned the face sheet for the box marked "Vocation." Her pulse quickened when she saw the words singer/entertainer typewritten therein. A smile of anticipation spread across her face, and her mind began a frantic search for the right words to say when they met.

With little else for her to do, the fantasy consumed the better part of the next hour. Sally only dimly recalled Miss Howell's admonition about mingling with the guests, relegating it to that corner of her brain reserved for annoying incidentals.

After endlessly rehearsing the utterly clever words she planned to say, Sally Kessler temporarily abandoned her daydream for the more mundane considerations of her job.

She leafed through the chart until she found the doctor's order sheet.

At first she read the order quickly, barely glancing at it. But then she went over it more closely and even had to scrutinize it a third time, letter by letter, before her mind permitted it to register.

Thirty-five hundred calories? Impossible. The amount was an absurdity for someone of Fontaine's height and weight, especially if that person were intended either to lose weight or to maintain it. What's more, the order called for eighty percent of the calories to come from carbohydrates. At best, the order was a simple mistake; at worst, sheer nonsense.

She pushed herself away from her desk and carried the chart into the hall. It was well after five, and the patients were scheduled to dine at seven. She followed the corridor to the circular rotunda, where she found the evening charge nurse seated at her desk. After introducing herself, Sally opened the chart and indicated the entry.

"I really wouldn't know," the nurse commented, giving her head a noncommittal shake.

"But just to maintain her weight she shouldn't need more than twenty-two hundred, tops. Right?"

"I honestly can't say. All I know is that I've seen Dr. Hume order amounts like that before."

"Yes, but—"

"And it *is* his clinic. Why rock the boat? Just do the calculation and don't let it bother you."

How odd, Sally thought. "Doesn't something about it strike you as peculiar?"

The nurse put down her work and folded her hands. She eyed the newcomer's name tag.

"Look, Miss . . . Kessler," she began. "Did it ever occur to you that things which are unusual in a normal hospital might be perfectly acceptable at San Sebastian? It's all part of the Spa's uniqueness. Dr. Hume is a genius at what he does."

"But don't you think I should notify him? I mean, the man is human. Maybe it's a mistake. We all have our bad days."

"Dr. Hume has standing orders not to be notified unless it's a life-threatening emergency. If you have a question, just jot it down. Send him a memo. That's what I'd do."

The reply made Kessler even more confused. She hesitated, not sure whether she should pursue the issue. But then she decided to persist.

"I don't get it. Isn't the patient's welfare supposed to take precedence over disturbing the doctor?"

The nurse's face wrinkled with the hint of a frown, an expression suggesting the remark was impertinent. Then she looked away and gazed at a far wall.

"What I like most about this job," she said in an offhand tone, "is the pay. Fantastic. I've got three kids to feed. I do what I'm told—I listen to orders, I follow regulations. I'm happy, the patients are happy. I've never had a serious complaint yet." She looked down at her nails, pushing back a cuticle. "So as far as I'm concerned, you can take all that high-powered nutritional advice they teach at the university and just file it away. That's the very same thing I told Miss Neal. She had an inquiring mind, too." She turned back to Kessler, her look an unwavering stare. "If you get my drift, Miss Kessler."

As they were talking, there had been the sound of approaching wheels, the muted rhythm of rubber trundling across the marble. Sally turned and saw Vincent pushing a stretcher, atop which a woman lay supine, her face swaddled with towels.

For the briefest moment, Sally's mind was tantalized by the thought that the woman might be Suzanne Fontaine. Yet before she had an opportunity to dwell on it, the entirety of her consciousness was drawn to a third individual—the man who led the processional.

The way he so completely captured her attention made Sally sure that the man was Dr. Hume, though Alice MacMurray's blandly flattering description had done nothing to prepare Sally for his physical aura. He wore a tailored suit of exquisite white linen. The bronze tone of his tanned skin contrasted sharply with the pale blue of his shirt—a hue that perfectly matched the color of his eyes, lacking only their sparkle. His straight black hair, streaked with gray, was carefully combed. Most extraordinary of all was his mouth, the two perfect rows of white teeth now smiling *her* way, Sally thought, in welcome.

"I'm glad Miss Kessler is so interested in nutrition," he said, in a delayed response to the nurse's observation. His deep voice had a tone of sincere cordiality. He reached out and gently grasped Sally's wrists, holding her eyes with his penetrating stare. "That is why I hired her."

Her mind flirted with all manner of rejoinder, but her thought processes were strangely awkward and clumsy, confounded by his charm and good looks. And so she stood there, saying nothing.

"I understand your predicament," he softly began. "And I sympathize with it fully. Did Miss Howell tell you that I once taught nutrition on the graduate level?"

She flustered, beginning to feel like a fool. "No."

He released her hands and began making a slow circle around her.

"That truly seems like decades ago. The science of nutrition was in the Stone Age then." He paused, touching a forefinger to his lips. "A fine school, UCLA. Is Professor Fulbright still chairman?"

"Why, yes," she replied, aware of how artless her voice sounded.

"Clever fellow. Brilliant, actually. He and I have shared countless thoughts over the years." He had come full circle and now stopped, facing her. "But just as we exchanged ideas, so did we have our disagreements. Oh, nothing drastic. Silly little issues, mostly—although we did vary on one fundamental principle. Understandable, of course. The academic world does tend to be rather inflexible."

He took her by the elbow and steered her aside, a few steps from the others. He leaned slightly closer when he spoke, as if sharing a confidence.

"It is those principles which are at the very heart of our success here at San Sebastian. And in time, you shall come to understand them. On that I give you my word, my sincere promise. As for the present, please try to accept the unusual for what it is: a special solution to a special problem."

"But only for special patients," she blurted, surprising herself with her candor.

He hesitated and then smiled, giving his head a considerate nod. "True." He gently wagged a finger at her. "You have a fine mind indeed." His finger slithered forward to seal her lips. "But not too fine, I hope." For a moment he stared at her in emphasis before looking at his watch. "Alas. Never enough time. We shall continue another day." He turned and issued a terse command to the orderly. "Vincent, take Miss Fontaine to her room. Good day, ladies."

With that, he walked briskly away.

Sally Kessler was dumbfounded. Caught between Dr. Hume's confidences and his sudden revelation of the Fontaine name, she stared in open-mouthed astonishment as the gurney bearing Suzanne Fontaine was wheeled past and out of sight. Sally was momentarily torn between her desire and her duty, but she docilely returned to her office.

She found it hard to resume her work. Despite Dr. Hume's allusion to certain principles, she was still nagged by the apparent illogic of the Fontaine diet. Sally sincerely wanted to trust, to be obedient, but her scientific training interfered with her ability to act on blind faith alone. Similarly perplexing was the charge nurse's indifference to Sally's legitimate questions. Did other staff members share the same attitude? With a shrug, she set about completing the dietary calculations.

The job was, as MacMurray had implied, ridiculously easy. By nine p.m., having completed working on the breakfast menus, Sally Kessler had largely forgotten her befuddlement and begun to concentrate on her boredom. There was little to do except read various texts, and no one to speak with. And then, of course, there was Suzanne Fontaine.

Sally felt a shiver of excitement. Here, she thought, at the Spa. Somewhere within these very walls.

A grin spread across her face. She closed the book she couldn't quite concentrate on, got up, and stretched. Her legs were stiff; she needed a walk. Just a little stroll, she told herself. Get acquainted with the place. And if by some miracle she should happen to meet Suzanne Fontaine. . . . Her smile widened. As she left her room, she was reminded of Miss Howell's instructions. But good God, she reasoned—this was a clinic, not Fort Knox.

Walking quietly, she crept into the corridor and proceeded in the direction the orderly had wheeled the stretcher. She walked on the balls of her feet. With each passing step, she was becoming aware of characteristics that distinguished San Sebastian from the other medical facilities she'd encountered.

The first was its peculiar configuration. Miss Howell had referred to it as a building within a building, but to Sally it seemed like a veritable maze. The interconnecting halls were wide enough and satisfactorily illuminated, but they were surprisingly short, having numerous turns and bends.

The second was the Spa's exceptional quietness, a quality which was making her increasingly uncomfortable. To be sure, it was night, and the patients slept. She was aware that the night shift in any medical facility could prove an unnerving span of time. Though Sally knew full well that San Sebastian was not a hospital in the traditional sense, it was a medical establishment nonetheless; and as such it was invested with that same nocturnal foreboding she had come to associate with medicine at midnight. With the hospital's public address system silenced and its overhead lights dimmed, the acrid odors of camphor, formaldehyde, and alcohol that drifted through the halls seemed to become a bit more pungent; and with its corridors darkened, the pervasive sense of illness and disease became disconcertingly prominent. Given the thick and hovering decay that defined a hospital's darkest hours, sound of any sort was perceived as a welcome intrusion.

But the Spa was not merely quiet, it was virtually silent. The deep and icy soundlessness was downright eerie. To make matters worse, she thought she was getting lost.

Rounding another bend, she came to a T-shaped intersection of corridors. She saw that she had come full circle.

25

To the right was the rotunda and its nursing station; to the left, another vacant hallway. She chose the latter.

Seconds later, what she saw made her trepidation disappear.

Before her stood a door whose silvery color matched the gleaming platinum of Suzanne Fontaine's chart.

She eased the door open. She stole on tiptoe through the short entryway, at the end of which was another door of similar hue. Sally's eyes widened in anticipation. The only sound was the nearly imperceptible scuffing of her shoes on the marble floor. Her heart was racing as one last time she practiced the apologetic tone of her well-rehearsed words: I'm so sorry, Miss Fontaine, I just happened to—

The hands were a pair of ragged claws that clamped onto her shoulders. Scared witless, Sally Kessler would have jumped if she had been able, but she was so nearly immobilized that all she could manage was a terrified gasp. Her head whipped around in a reflex of animal fear, until her eyes met those of her assailant.

It was Vincent. In that moment of recognition, the frightful pounding of her heart eased, and Sally willed herself to relax. She was silent, waiting for him to speak. Yet he replied to her muteness with a stony silence of his own, holding her tight as his gaze bored through her.

"Please." She winced. "You're hurting me."

Though he spoke without bitterness, his tone was recriminatory. "Where are you going?"

"My shoulders." She grimaced. "For Heaven's sake, let me go."

He slowly released his grip, not taking his eyes off her. Regaining her composure, she rubbed her shoulders and stared at him defiantly.

"You could've broken my arms."

He ignored her observation. "Didn't Miss Howell tell you to remain in your office?"

"I was taking a walk. Just a simple walk. Looking around, you know? First day on the job."

"Take walks on your own time. Not Dr. Hume's. And we don't look around at San Sebastian."

"For God's sake, why does everyone sound like there's something to hide around here?"

She was surprised by her petulant tone, annoyed at it, even. For although his expression seemed calm, she sensed that he could easily be provoked into striking her. She instinctively knew that Miss Howell had been right: the man would indeed do anything for Dr. Hume.

"Dr. Hume doesn't appreciate that sort of question. Go back to your office."

"Look. Can I talk to him?" She was watching him closely, all her senses taut. "One of his patients—"

She saw the movement of his arm and reacted instantly, leaping a full step backward before he could seize her again. "All right, already. You made your point. I'm going. You don't have to break my damn wrist, for Christ's sake."

He watched as she slowly retreated down the corridor, never once releasing her from his stare. She made one last stab at impudence as she rounded the corner.

"Harassment's illegal, you know. Job discrimination." Then, less certainly, "At least that's what they taught at UCLA."

In fact, he didn't know—the thought had never even occurred to him. To Vincent, all that mattered was that his employer's dictates were followed to the letter.

To Sally Kessler, however, such blatant persecution must be reported. Which is precisely what she did the following morning, both to the state attorney general's office and to Miss Howell.

Two days later, she was once again visiting the UCLA job procurement counselor, trying to explain how patently unfair it was for her to have been peremptorily dismissed without any explanation.

Chapter Three

What had happened to her strength? Suzanne Fontaine wondered. She climbed out of the California Spa's heated indoor pool and stood breathlessly on the coping, shaking the water free from the thick tassle of her blond hair. As usual, Dr. Hume had instructed her to swim alone. On every previous visit to San Sebastian, she had swum for hours. Yet today she had scarcely swum four laps when, unaccountably winded, she was forced to stop.

Had she picked up a virus? Fatigued, she stood there limply, chin on chest, letting the warm rays of the February sun that streamed through the skylights knead the knots out of the muscles of her back and shoulders.

She threw a towel around her tanned neck. Plodding out of the pool enclosure, she followed the narrow passage that led to the adjoining sauna. Occasional droplets of water marked a path that trailed her across the marble floor. As she walked, she self-consciously thumbed the elastic of her sleek maillot down over the briefest exposure of her buttocks. God, the damn thing didn't seem to fit any more. Had she actually shelled out seven hundred bucks for a custom suit just to have it ride up like cheap nylon?

In the cedar-lined sauna, no sooner had she settled onto a wooden bench than she wriggled and shot up again, giving a loosening tug to the edges of material that creased her groin. It was no use; even with the soothing heat, she still felt uncomfortable. She would simply have to change. Yet despite her willingness to blame the ill fit of the swimsuit for her discomfort, the back of her mind harbored the inadmissible thought that the flaw lay not with the tailoring but with herself.

She pressed a buzzer to summon the orderly who always accompanied her. Moments later, he dropped her off in her bedroom and closed the door. Inside her quarters, the most direct route to the bathroom wound past an antique tea wagon that rested at the foot of her bed. Among the items atop it was a neatly folded Los Angeles newspaper, beside which was a porcelain bowl that was filled with precisely the four ounces of dried fruit and high-protein seeds Dr. Hume referred to as "health mix," part of her daily diet. Suzanne's gaze fell on the crockery, and she sensed her pulse rate soar frighteningly.

She quickly looked away and made a circuitous detour around the wagon. Since her arrival at the Spa a week before, there had been something peculiar about the sight of food—any food—that tempted her unbearably. She was becoming positively mortified by it. In the past, she had never had any trouble adhering to the diet prescribed for her. Call it motivation: however appealing other foods might be, she never had the slightest temptation to stray from her dietary routine.

Now, though, she had begun to suffer pangs of hunger sharper than any she'd felt in years, since the days of obesity that defined her young adulthood. Even more appalling was the fact that they weren't really pangs at all, but a more sinister craving—a terrifying compulsion to eat it all, to cram her cheeks in that nervous, nimble-fingered drive of the truly starving.

She quickened her pace and shut her eyes, biting her lip to make the image disappear, not really relaxing until she reached the confines of the bathroom. Although she had no proof, she was beginning to think that her change in appetite was in some way related to her arrival at the Spa. It was something she would definitely have to discuss with Dr. Hume. With *anyone*, for that matter.

After changing into a robe, she retrieved the newspaper and stretched out on her bed. Out of habit, she automatically turned to the entertainment section, where she was surprised to see her name headlined in the lead article.

Beneath it was a lengthy piece of dubious journalism she would nonetheless have to review. But before she could begin, she was distracted by a familiar face in a photo midway down the page.

She smiled, adrift in a flood of memories. The photo of Jacqueline Ramsey was a good one; she looked gorgeous, as usual. And what is my darling up to now? Suzanne thought. She read through the article hastily, breaking into hearty laughter at one point, laughter that bespoke fond reminiscence. Then she reread the piece more slowly, the laughter bringing tears to her eyes. God, she'd known Jacqueline so well. . . . She could just picture Jacqueline's indignation at what had been printed.

"Oh, Jack, you sweet dummy. You are positively scandalous," she said in a tone of soft consolation, gently stroking the photo as one might caress a pet animal. "Serves you right for being so accommodating." Then, more faintly, "We never dreamed it would come to this, did we?"

She leaned back on the bed, dabbing the moisture from her eyes. She sighed, not quite ready to tackle the article dealing with her, when there came a knock at the door.

Suzanne sat up, puzzled. Although she didn't wear a watch, she knew it was approximately four p.m.—a time she was ordinarily supposed to spend resting, undisturbed. She debated ignoring it. Yet after another knock, she pushed herself out of bed and tiptoed across the carpet, wearing a look that was part perplexed, part indifferent. The instant she opened the door, however, her expression changed to one of delight. It was Dr. Hume. Suzanne smiled and drank in the rich baritone of his greeting.

"I hope you are not offended by this little liberty I have taken with your daily routine."

"No, not at all," she quickly reassured him. She paused to allow him to continue, but he didn't. "Is there something wrong?" she asked. She felt a sudden apprehension, reacting to it with a verbal spasm—rushed words tinged with forced laughter. "I mean, you're not canceling our dinner tonight, are you? Flying away to one of those medical conventions I always wondered about?"

"Nothing of the kind. I trust you have not overlooked that we dine precisely at seven?"

"Are you joking?" she said, touching her bosom with her hand. In truth, she was not terribly keen about the meal; but the thought of his being unavailable nearly put her into a panic. She sighed with audible relief. "I'd sooner cut off my right arm."

Again, his smooth and charming laughter.

"No need for such drastic measures, I assure you." He took a deep breath, as if preparing for a lengthy exposition. "Suzanne—" he began, then stopped unexpectedly.

She cocked her head to one side, a posture of uncertainty. "Yes?"

"There is something I would like to discuss with you when we dine. A small matter, to be sure. I only mention it now to allow you to give it some thought prior to our negotiations."

She wasn't sure she heard him right.

"Did you say negotiations?"

He waved his hand in the air. "An insignificant business transaction, actually. It's fairly straightforward, and all I require is your signature. I shall elaborate on it a bit later: in essence, I have come to the conclusion that the time has arrived to discuss a redistribution of your assets."

Suzanne thought that over the years she had become accustomed to his verbose way of speaking; yet what in the world was he talking about now?

"I'm sure you're making perfect sense, but for some reason I don't follow you."

"No need to trouble yourself with the mundane details." He laughed. "As for now, simply continue to concentrate on your magnificent singing without dwelling on the fine print of our merger."

"*Merger?*"

His reply didn't skip a beat.

"You incorporated your talent not long ago, did you not, Suzanne? Formed what is known as a personal holding company, with 200 shares of common stock outstanding, of which you are the sole officer, proprietor, and shareholder?"

"Yes, but how did you—?"

"It is a matter of public record," he replied. "I make it my business to keep abreast of all aspects of my patients' lives, so as to be aware of everything that might affect their welfare."

"I see," she said, not really seeing at all. "But what was that you said about a merger?"

"Dearest Suzanne, *do* leave the annoying minutiae to me. I can more properly do justice to a summary of this transaction later, after you are more relaxed, unencumbered by the pressures of day-to-day life outside San Sebastian. These can be subtle but destructive pressures, though they are pressures which—I regretfully add—are already exacting a pronounced effect on your psyche. By transferring all your stock to me, you will significantly diminish that troublesome burden."

Her mind spun, so totally unprepared was she for what he glibly made seem the most casual of proposals. Yet she could barely grasp the concept, much less the staggering implications. She struggled for the right words.

"My stock? You want all 200 shares of my stock?"

His tone was sympathetic, even reassuring in its paternal way.

"Dear Suzanne, do not try to comprehend all this prior to this evening. I fear you already misunderstand the little I have said. As for myself, I need nothing. It is not *I* who wants. It is *you*. Though you are not consciously aware of it, you desperately want to defuse the tensions caused by your business dealings. I thoroughly concur with that subconscious assessment—and I am bound, both medically and ethically, to honor your wishes. In fact I venture to say that continuation of your treatment here is contingent upon your acquiescence in this matter."

Her heart turned to gel, a quivering aspic that swelled chillingly in her chest. The mere thought that he might interrupt her treatments was enough to make her legs tremble. She was convinced that without her therapy at the Spa, she would revert to that obese forerunner of her present self, the sowlike creature she had been before the remarkable metamorphosis that eventually enabled her to rise to stardom. For his orchestration of that transformation, she adored him and would be eternally grateful, forever mindful of his admonishment to return to the Spa twice yearly.

Yet, stock? Her success as a vocalist, both musically and financially, was something she had achieved alone. Although she was thankful to him, her success was not something she could simply give away. Yet in the few years she had known him—revered him, followed his instructions to the letter—she had never known him to lead her astray. True, what he was now suggesting had the blatant hallmarks of a bribe. But was he right, perhaps? Could the vague and unsettling anxiety she'd been experiencing be somehow related to the financial pressures that accompanied her ascent to celebrity? Her reply was subdued.

"I honestly don't know what to say. But if you think it best. . . . Naturally, I'll have to talk it over with my accountant."

"That is something I must forbid. You must decide tonight."

She was stunned by the sternness of his reply. *Forbid?* Who was he to forbid her anything? She became a soldier out of step, disoriented and confused. Her voice modulated in an attempt at apologetic persuasion.

"You can't expect me to make this decision alone. I pay people to decide these things for me, people that I trust, that—"

"You need trust only me, Suzanne. It is for the best. Until seven, then."

He softly closed the door and was gone.

Dazed, Suzanne stood there for several moments before she returned to the bed, onto which she collapsed. Yet despite her outward appearance, her mind was a frenzy of disconnected thoughts. She was busily calculating her financial net worth, pondering the implications of entrusting someone with all of what it had taken her years to achieve.

She could make no sense of it. She desperately wanted to speak with someone—not only to verbalize her fears, but also for reassurance and support. She had business associates too numerous to count, chums and buddies galore;

but now she longed for that true friend, someone in whom she could confide, in the manner in which she had been able to let her heart out to Jacqueline in her youth. Although they were separated by years and miles, Jacqueline was the one person who might really understand, having shared the torment and turmoil of their childhood together.

Yet she had no such friend at San Sebastian, and calls to and from the Spa were prohibited. Even if she'd been permitted to call, Suzanne thought, what would she tell Jackie? Jackie knew Dr. Hume as well as she did—had even introduced Suzanne to the Spa. She would never believe this.

Honestly, she consoled herself moments later: she probably hadn't heard him right. She must have been mistaken; no one would make such an outrageous demand. A merger—well, maybe. Certainly, she reasoned, she owed him that much. Her indebtedness was something that transcended mere dollars and cents. And thus she mentally passed the next several hours, vacillating between rationalization and disbelief.

Shortly after seven, they dined alone on the Spa's private terrace. While the first course of melon was being served, he remarked how splendidly she had done since first coming to the Spa. And then, in smooth and polished tones delivered so casually that he might have been commenting on the weather, he outlined a plan that would grant him complete and absolute control of her business holdings. In a word, whatever would henceforth accrue to Suzanne Fontaine was to be his and his alone—allowing her a reasonable percentage, of course.

Her fingers turned to ice. She now knew there was no chance that he was joking. His blue eyes reflected the steely, matter-of-fact glint of ultimatum.

"I'm sure you find yourself able to agree to this, Suzanne. There is nothing more tiresome than unnecessary bartering."

"I can believe that," she replied, trying to remain calm. She wiped her dry lips with the back of her wrist.

He paused, giving her an opportunity to continue, but she refused to take it. "Well, Suzanne? I await your decision."

"I realize."

He gave a sigh of patient deliberation.

"Let's not play cat and mouse, shall we? All I require is a simple yes or no."

"But it's not fair!" she shot, her gamesmanship suddenly gone as she stabbed an outraged finger defiantly toward him.

"Fair? And just what is fair, Suzanne? Obesity and failure—are they fair? And what of success and stardom? You are, after all, my creation. Without what I have done, all those awards you treasure—the Grammies, the gold records and platinum albums too numerous to count—would never have been yours. So let's not talk of fairness. Fairness is not the issue here at all."

"But you're talking about all I represent, everything I've worked for! Do you expect me to hand it all over just like that, one two three, when it's taken me—"

"*Do* be realistic," he interrupted, smoothly folding his napkin. "You are forgetting your sense of priorities. It would be foolish to overemphasize simple business matters at the expense of one's physical image."

"You're not even listening. I haven't finished!" She felt the tears coming, and she tried to suppress them while she looked slightly beyond him, as if peering at a distant horizon. "Oh for God's sake, what's the use. You have absolutely no feeling for my feelings at all."

"Do I take that as a negative reply?"

"I *can't*, I tell you. I won't!"

His slow exhalation was the essence of strained remorse. "Very well, then. But I must inform you that there may be certain . . . consequences . . . to your decision. No doubt you have already begun to notice them."

She instantly felt cold.

"I don't know what you're talking about."

"Little things, to be sure," he explained. "Inconsequential to most people. The strange way a swimsuit might no longer fit, for example. Or a peculiar attitude toward something as simple as food."

It was still the same face, her face; but it suddenly seemed much older, as if she had aged ten years all at

35

once, her skin a sallow, leathery texture. Her voice weakened to a whisper.

"You're just inventing that."

"Am I? We'll find out about that, won't—"

It was she who broke off the conversation, horrified by his implication, leaping to her feet and running back to her room. She slammed the door behind her and breathed heavily, trying without success to deny her abject fear. For long seconds she just stood there, all muteness and marble—able only to stare.

Chapter Four

Central Park South was a boulevard not known for its professional offices. It was a primarily residential street whose impressive northward view looked out upon hundreds of acres of park space in the interior of Manhattan. This was not to say that such offices didn't exist; indeed, it was in one such hidden vestibule that Dr. Richard Manley had set up shop. Perhaps the choice of location was a reflection of his character. It had never been his nature to follow the crowd, as might have been suggested by an address in Doctor's Row on Park Avenue. But then, perhaps it was also an indication that he was not terribly keen about his work, for although he excelled at the clinical aspect of his specialty—psychiatry—he found it much too mundane to keep him mentally stimulated and professionally satisfied.

He might have abandoned the field entirely, had he not become fascinated, during his residency, with basic research. Experimental investigation was necessarily limited, since its medium was the mind, not the test tube; yet ongoing research was necessary in organic psychiatry—that aspect which dealt with the role of physical and metabolic disorders in the genesis of mental aberration. Early on, he'd received a sizable grant from the National Institute of Arthritis and Metabolic Diseases, a division of the National Institutes of Health. NIAMD was interested in establishing protocols for studies on the psychological underpinnings of metabolic diseases, many of which had a component of obesity. It was precisely this area that held such intrigue for Manley. His credentials were perfect; thus he'd been awarded the grant. Over the next few years, he developed considerable expertise in the field of metabolism—knowledge that perfectly complemented his psychiatric abilities. Thus, when his office sessions were over, he enthusiastically returned to his studies at the university.

Still, his research appointment paid next to nothing; it was the more lucrative private practice that enabled him to pay the bills. By sheer luck, one of his first referrals had been a rather trendy, well-to-do woman with a penchant for gossip. Her word of mouth helped his small and limited practice grow to acceptable proportions, one which seemed all the more enviable in that his clientele were generally considered to be among the city's most monied and exclusive individuals. He soon observed that they seemed to have a universal complaint: boredom.

Manley's professional personality was a perfect mate to his patients' common neuroses. He listened intently and spoke almost never. It was not unusual for whole days to pass without his uttering a word, other than to indicate the start and finish of each session. Observing him, one might think him insensitive; in fact, he cared deeply for those who sought his care, but he also understood that there was little his select group of patients either needed or wanted other than to use him as a sounding board. In that, he was happy to accommodate them. His prescription for professional success was minimal talk, virtually no intervention, a ban on unsolicited advice, and absolutely no involvement.

Now, however, he was very much involved, although not with a patient: he was far too principled for that. He'd had ample time to think about that involvement during this psychiatric convention, for in the midst of a lecture, images of Jacqueline had wandered through his mind and disturbed his concentration. Now, for the first time— physically separated from her as he was—Manley admitted to himself how deeply he loved her.

He was surprised how the confession contented him. When he returned his concentration to the lecture, it seemed unimportant that Jacqueline was interrupting his train of thought, for he understood the topic quite well. What he understood far less was Jacqueline: her moods, her perspectives. Every time he came to conclude that he at last knew her reasonably well, she would surprise him with some whimsical statement or action. That was simply the way she was: endearing, confusing, but adorable.

Except, he thought, when it came to her weight. Her behavior in that regard was an obsession. Nothing underscored her attitude toward her self-image more than what had occurred when they had dined with Jacqueline's mother.

It had been more his suggestion than hers, though in the end her initially indifferent acquiescence changed to lukewarm anticipation. Partly, Manley had suggested the three way get-together because he was perplexed by Jacqueline's ongoing ambivalence toward her mother—a vacillation in which her words ping-ponged back and forth, at one moment admiringly devotional, at another clouded with overtones of resentment. Whatever the explanation, if he wanted to get to know Jacqueline more closely—which he was pleasantly surprised to admit that he did—he had to understand more about the ticking of her psychological clock. This ultimately prompted his suggestion that they invite Jacqueline's mother to drive down from Connecticut and dine with them in Manhattan.

From a culinary point of view, their meal at the chic midtown restaurant had gone smoothly enough. Tasteful appetizers, and wines that were remarkably inexpensive for their quality. And after a momentarily awkward introduction, Manley and Mrs. Ramsey had hit it off well together. She was outspoken and candid. She didn't hesitate to remark that she was delighted with her daughter's new beau—a bold comment which left Manley temporarily speechless, and which drew a slightly embarrassed, if unconvincing, protest from Jacqueline.

As the evening wore on, Manley had found Maureen charming and witty, an excellent raconteur whose tales about Hollywood were endless. She had the most extraordinary eyes, with a golden glint similar to Jacqueline's.

From time to time, Manley had cast a surreptitious glance Jacqueline's way. She appeared to be listening contentedly, and her expression revealed the sort of pride that usually solidifies an innate bond between mother and daughter.

When dessert was served, Manley had subtly maneuvered the conversation in the direction of Dr. Hume. Without being overly provocative, he had hoped to learn something more than what Jacqueline had already told him, especially since he knew it was Mrs. Ramsey who had subsidized Jacqueline's initial trip to the Spa.

"How did you first learn about Dr. Hume?"

"I don't recall, precisely," she said, gazing beyond him in reminiscence. "It was when I was recuperating from my accident. Indolent as a sloth, then. And I had gained considerable weight." She cast an eye at her daughter. "Nowhere near as plump as Jacqueline once was, but still on the pudgy side."

His eyes flicked toward Jacqueline, whose expression retreated into her best "how dare you" look.

"You needn't remind me, Mother."

"Oh, pooh. That was ages ago." There was a long uncomfortable moment. Then, brightly, "And anyway, look at you now."

Jacqueline folded her arms recalcitrantly. "I still wish you hadn't mentioned it."

Maureen smoothed her dress over her knees, a gesture that seemed to brush away her daughter's protest along with the crumbs. She smiled and daintily tugged an earlobe. "Whatever you say, darling."

Manley couldn't tell if Maureen's smile was genuine or merely a token grin. She was, after all, an actress. She let out a conciliatory breath and eyed Jacqueline in silence. During that hiatus, Manley sensed Maureen's remarkable electricity. He also developed a feel for Jacqueline's stubbornness, as she avoided her mother's gaze and looked obstinately down at the tablecloth. Manley thought it best to change the subject. He cleared his throat and once again inquired about the Spa, asking both Maureen and Jacqueline to describe it.

Maureen was the first to reply. "You really must go

there sometime. Marvelous place—one of a kind. From what I've heard about other spas, there's no comparison. San Sebastian is a rich man's soup to nuts. And then of course there's the good doctor."

"He's really what makes the whole thing work," Jacqueline affirmed enthusiastically. "Without Dr. Hume, everything else . . . I don't know. It just wouldn't be the same."

Manley listened in silence as the two Ramseys shared reminiscences. It was clear that they were both enchanted with Dr. Hume. As they recounted their experiences during their numerous visits, it came as a surprise to Jacqueline that there were differences in their treatment.

"You honestly don't use the Nautilus?"

"Never. Dreadful machine. Dr. Hume and I have an unwritten agreement."

"What?"

"That my fortnight at the Spa is to be one continual massage." She smiled. "Interrupted only by my dieter's dinner with him. You have no idea what a charming conversationalist he is."

"I dine with him too, Mother."

"Yes, yes. Of course you do. That was my suggestion."

Jacqueline was stunned. "What do you mean?"

"Dr. Hume is such a busy man, darling. But I insisted that Maureen Ramsey's daughter must have equal time with her host."

"Are you implying that he dines with me as a courtesy to you?"

"Merely a suggestion," Maureen shrugged. "But one I'm glad he decided to heed."

Manley had the distinct impression Maureen's disparaging comments were unintentional. He sincerely doubted she was aware of the subtle effect of her words. His expression turned to a distant stare of concentration.

"Are we boring you, Richard?" said Maureen.

"Sorry, not at all. Ears of stone. Mind was wandering a little."

"A sure sign of approaching age. I hope your other powers haven't abandoned you as well." She gave her daughter a duly ambiguous smile.

41

Jacqueline reddened. "Mother, you are a scoundrel."

"I should certainly hope so. Otherwise life gets rather dull."

Manley paid the check and they left. Outside, it was a clear night, the cloudless Manhattan sky an inky blue mantle. The air was mild enough for a stroll. Their restaurant was on First Avenue, and they decided to walk to the promenade by the East River.

"Jacqueline tells me you were an athlete," Maureen said.

"At one time."

"Hockey, wasn't it? Do you still play?"

"Oh, keep my hand in."

"Leagues, that sort of thing?"

"No, just a little simple skating. Exercise is my only consolation."

"When do you find the time? I thought doctors worked such long hours."

He launched a guilty shrug. "Hardly. A few years ago, maybe. When I was in residency training."

"And now that you're your own boss?"

"I plead the Fifth. Can't let truth tarnish the profession's image."

Arriving at the river, they sat on one of the walkway's many vacant benches. Looking toward Queens, they could easily make out the Roosevelt Island tramway, while farther to the south, the graceful span of the Brooklyn Bridge glowed like a strand of incandescent pearls.

"Leg all right, Mother?"

Maureen waved her hand. "The slightest of aches."

"How did you injure it?" Manley asked.

"It was my skull, actually." There was a windy gust, and delicate fingers of chill crept up her cheek. She hiked the mink collar higher about her neck. Her hand strayed to the stylish tresses that covered her ear, and she traced the long scar that was hidden beneath her hairline. "Fractured it in a fall on the set. Klutzy. Anyway, there was surgery. I had some sort of clot. The limp is merely the result. Or do you doctors call it 'sequelum'?"

He laughed lightly. "Only to impress people. Who was your surgeon?"

She pulled her nose. "Someone at Cedars. . . . Funny. Can't remember his name for the life of me."

"Dr. Hobson," Jacqueline reminded.

"Oh, yes. Hobson."

"A neurosurgeon?"

"I honestly don't know. But he certainly was Johnny on the spot, then. Brilliantly unconventional techniques. I was told he saved my life."

"Not easy to repay that sort of debt," Manley commented, casting his psychological net upon her emotional waters.

She managed a mirthless little smile.

"Good Lord, easiest thing in the world. Simply a matter of a woman utilizing her biologic skills. And I might have kept right on paying him, too, if he weren't so pathetically uncarnal."

Manley and Jacqueline laughed in unison.

"You are hopeless, Mother. Utterly hopeless."

"No argument there." She eyed a distant star. "My own fault, though. Never had enough patience with men."

Jacqueline shrugged lightheartedly. "If we pool our talent, maybe we can still fix you up with a refined old country doctor."

"Not too old, darling." She left a pause. "Another doctor. . . . No, that really wouldn't do. Nothing personal, Richard."

"No offense taken."

"It's just that where eroticism is concerned," she went on, "doctors are so incorrigibly ignorant. Except for psychiatrists, perhaps." The look she cast his way was vaguely suggestive. "The maddening thing is that you would think they should know *something* about a woman's anatomy. The basics? But when it comes to passion, doctors are peerlessly dumb." She reached out and patted his knee. "Present company excepted, of course."

He gave a cluck of amusement. "How would you know?"

She looked at Jacqueline and feigned seriousness. "Is this man pretending innocence?" Then, to Manley, "Everyone knows what goes on with psychiatrists. All that hanky panky—common knowledge. Are you trying to imply the field is boring?"

"The very height of tedium."

"I have firsthand knowledge that is not the case."

He shared a glance with Jacqueline. "I hesitate to ask how."

"No secret. An occupational hazard—nature of the beast. In theater, everyone's under analysis at one time or another."

Jacqueline's surprise was genuine. "I had no idea. Recently?"

Maureen waved at the air with her hand. "No, it must be ages."

"Before Father?"

"Afterward, darling. I'm no trollop." She glanced at the swiftly moving current. "If I recall, you and I weren't speaking much then. It was long before I went to the Spa. I became quite an eater in those days following your father's death. A drinker, too. Made an utter pig of myself. Thought a shrink would help, you know? No such luck." She paused, organizing a thought. "After several sessions I remember his telling me that he couldn't unearth a psychological cause for my weight problem, and that it was probably due to drinking." She chuckled at the memory. "I assured him that it was quite all right. I promised to return when he was sober."

From Jacqueline, a squeal of delight.

"As for his finer points," Maureen went on, gazing afar, "must be those couches." She turned to Manley. "Magical effect—don't you think?"

He smiled and shook his head. "I honestly can't say."

"My, his very words. Amazing how you all mumble so noncommittally. Not that speech mattered much in his case." She cocked her head to one side in reminiscence. "The man was insatiably libidinous. But it was really splendid. How naughty, Christ." She lightly shook her head at the memory. "And those Ben Wa beads, or whatever he called the damn things. . . . Sensational, absolutely."

Manley tried to retain his aplomb, but he too broke up.

Jacqueline chortled while looking down at her feet.

"There's hope for you yet, Mother."

"Think so?"

"A column, I think. 'Maureen's advice for the lovelorn.' "

44

Maureen digested that, then reluctantly nodded her head. "If all else fails." She faced Manley. "Nothing short of incredible that I wound up with a daughter like Jacqueline."

Jacqueline's smile turned nervously formal. "In what way?"

"Your love life, darling. Not at all like mine. Must be your father's side of the family: good Mormon stock. Why, when you were a teenager, you were a positive pillar of the community."

Jacqueline's lips tightened. "No use boring Richard with tales of my wasted adolescence."

Manley felt the tension mount. He said nothing, letting his glance pass from one woman to the other.

"Hardly wasted; would that it had been. Why when I was that age, all I dreamed of was being au pair in a bordello. I dare say your teenage years were shamelessly virginal." She thumbed a nostril. "Totally innocent. Pity."

All humor had left Jacqueline's face. "I don't see how that's anyone's business but mine."

"Oh don't be so pious," said Maureen, looking away as she brushed back her hair. "From what I've heard, you've more than made up for it now."

Jacqueline turned away and looked across the water. Then her eyes filled with small tears that threatened to run down her cheeks; she rose silently to her feet.

Manley's quick eyes read the deep hurt in Jacqueline's expression. While Maureen nattered on, oblivious to the quiet upheaval beside her, he got up and grasped Jacqueline by the wrist. She needed only his firm touch to compose herself. Thus calmed, she turned back to recreate the threesome.

Chapter Five

"Where the hell are those restraints? Jesus Christ, where *is* everybody?"

The patient beneath him fought back with surprising strength, considering the fact that she was both slender and petite. The woman tried to struggle to a sitting position, her arms pinioned by the medical resident. Detached intravenous tubing dripped into a widening circle of liquid that pooled on the floor next to a dislodged stomach tube. The patient had ripped both tubes from her body.

It was shift change. More help arrived as the night crew showed up for work. Soon a phalanx of nurses and attendants subdued the patient, fastening her wrists and ankles with sturdy leather restraints that attached to the bed's metal siderails. A medication nurse drew up a yellow liquid into a syringe, dabbed the patient's shoulder with alcohol, and gave the injection.

"Ten of valium?" asked the resident.

"Right."

"Get me a hundred of secobarb for IV push. She's a bull."

"*Please*," pleaded the patient, struggling to free herself, as if she desperately wanted to clutch the warm and reassuring hand of the nurse nearby. Her suffering face turned toward the resident. "Please, help me!"

Tears filled her eyes, redrimmed and sunken.

"We're trying, Miss Fontaine," said the resident, truly touched by her misery despite the strained patience of his tone. "But help us out, huh? Keep your hands away from the tubes."

The sedative began to take effect. The patient slumped back against the mattress, resistance gone, the sound of her sobbing muted by the drug. A nurse attached fresh tubing to the IV bottle and readied it for the doctor. He applied a tourniquet and slapped the patient's forearm to make the veins distend.

The woman's skin was parchment thin. At length the resident found the faint blue streak he sought and plunged the needle home. He adjusted the IV's rate of flow and fastened the tubing in place with enough tape to discourage the most demented of individuals. The nurse handed him the syringe of secobarbital, and he injected it slowly through the tubing. Within seconds, the patient's crying ceased. She was asleep.

"Are you going to put back the N-G tube?"

"Not while she's sedated. Too risky. In the morning, I guess, after we all get some sleep. Just keep that damn IV going—and for God's sake, keep everyone away from her restraints."

They left the room en masse. As the resident returned to his on-call room, one of the night shift nurses greeted him by name. He turned, saw her tanned skin, and smiled.

"Janet—you look super. How was Maui?" he asked, wondering if she had been screwing her brains out while she was away.

"Absolutely fantastic. Best week of my life. You have no idea how much I detest having to come back to work," she replied, hoping her casual attitude would conceal the fact that she had been screwing her brains out.

"I can imagine."

She was suddenly serious, gesturing down the corridor with a shake of her head. "Is that patient Suzanne Fontaine?"

"The one and only," he nodded. "Brought her in the night before last."

The nurse was clearly bothered.

"I can't understand it. I caught her show at the Forum just a few months ago. She seemed fine then. What in God's name happened?"

"Anybody's guess," the resident shrugged. "She was comatose when they brought her in. Very peculiar story."

"Drugs?"

"We figured that, too, at first. But, no—she was clean. Apparently, she somehow locked herself in a bathroom. The housekeeper found her unconscious."

"From what?"

"We don't know. No, I take that back—we don't know *why*. But clinically, it looks like bulimia."

The nurse frowned as she tried to recall the word.

"Binge eating?"

"Right. You know, like in anorexics who stuff themselves and then barf their brains out? Only she passed out before the puking stage. Christ, you should've seen all the crap we drained out of her stomach."

The nurse was flabbergasted.

"Does anyone know why she did it?"

"No, she's not really all there," he said, tapping his head. "It might be some sort of metabolic problem. Her albumin is off the scale, her electrolytes are totally screwed up, and every time we turn our backs she's wolfing down some other patient's food. I mean, can you picture that? One of the world's top singers, zipping in and out of rooms like she's a food processor? Some old wino down the hall nearly had a heart attack when she jumped on his bed and swiped his broccoli. It got so bad that we finally had to put her in restraints."

The nurse paled. "I just can't. . . . How *awful*."

"You're telling me. It's really hard to believe that in this day and age, in what's supposed to be one of the finest fucking hospitals in LA, a patient can damn near eat herself to death."

Perplexed, the nurse slowly shook her head.

"I've been a big fan of hers for a long time, back to when hardly anyone knew her name because she was so fat. She used to work weekends at little places—you know, like Sweeney's, and The Cellar? And then, when she lost all that weight a few years ago, it suddenly seemed like the whole world noticed her."

"I remember that. Do you know if she went to some sort

48

of clinic? That's the big question mark on her chart. We'd love to get hold of those records."

"Maybe. I'm honestly not sure." She hesitated before changing the subject. "But—bulimia? That's insane."

"That's what the shrinks say, too. That she's nuts. They'd love to transfer her to the psych unit if we can shape her up." He paused. "You know what's the funniest thing, Janet?"

"What?"

"Well, not funny exactly. It's . . . sad. 'Pathetic' would be a better word. I've been with her almost every minute since she was admitted. Most of the time, she's delirious. But sometimes she sort of snaps out of it, and she says the strangest things."

"Like what?"

"Well, take this morning, for instance. I thought she was asleep, and I was sitting on her bed, listening to her chest. Suddenly her eyes flashed open and she grabbed my wrist. There were tears in her eyes. She begged me—I mean really pleaded—not to let her die. And then she closed her eyes and drifted off again. It was the saddest thing I've ever seen."

"That poor woman."

"The thing that bothered me most was—well, she had such a sincere tone in her voice. She sounded absolutely terrified. As if . . ." He halted.

"What?"

"As if she weren't in control of what was happening." He forced a smile. "Which is pretty ridiculous, isn't it?"

"I still don't understand what the problem is. Can't you just keep her on IV's until this metabolic thing or whatever it is corrects itself?"

"Sure, if she'd cooperate. But somehow she manages to pull out her plumbing faster than we can put it back in."

"Why in the world does she *do* that?"

"Who knows? The shrinks say it's a death wish."

"But you don't believe it."

"Her eyes, Janet," he said, reaching out to touch the bridge of her nose. "You'd have to see her eyes when she talks. Then you'd understand."

49

Even at night, the hospital floor was chaotic. There was an unusually high number of postoperative patients requiring constant care, and the burden of the fifty-bed ward was proving too much for the single RN and three nurse's aides on duty. Ordinarily, a patient of Suzanne Fontaine's stature would have had a private duty nurse. Yet such assistance had to be requested by the family, and as far as anyone knew, the female entertainer had none. Thus it fell upon the head nurse to check the woman's IV, vital signs, and restraints at midnight. Noting that the patient slept, she'd left her alone, understanding the importance of rest in the treatment of the acutely ill.

A presence hovered in the corridor's far, dim recesses. Ghostlike crept the shadow, though uniformed like the rest, gliding darkly along the hall and into the room unseen. Strong hands undid the leather manacles and then quickly disappeared, but not before the nearby stairwell door was wrestled open.

The nurse returned at two, on schedule, and heard the dripping. Puzzled, she turned on the overhead lamp. Droplets of IV fluid fell into a puddle on the floor from the severed end of the tubing, and the leather restraints hung loose and open. The patient was gone.

The nurse immediately called Security and notified her aides. She knew the patient couldn't have used the elevators: their banks were in plain sight, adjacent to the nursing station. Leaving the aides in charge, the nurse and a guard began a hurried room-to-room search, but found only those patients who belonged. And then they noticed that the fire door was ajar.

The stairwell was dark and quiet. They tiptoed apprehensively from step to step, ears straining for the sudden cry or moan. But they heard nothing. Three floors below, they reached another usually locked door that was now strangely open. Ordinarily, the employee cafeteria was closed from ten p.m. until six in the morning. Creeping inside, they cautiously switched on the lights, but saw only the orderly formations of vacant tables with chairs propped atop them. A soft hum whirred from within the darkened kitchen beyond. The guard turned on his flashlight and then slowly proceeded inward.

Food was strewn everywhere. It spilled from the enormous humming refrigerators onto neatly washed tile, and from stainless industrial countertops into large sinks nearby. The yellow halo of the beam inched across the room's dark contour until finally it came to rest on the grotesque form of Suzanne Fontaine.

Clad only in a soiled hospital gown, her body was propped up against a wall. She appeared astonishingly heavy, but it was a pathologic heaviness: her sallow flesh was swollen, puffy, with a waxy tightness like a boiling sausage whose skin is about to burst. Beneath the hiked-up gown, her abdomen was hideously distended, like the belly of a pregnant woman. But most curious was the food about her. One hand held a roll, half eaten and crumbling; the other clutched a chicken drumstick, most of its meat gnawed away to expose decaying yellow bone.

As the pale light framed the body, Janet recalled what the resident had said about Suzanne Fontaine's eyes. Now those same familiar eyes were fixed in an expression so profound that even Janet was touched by its inherent terror the instant before she screamed. The guard gaped downward, speechless. Suzanne's features evinced unspeakable horror, as her thin lips stretched into a terrified rictus; and her drying eyes, frozen in fear, stared back at them.

Chapter Six

She wallowed in the muck and managed to right herself on hands and knees, elbows mired in barnyard excrement. Beyond the pigsty fence, a wobbly-legged calf fattened itself, lapping milk from a trough until its belly was as round and swollen as that of the bean-fed horse that grazed beside it. In the corner of the pen a huge porker grunted among worm-bored cobs of corn. He was fat and sleek. The sow beside him lazed in the mud, giving suck to rotund piglets covered with slime.

She crept forward through the ooze, pawing past the warm and steamy dung, snorting at the fetid odor that filled the snout of the swine. She reached the litter and thrust her hands among the young, casting them aside in a chorus of guttural squeals. Wet and exposed, the sow's firm teats beckoned, moist pink slugs that glistened in the sun. Jacqueline's eyes fixed on them. She savagely fought off the other hungry pigs as she opened her quivering mouth and slowly, slowly lowered her lips. . . .

She awoke in a fit of shivering and bolted upright in bed, staring sightlessly around her room. Then awareness replaced apoplexy, and slowly she lay back, shuddering, against sweat-soaked sheets. The man beside her remained asleep, undisturbed. The ghostlike rumble of her dream receded, and her thoughts turned toward her physical being.

As always after that nightmare, her skin was cold and damp. Her fingers wandered fretfully along her body. She probed here, tested there, tensing against the horror of her greatest fear—that she would one day suddenly awake to rediscover herself fat, even more obese than in her former days of hurt and misery. But once again, as always, her hands found only the slender curves of her present self.

Her fluttering hands inched across her chest, grazing her nipples. She clutched her bare breasts, where she clung quivering, as if their firmness were the only thing that could reassure her and stifle her silent scream.

Chapter Seven

Rick prepared to leave for an early conference at the hospital while she was just beginning to wake, stretching under the sheets. He kissed her and she smiled, eyes still closed, nuzzling her cheek to his lips.

"Coffee's by the TV," he said. "Meet me back here at six?"

"Hmmm," she agreed, her nightmare gone and nearly forgotten, leaving her heavy with the lazy feeling of warm slumber.

She could now afford the luxury of arising slightly later than she had when she starred in the soaps. Recently, after she finally dragged herself out of bed, she had begun to watch the morning news while dressing, giving most attention to those three-minute slots devoted to celebrity headliners.

He put on his coat in the entrance hall and was about to depart when she slid into view, wearing one of his over-sized shirts, loose wisps of bedroom hair curled softly about her bare neck. He watched silently from behind as she glided across the carpet, graceful as a cat. He adored her figure—her long, slender legs, her tight buttocks. He knew he was coming to adore everything about her. Smiling to himself, he slipped quietly out the door.

Jacqueline took a sip of her espresso while she concentrated on the telecast.

At the mention of Suzanne Fontaine's death, Jacqueline suddenly blanched. When in-concert closeups of the svelte songstress appeared on the TV screen, Jacqueline was violently jolted into a dry-throated wakefulness. The cup and saucer began to vibrate in her hands.

Clutched in her white-knuckled fingers, the handle snapped cleanly off its stem. The cup tilted to its side, first spilling its contents on the rug before plummeting downward end over end, where it shattered into countless shards.

For an instant she thought she wouldn't be able to breathe. Somehow she managed to put down her saucer, after which both her numb hands drifted helplessly toward her throat, where they hovered uselessly about her open collar. Later, she would have no memory of stumbling backward to the couch, into which she collapsed in something akin to a swoon. The nearby words and pictures became a blank.

Dear God, not Suzanne! And then, all of a sudden, Jacqueline was overcome with remorse. She was too stunned to experience the initial anger that accompanies personal loss. Instead, her eyes filled with bitter tears.

If she was mad about anything, with anyone—Jacqueline was angry with herself. She'd allowed more than a year to go by since last speaking with Suzanne. Oh, she knew the latest rumors, heard all the gossip; but it was hollow, grapevine talk, with none of the warmth found in the simplest of personal hellos. Damn her procrastination! Why, if. . . . She slumped forward and dabbed her moist eyes with her shirttails, gazing once more towards the TV. Images of her childhood friend still flickered dispassionately on the screen. The series of portraits of Suzanne was hauntingly familiar. Even more unsettling were the full-length photos that revealed Suzanne's figure—stunning curves in a fringed black dress, a tight and alluring body that for some reason bore the strangest resemblance, Jacqueline thought, to her own. Dear, *dear* Suzanne!

Jacqueline looked up, staring straight ahead. The funeral. There would be a funeral. Maybe if her director would. . . . And if she could manage to book a flight. . . . Suddenly she clenched her shaking fist and pounded its white knuckles into her lap. Damn, oh damn! Her schedule was so tight she didn't have even one day to spare.

Jacqueline rose to her feet, her expression one of anguish

and guilt. She thumbed away a tear, sniffling as she shook her head. It was all so senseless. As she started toward the bathroom, the only thing that consoled her was the memory of how she had introduced Suzanne to the Spa. How happy that had made them both!

Jacqueline took a soothing hot shower, and then rouged her still-pale cheeks. When she was finished she toweled dry and tried to calm herself with deep, relaxing breaths. Yet despite doing her best to suppress her reaction to the shocking news about Suzanne, Jacqueline felt not only grief but a peculiar apprehension.

What was it? she worried. Rehearsals for the show were going smoothly; it couldn't be that. Her social life was full and vibrant, with none of the errant publicity so apt to perturb the prominent. No, it wasn't that either.

She donned her undergarments and inspected herself in the full-length mirror. Where her figure was concerned, Jacqueline was her harshest critic. Her body was her stock in trade; she valued her judgment of it above all others'. It was her meal ticket, her entree into all that she now held dear—the feverish dancing at Claudine's, the elegant parties thrown by Calvin, the last-minute soirees where small galaxies of notables swarmed together, whispering hushed confidentialities.

These people had no real use for her, of course, for Jacqueline the person; she was far too astute to believe that they had. Despite their grudging acknowledgment of her skill as an actress, her worth to them clearly lay in what she had come to represent: the body incarnate, divorced from the soul that governed it—the female figure against which all others were compared. They would give her little looks. Fingers touched her bare arm when she passed, conveying a hint of intimacy.

At her appearance, women undid yet another button on their blouses to bare a bit more bosom, and men embraced her with a lingering familiarity whose only justification was biologic.

She did not resent the fact that she was something of a symbol. Rather, she cherished it, for it represented the ultimate reward for one who had once loathed herself. Her body now defined her existence. Yet though it gave her life, it also raised the ante, and it now personified everything she had to lose.

Jacqueline took in her mirrored image and slowly bit her lip. She pouted. Years of self-appraisal told her that something in the reflection was not quite right. Was it the bra? It was the same style she'd worn for months. Only . . . she slipped out of it and put on another. Once again, fine lines of worry crept across her forehead.

It was getting late; she had to finish getting dressed. Unnerved, she stepped into her loden green wool skirt and pulled on a beige boat-neck cashmere sweater tunic. As was her custom, she first assessed the way the cloth matched her eyes. Her hazel irises were gold spotted. Satisfied, she ran a brush through her long auburn hair and then halted, again studying her reflection. She adjusted what she thought was an imperfection in the fit of the cashmere, but it wouldn't hang true.

Didn't I just have this cleaned? she wondered.

She stepped into her shoes and notched a belt around the sweater's waist, fidgeting when the clasp seemed unexpectedly tight.

"Damn it," she muttered. She would *have* to have a talk with the woman at the cleaners.

Her hands were trembling as she hurriedly threw on her cardigan, slipped into her coat, and left. Within the hour she was at work, entering via the stage door en route to her room.

Her practiced eye took in the casual strolling of the stage crew. Their nonchalance revealed that they had not yet heard the bulletin about Suzanne Fontaine. They would learn about it soon enough, Jacqueline thought, but for now, it was just as well. Her friendship with Suzanne was well known, and right now she couldn't bear any expressions of sympathy.

Within minutes she was changing clothes once again, for rehearsal. She tried to loosen the costume's waistline.

"Oh, balls. Did you take this in, Phoebe?"

"No, Miss Ramsey. It's just as you left it yesterday."

"Who else does alterations?"

57

"Only me."

Jacqueline was growing increasingly annoyed at the woman's disclaimer. Obviously, there had been some mistake.

"You don't suppose you intended to take in someone else's waistline and did mine by accident?"

"Certainly not."

"Mr. Berson didn't ask you to do it? Come on," she coaxed, her sugary voice a conspirator's tone. "You can trust me."

"Miss Ramsey, I wouldn't alter one stitch of a performer's costume without her knowledge, and definitely not behind her back!"

"Then why the hell does it feel so tight?"

"You might know more about that than I, Miss Ramsey."

She looked down her nose at the costume designer.

"Just what are you suggesting, love?"

"It's really not my place to say. But I've known many an actress to wear her wardrobe a bit thin as time goes by."

Why of all the nerve, Jacqueline silently fumed. The older woman strolled away with sedate dignity, leaving Jacqueline in a state of consternation.

She walked out of her dressing room, stormed down the hall, and barged into Sheila's smaller quarters. Sheila, who had been in the midst of blowing a bubble, watched as its pink sphere collapsed onto her round nose.

"Just call me gumface," she sighed.

Jacqueline fought off a smile as she studied Sheila's face. Sheila's expression bespoke ignorance of Suzanne's tragedy, something for which Jacqueline was thankful.

"Do you know that witch who does the alterations?"

"Sweet old Phoebe?"

"Look at this getup," she said, pinching the cloth. "She had the nerve to take in the waistline without letting me know. And when I asked her about it, she flatly denied it and ho-ho-ho'd that I was getting fat!" She smiled uneasily, trying to laugh it off, but Sheila didn't smile back. "Just who the hell does she think she is?"

Sheila pried away the gum's pink flecks.

"Well well well. You too are human."

"Ah." Jacqueline watched her friend watching her. "You think I'm thin-skinned."

"It happens to us all. Our strengths become our greatest liabilities."

"I see."

Having plucked off the sticky residue, Sheila resumed chewing as she studied Jacqueline's reflection in her makeup mirror. Perhaps she underestimated the sense of threat her friend genuinely seemed to be experiencing. After all, unlike Jacqueline, she had always been overweight, not simply during the decade of her teens. Yet inasmuch as Jacqueline was her dear friend, Sheila knew she could no longer forestall the inevitable. She had been waiting for the proper moment to arise for days—and that moment was now.

"Jackie, sit down a moment, huh?"

Jacqueline slowly sat down in bewilderment. Sheila pursed her lips, composing her thoughts.

"Look, I hate to be the one to tell you this," Sheila began. "But if I don't, who will?"

"What on earth are you talking about?"

"I'm talking about you, darling. Dear old Phoebe was just trying to be kind." She paused and looked Jacqueline directly in the eye. "The terrible truth is that you *have* put on four or five pounds."

Jacqueline was flabbergasted. Her voice weakened to a whisper.

"But . . . that's impossible."

"Says who?"

There was a wild look in Jacqueline's eye, panic in her speech.

"You know I haven't gained an ounce in three years, since I began the treatments! Where do you think I disappear to every six months? As long as I keep returning, they said that . . ." Her fingers were butterflies that fluttered to her lips. The sudden terror that seemed to grip her was frighteningly real. Her mouth turned to parchment, and her hollow voice grew hoarse. "Oh, Sheila, if I ever gained weight again, I think I would *die*."

"Spare me the melodramatics, it can happen to anyone.

Look," she encouraged, "we'll start going to a health club, and—"

"You don't understand!" Jacqueline cried in horror. "It's not supposed to happen, that's all."

"And neither is faggotry. Why don't we have lunch together?" she smiled. "We'll have you shipshape in no time."

Jacqueline couldn't reply. She shuffled expressionlessly from the room. In the corridor, she unconsciously fingered the ring on her right hand. She slowly stopped walking and twisted at the band's peculiar constriction. Why, it had never. . . . Don't be silly! she scolded. It was *bound* to feel tight just before her period.

Later, at rehearsal, Jacqueline's performance lacked its usual luster. Inevitably, word of Suzanne Fontaine's death had begun to circulate through the cast. The hushed whispering of people huddled together broke off whenever Jacqueline turned their way; most politely avoided making eye contact with her. Though she refused to admit it, and though she thought she was behaving in the grand tradition of the show that must go on, she was acting mechanically, with little feeling or emotion. Others noticed it; the director asked if she were all right. She replied that she was fine, just felt a little tired.

She coasted glassily offstage, ignoring the twitch that fluttered in her eyelid. She forced a weak smile, convinced that what Sheila had said was absolutely preposterous.

She passed the entrance to the empty masseuse's room—quarters Mr. Berson had so thoughtfully provided the performers. Jacqueline stopped and gazed at the floor-to-ceiling mirror that bordered the far carpet. She studied her reflection as she slowly ran her palms down her sides, sliding from breast to hip. Under her costume, her figure still felt soft—but dumpling soft, even lumpy. She took her hands away. Damn this heavy fabric!

Disregarding the mirror, she ventured further into the room. Beyond the massage table was an upright doctor's scale. She touched its weight arm, perfectly zeroed; it drifted slowly upward, the arc of a pendulum. Should she . . . ? *Don't be absurd!* she thought. She hadn't weighed herself in over a year, because her weight never varied at all. There was certainly no reason to start now simply because others were acting so childishly.

She hurried from the room, determined to unwind the tense spring that coiled about her spine. Behind her, unseen, the arm of the scale slowly nodded up and down. Jacqueline desperately willed herself to relax, but she couldn't. Now trembling, she tried to avoid grappling with her innermost fear; for to do so would lead her to the conclusion that it was actually starting to happen—that her dream was not a nightmare after all.

PART TWO

From the Previous December

Chapter One

A stack of messages awaited Jacqueline Ramsey when she was finished on the *Hospice* set. They were neatly piled on the corner of her vanity like so many discount coupons, clipped together by the studio's receptionist in the order of their receipt. Jacqueline sighed, more from ennui than fatigue, and sat before a makeup mirror that was studded with incandescent pearls arranged in an arc. She was bloated with apathy; it would take an infinity of moments to summon the incentive necessary to wade through the chits of handwritten scrawl. She skirted the responsibility by taking off her makeup.

"Ah, me," she whispered to her reflection, when the heavy rouge was finally removed; yet her tone belied her deep contentment, a childlike satisfaction at what she saw in the mirror.

She began to sift through the messages with all the enthusiasm of a well-fed lioness at nap time. Most of the jotted communications were insignificant callbacks that could easily be handled by her agent. The last scrap of paper, however, made her sit up and take note. Her eyebrows arched in surprise, and an easy smile dispelled her fatigue.

"Sheila?" she announced, as if she needed to mouth the name to convince herself. "Here? *Now?*"

She hastily jabbed at the buttons on her telephone. She cocked her head to one side while the phone rang, smiling at a memory that surfaced while she waited to hear the voice she knew so well.

"Laverne!" she proclaimed gaily when the phone was answered.

"That could only be Shirley," responded the other party.

In the excited conversation that followed, Jacqueline insisted that Sheila leave her midtown hotel immediately and take a cab to the West Side studio. It was time for celebration, not amenities: Sheila was back. Further chit-chat could await their reunion. Jacqueline hadn't seen her chum in two years.

She phoned the studio doorman and told him to expect a Sheila Hastings. Then she slipped out of the white nurse's garb most scenes called for and found her jeans in the wardrobe chest. Filled with renewed energy, she brushed her long hair once again, taking a full ten minutes in the process, chuckling to herself all the while like a madwoman. She had just pulled on a loose-fitting top when there came a knock at the door.

She hurried across the room and flung the door wide.

"Ta-da!" she bubbled, holding her arms out wide.

Sheila walked in without need for prompting. They immediately embraced, hugging closely, patting one another on the back as if encouraging a burp from a baby. Jacqueline pulled away to arms' length, radiant.

"You scoundrel! Why didn't you tell me you were coming?"

"Ah, the element of surprise," Sheila replied, in Brooklyn tones that now sounded very British. "If you'd known, you'd probably be decorating another crate of lubricating jelly by now."

Jacqueline reddened at the memory.

"God, I nearly forgot about that. Weren't we terrible to him?"

"You mean sending it COD, or having it delivered on his birthday?" She dismissed Jacqueline's look of guilt with a wave of her hand. "The guy deserved it. Anyway he's probably thanking us by now. People like that are better off out of the closet."

Sheila shrugged out of her heavy winter coat, and Jacqueline draped it on a hanger while her guest settled into one of the director's chairs that cluttered the room. She had brought a stack of newspapers with her.

"Speaking of queens, that's what they're calling you in London these days. 'Queen of the soaps.' " She paused. "Funny, you don't look any different."

"Neither do you."

Glowing, Jacqueline studied her friend's face appreciatively. Sheila hadn't changed a bit. Her familiar cheeks were puffy and red, and she had lumbered in like an overweight matron.

Sheila leafed through the newsprint that lay on her thighs.

"Got to keep track of you, though. Blink my eyes and you've had another abortion. Or is it an engagement?"

Jacqueline glanced at the lapful of sensationalist weeklies.

"God, where'd you collect all those?"

"In the hotel lobby. Amazing what they sell these days. I would have preferred *High Times*. Let's see, now," she continued, as she slowly turned the pages. "My, you have been naughty. Where *do* you find the time?"

"Give me that!"

Jacqueline good-naturedly snatched the tabloid away while Sheila dived into the one beneath it. Jacqueline smoothed the cover. No wonder, she thought. It was *Score*, the gossip journal with the widest circulation and the least emphasis on editorial scruple. She scanned the headlines.

" 'Miracle Baby Survives Brain Transplant'?"

"Keep going."

" 'Salmon Sperm Reduces Cancer Risk'?"

"In the center, darling."

She waded through the pages toward the paper's mid-section.

" 'We Met After He Spit On My Shoe'?"

"Dummy—on the opposite page."

"Oh, yes," Jacqueline noted. " 'Hospice Star J.R.: I'm In Love.' " She read the article's first few sentences. "I wonder why Bernie didn't mention this piece to me?"

"He's your agent, not your lawyer."

"I can't yawn my way through this whole thing, Sheil. Who do they say I've fallen for this time?"

Sheila clucked devilishly.

"Christ, Jackie—you're supposed to have been sleeping with the guy for three months, and you still don't know his name?"

"C'mon, who?"

"Nick Tucker."

"You're kidding," she said, crumpling the paper as she looked away with a sudden expression of disgust. "I think I'm going to vomit."

"You ain't heard nothin' yet," Sheila continued. She folded a page and passed it to Jacqueline to inspect. "Really, my dear, why didn't you tell me that it wouldn't matter if your mate were impotent?"

"As long as he can cook," Jacqueline sighed. Wearily, she took the folded paper and gazed at the spot Sheila indicated. " 'What Jackie Ramsey Wants Most In A Husband,' " she recited. "This should be interesting." She read on. "God, where do they dream these things up? I wish I knew as much about my sex life as these writers do."

"How disappointing. Does that mean you really don't get it on with chimpanzees?"

"Not this week, anyway."

Sheila was surprised by her friend's unexpectedly despondent expression. She took the paper away and tossed it toward the trash. "Hey, that's not the Jackie I know. Get your chin off the floor. We could both still be waiting tables, you know."

Jacqueline brightened.

"You're right," she laughed. "I just need to be reminded every once in a while. Did you call Grace yet?"

"I thought we might surprise her together."

Jacqueline beamed, pointed a finger at her, and pulled the imaginary trigger.

"Perfect!"

Jacqueline bounced enthusiastically from her seat and went to the closet to dress for the cold outside. Sheila watched her bundle up, and she smiled. Even her insider's eye couldn't detect any change in Jackie's appearance since the day Sheila had departed for England. Though it was winter, Jacqueline's long, auburn hair seemed streaked by the sun; her lips held the same sparkle; and the faint coppery hue of her skin hinted at the glowing tan of summer past.

Jacqueline was tall, over five-seven, and her fur coat merely accentuated her shapely figure, rather than overwhelming it. Her legs—stunning, even in jeans—were her most outstanding feature. Of course, it hadn't always been that way, Sheila recalled; yet even in the days when they were both fat and unknown, Jackie's legs were striking.

She thought about that—the sameness of it all—as they locked arms and strolled from the studio. Some things never changed: the way Jacqueline cocked her head to one side as she nattered on about whatever came to mind, the obvious strength of her personality and character, yet the frenzied element in her chatter that a once-fat girl cannot shed as easily as she might slough surplus pounds. God, she had done that handily, Sheila thought—miraculously, almost—going from heavy to slender in what amounted to a matter of weeks.

The studio doorman had summoned a cab, and he held its door open for them while he waited curbside. A trio of paparazzi had stationed itself just beyond the building's entrance. As the two women stepped outside, they were battered by the wind, their ears filled with the metallic sound of autowound cameras as shutters clicked and film advanced.

"Come on, Jackie, how about a smile?"

"Can you give us a profile, Jackie?" prompted another, shooting constantly. "And can we get a peek at that figure?"

Sheila saw the hint of a smile creep over her friend's face, and she was warmed by it. She knew how Jacqueline truly adored the newfound attention lavished upon her.

"Not tonight, guys. Gotta keep the buns warm."

They tumbled heavily into the taxi's back seat, jostling Jacqueline's oversized sunglasses. "My incognito shades," she called them, as she adjusted the frame.

Sheila insisted they first stop at Bloomingdale's. Having been away for two years, she said, she wanted to savor the smell of dollars and capitalism again—a scent quite unlike that of the British pound. Anyway, Bloomie's was near

Grace's place. But once there, Sheila was so overwhelmed by the volume of polyester on display that the duo returned outside almost immediately.

Given the proper combination of a northerly breeze and turbulent airflow off the East River, New York's Third Avenue had the capability of being one of the most profoundly windy streets in the city. On that cold and gray evening, fifty-mile-per-hour gusts sent hats flying, and the detritus of midtown life filled the air with a face-stinging testimonial to the inefficiency of the city's sanitation system. It was nearly dinner hour, and the street was crowded with men pressing their faces further downward into collars already hitched high and women holding coat hems tightly to their thighs as their colored scarves flapped in the wind like woolen pennants. It had begun to snow, and the pelletlike flakes had a blinding quality that made passage all the more treacherous.

An exception to the frantic scurrying was posed by two young women who strolled arm in arm, mindless of the snow which clung to their coats. Crossing Sixtieth Street, they spotted the coffee shop in the distance. Moments later, Jacqueline and Sheila arrived at their former place of work.

The front step was covered with a thin layer of snow. As fate would have it, Sheila avoided the numerous fresh footprints there, and the sole of her boot planted on the only slick spot on the doorstep. Viewed from within the cafe, her legs appeared to fly straight out from under her, as if in practiced pantomime. For a fraction of a second Sheila seemed to float in midair before she fell heavily to the stone.

Stunned by the quickness of the spill, Jacqueline gazed downward in open-mouthed paralysis. Sheila was testing her muscles when someone appeared in the doorway.

It was Grace. Seeing that her ex-employee was unhurt, she managed a pathetic smile before she slowly shook her head. Sheila looked up.

"Surprise!"

"I should have known," Grace lamented, in a dour tone that was belied by her grin. "If it ain't Laverne and Shirley."

70

"Don't lie: aren't you delighted to see us?"

"This is Sheila's rendition of dropping in," Jacqueline added.

Grace extended her arm downward.

"You're a sorry sight. Give me your hand, kiddo."

With that, she helped Sheila to her feet. Sheila brushed the snow from her coat and patted her hips.

"Sometimes that extra padding comes in handy."

"Come in, you two. It's freezing out here."

In the cafe, the handful of patrons, having witnessed Sheila's flop, were staring her way with curiosity. Sheila disarmed the diners with a smile, after which she bowed.

"Thanks, folks. My next number will be in ten minutes."

She took off her coat, slung it over her arm, and retreated behind the counter to an obscure corner already occupied by Grace and Jacqueline.

"You learn that in London?" Grace quipped.

"No. In England they fall on their faces."

"Careful, luv. My mother's name was Chamberlain."

Conversation momentarily halted—that instant of awkward silence when the departed return to the fold. The joy of their reunion was obvious, like an emotional tether that linked the three of them. But finally Jacqueline yielded to the mounting tension.

"Just like old times, Grace?"

The hard-nosed cafe owner was touched.

"Yes," she admitted as tears rimmed her lids. "I could close my eyes and forget you two had ever gone."

"Aw, Christ," said Sheila, extending her arms like gull wings and drawing the three of them close. They huddled together like football players. "Tell you what—would it make you feel better if I cleared the counter?"

"Go on!" Grace chided as she wiped her eyes and pulled away. "This one I can watch on TV every day," she said, indicating Jacqueline. "But you—you owe me some filling in. Writing only twice a year. . . . What am I to think? There's a lot more I want to know than the scraps I learn from Jackie."

Sheila took a deep breath.

"Hold your hat, Grace," she began, with a wink. "I'm

an honorary Member of Parliament, my tour of the garrison in the Falklands is over, and I don't care what the papers say: Prince Andrew and I are finished."

The three of them went on like that for the next hour, their conversation sometimes serious, at other times a charade that reflected the exhilaration of their reunion. In slivers, Sheila recounted her experiences as a little-known American actress working in British theater, until the whole that emerged was a fairly accurate summary of her tribulations on the London stage. Grace kept interrupting the recitation with her duties at the counter, bouncing back and forth like a deli pro, missing an occasional phrase but never the substance of the conversation.

"You're not going back, then?" Grace asked Sheila.

"Not this year. The play had a good run. Eighteen months isn't bad for London. But I just wasn't up to going on tour. So hold on, New York—I'm back. Think there's anything in this town suitable for a person of my considerable stature, Jackie? I only have to lose about a hundred pounds."

Jacqueline pursed her lips in reflection.

"Let's see . . . PBS needs a woman for a kids' special. You get to dress up like an ostrich."

"Sesame Street?"

"No, different. A one-shot deal."

"I always liked feathers."

"You have to be at least six feet tall."

"So I'll wear heels." She absentmindedly opened the door to the stainless-steel refrigerator and extracted a large, oblong fruit. "What the hell is this?" she asked Grace.

"Papaya."

"Ah, just what the doctor ordered."

She found a paring knife, peeled off the thin skin, cut the flesh into wedges, and mixed it with drained pineapple chunks. Jacqueline and Grace watched her with curiosity.

"I thought you were sticking to skim milk and cold cuts," said Jacqueline.

"That was last week. It didn't work; I didn't lose an ounce. Too much animal fat, I bet."

"That's the whole diet? Pineapple and papaya?"

"Hell, no," she said, cramming her mouth with the concoction. "You can have almost any fruit you want. Unlimited, lots of variety. How's that grab you?"

Grace thought for a moment.

"It sounds like an explosion diet."

Sheila put down her spoon. "A what?"

"If I just ate fruit, and nothing but," she continued. "I'd have enough gas to float the Goodyear blimp."

Jacqueline looked at Sheila and smiled. It felt good, having her back—comfortable and warm and familiar. She had had no one to confide in since Sheila had gone, no one she could trust with that same degree of confidence.

She gazed outside. The snow had stopped, but the fierce wind still whipped with intensity. The last customer left, and Grace went to clean the vacated booth. A Walters interview was just beginning its broadcast, and both younger women looked up to study the televised special.

The woman being interviewed was a film star whose heyday had been twenty years before. Yet even now her infrequent cinematic roles commanded seven-figure sums. Despite her decreased activity, she was very much in the public eye, alluded to in the same whispered tones the gossip columnists reserved for the likes of Princess Caroline or Jackie-O.

"Isn't she something?" Grace said admiringly. "I've seen every one of her pictures at least twice. Now that's an actress."

"You're nuts," Sheila replied. "She has about as much talent as an Australian dingo. All she could ever do was spread her legs—and now she caps it off with a little kiss and tell. Don't you think so, Jackie?"

Jacqueline didn't reply. She was mesmerized, absorbed by the woman's physical image. She felt an inner chill, and the tiny pulse in her temple stepped up its cadence.

She gazed at the screen through fish-bowl eyes that magnified imperfections. The generation past had not been kind to the woman. Her battle with her waistline was well known and often publicized. Yet what some might dismiss as a minor skirmish now appeared to Jacqueline as the most horrifying sort of carnage. She saw it as a terrifying transformation: the woman's lower lip billowed downward to merge with a ripple of chins, and the sagging folds of skin beneath her once-smooth cheeks were pig jowls that disrupted an otherwise straight jawline. They hung there, loose and flapping when she talked, taunting Jacqueline by their very existence.

Chapter Two

Allison Wade was finally about to admit her love for Brandon McCall, but McCall was dying of leukemia, and Allison's best friend and fellow nurse Margo Tyler saw what was happening and warned her against it, for after all, wasn't that what the cool-headed but sensitive Allison always preached about involvement with the patients, because it was madness, for all their patients in the city's largest hospice were doomed, and yet McCall was a gifted young poet whose poems to Allison seemed all the more touching after he was jilted by Erica, and it was something Allison could never forgive Erica, but also something which only served to draw her closer to McCall, for she felt especially attached to him now that his physician, Dr. Bradley Worthington, pronounced his case hopeless. It was time for their first kiss.

"Places," called the set director.

Jacqueline returned from makeup with her long hair once again tucked up tight under her nurse's cap. A low whistle followed her as she strolled toward the set. She turned to see one of the new stagehands gaze admiringly at her figure. Jacqueline acknowledged the overture with a faint smile.

She momentarily reflected on her figure with intense satisfaction. It was largely because of her shapeliness that—when she wasn't occupied with the show—her agent had arranged other commitments for her, usually short photographic sessions. Her portrait adorned the cover of many a fashion magazine, though she was surprised to find that she was far more comfortable posing in beachwear or leotards, often for articles on physical fitness. She did for tights what Brooke Shields did for jeans. Early on, she had developed her own style of aerobics. When the highlights of "Jacqueline Ramsey's Slimnastics and Dancercise" were featured in *Newsweek*, the magazine sold more copies than at any other time in its history. Jacqueline was elated. She was obsessed with the idea of being thin, of working at being thin, of getting involved with being thin in every way possible—because thinness had brought her so much happiness.

The scene wasn't going well. Jacqueline wondered if it stemmed from her lack of experience doing love scenes. In the three years since *Hospice* had rocketed to first place in the ratings among afternoon soap operas, she had kissed only three other men before camera—yet those scenes had been takes the first time taped. However, the viewing public had perceived those episodes as Allison's innocent flirtations; this was to be her first true romance.

No, she concluded, it wasn't she; she wasn't the one who convulsed in laughter during the first two takes—it was the actor who played McCall. She smiled to herself: Morrison always picked the worst times to crack up.

"Keith," said the director, "could we possibly try it this time without you winking at the camera or feeling Jackie's tits?"

"Sir, I am the utmost of professionals."

"And you, Jackie?"

"What should I do if he gets a hard-on?"

"Oh, Christ. Can't you guys be serious? We're already thirty minutes behind. Screw his hard-on."

"You want me to screw his hard-on?"

"She's a real go-getter, Mr. Hammill," said Morrison. "I'll back her up all the way on that."

"I give up," the director shrugged. "You kids want to play, go ahead. Just let me know when you're done."

"Jackie, what a genius idea!" said Morrison. "Look, we'll do the scene blue, auction the tape for cable rights, and then do it straight. Here, let me help you out of that dress," he said, proceeding toward her top button.

She waved him away good-naturedly and took her place on the set. Morrison sighed, checked his hair, and joined her.

"Some women have no business sense," he mumbled.

The lights went out and the cameras drew in tight. It was a close-up, filmed on a bed. The script called for Nurse Wade to have a lengthy bedside talk with her patient, a chat that would become more and more intimate until the moment of their kiss. The dialogue had gone well before their embrace ended in disaster. Now, ready again, they resumed their postures and were preparing for the take when Morrison began wriggling.

"I bet they didn't change the sheets," he grumbled.

"Keith, please!" said the director. "Get started, huh?"

"Yes, sir. Yes, sir."

An hour later, when they finally finished what was intended to be an eighty-second scene, Jacqueline returned to her dressing room, smiling lightly. In the end, it had come off well. Morrison was such a flake. From some of his remarks, though, she wondered if he truly thought her private behavior was as colorful as the weeklies portrayed it. She rarely spoke about her personal life on the set, for there was not all that much to speak about. She had worked from dawn until well after dusk, fifty weeks out of the year, for three years running. And with a script that always called for a minimum of thirty pages, with a maximum of sixty—who had the time? It amazed her how enterprising photographers managed to ferret her out on the infrequent occasions she socialized, and then to use the pictures as frontispieces for story after story about her loves and secret desires.

Her sex life, she reminisced coolly. They should only know how badly it had begun.

The small car's heater fought with the winter chill but lost, and the windows misted with the fog of their breath. Her date's fingers were icy talons that urged her wrist toward his lap.

"C'mon, sugar, I know you want it. Who're you saving it for?"

"Could you please take me home?"

"Sure, just let me touch you a little . . . there."

"I asked you to keep your hands off me." How adult he had seemed at first, she reflected. How collegiate; yet now it was clear he wanted the same thing as all the others.

"Hey, loosen up. Sixteen isn't so young."

"My mother will kill me if I'm not home by twelve."

In the parked car, his breath became as frosty as the sudden tension between them. Then he was all sweetness again, nuzzling her cheek and neck while she sat rigid.

"Tell you what . . . If you're in such a hurry, all you have to do is go down on me, hmmm?"

"You're disgusting."

He pulled away in a huff and started the engine.

"Is that right? Let me tell you something, sweetheart. You're no prize package yourself. If anybody's disgusting, it's you. Everybody thinks you're a pig, you know that? You belong in a barnyard with all the other fat hogs!"

Even now the adolescent memories were chilling. Her hand was trembling when she closed her dressing room door. She blanked out all thoughts by leafing through her messages. Among them, a call from Sheila, and a message from her agent about doing the Donahue show Christmas Day. Why not? she thought to herself. They weren't taping that day, and her mother wouldn't return from St. Thomas until after New Year's. She dialed her agent first and began talking while she slipped out of her costume. She abruptly stopped speaking, her skin slightly pale.

"God, what a coincidence. . . . No, just something I was thinking. Out of all the stars who were once heavy, they should choose me. . . . You're kidding! Richard Simmons, Lorraine Taylor, and who? . . . No, I never did. . . . All right, if you think so. Tell them I'll do it."

Jacqueline hung up with uncertainty, her thoughts still mired in the icy slush of humiliation that constituted days past but not forgotten—the days when she first arrived in New York.

❧

It wasn't until then, when she was twenty-one, that she learned never to weigh herself more than once a week: greater frequency prompted discouragement. She felt as if she were starving. For days she had eaten only fish, but it wasn't satisfying; a constant gnawing sensation tugged at her stomach. She guessed she had lost at least five pounds. Yet when she disrobed for her ritual Saturday morning weigh-in and stepped on the scale, her expectations turned to disillusionment. She got off, looking utterly forlorn, having noted that the scale registered less than a two-pound weight loss.

She turned on the shower, appraising her figure in the mirror as the water warmed. Was she really "big boned," as her mother had suggested? Her bones had never struck her as particularly large. Perhaps it was just another euphemism for being overweight, just as "baby fat" had become a "hormonal condition" when she was an adolescent. Her figure was, in fact, rather good, when each area was considered separately. Her breasts were full and round, her legs were shapely, and her face had striking features. But the total was more than the sum of its parts, and she had learned long ago that one hundred seventy pounds was simply too much to be carried on her frame. And the greatest insult, the harshest blow to her ego, came when she occasionally overheard people whispering, "But she has such a pretty face."

Her overweight would be so much easier to accept if she were ugly. Then, she thought, she wouldn't care. But she did have a pretty face; she had known that for years. It could be a beautiful face, a stunning face, if it weren't trapped in a mold of corpulence. Admit it, she told herself as she stepped into the shower. You are just plain fat.

She was no stranger to dieting. She had been an ardent devotee of each new weight-loss fad for years, ever since she had been a plump fourteen-year-old a decade before. Over the course of that time she had lost thousands of pounds, only to regain them. There was no magic combination of foods she would not try. At various times, her refrigerator resembled an international food cooler, as the prosciutto and Genoa with Vichy water diet was supplanted by the oriental rice and macrobiotic diet, which preceded the Scandinavian high-protein egg and soy bean diet, all liberally interspersed with sushi, goat's milk, and bean curd. Now, it overflowed with fruits domestic and exotic, a colorful mixture of red grenadine, green kiwi fruit, casaba melon, guava, and tamarind.

Drugs were of no help. The amphetamines a friend gave her in college paradoxically stimulated her appetite rather than suppressing it. And once, in desperation, she had tried the standard doses of thyroid, digitalis, and diuretic, a combination that worked particularly well for another acquaintance; but it was a mixture which landed Jacqueline in the hospital with dehydration, a low potassium level, and an irregular heartbeat.

She had even succumbed, two years before, to her greatest aversion: sports and exercise. After several days of diligent jogging, her painfully swollen knees and ankles led her to a doctor, who diagnosed the condition as chronically weak ligaments. The ultimate irony occurred when he told her that she could resume jogging only if she first lost a great deal of weight. It was a no-win situation she was happy to part with. Not that she didn't exercise at all: on Mondays and Thursdays she attended dance class near the Actors' Studio, and every morning and night she did Jane Fonda's special tummy and buttocks tightening exercises. Afterwards, she felt tight, but still fat, concluding that tightness was an asset only if the underlying muscle could be seen.

In truth, when Jacqueline was painfully honest with herself—which was quite often—she was forced to admit that each fad, each new diet, did work, if continued. The problem lay not with the diet; it lay with her. Her poor self-image hurt her confidence and disturbed her perseverance. At any minor setback, any hint that the pounds wouldn't magically disappear with the latest dietary gimmick, she would cave in. Inevitably, as her weight loss would plateau, she became discouraged. Unlike her dietetic fare, the eating binge that ensued was purely American, and she would gorge herself on deep-dish Chicago pizza, Big Macs, Super Tacos, and Wednesday is Sundae at Carvel's.

That morning, however, her discouragement was not so profound. She was to meet her agent just before ten at his West Side office. Bernie Sokol's clientele consisted largely of relatively unknown actors and actresses like Jacqueline; she had met Sheila through him. He'd helped her land several bit parts, none of which led to greater recognition of her talent. Now, though, she had a specific part in mind. And she wanted that role desperately.

She got dressed and breakfasted on a banana and a canned pear half. She counted the times she chewed, eating slowly, using behavior modification techniques to control her appetite. They never really worked for her, but their distraction did help take her mind off her hunger. At nine-thirty, her thoughts filled with visions of eggs Benedict and thick rashers of bacon, she left her apartment.

Her agent's office was a low-budget operation, a second-story walk-up many blocks from the high-rent district. Jacqueline mounted the rickety wooden stairs that led to his door. The sign upon it read, "Bernard Sokol: Casting and Production." She always smiled at that. The closest Bernie came to production was the two children he had fathered by his first wife. She rapped firmly on the door.

"Come in. It's open."

Jacqueline turned the handle and walked in, casually looking about the room. Framed, autographed photos of celebrities adorned the plaster walls. None of the actors was a client of Sokol's, though when he spoke he continually referred to them as if he were on a first-name basis. Sokol was a balding, cherubic man in his fifties. As usual, he was sitting behind his desk, chain smoking and rereading a dogeared edition of *Variety*. He put the tabloid down.

"Jackie, bubbie, you look ravishing."

"Can it, Bernie. I'm about as ravishing as Mother Goose."

"Never dismiss a compliment, Actor's Rule Number One."

"I wouldn't if I were Bo Derek." She sat by his desk. "But thanks, anyway. Did anything come in this week?"

" 'Fraid not. Wish there was. Gotta pay the rent, you know."

"Nothing? Not one thing?"

"Nope."

"Oh." Jacqueline looked down at her hands. "What about the Jones production in the Village?"

"Harlem Workshop? Forget it. Blacks only. But don't worry. I'm getting some stuff ready for summer stock."

"Bernie, I can't wait until summer. I want to work now!"

"What's the matter? Money problems?"

"No. I can manage. It's just that . . . it's been three years now, and I'm still waiting."

Sokol laughed, cigarette smoke spiraling from his nostrils.

"You know what? If I had a dime for every kid who had a part in college drama and then thought he was ready for Broadway, I'd be in Beverly Hills myself." He stubbed out his cigarette and leaned toward her. "Look. Do yourself a favor. Swallow your pride, huh?"

"I have been, ever since I came to New York."

"You know what I mean. For Chrissake, don't be so stubborn. Give your mother a call. She's got contacts I could never get. Why spend your life being a martyr?"

She stood up.

"We've been through this before, Bernie. If that's all you've got to say, forget it." Nearly at the door, she stopped and turned back to him. "I signed up for the *Hospice* audition next week."

"Oi, I got a masochist on my hands. You asked me before, and I told you. It's not for you."

"I've seen the script—"

"So have I," he interrupted. "There's nothing for you. Which part were you thinking of?"

She hesitated. "Female lead."

"You gotta be kidding."

"But it's perfect for me! I can do those lines, know them inside out—"

"Sure, sure." He blew out smoke into the air, looked at

her, and saw the distress on her face. He waved at the bluish haze. "Ah, I'm sorry." He got up and walked over to her. "You know your problem? I'll tell you. You do have talent. Lots of it, a helluva lot more than your mother did. Sure you can read those lines. I know that. But it's the image, kid. These days, everything is image, packaging. You try for the lead in a hot soap, you gotta have the goods. Up here," he said, pointing to her head, "you got 'em in spades. But the rest? Come on, face facts. Just look in the mirror."

"I know I can lose the weight."

"You gonna knock off forty, fifty pounds by next Wednesday?"

"No, but I'm sure I could once I got the part."

"Who's kidding who?"

"It's the truth. I know I could!"

"The truth? You want the truth? Okay. Truth is, there's no one in town who's gonna hire some fat bimbo just because she can read well."

She reddened.

"Thanks, Bernie. You really have a way with words." She turned away and hurriedly left his office.

Jacqueline descended the stairs and walked home. She turned down Broadway, heading past the glare and garish neon as she passed Forty-second Street. Billboards were everywhere, placards for plays and movies and porno shows. She couldn't help looking at them, at the scores of beautiful, sensuous women who seemed to stare back at her, all of them provocatively, enviably thin.

❧

Jacqueline didn't want to discuss the *Hospice* love scene, but Sheila pressed her for details.

"Gawd. Don't make it sound so unpleasant."

"All I did was pucker up."

"Yeah, and the Pope's a Moslem. You trying to tell me you felt nothing? Not even an eensy twinge?"

"Well . . ." Jacqueline hedged.

"That's more like it! Give."

"All right. To start with, he has these thin lips, you see—"

"Yeah, tell me about it."

"—but they're very soft."

"That's the stuff," Sheila prompted attentively.

Jacqueline glanced over her shoulder to see if the people in the next booth were listening. Then her eyes narrowed, and she hunched over their restaurant table with a conspiratorial whisper.

"He told me we were just going to practice, you know, to get the take right."

"I knew it! He's got that devil in his eyes. And?"

"He started moving his mouth back and forth real slowly. . . . And then I felt his tongue slide across mine."

"Oh my God I'm going to faint."

Jacqueline picked up her drink and sipped it, all the while concentrating on Sheila, whose eyes were wide and staring.

"When he sucked on the tip of my tongue, I got these little shivers. He touched my neck with his fingers, and then his hand started to move—you know—downward?"

"I can't believe this," Sheila puffed heavily. Jacqueline's recitation momentarily halted, and Sheila tensed. "Come on, Jackie, you can't stop now. What happened, already?"

"You really want to know?"

"Jesus, what's with you? Tell me!"

"Well," she resumed, "his lips sort of edged up to my ear . . ."

Sheila unconsciously fingered her earlobe.

". . . And then his mouth opened . . ."

"Yes," Sheila whispered.

"And then he told me he had herpes."

Sheila stared at her dumbly. Her lower jaw slowly fell, forcing her lips apart.

"What?"

Jacqueline guffawed, a horselike snort that made her spill her drink. The charade had gone far enough; she knew she had been convincing, but she could torture her friend no longer. Sheila wore a look of dismay. Then her consternation vanished, and she flushed at being taken in;

but she was quickly caught up in the contagiousness of Jacqueline's laughter. She lightly spanked Jacqueline's hand.

"You little shit," she scolded. "Gullible's travels. And here I sat believing all that crap."

Jacqueline wiped tears of laughter from her eyes.

"Really, Sheil, you make it sound like London's on another planet. Didn't you read the papers over there?"

"All I 'ad time for was the telly, luv."

"I hate to be the one who breaks this to you, but Keith has Queer's Disease."

Sheila slumped back against the booth's cushions, clearly shocked.

"You have got to be kidding."

"Scouts honor."

"I can't believe it," she said, slowly shaking her head in disappointment. "Keith Morrison, the one great love of my life—*maricon?*"

"He's put the make on half the guys in the cast."

"Oh, God, kill me!" she cried theatrically, throwing back her head and looking toward the ceiling. "Let it not be so!"

"Sheila," said Jacqueline, glancing around, "you keep carrying on like that and someone's liable to walk over and do a Heimlich maneuver."

"Don't knock it, it might be my best shot at romance." She was still flabbergasted at Jacqueline's revelation. "This is too much. Why'd you do that to me?"

"I just couldn't resist."

"I swear my pants were getting wet just listening to you, like the first time I got fingered. Christ, Keith Morrison— God, what a buster! Jeez, I hope the boys in the band don't hang around my new show."

"Rehearsals start Monday?"

"Bright and early."

"You don't exactly sound thrilled."

Sheila lit a cigarette in contemplation. "It's a very good opportunity."

"My, how tactfully put. 'Chance of a lifetime'?"

"Hardly." Sheila shook her head. "My role is like linoleum—it's everywhere, but you don't see it. Not the sort of thing Emmies are made of. The female lead—now that's the hot spot."

"Meeghan Fleming?"

"They're going to invest their money in that primadonna. Propping up her role, spotlighting it. I got a peek at the advertising budget. It looks like a tally sheet for the Federal Reserve."

"And here I thought you liked her."

"I admire her," said Sheila, inhaling deeply. "Underneath that put-on moodiness, she positively oozes talent. More than I thought at first. In some ways she reminds me of your mother."

A dark and brooding silence interrupted Jacqueline's cheerfulness, and she momentarily looked away in bittersweet reverie.

❧

"Thank you very much. We'll let you know. Next, please."

The discouraged young actress managed a polite smile before she left the set. A plump young woman took her place, walking enthusiastically to the chalk mark on the studio floor, script in hand. Despite her agent's objections, Jacqueline was determined to try out for *Hospice*.

"Hi," she beamed.

Seated thirty feet away, the two men exchanged glances.

"Is she for real?" whispered the producer.

"Something familiar about her," the director replied. Then, more loudly, "What's your name, sweetheart?"

"Jacqueline Ramsey."

The director hesitated. "Maureen's daughter?"

"Yes."

"I see the resemblance. How is your mother, anyway?"

"She's fine, thank you."

"All right, Jacqueline. Take it from the top on eighteen."

She commenced reading, channeling all her force and energy toward the two men nearby. Though the producer sank lower and lower into his chair, the director listened attentively. Jacqueline finished the passage and looked in their direction.

"How was that?"

"Not bad. Let me hear you do the monologue on forty-two."

Out of earshot, the producer turned to his colleague. "You can't be serious."

"She's good, damn good. Better than her mother."

"But she's a cow."

"Hmmm," the other man murmured, pressing a pencil eraser to his lips. In moments she had finished, and he waved in her direction. She walked hopefully toward them.

"Miss Ramsey," the director began, "you have the potential to be a fine actress."

"Thank you," she glowed.

"You have poise and charm and you strut your stuff better than most actresses twice your age. You're the finest we've seen today."

She was ecstatic. "Do I get the part?"

The producer snorted and snapped at the man beside him. "Are you out of your mind?"

The director ignored him. "I'm afraid not," he told her. "There's no question about your qualifications. But I think the problem is as obvious to you as it is to us."

"If you're talking about my weight, I've lost fifteen pounds in less than ten days," she fabricated. "I was one twenty a year ago, and I could be down to that in another few weeks."

He frowned. "Let's be honest with each other. I remember seeing you in the Player's Production that had a short run about a year ago." He paused, and Jacqueline reddened. "Do you get my drift?"

"I'm sorry, Mr. Hammill. But if I get the part, I can lose the weight, really I can."

"You realize we tape the pilot in less than a month, don't you?"

"I understand that, but—"

"Tell you what. You come back in three weeks weighing the one twenty you mentioned, and I'll be happy to reconsider."

"But if you'd just—"

"Look, kid," the producer interrupted. "Alan's being

generous with you. But I'm not. There's no place in my show for a fat broad with talent. Now I'd appreciate it if you'd get lost, because you've wasted enough of our time already."

"Jesus, Oscar," said the director.

"I suppose you think you're doing me a favor by being painfully blunt?" she shot at the producer.

"Yeah. I am. It pains me no end. Now scram."

Furious, she turned on her heels and stormed away, stopping halfway across the set.

"I'll be back, Mr. Hammill. You'll see me in three weeks."

"Sure you will, kid," said the producer. "That's when we'll be casting for Barnum and Bailey."

Outside, as she shivered in her coat, the stinging words reverberated in her ears. Her tears were salty warm, but she tried to ignore them as she walked, head held high, sniffling her way into Central Park. It was an ice skater's day, the sky blue and cloudless above the Wollman rink, and she watched the lithe skaters whirl in the bright winter sun. Farther on, she came to the children's zoo, now nearly deserted as she wandered along the path, glancing at the sign for the elephant.

Not an elephant, she thought. A hippo. He was right. I am nothing but a gargantuan circus animal!

Her self-pity turned to loathing, and then anger took its place. She hurried out of the park, feeling utterly despicable, enraged at herself. The chance of a lifetime was there, hers for the taking; but it was slipping right through her fingers. She crossed Seventy-second Street, saw her reflection in a storefront window, and glared at it. You are repulsive!

Nearing her apartment, she impulsively entered a delicatessen, where she purchased a half gallon of butter pecan ice cream and a bag of chocolate cookies. As soon as she was home, she threw her coat on the floor and went straight to the kitchen. She began to devour the ice cream straight from the container, one enormous spoonful after the other, barely tasting what she swallowed, pausing only to rip the cellophane wrapper off the cookies. Soon her squirrel-stuffed cheeks were filled, and yet she consumed bite after bite, a famished child at a birthday party who quickly sports a mustache dotted with crumbs. Only when the container was nearly empty did her ravenous behavior subside, and as the ache in her stomach diminished, she dropped her spoon into the now melting contents and pushed away the few cookies that remained.

Damn you! she thought. You are nothing but a pig!

Her mind was as filled with repugnance as her belly was with sweets, and in a desperate attempt to purge both, she suddenly ran to the bathroom and forced her fingers down her throat. The relief that followed was swift but incomplete, for the mind could not empty itself in the manner of the body.

Later, alone in her bedroom, shades drawn to insulate herself from the outside world, she slowly took stock of her situation. Self-deception could carry her only so far; she had tried, and it had failed. Yet she was desperate, and in her moment of need, it was clear that there was only one place she could turn. Resignedly, she rolled onto her side and reached for the telephone, dialing the one number she had vowed never to call.

"Hello, Mother?"

Chapter Three

The midmorning talk show was just underway, with the host greeting the audience and the viewers. After making the traditional Yuletide pleasantries, he launched directly into the topic at hand.

"It may seem inappropriate to discuss it on a day when Christmas stockings are filled with what some call junk food and when many families will be settling down later to an enormous dinner. But our subject for today is that perennial, unpleasant bugaboo, dieting. Or more specifically, keeping the pounds off after they're shed. Many of us have gone through the torture of one diet after another, endlessly—and some have even succeeded at getting down to their ideal weight—only to find that a few days later their weight shoots up again and the whole spiral starts once more. By a show of hands, how many of you has that happened to?"

There were sympathetic nods and a chorus of murmuring as dozens of hands were raised.

"It's a familiar and frustrating experience that often leads to even worse dietary habits than before. Spending their holiday with us today are four diet experts whose names are household words across the country. I can honestly say I can't recall ever doing a show before with such a star-studded panel. They're here to share their past problems and advice with us in what I think you'll find to be one of our most fascinating shows ever. We have a commercial message, and then we'll be right back. Stay with us."

It was only a slight mistruth that all the guests needed

no introduction. Though most people were familiar with the names of Simmons, Ramsey, and Taylor, few viewers, if any, knew of Dr. Richard Manley. During the pause, Manley took a cool sip of water and shifted uncomfortably in his seat, caught in the stage lights' bright glare, acutely aware that he had been excluded from the casual show-business chatter of the three people beside him. He was a last-minute replacement on the show. Originally scheduled was Dr. Robert Morse, author of an international best-seller on dieting, but Morse had been forced by an emergency to cancel his appearance. The show's producer understood the importance of balancing the panel with a physician. However, unable to locate another weight-loss expert on such short notice, he decided that a legitimate researcher might fill the bill. Thus Manley had been summoned, and he had agreed—reluctantly—to appear.

After the station break, the guests were greeted by an enthusiastic audience. Jacqueline wore a form-fitting dress of clingy gray silk that made her the center of attention. Ultimately, Manley was introduced, and the host listed his credentials as those of both a practicing psychiatrist and a researcher into the psychiatric aspects of metabolic diseases, many of which had a component of obesity. That was Manley's only appearance on camera during the show's first half; for the next thirty minutes, he was virtually ignored.

The initial segment of the show was part confessional and part group therapy, interspersed with liberal doses of laughter, wit, and shenanigans. Most of the audience was aware of the sometimes farcical tribulations of Simmons and Taylor. It came as a surprise to many, however, that Jacqueline Ramsey had ever been overweight: her image had been that of the beautifully slim star of the greatest smash to hit daytime TV. When the host brought the questioning around to Jacqueline, her bubbly though embarrassed expression revealed that she was still not quite comfortable with the calls and whistles that greeted her.

"Well," the host interjected, "we haven't had an audience this appreciative in a long time. I suppose you must be accustomed to it by now."

"Not really. It's one of those things that's hard to get used to."

"You certainly handle it with poise and charm," he said, turning to look at the camera. "We have to break away for a moment. But we'll be right back to hear the untold saga of Jacqueline Ramsey."

When the lights dimmed, the host and the show's director had a hurried conference. Word had come from the network that the televised audience share was tremendous and growing; they had to save their trump for last. When the show resumed, the host temporarily abandoned Jacqueline and directed several pertinent medical questions to Manley.

Before his first reply, Jacqueline and Manley exchanged stares for a fraction of a second, though it seemed much longer to her. She felt a peculiar attraction to him. When they were backstage before the show, she had been struck by the way he carried himself—the loose tilt of his head, the offhand manner in which he leaned against the wall—all of which conveyed a rugged body language she found very appealing. Now she was impressed by the way he talked. He spoke in a friendly, casual manner, almost aloof, more like a spectator than a performer.

Manley's responses first alluded to the psychological impact on those whose initial success at dieting began to falter, and of the accompanying poor self-image, the resultant frustration, and the sometimes overwhelming guilt. Then he addressed some of the new and controversial views of dieting held by many in the medical community: the decreasing emphasis on simple dieting alone, which seemed to initiate a self-defeating vicious cycle; the lesser role played by low-calorie, high-protein diets; and above all, the reason why increased activity often succeeded where dietary measures alone failed.

"I couldn't agree more with Mr. Simmons," he summed up. "The key issue is when doctors will stop handing out preprinted 1000 calorie diet plans as if they were a panacea. I'd much prefer that they simply sit down with their patients and work out a reasonable exercise program with attainable goals."

"Then you would take issue with the doctor-authors of every bestselling diet book in the past decade? Are you trying to tell me," said the smiling host in a tone of joking indignation, "that all the protein I ate and all the water I drank was for nothing? Not to mention the hours I spent in the john!"

A wave of understanding laughter rippled through the audience.

"Not really," Manley replied. "It's the motivation that counts. If you at least have the incentive to *start* a diet, that's the most crucial step. Then it becomes a question of transferring that incentive to a well-thought-out plan of increased physical activity. But I can't honestly say that most of the diet books I've seen are worth either their price or their toll on the psyche."

"So what *is* the secret to losing weight?"

"There is no one secret. It's simply the age-old formula of exercise, proper nutrition, and a modicum of perseverance."

"I was afraid you were going to say that," said the host, feigning a wince to the accompaniment of tittering in the audience. "Dr. Richard Manley, ladies and gentlemen." There was polite if restrained applause. "We'll speak with the star of *Hospice* when we return."

Off mike, the host turned to Manley. "It's refreshing to find someone who isn't trying to make a buck with the latest crock of dietary mumbo jumbo."

"Thanks."

"Jackie," he said, turning her way, "I'm not ignoring you—promise. We're saving you for the finale."

"I pretty much figured that out," she smiled.

"Has anyone told you how much you resemble your mother when you smile?"

"Yes, all the time."

"Such a remarkable actress. She did the show a few times."

"Ten seconds," said the set director.

The host walked casually back to his stage mark. Only Manley noted the distant expression that glazed Jacqueline's eyes.

Jacqueline had the opportunity to recall the telephone conversation with her mother countless times during her first flight to the spa. In the days before her departure, Jacqueline had done her best to keep her mind blank, trying not to dwell on the chat with her mother, as if the issue would disappear if she swept it under a mental rug. She packed and unpacked her bags daily, notified her neighbors about her impending two-week absence, and okayed the trip with Grace, who said she could manage just fine with Sheila. Yet now, in the isolation and solitude of the transcontinental flight, her mother's words loomed in her mind as stark and as gray as tombstones.

Their conversation more closely approximated reconciliation than recrimination, free of the I-told-you-so's that would have doomed the dialogue. Indeed, Jacqueline should have expected this, for it was she more than her mother who had been instrumental in widening the distance between them. It was she who had rejected her mother's advice, she who had determined to chart her career without assistance or intervention, and in the end, she who had come full circle, returning to her mother for warmth and comfort as she had done so often as a child.

Their schism began as a simple difference of opinion in Jacqueline's final year at the university. Her mother, aware of the keen mind her daughter possessed, suggested a professional career in law, medicine, or journalism. Jacqueline would have none of it. After she overcame her adolescent shyness, her personality blossomed in college, and she grew enamored with drama, the same passion that had claimed her mother a generation before. Her mother cautioned, and her mother warned: the road to success in acting was fraught with difficulty, and the weak-willed or those lacking in ability littered the wayside like so many ashes fallen from the cinderman's cart. Moreover, she added, it was an industry in love with its own glamour, one in which a slender waist and large breasts went further than a pocketful of talent. It was on this latter point that they differed least: her mother openly acknowledged Jacqueline's obvious dramatic skills. Yet in the end Jacqueline became convinced that her mother's caveats stemmed in large part from Jacqueline's weight. Thanks for the encouragement, Mom. But I can lose that weight. And when you see my star rising, you'll know I did it on my own.

Jacqueline knew her mother could have been of considerable help. A successful actress in her own right, forced by injury into early retirement, she could have pulled the strings to gain the exposure so necessary to Jacqueline in a business where one's contacts were as important as one's credentials. Yet Jacqueline insisted on going it alone. She would garner the success she saw as inevitable without a handout. And so the row became a rift, and the rift a widening filial void, as Jacqueline let the calls and letters go unanswered, eventually making her way to Manhattan armed only with a heartful of ambition.

Still, they did speak with one another, albeit infrequently. Jacqueline was civil, polite. Yet beneath the courteous tones of their speech was the slender thread of discontent that precluded any show of the tenderness and affection they had shared when she was younger. Deep down, Jacqueline yearned for the day she could return to her mother in triumph, having gotten the big break that would lead her to stardom. But it was not to be. The three years following her graduation were lean, discouraging times that saw her hopes turn to despair. Thus did she finally admit defeat, vanquished by her physical size, and in surrender called her mother, who helped her cast off the albatross of obesity that she had worn like a badge of failure.

"Mr. Hammill?"

"Yes?" he said, turning to stare at the lovely young woman.

"I'm back."

"Back?" he said, as the spark of recognition began to grow.

"In three weeks, as you said. But I'm afraid I didn't keep

my end of the bargain. I'm not one twenty." She smiled. "I'm less."

"Ramsey . . . Aren't you Jacqueline Ramsey?"

She nodded. "How do I look?"

"Marvelous, as if you didn't know! How in the world did you do it?"

"It's a long story. But I'm going to hold you to your word, Mr. Hammill. You said you were willing to reconsider."

"Yes, but . . . I'm afraid the matter has already been decided. We signed the female lead over a week ago."

"Please, give me a chance to go over the lines again. It won't take much of your time. I think you owe me that much."

"It's not that simple. Contracts have been signed, and we start taping this Friday."

"I'm sure the network has good lawyers, if it comes to that. And I know the script by heart. You said I was the most qualified for the part. Please, just give me another try."

Hammill was torn. The busty imbecile who had gotten the role was hardly his favorite actress. There was no question that Ramsey, by some miracle, was now physically her peer; technically, it was no contest. Still, production had begun, and promotion and publicity were in full swing. Yet he had given his word.

"Okay, but I'm not making any promises. We'll go to the set next door to avoid an uproar."

Ten minutes later, on the unlighted sound stage, Jacqueline delivered her lines with verve and polish. Hammill stood fifty feet away, arms folded across his chest, watching her intently, impressed by her remarkable performance. Another man approached him, walking quickly across the studio floor.

"Alan, where the hell've you been? I was—" He slowed, suddenly noticing Jacqueline. For several seconds he was speechless. And then, to Hammill, "Christ, she's beautiful. What a body."

They watched in silence. Jacqueline's poise and talent were irrefutable. She was the most natural of actresses, born for the stage. Hammill asked her to repeat the long monologue she'd done for him weeks before. She began without needing a cue.

"Where the hell was she when we were casting?"

"Just listen, Oscar."

They listened, impressed. When Jacqueline was finished, she simply stood there, looking their way.

"Who is she, Alan?"

"You have a short memory, Oscar." He reached for the phone to make the first of numerous calls that would be necessary. "I'll reintroduce you in a minute. After that, I'm going to need every bit of your help to keep us out of one Godawful lawsuit."

❧

The talk show host continued the live interview.

"As Maureen Ramsey's daughter, and as someone with such obvious talent, why did you delay your acting career until the start of *Hospice* three years ago, when you were already the ripe old age of—what? Twenty-five?"

Jacqueline nodded and shrugged. "I couldn't get a job."

"Seriously?"

"Yes. I've always been interested in acting. The problem was that ever since I was a kid, I was terribly heavy. 'Fat' would be more accurate."

"Most people watching today would find that astonishing. I would venture that the average *Hospice* viewer thinks of you as forever slender."

"Just the opposite. I think I experienced the same humiliations and disappointments as fat children everywhere. Obesity leaves an indelible mark on you; it's something you never forget."

"You've been in New York since . . ."

"I was twenty. Looking for parts, trying to line up a job, the usual. I simply couldn't get anywhere because of my weight. And then, one day, I lost it."

"In one day?"

"No," Jacqueline laughed. "It took me two weeks."

"How much did you lose?"

"Fifty-two pounds."

The audience murmured, and the host wore a look of amazement.

"That's phenomenal. How did you accomplish that?"

She replied without missing a beat. "I went to the Spa at San Sebastian."

The host wrinkled his brow in recollection.

"San Sebastian . . . What can you tell us about it? I vaguely recall that it's on the west coast."

"Yes, southern California. It's a small clinic."

"Do all of the Spa's clients have success similar to yours?"

"I honestly don't know. San Sebastian is small and lovely, and each patient is so carefully attended to that I never have the opportunity to meet anyone else. But I would imagine they probably do as well."

"You say 'never have'—do you return periodically?"

"Yes, every six months or so."

"Have you ever run across that sort of progress, Dr. Manley? Are you familiar with the work at San Sebastian?"

"Taking your second question first, the answers are 'no' and 'never.' "

Jacqueline looked his way with annoyance. Did he think she was lying?

"I guess it's hard for some experts in the field to admit that somebody else might know something they don't," she said coolly.

"How do you respond to that, Dr. Manley?"

"I'd be interested in learning what Miss Ramsey's secret is and what their program is at her spa."

"It's not a secret." She paused, growing increasingly angry at him, but uncertain how to reply. The staff at the Spa had never discussed it with her in detail.

"I'm curious, Miss Ramsey," Manley continued. "What did they do to you out there to produce such spectacular results?"

She reddened. "I . . . I'm not sure."

"I don't doubt Miss Ramsey's sincerity," he went on. "But I question her veracity. If what she claims were true, so many people would head for California that the state would split right down the San Andreas fault and fall into the Pacific."

The audience laughed. Jacqueline was mortified. She turned to stare at Manley, her gaze icy.

She was waiting for him in the hall when he left makeup.

"Dr. Manley?"

"Hello, again," he said. "How do I look without eye shadow?"

She ignored the remark.

"I don't know what you were trying to do out there, or what made you say what you did. But I want you to know that I think you are an absolute bastard!"

"Now wait a minute—"

"No, *you* wait!" she fired, furious. "What makes you think you're entitled to embarrass someone, to publicly humiliate a person, just because you've got an MD attached to your name?"

"Oh, please. You're not going to pretend you were serious, are you?"

"I most certainly was! You may meet a lot of pathologic liars in your business, but I resent it when you imply that I'm one of them!"

"Look, Jack-O—"

"The name is Miss Ramsey, if you don't mind!"

He shrugged. "Whatever you say. You're right, I run across a lot of weird people. I've also known some others who tend to stretch the truth a little. And I frankly don't see why you should get so high and righteous when you get caught in the act."

"How dare you!"

"Easy. I deal with facts. You know as well as I that it's impossible for anyone to do what you said. I don't care if you're a big star or not. I just think it's pretty low to go around misleading millions of people."

She glared at him, enraged by his accusations. She had no idea how to convince him, or if she should even try. "I guess it gives you a real thrill to tell me off like that."

"Look, Miss Ramsey. I don't want you to think I was attacking you personally, and I don't get my jollies out of being the Ralph Nader of medicine. I just think that there are millions of fat people out there, and they should know hype when they hear it."

They were approached by a cheerful young woman who resembled an oversized panda. She was looking flirtatiously at Manley as she linked arms with Jacqueline.

"I hope I'm interrupting," said Sheila. "I just developed this horrible psychosis. Do you have a card, Doctor?"

"The Doctor's not seeing new patients," said Jacqueline.

"I—" he began.

"He discovered something horrible about himself," Jacqueline continued, "and he's thinking about seeing his own doctor." She turned to Sheila. "He just accused me of inventing the story about losing fifty pounds."

"All I said was—"

"Why are the handsome ones always such shmucks?" Sheila said to Jacqueline, slowly turning her around by the elbow. "Come, darling. Let's go to the nearest construction site and look for some real men." They began to walk away. "If you ever get out of therapy," she called to Manley over her shoulder, "I've got great insurance."

Manley watched them depart. Had he been mistaken? He knew he had been pretty rough on her, yet what she claimed was patently absurd. Then again, he wondered, was it?

Chapter Four

On average, Manley lectured to the medical students once every six weeks, touching on various topics in psychiatry, pharmacology, or basic science. His present lecture, on physiology, covered the fundamentals of obesity. He periodically updated his notes to keep apace of recent developments in the field. After his appearance on the talk show, he had been inundated with queries about the simplest aspects of weight control.

The lecture hall was uncommonly crowded for a Friday. Scores of matronly nurses and paramedical personnel stood in the rear or flanked the exits. Manley walked back and forth as he spoke, surprised by the turnout, understanding the success of physicians who specialized in bariatric medicine. He had a provocative, Jesuitical style of teaching that brought the subject alive.

Yet despite the obvious attentiveness of his audience, he was distracted. The image of a lovely young woman he'd so recently insulted drifted in and out of his mind like a tantalizing fog. It was all he could do to maintain his concentration.

Toward the end of his presentation, he briefly commented on the tenuous relationship between dietary fads and physiologic reality. With compendious logic, he dismissed such topics as vitamin B-15, dolomite, and starch blockers as spurious notions with no basis in fact.

"Obesity, then, suggests an excess of body fat, whereas overweight means that the body weight is in excess of some arbitrary standard. As we've seen, thirty-five percent of the adult population is obese, though a specific medical cause can be found in less than five percent of cases. And obesity—directly or indirectly—probably accounts for fifteen to twenty percent of the adult mortality rate. One of your many future goals as physicians will be to deal effectively with a phenomenon that will threaten the well-being of many of your patients."

There were numerous questions from the assemblage. Most dealt with common approaches to the treatment of obesity, the value of appetite suppressants, or personal dietary dilemmas. Manley briefly replied to the questions in the short time remaining. Then he straightened up his notes as the listeners slowly filed out, wondering if any of these doctors-to-be would be the one to discover a revolutionary breakthrough in the treatment of the obese. His thoughts abruptly shifted again to Jacqueline Ramsey.

Assuming, he mentally amended, such a breakthrough had not already been discovered.

Later that afternoon, it took him more than five hours to drive from his apartment to his home in upper New York State. The secluded house in the Finger Lakes region was more of a wilderness cabin than a weekend retreat. It was far off the beaten path, virtually hidden, miles from the nearest highway, located deep in a forest whose tall trees bordered a blind cove. He arranged his work schedule so that he could leave no later than noon on Friday, returning home late Sunday night. He always went alone, except for the company of his dog, Dart. Inclement weather was no factor. He would brave the fiercest of blizzards in his four-wheel-drive vehicle, whose road-hugging traction now served him well when he turned off the old lumber road in the final two-mile stretch that wound through the woods to his cabin.

When he had built the cabin, six summers previously, he had had no idea that it would become the idyllic haven he dreamed of. He originally intended it as a sanctuary, a place where he could escape from the frenzied tumult of city life to the solitude of the wilderness. It proved to be all of that and much more. He had come to know nature, learned to understand the ways of forest animals in their own uncluttered habitat. During the summer, he would spend entire days on the lake, lazing in his canoe or fishing for bass or trout from the shore.

And then there was Ben. A retired trapper—part mountain man, part philosopher—he had come to befriend Manley when he was convinced of the younger man's sincere intention to leave civilization behind. Manley didn't hunt, but they fished together, prowled the woods together, and spent long winter hours before the fire in idle contentment.

Ben was a recluse. He would keep to himself for months at a time before he would mysteriously appear, bringing an offering of firewood or freshly killed game. He was a reticent sort; yet when he spoke, his words were pithy and instructive. There was little, if anything, that he did not know about the forest. His knowledge was voluminous, but he never flaunted it, speaking instead in easy monosyllables. It revealed itself in pieces, glints of insight that, taken together, were astonishingly profound observations from a man who had little formal schooling. Alone, he'd discerned the workings of the jack o'pulpit in dark forest reaches. His understanding of nature was gentle and philosophic. Reduced to its most basic form, his simple reasoning was that everything in nature had its place.

Manley had taught him to play chess, and Ben had taken to the game with uncanny ability. He would silently tug on his pipe, pondering each move, while smoke curled in wreaths about his long white hair or rose up in little ripples that played at the fringes of his short-cropped Hemingway beard. Manley had a deep affection for the man, overshadowed only by the devotion of Dart. He often wondered which way the dog would turn if both men were to call his name at the same time.

The snow came up to the vehicle's bumper. It was nearly dark. Dart, asleep for most of the trip, was jarred awake as the vehicle drove through ruts and over fallen limbs, while Manley followed the forest landmarks he knew so well. Suddenly Dart sat up and began barking loudly, looking through the window and off to the right. Manley braked to a stop. The dog's bark had a plaintive whine, and his downturned ears indicated excitement rather than danger.

"What is it, boy? One of your wild cousins in heat?"

He leaned over and opened the door. Dart leaped out and bounded out of sight through the snow. Seconds later, there came the sound of continuous yelping. Manley smiled. He turned off the motor, put on his boots, and followed Dart's trail through the white fluff.

Soon Dart came into view, leaping playfully on his hind legs. Manley glanced at the snow. The dog had found Ben's tracks, and the gamy scent that filled the air indicated another presence, perhaps that of a fine buck. Soon they returned to the van for the final leg of their drive.

They ate well that night. The scent Manley had detected was indeed a buck's—a whitetail stag Ben had neatly dispatched with his Winchester. Ben had butchered the deer and placed the bulk of the cuts into the bin of a makeshift outdoor freezer outside of Manley's cabin. In the cabin, the lingering aroma of pipe tobacco indicated that Ben had only recently departed. Manley roasted the choicest steaks over a blazing open fire, giving the scraps to Dart. After the meal, the dog lay at his feet, gnawing a bone. Manley gently rubbed the scruff of Dart's neck while he gazed at the embers that glowed in the hearth, feeling very much like a woodsman returned from the hunt.

Thoughts lost in the crackle of burning wood, he saw the glint in her eyes, the curious flecks of gold—eyes warmer than all sensibility. Strange that he should be thinking of her now. What would Ben have said? But then he pictured the old man's weathered face, the twinkle in his eye. At the root of everything, Ben taught, there was reason.

"I learned a long time ago that the greatest privilege in life is to be placed on this earth as an observer," Ben had said. "You watch, and you learn. You may not *understand*, but that comes slowly. Sooner or later, you discover the reason for it all. It may be an odd reason, or even a wicked reason. But if you search hard enough, you'll find it."

"How do I do that?"

"The trick," the old man had said, "is knowing where to look."

A while later, Manley tonged a log onto the dying fire and went to the large bay window that overlooked the lake. Outside, the sky was cloudless, the moon full. The hard ice on the cove was a mirror reflecting the bright light overhead. On impulse, he went to the closet and got his skates. Dart leaped to his feet and excitedly wagged his tail. Soon, after donning his parka and getting his stick, Manley followed the dog outdoors.

The air was frigid, calm, and still. Their breath was a cloud of frosted vapor that trailed them lakeward in a thin white mist. Manley sat on a felled log and laced up his skates. Dart was already on the ice, running and sliding across its surface like a circus clown. Moments later Manley was on the lake, gliding gracefully in long, forceful strides reminiscent of his days as an all-star collegiate defenseman.

He found three small logs and arranged them into a U-shaped goal. Dart, a practiced hockey veteran, barked loudly and stood his ground in front of the wood as Manley put his stick to the ice, pushing the tennis ball puck before him. He skated in widening circles, building up speed, eyes fixed on the goal. Dart was motionless, intent on the ball, his pointer's tail straight as a staff. Abruptly, Manley changed direction and streaked toward the logs. Dart tensed and braced his legs in a canine crouch. When Manley was twenty feet out, he swung his stick and rifled the ball toward the center of the U. The slap shot lifted off the ice, streaking higher and higher like an arrow. Just at the right moment, Dart leaped into the air and clamped the ball in his teeth. Manley skidded to a stop, a glistening spray of fine ice showering off his skates. He bent down and patted the dog affectionately on the head.

"Good boy, Dart. Good boy! I bet you're the only one who can stop Gretzky!"

Dart furiously wagged his tail, dropped the ball at Manley's feet, and licked his face.

Chapter Five

He called to her by name, but the harsh wind drowned out his words. Manley quickened his pace to match her long strides. He tapped her shoulder. Sheila whirled with a snarl, arm somewhat comically raised in a karatelike posture that caught him completely by surprise. While he was deciding whether to laugh or to apologize, she spat out a warning.

"Start up with me and kiss your balls good-bye."

"Miss Hastings? Sheila?"

There was a glint of recognition, and her arm lowered.

"Full marks." She scrutinized him approvingly. "I know those brown eyes from somewhere."

"Jacqueline Ramsey introduced us after the talk show."

"Ah yes. The naughty doctor who fancies himself a psychiatrist."

She tried to effect a withering stare, but it turned into a look of bawdy approval.

Manley nodded. "The same. Could I speak to you for a minute?"

"I know I should tell you to piss off and go to hell. For Jackie's sake." She clasped her hand theatrically to her breast. "Yet I am a woman totally lacking in dignity. What's on your mind, cutie?"

"Just talk."

"Talk? How utterly insulting. I was hoping for more."

He nodded toward a cafe across the street.

"Care for a drink?"

"Tea, darling." She unexpectedly took him by the arm and led him expertly through the traffic. "I know the owner here. For a few bucks I'm sure he could round up a couch for you."

"I wasn't intending a heavy analytical discussion."

"Nor I."

They reached the other side of the street and entered the establishment. The proprietor escorted them to a corner booth. While Manley helped remove her coat, a waiter took their order. Sheila plunked her elbows on the table, and her head shivered forward at him before settling into the bowl of her hands.

"Your credentials sounded very impressive on the show, Dr. Manley."

He gave a modest shrug.

"I think they overplayed it a little. And it's Rick."

"An undeniably delicious name." She raised her eyebrows at him, let them drop, and turned serious. "Before we begin, Doctor, I must warn you that sex is constantly on my mind. Black leather. A whip. Spiked heels."

"Sheila, I—"

"I wear nothing under this. But you needn't feel insecure."

He smiled. "I have a sneaking suspicion I'm getting absolutely nowhere."

"Entirely up to you, darling. Don't let it bother you that I'm a quick lay." She lifted a daisy from a nearby bud vase and began to pluck its petals. "He loves me, he loves me not . . ."

"Could I possibly talk with you about Jacqueline Ramsey?"

She threw him a look of disappointment and nipped the flower off its stem.

"Pig. Using me like that. How hateful."

"Very much what Miss Ramsey said to me. She thinks I'm a bastard and a chauvinist pig."

"Language like that from such a lovely girl! Shameful. Probably right, though."

"Now wait. The fact is—"

"Let me guess," Sheila interrupted. " 'If only she knew me better'?"

He turned away from her stare, disconcerted.

"Well, something along those lines."

"And you want me to help."

"I want you to listen to my side of things. I think she completely misunderstood me."

"And after you let your wretched heart out to me, and once I've conceded that you are a truly adorable man, then what? I should smooth things out with Jack so the two of you can play a little smoochie?"

"I merely want to make a position statement."

"Positively political."

"After that, we'll see."

Sheila sighed. "It boils down to my running interference for you."

"I wouldn't exactly put it that way."

"However you put it, you *are* a bastard."

He was startled by her serious tone. Apologetically, "Sheila, please don't misconstrue—"

"You men are all alike," she softly clucked, twisting to make room for their drinks. "Rainbow chasers. I sit here before you, a totally wanton woman, willing to do your kinkiest bidding." Her gaze swiveled to follow the departing waiter. "Dear, dear, what a delightfully compact behind."

"Are you saying you won't talk about her?"

"My you are persistent," she said, turning back to him, "which ordinarily would make me want to tell you to bugger off." She gave him a contemplative look. "However, in your case I may make an exception. Only because I remember the way Jackie was looking at you. I know what Jackie's thinking, you see, despite her tone of voice." She paused. "No doubt this little confession makes your black heart go all atwitter?"

"I'm not sure what you mean."

"Oh, I think you know. Simple psychology. Or is it chemistry? Whichever. Ah, me," she sighed loudly. "Another one that got away without so much as a nibble." She eyed him seductively and undid the top two buttons of her blouse. "If you promise to stop staring at my breasts in that crudely obvious way, I'll tell you whatever you want."

Manley laughed. He touched Sheila's hand, aglow with a feeling of kinship.

"Jackie, at heart, is probably the sweetest person you could ever meet. Loyal, trustworthy. Literally take the shirt off her back for you. Which is something I doubt you would object to."

"I honestly hadn't thought that far ahead."

"Pity. I've seen firsthand what you're missing. But it wasn't always that way, you know. Which is why she was so resentful of your poking fun at her, suggesting that she was lying."

"I didn't mean to imply that at all. It just sounded too incredible."

"Well, how's this for credible? Remember *Indigo Caper*?"

"The Suzanne Fontaine film? When she was a kid?"

"*And* Jackie Ramsey film. They were costars, but for some reason most people remember Suzanne."

"God, that was ages ago. I didn't realize."

"Jackie was eleven, Suzanne ten. Suzanne did one picture after that, and Jackie had one in the works. But it got scrapped."

"Why?"

"She grew tits, for one thing. Kind of destroyed the pixie-ish image they had in mind. For another, she got fat. And I don't mean a little baby fat. She gained forty pounds in about a year. She once told me she weighed one fifty on her thirteenth birthday. Now, that's *fat*. And after that there was no end in sight."

Manley sipped his drink and toyed with a breadstick.

"Adolescent obesity is a tough nut to crack. So many factors involved. Peer pressure, awakening sexuality, parental attitudes. All have their impact on the kid's self-image."

"I'm sure whatever you're mumbling is true. You're the doctor. But I doubt Jackie ever thought of it in precisely those terms. All she knew was that she was a blimp."

"She told you all this?"

"Surprised? Fatties *do* talk—but only to one another. We roomed together when we first came to New York." Her gaze grew distant. "She used to have this recurring dream. Couldn't fall asleep after that."

"A nightmare?"

"Yes, but she never actually discussed it with me. She

would only let on that she dreamed she physically became a pig. No doubt that means something profound to you."

He looked away reflectively. "I suppose that could account for it."

"For what?"

"Her reaction. If she truly were that obese—"

"She was. I've seen her hidden album of snapshots that all us fatties keep hidden away."

"—then she'd resent anyone who impugned her sincerity."

"Splendidly put, whatever impugn means."

He swirled the melting ice in his drink.

"It's too bad her family couldn't help out. Parents with children who share the same career can be mutually supportive."

"Mums? Sweet old Maureen?"

"Why do you say it like that?"

"She's all charm, Maureen. Publicly. But somehow I can't picture her as supportive."

"No?"

"Jack never said as much directly, but I'd wager there was a bit of competition there, luv. What time is it?"

Manley showed her his watch and nodded at her saucer. "Another cup of tea?"

Sheila lifted the limp teabag. "It's hard to think of this dreadfully insipid stuff as tea, but yes. Some other time, though." She reached for her coat, then turned to him with one eyebrow uplifted. "Unless, of course, you won't reconsider sharing some delightfully obscene perversion?"

He smiled and gave his head a polite shake.

"My ego thanks you for the flattery."

"How disappointing." She buttoned her coat. "As for Jack, I might be able to put in a good word or two for you. And I should mention that she's a soft touch for flowers."

"Before you go," he said, rising beside her, "tell me something."

"Anything, darling."

"This business of Jacqueline's weight loss . . ."

"Is a fact, Doctor. I don't know precisely how she did it, but I can vouch for its occurrence exactly as she said."

"But how—"

Her forefinger silenced his lips.

"Why don't you ask her yourself?"

She turned and left, leaving him to ponder how he could implement her suggestion.

Chapter Six

"It's the second time he's called, Miss Ramsey," said the wardrobe clerk.

Jacqueline glanced at the blinking light on the dressing room phone. She never thought he would call, though she now wondered if she hadn't secretly hoped he would. And then there were the flowers: not the typical gaudy floral displays or the dozens of roses with tight hothouse buds, but an unpretentious arrangement of violet crocus and yellow daffodil. The simple card that accompanied it read, "I'm sorry—Rick Manley." She picked up the telephone.

"Yes?"

"Sorry to disturb you, Miss Ramsey. I just called to apologize for some of the things I said on the show last week. I had no right to come down on you that hard."

"No, you didn't."

There was a pause; neither of them could think of what to say.

Finally, "Apology accepted?"

Jacqueline smiled. "Accepted."

"Maybe we could seal the truce over a cup of coffee. I know you're busy, but it would make me feel a lot better if I could say I'm sorry in person."

She began to think her initial impression of him was correct.

"All right." She gave him the address of Grace's coffee shop.

She met him a short while later, after evening rush hour. The cafe was relatively uncrowded; most people were scurrying home. While Manley ordered only coffee, Jacqueline confessed she hadn't eaten yet. Familiar with the menu, she called out her requests to Grace. After taking their order, Grace stayed a polite distance away, occasionally looking at Jacqueline with a knowing wink. Manley was well into his second cup of coffee—and Jacqueline midway through her meal—before either of them could relax. She sensed he was holding back, wanting to ask something but waiting for the proper moment. She asked him if he had always lived in Manhattan.

Manley told her how he had come to New York. After graduating from Boston College, he had very nearly tried to become a professional hockey player. He had promising offers from various clubs. He knew he was good—maybe even as good, eventually, as a Potvin or an Esposito. But he wasn't sure he had the patience to endure the lean years in minor league play, always exposing himself to injury, before he earned a berth in the NHL. Therefore he'd entered medical school in New York, having developed a liking for medicine during his undergraduate major in psychology.

He'd explained that after medical school had come residency training in the field of psychiatry, and then he had gone on to tell her why he had turned from the practical side to basic research in psychiatry midway through his training.

"Do you work with animals?"

"God, no. I hate animal experiments. I can't stand to see them suffer—never could. I'm forever letting them out of their cages."

Jacqueline laughed. She was growing fond of this man, and she thought she could understand the reason behind his cheerfully rugged mannerisms. Deep down, he was still a child at heart, a child gleefully playing outdoors; or at the very least, he was a grown man who retained a child's sensitivity.

As he spoke, Manley was watching her. She was an attentive listener, with none of the snobbery he so often associated with successful entertainers. He began to under-

113

stand that success was indeed rather new to her. She had a bubbly enthusiasm that was almost infectious.

Finally the moment had arrived.

"I don't see that much of a resemblance."

"Between what?"

"You and your mother," he began, broaching the subject obliquely. He had been waiting for the verbal entree; and now that he had it, he watched her, noting the subtly brooding cast that came over her features.

She averted her eyes.

"Is there supposed to be?"

"That's what they thought on the talk show."

"Oh, that. Everyone says that, but I agree with you. I think I take after my father. He's dead, you know."

"I wasn't aware."

"He died in a car crash when I was twelve. My mother was injured, too, but she pulled through all right," she said, with the faintest suggestion of ambivalence.

"Does that disappoint you?"

"Disappoint me? Why in the world should it?"

"Just because of the way you said it. I get the impression of some unfinished business between the two of you."

"Unfinished business," she slowly replied, mulling over the phrase. "Yes, I suppose you could say that."

"Like to talk about it?"

"Ah," she said, aiming a pistol finger at him. "The psychiatrist speaks."

"Let's just say I'm curious."

"About what?"

"There you go again. Evasive."

Jacqueline felt surprisingly at ease with this man. Something in his manner encouraged her to reveal emotions she'd always kept hidden. She made a palms-up gesture of cooperation.

"All right. What do you want to know?"

"Whatever you want to tell me."

She sighed. "This is getting us nowhere."

"Your mother's accident, then. What happened after that?"

"Nothing," she quickly replied. Then, after a moment's reflection, "Or everything. Depends how you look at it."

"How do *you* look at it?"

"I can't get out of this gracefully, can I?"

"It seems important for you not to talk about it. Painful memories?"

"Not terribly painful, no. Well . . . a little. Maybe."

"How so?"

She looked beyond him toward a horizon of distant reminiscence.

"I guess it all started after I made *Indigo Caper*. Did you see it?"

"Yes."

"My father was still alive then, and he was thrilled. I'm an only child. My parents doted on me when I was younger. But after that film, Mother seemed to grow . . . distant."

"In what way?"

"It seemed she no longer had time for me. We stopped doing things together. And whenever we did, I felt like some Godawful excess baggage she was forced to lug along."

Guilt, thought Manley. Feelings of rejection.

"And it was your fault?"

"Was it?"

"I'm asking."

Jacqueline reflected. "I guess I thought so at the time. I remember wanting to do things to please her. I suppose I wanted her praise, but I no longer seemed to get it. At night I would lie awake wondering what I was doing wrong. Does that sound right?"

"It's not a question of wrong or right. It's how you felt about it. You mentioned praise. Another word might be more appropriate."

"Which?"

He shrugged.

"Recognition. Attention."

"Attention," she faintly seconded, running a finger around the rim of her cup. "I never really thought of it that way."

"It must have been an uncomfortable feeling."

"Very. Yes, very."

"And once your father died, it got worse?"

"How did you know?"

"Not hard to figure out. Here you went from one hundred percent recognition as the center of your parents' attention to fifty percent. Then, after the movie, to zero. All in a relatively short time span. That can have an impact."

"In what way?"

Manley made an expansive gesture with his hands.

"When an individual is suddenly deprived of affection, he may try to regain it from another source. In a teenage girl that source might be boys. The classic example is the adolescent girl who becomes the easy make on the block."

She gave an amused whiff of a smile.

"That might have been interesting. But I never really dated until I was much older."

"Why was that?"

"I got fat. Grotesquely fat, to the point where I was terrified of being seen in public."

"It could be that was your way of solving it, then."

"What was?"

"Food. Food can be a tremendous source of affection. It becomes a reward. Do you see what I'm driving at?"

"Yes . . . Yes, I do."

"The problem is that it also becomes a vicious cycle: the more you eat, the fatter you get. The fatter you get, the worse you feel. The worse you feel, the more you eat." He paused, watching her nod in slow acquiescence. "What did your mother think of your change in eating habits?"

"It didn't seem to bother her. She kept telling me not to worry about it. In fact she even brought home more for me to eat. Cakes. Danish."

"How did that make you feel?"

"Angry," she said without hesitation. "Furious, sometimes. But for some reason I would eat it anyway."

"That made you resent her?"

"Oh, definitely."

He hesitated, looking down at the table as if reaching deep inside himself for a comment.

116

"Did you ever wonder, Miss Ramsey, how your mother might have looked at things?"

"Not exactly. Should I have?"

"Again, it's not a question of should or shouldn't, wrong or right. But for the moment let me put myself in her place. From her point of view, *you* might have been the threat."

Her expression turned disbelieving.

"Come on, I was no threat."

"Not physically, no. And as someone who adored her mother, to use your own words, there would be no reason for you to suspect that she might harbor negative thoughts toward you. Yet consider how she might have viewed it. Let's say that she *was* at the height of her career. That meant she could go in only one direction: down. At that point, if her daughter suddenly stole the show—quite literally—she may have indeed felt threatened."

"Do you think so?"

"Certainly possible. And if she did, she may have reacted to that threat with resentment. In which case the things you've blamed yourself for all these years—what you describe as your resentment—might merely have been a very human response to her resentment."

"You make it sound so simple."

"Of course it's not. I'm oversimplifying to make a point. But I think it's worth trying to understand things as seen through your mother's eyes."

She looked away. "I have tried."

To Manley, it sounded like a textbook case of parent-child jealousy, but one which smacked of subtle sabotage. What he could not understand was Jacqueline's current attitude toward eating. He imagined she would have been extremely careful about what she consumed. Yet throughout their discussion, she seemed to be continually nibbling.

"How can you get away with that?" he asked, motioning to the empty plate beside her. "Spaghetti, a bagel, and now the French bread. Aren't you concerned about your weight?"

"Of course. The idea of getting fat terrifies me. But to me, this isn't overeating. It's following doctor's orders."

"You're allowed unrestricted junk food?"

"Carbohydrates. I'm supposed to eat a lot of carbo-hydrates: pasta, bread. The things I used to hate myself for eating when I was growing up."

"That's a switch."

"I know. As you can see I'm not exactly stuffing myself, but I do stick to those general guidelines. I *would* be worried if I didn't eat as instructed."

"With my background, you can understand why I'm a little skeptical about how quickly you lost weight, can't you?"

"Of course. I'd probably feel the same way."

"The problem I have, Miss Ramsey—"

"I think we can skip the formality and switch to Jacqueline, all right?"

He smiled. "Okay. But only if you call me Rick. Yet I can't deny that I'm having a lot of trouble buying the logic in what you're saying."

She smiled back at him. "We're not going to get into another big argument over this, are we?"

"I hope not. But as a researcher, it's frustrating that I can't figure out what's going on in a field in which I am supposedly an expert."

"Why don't you call them at the Spa?"

"Maybe I will. But didn't they give you any clue at all?"

"Not really. It seemed pretty straightforward. There was the diet, of course. And during the day, personally supervised exercise." She paused and reflected. "The only thing you might consider unusual . . ." She shook her head. "No, forget it. I'm sure it was nothing."

"Tell me anyway."

"Oh, I was just thinking about the way I sleep when I'm there."

He laughed. "I never get a wink on a strange mattress either."

"But that's just the point. I sleep wonderfully. Some-thing in the air, I suppose. Or maybe it's my digestion."

"Nothing like hot chocolate before bedtime."

"You're not far off. Part of their diet is a late-night

snack. Must be their equivalent of cookies and milk. It's amazing how I start to nod off right after that. I'm zonked in fifteen minutes. Eight hours of sound, dreamless sleep."

"Uninterrupted?"

"Yes. Isn't that strange? You see, for as long as I can remember, I've always gotten up twice during the night. But at San Sebastian, never. I sleep straight through until morning."

"You make it sound like you were drugged."

She smiled and rebuked him with a little wave of her hand.

"No, they frown on pills and shots. They say it's not natural."

"Aren't you worried by such unusually deep sleep?"

"Worried about what?"

He shrugged. "A lot of things. Being sexually molested, for instance."

She laughed. "You've never seen pictures of Dr. Hume, have you."

"Who's Dr. Hume?"

"The director of the Spa. He's the most gorgeous, charming man I've ever met. If he did molest me, my only regret would be that I wasn't awake to enjoy it."

She looked at the clock and took one last bite of bread.

"God, it's late. I have a long script to go over tonight." She got up and put on her coat. "Don't worry about the bill. Grace insists it's on the house. She says business began to boom once word got around that I used to work here." She did the last of the buttons, and her laughing expression softened. She looked down at him fondly.

"The flowers were very sweet, Rick."

"I forced those bulbs indoors, in a little place I have upstate."

"Maybe you'll let me see it sometime. Ciao."

She turned and was gone.

He stared at the door long after she left, darkly wondering if what she said could be true. She certainly seemed to believe it. As a psychiatrist, he was worried about her nights without recall. Two weeks of nights without memory, a fortnight under another person's control. Who knew what kind of subconscious scar that might leave? He had seen her hesitation, the hint of worry that surfaced when he'd begun to question her in detail.

He was also worried about her. She was so gay, so carefree; yet beneath her childlike joy was a fierce will, a granitelike determination. He didn't doubt for an instant that she'd do virtually anything to stay thin.

There's a reason for everything, Ben had said. Manley didn't understand that reason; nor, apparently, did she. But now he wanted more than anything to figure it out.

Chapter Seven

Jacqueline leaned against the headrest as she sat in bed reviewing her *Hospice* script, steadying its pages on her propped-up knees. After several minutes of concentration, she took a breath and let her head fall back against the bolster. She rubbed her eyes and gazed around the room at her plants, noting how each fit perfectly into its own sculpted niche in the decor. Of course it hadn't always been that way. She closed her eyes and thought back several years to the time she roomed with Sheila. Their last days as roommates, not long after Jacqueline had won the lead in *Hospice*, had been a changing point in their careers.

Jacqueline smiled at the recollection. The apartment they had shared was scarcely one-third the size of her present digs. Its kitchenette was minuscule, not much larger than a walk-in closet. Whereas the newly slender Jacqueline could move about it freely, its cramped contours considerably restricted Sheila's movements; but she had nonetheless managed to maneuver within its confines, somewhat clumsily, Jacqueline recalled, to prepare countless meals and snacks. Each night Jacqueline had returned from work, Sheila had been in that kitchenette, preparing the customary pot of coffee they had shared while rehashing the day's events.

They had been very close, as roommates went, sharing many of the same hopes and frustrations. One of the few things on which they differed was their orientation toward men. Whereas Jacqueline had been—according to her recol-

121

lection of Sheila's description—"ingenuously naive," Sheila had related to the opposite sex with a down-to-earth candor she referred to as "disappointingly lewd," in the sense that her unfettered interest in such matters had always exceeded that of the men she encountered. And then, once Jacqueline's role in the soap opera was secure, Sheila had decided to move on, over Jacqueline's protests.

Sheila had opted for a chance at English theater. It was partly, Jacqueline remembered Sheila saying, to keep from crowding Jacqueline, whose success demanded more breathing room, and partly because Sheila had hoped that—contrary to public perception—British men might prove more responsive to her overtures than had their American cousins.

"Wrong again," Jacqueline said to herself, still smiling in dreamy reflection.

Thinking back, she remembered how intent Sheila had been on meeting Jacqueline's mother before her departure. After all, Sheila had maintained, how often did a struggling actress—or anyone, for that matter—get to meet a star of such considerable fame? Jacqueline had finally given her promise. They had agreed to make the trip to Maureen's estate shortly before Sheila's transatlantic crossing.

Jacqueline's smile lessened as she recalled the conversation that had preceded their visit. She had just shuffled into their apartment on that cold night, tossing her coat on the couch as she collapsed wearily beside it.

"I think I could sleep all weekend."

"Why you unprincipled conniver. Barely home and already trying to pull a fastie? Forget it. We're leaving tomorrow at eight sharp."

"Wouldn't you rather sleep late?"

"No."

"It's at least a two-hour drive."

"Worry not. I never get carsick."

"Sheil . . . are you sure?"

Sheila pointed an insistent finger at her. "There's no way I'm letting you forget your promise, sweetie, so don't try to weasel out on me now. And it's not the Marquis de

Sade, for God's sake. It's your mother. How long has it been since you've seen her?"

Jacqueline looked upward in contemplation. "Two years. Maybe three."

"You mean she's never seen you thin?"

"Not in person, no."

Sheila shook her head.

"I can't understand you. Not long ago, you could have understudied Shamoo the Whale. Don't you think your mother would be proud of the way you look now?"

"I honestly don't know what she'd like. All I'm sure of is what she doesn't."

"Meaning?"

Jacqueline's eyes narrowed, a distant look.

"Mother is . . . I don't know. It's hard to explain. Maybe it's just some of the things she says." She paused, reflecting, and her stare deepened in concentration. "Or the way she says them."

They arrived at Maureen Ramsey's Connecticut estate late the following morning. Sheila's excitement was obvious; she was loquacious, giggly. Outwardly, Jacqueline appeared subdued. Inwardly, however, she was truly eager to see her mother again, even daring to hope that they might somehow recapture the warmth and closeness she remembered sharing when she was growing up. Until today, all she lacked was the courage. And now Sheila's insistence provided that.

Sheila fidgeted with her hair as Jacqueline rang the doorbell.

"This perm's a frizzball, isn't it?"

"It looks fine."

"What do I call her? Miss Ramsey?"

"Sheila, honestly. Maureen. Just call her Maureen."

"Do I bow or something? Curtsy?"

"Just be yourself."

"Christ, if I do that we'll wind up in jail."

A maid opened the heavy front door. Jacqueline cautiously entered the manor, trailed by an uncharacteristically sheepish Sheila.

"Jacqueline!"

Maureen Ramsey smiled broadly as she called to her from across the room. She was holding a cane, and she dragged one leg slightly as she crossed the floor.

Touched by her mother's smile, Jacqueline advanced more quickly. Soon mother and daughter were sharing what appeared to be a genuinely warm embrace, clinging with the intensity of long-lost friends. Finally her mother pulled away and admired Jacqueline at arm's length.

"Here, let me look at you. My, you are stunning!"

Beaming like an adolescent, Jacqueline made a slow circle as she stood in place. "Isn't it fantastic?"

"Incredible. Simply incredible."

Jacqueline was delighted, and she spoke with mounting enthusiasm. "Did you see the show, Mother?"

"Oh, I haven't missed a day. You are wonderful in it." Slowly, her gaze drifted in the direction of Sheila. "And is this the delightful roommate I've heard about?"

Jacqueline whirled around, abashed by her gaffe.

"I'm sorry, Sheil. Atrocious manners. Mother, this is Sheila Hastings. Sheila's more than a roommate," she confided, drawing Sheila forward by the wrist. "She's my dearest friend."

Sheila gawked self-consciously as Mrs. Ramsey extended her arm in welcome. Yet once their hands clasped, Sheila's diffidence vanished, falling away like a veil.

"It's a pleasure, Sheila."

There was a long moment as Sheila collected herself.

"For me more than you, Miss Ramsey."

"Please—call me Maureen."

"I can't tell you how long I've looked forward to meeting you," Sheila prattled like a gadfly, furiously shaking the older woman's arm as if it were the handle of a water pump.

"Thank you," Maureen said, politely prying her hand away. "Come, let's sit down."

She escorted them into the living room, where they took seats around a low coffee table. Maureen leaned forward and eagerly addressed her daughter.

"Is the rumor I heard about the ratings true?"

"Right to the top of the charts, in two months!" Jacqueline nodded with a smile.

"And been there ever since," Sheila added.

"You must be thrilled."

"Oh, Mother, I am so terribly happy!"

Maureen lightly placed her hand atop her daughter's. There was a tone of affection in her voice.

"And I am so terribly proud of you, Jacqueline."

"Mother," Jacqueline replied awkwardly, her eyes moist with joy. She gratefully squeezed the hand that touched hers. "I couldn't have done it without you."

"Or without Dr. Hume."

"No." She nodded in the direction of the maid, who had been discreetly standing in the background waiting to serve tea and pastries. "When I think back to the days before you arranged for my trip to the Spa, it's as if . . . as if I lived in another world. Wasn't it, Sheila?"

"Positively alien."

"I'll never be able to thank you enough, Mother."

"Nonsense! Seeing you happy is thanks enough for me. But has your life really changed all that much?"

"Completely. You have no idea."

"Has it, now?" said Maureen, with a suggestive twinkle in her eye. "That leads to the question I've been waiting for. The one about all the delicious men in your life."

Jacqueline shrugged. "There really haven't been that many. Not that I haven't had plenty of offers. It's just that I've been working so hard, I haven't had the time."

Sheila's laugh was an abbreviated snort.

"Don't believe a word of it. Jackie attracts more men than a dog does fleas."

Jacqueline reddened in embarrassment. "Oh, you're hopeless, Sheila."

"Should I name 'em?"

Maureen clapped her hands delightedly, wearing a look of salacious anticipation.

"Ah, here comes the good part."

"Well," Jacqueline admitted, managing a little grin, "I may go out sometimes. Nothing on a regular basis."

"Jackie, darling," Sheila inflected, "surely you recall what happened to Pinocchio's nose?"

"Sheila," Jacqueline replied as she raised her eyebrows, "you wouldn't by any chance be trying to give Mother the wrong impression? Name one."

"*One?*" She turned to wink at Maureen and whispered in a conspiratorial murmur. "Would you believe dozens?" Then, to Jacqueline, "How's Roger Markham? Just for starters."

"Oh, Sheila, really. I haven't seen him in months."

"Not the offspring of a certain actor by the same name?" asked the older Ramsey.

"You've got it, Mo."

"Dreadful man, Roger senior. Well, not totally dreadful. He did have at least one stimulating aspect."

Jacqueline grew curious. "I didn't know you dated him."

"Of course I didn't. At least not in the ordinary sense of the word." Her face brightened with a faint smile. "However, there was a time, when I was pregnant with you, that I thought Roger might be your sire. It turned out that he wasn't, thank goodness. Not that I ever mentioned the nasty business to your father."

"Mother, you were positively scandalous!"

"Utterly outlaw," Sheila scolded, nodding her head delightedly.

"Most definitely. And I loved every minute of it. Might even have divorced your father if Roger weren't a Leo."

"Bad sign," Sheila agreed.

Jacqueline's eyes rolled upward, and she released an exasperated sigh. "Now you've done it. There goes the ball game."

"Done what, darling?"

"Astrology. Sheila's bonkers about it. Known to talk your ear off."

"As well she should. It's a science, you know. Wouldn't you agree, Sheila?"

"Totally."

"Take Roger senior, for instance. As a Leo, he considered himself a born leader, while others thought he was simply pushy. But then most Leos are nothing but bullies.

And Roger was terribly vain. He couldn't tolerate honest criticism. Disgustingly arrogant." She hesitated and raised her eyes, peering into the distant past. "Leo people are such thieving bastards."

Jacqueline smiled to herself, giving her head a little shake. Her mother had always been so outspokenly candid. She leaned forward and helped herself to a large croissant-like pastry comprised of buttered dough without custard filling.

"Do be careful," her mother said. "Rather fattening."

"It's all right. All part of my diet. Sort of therapeutic, as long as the carbohydrates aren't pure sweets."

"You don't say. Strange how Dr. Hume forbid me to touch the stuff. Nothing personal, darling—but how much do you weigh?"

"About one fifteen," Jacqueline said, feeling an uncomfortable self-consciousness when she took another large bite.

"Really, now. Can't fool dear old Mums."

Jacqueline stared at her with mounting annoyance. "I'm not fooling, Mother."

"Yes . . . ," her mother replied, letting her gaze slowly run the length of her daughter's seated figure. "Perhaps it's the camera. Celluloid can be so insulting. Adds ten pounds, you know."

Jacqueline felt the muscles in her face tighten in mortification. How thick the air seemed then, how difficult to breathe.

Even now, after three years of success with *Hospice*, she still wondered whether her mother could ever be completely satisfied with her.

The four of them—two producers and two actresses— sat mute and immobile backstage of *Hospice*. It was up to Jacqueline to speak. Sheila was at her side; Emil Berson sat opposite, hunched forward in expectation, and Alan Hammill was in between, arms folded across his chest, lips pursed in a pout. Though still stunned, Jacqueline maintained the sculpted grace of a statue.

127

"I don't know what to say."

"Just say yes," Berson said, "and leave the rest to me."

"Sheil? Did you know?"

"I'm just as surprised as you."

"Do you think I should?"

"I think you'd be crazy not to."

Jacqueline mulled over the reply and then turned to Hammill.

"How about you, Alan? I imagine you're not exactly thrilled about this."

"I'm not. But it's your career. I just want you to know that Emil and I have known one another a long time, so everything is up front and out in the open as far as I'm concerned. Whatever you decide is up to you."

"It's so sudden . . . Look, I'm going to call Bernie."

"I already spoke with him," said Berson. "He's *dying* for you to take it. I made him promise to give you twenty-four hours to think it over before he pounced on you."

"God."

Jacqueline pushed up out of her chair and walked slow circles around the others.

"I suppose I should be flattered. Jesus, that sounds terrible—I *am* flattered. But you're talking about a whole different ball game. I don't know if I could cut it."

"Oh, come on, you've got to be kidding," said Sheila.

"Sheil, I haven't done live stage since college. All I know is soaps."

"If I thought that, I wouldn't have offered you the part," said Berson.

"But how could I just drop everything here on such short notice?"

"Jackie, I'm pressed for time myself," said Berson. "I have to know by tomorrow. But you certainly shouldn't worry about leaving the show. Alan's an expert at knocking people off."

"I beg your pardon?" Hammill said with smiling indignation.

Jacqueline stopped pacing before Hammill's chair.

"Alan, be honest with me. Do you think I could do it?"

"Hey, that's putting me on the spot."

"But I have to know. I trust your opinion on this more than anyone's."

Hammill looked back at her and exhaled thoughtfully.

"I don't know why you always sell yourself short. You have this underlying compulsion to look at yourself as a one-dimensional actress. But you're not," he said. "So at the risk of losing the biggest star I ever directed, I have to say yes. There's no question you could do it."

That seemed to settle it for Jacqueline. At length, the informal conference broke up. Jacqueline promised her reply by the following day. She and Sheila put on their coats when the two men were gone.

"Sometimes I think you're nuts."

"I'm no Meeghan Fleming."

"Thank God for that. You're a thousand times better."

"But to just up and leave . . ."

"You're unbelievable. You make it sound like you're entering a convent," said Sheila with exasperation. "This chance is the stuff that dreams are made of—but to hear you talk, it's like you were losing your job."

Outside, they quickly found a cab and settled inside.

"Why did she quit?"

"I don't know. And who cares? Maybe somebody was honest enough to tell her she had BO. But what does that have to do with you?"

"I suppose nothing."

"Precisely. If you don't take her part, you ought to have your head examined."

"I wonder what Rick would say?"

"I said head, darling, not the parts he's been examining."

"Sheila, if I didn't know you better—"

"Yeah, I know, you'd tell me off. But I can read between the lines."

"Christ, I haven't seen the guy that often."

"How many times does it take?"

"You're impossible."

Jacqueline shivered in the back seat of the cab, no longer aware of Sheila's banter.

The lead role in a major Broadway production was a guarantee of career success. Still, a plague of uncertainty infected her self-confidence. She began to picture herself onstage, before a live audience. Yet no matter what costume she wore, the image that came to mind was that of an unmistakably obese woman.

The time was approaching for her semiannual pilgrimage to San Sebastian. She envisioned Dr. Hume's warm face, heard his words of comfort. If anyone could encourage her, she thought, it would be he.

An idea unexpectedly occurred to her, but she decided to wait until later, until they had nearly finished their dinners, before she broached the subject with Sheila. Her lips tightened with distress as she watched her friend lighten her coffee.

"Sheila, do you really need that much cream? And that dessert is so fattening. Why don't you skip it?"

"Not to worry, dearie. Extra calories make me lovable."

But Jacqueline did worry. She toyed with a crust of bread as she watched her chum consume the dessert, suddenly overtaken by a feeling of intense affection that brought tears to her eyes. She would do anything for Sheila, if she could; and despite Sheila's occasional protestations of satisfaction with her weight, Jacqueline suspected it was all a pretense. She could not conceive of anyone not wanting to be slender, if given the opportunity. And now the opportunity was perfect.

"When was the last time you were in California?"

"Never ever. Too much sun can give you cancer."

"How could you miss Disneyland?"

"Not to worry. All seven men in my life have been dwarfs."

"Sheil, what would you think about going to San Sebastian with me?"

"Golly, do I look that fat?"

"Seriously."

Sheila shrugged. "I never really thought about it. And on my salary, I don't exactly have the money."

"I mean as my guest. You know I'm due at the spa next week—the *Hospice* script already allows for my being away. You're such a quick study that I bet if you asked Emil for two weeks off, he'd give it to you. We'll still have plenty of time to rehearse when we get back."

"Whatever did I do to deserve this? Christmas is over, you know."

Jacqueline touched her friend's hand. "Consider it an investment," she smiled. "If I keep you happy, I keep me happy."

"Ah, to be a size twelve again. . ." She arched her eyebrows in contemplation. "Saint Jacqueline," she said thoughtfully. "It has a nice ring to it."

"So you'll come?"

"Of course, darling. I'm not as stupid as I look." Touched, Sheila squeezed Jacqueline's hand in grateful reply.

The following day, Wednesday, Jacqueline told Hammill her decision. He fully expected the answer she gave but looked sad nonetheless. Jacqueline hugged him and kissed both his cheeks. There followed a hasty meeting with the cast members. When the announcement was made, their congratulations were tinged with annoyance; any decisions affecting the star would have an impact on them. Then the screenwriters quickly assembled to discuss how to adjust the script for Jacqueline's final appearance. At least they would have the two weeks she was away to make the scene as dramatic as possible. Jacqueline was promised such a romantic demise that she wondered if she ought not resurrect herself someday.

She was immensely relieved. The awkward moments were over. After she completed the current week's shooting on Friday, she could look forward to the spa. Rick was taking her to dinner and a hockey game on Saturday before she and Sheila boarded their plane Sunday morning. It would be a fortnight later before the truly hard work would begin.

❧

"Keep your eyes on number ninety-nine. Watch the man, not the puck."

"Isn't he the one who scored the first goal?" she asked, shouting to be heard over the crowd noise.

"Right."

It was midway through the two-minute power play. The goalie had already made two spectacular saves at point-blank range, but the defense was unable to wrest the puck away from the attackers. The action was too fast for Jacqueline. She followed Manley's advice and watched ninety-nine, who seemed to glide haphazardly back and forth in front of the goal, with no specific pattern. One of the wingers set up at the blue line and slapped a long, low shot toward the net. The puck was wide of the goal and caromed off the boards. Behind the net, another attacker got his stick on the rebound and slid toward the crease. Suddenly ninety-nine, as if by design, was right in front of the net. The short pass from the post zipped his way. With a lightning backhand flick, his stick lifted the puck into the open corner of the net beyond the helpless goalie's glove.

"I saw it! That time I saw it!" Jacqueline said. "How did he know where to stand?"

"Instinct. The guy's uncanny."

Jacqueline watched Manley applaud along with the rest of the spectators. He was obviously fascinated by the quality of play, but it was the fascination of a craftsman admiring another craftsman's work. She wondered if the mark of success was having one's own color commentator.

"You miss playing, don't you?"

"Sometimes. But when I made my decision, shrinking people's brains in an office seemed a lot better than beating 'em out on the ice."

"And now?"

"There was another factor, too," he said, pointing to his nose. "See the way it's bent? I broke it three times. I thought I'd better get out while I still had all my teeth. Ever see a hockey player smile?"

She had. Ever since she had become a celebrity, she had met quite a few men, from all walks of life. It seemed that someone was always entertaining, and the parties were incessant. She was introduced to countless actors, many of them attractive leading men, as well as numerous professionals, businessmen, jocks, and artists. She found it hard to befriend them. Almost to a man, they seemed glib, calculating, and emotionally distant. And unlike her former male friends—in days gone by when she was fat and unknown—they all appeared to have one goal in common: getting it on with a young starlet. Initially, their attentions had flattered her; but flattery had soon turned to resentment, and it was not long before she began to wonder if something were wrong with her, since none of the men she met seemed interested in letting his hair down, in having a frank, honest discussion with her, or in treating her like an individual. None, that is, until Rick.

He seemed terribly self-confident. On this, their third outing together, flashbulbs popped whenever she was recognized in the crowd. This never appeared to throw him off stride; in fact, she thought he found it rather amusing. Yet although she was clearly the center of attention, she noticed that quite a few women were casting looks his way, too. It was something he must have grown accustomed to, and she admired the way he handled it with a low-keyed grace quite unlike the swaggering self-importance of other beautiful people. Whereas this distinguished him from the other men she met, she began to wonder if he found her as interesting as she did him.

She wished she didn't have so much packing to do, but the following day promised to be hectic. After the game, they drove directly back to her apartment, a fashionable condo at the top of the Village that she was endlessly redecorating. He parked a few doors from the entrance.

"I'm just having coffee," she said, "but I can offer you a drink if you'd like to come in for a while."

"Have to run, Jack. I'll take a raincheck."

She looked at him, bewildered, starting to feel her old fat girl's insecurity returning. After all, she wasn't exactly trying to lure him into bed. Yet after their first encounter in the coffee shop, the prospect of anything other than informal conversation didn't seem to interest him at all. He certainly didn't strike her as the kind of man who might feel threatened by her. Why, then? Did he have a girlfriend? All she wanted, she reasoned, was to get to know him a little better, and then, maybe, to . . . what? She hadn't really thought about it. She reached for the door handle.

He saw the hurt in her eyes and instinctively took hold of her wrist.

"Hold on, kid."

He slid across the seat and kissed her softly on the lips. Then he pulled away, gazing into her eyes, gently touching her cheek. "I don't want you to get the idea that I'm giving you the runaround." He kissed her more deeply this time, and she kissed him back.

When their lips separated, she put her arms around his neck, lowering her face until her forehead rested on his chin.

"You're enough to give me a complex, you know that?"

"That's not what I had in mind."

"What exactly did you have in mind?"

He lifted her chin with his fingertips.

"Didn't your mother ever tell you," he began, pausing to kiss her on the lips, "that there are some things," again, a kiss, "you never ask?" he said, ending with another kiss.

"No, but she did tell me about doctors."

"Really?" he smiled.

"It had something to do with keeping them away with apples. And you know what?" she said, drawing his face nearer.

"Hmmm?"

"I hate apples."

Now she kissed him, lips soft and open, a long, tender kiss that ended in a warm embrace.

Finally she leaned back against the car door. They gazed fondly at one another, and she took hold of his hand. An occasional passerby glanced at the car and then looked away. She watched them come and go.

"I could never do that before."

"I thought you did it rather well."

"No," she laughed. "I mean kiss in public. I suppose that has some profound psychological meaning."

With one hand, he unbuttoned her fur coat.

"I suppose."

Her skin was so lovely, so tempting. He watched the small pulse beat in the soft skin of her neck, and he touched it. He traced the path of the throbbing vessel down to where it disappeared under her collarbone. He widened the lapels of her blouse, rubbing his fingertips across her velvety, unblemished skin. He slowly undid her top button. She gently took hold of his hand.

"Rick," she said. "Not here."

He smiled. "Just brushing up on some anatomy."

"I really do have some lines to go over and some packing to do. And didn't you mention a raincheck?"

"Yes," he nodded, looking away.

As he replaced the key in the ignition, Jacqueline searched his face. She was suddenly worried that he misinterpreted what she had said as the words of a tease.

"I'm sorry," she said.

"About what?" he smiled. "I know psychiatrists are supposed to be open-minded, but I've never done it in the middle of a city street either."

"There will be another time, then?"

"Jax, I said raincheck, not rainout."

"Good," she said, leaning her head against his shoulder. "I want there to be enough time."

"I heard it only takes five minutes."

He was hopeless. She smiled and shook her head in desperation.

"You don't strike me as the type who's interested in a quickie."

Manley stared at the entrance to her building for long moments after she was gone. He could still smell the cachet of her perfume, hear the sound of her voice. No, he thought. Not a quickie. Certainly not with her.

Some time afterward, he sat in his apartment, wearing his robe and with his feet propped up on a chair. His memories were still in the fond place he'd left them an hour before. A sheaf of papers lay at his side, a doctoral dissertation that needed evaluation and comment by Monday morning. After cursorily scanning the pages, he realized it was hopeless. He couldn't concentrate. He put them down and picked up a box of dog treats.

"What do you think, boy?" he said to Dart, casually flipping the small biscuits to the dog, who caught them in his teeth. "You know me better than anyone. Except Ben, maybe. Any reason for me to be worried?"

The dog whined and stretched out on the rug.

"This has got to stop. I can't have some woman screwing up my work like I was a bloody sixteen-year-old. I don't suppose you know about that kind of stuff, huh? Except maybe for that Irish setter down the hall? Ah, Christ."

Feeling ridiculously sentimental, he tossed Dart the last treat and tried to go over the papers again. It was no use. The more he looked at the pages, the more he saw her face. There came a knock at the door. Dart sprang to his feet, loping across the carpet with a suspicious growl. He reached the door, sniffed, and began to wag his tail.

Manley opened the door and smiled broadly. It was Jacqueline.

"Jack! I didn't know you made house calls."

She wasn't sure what to say, social boldness not being her strong suit. And then there was the lie about her lines; she hadn't yet told him about her changing career. Shyly, "Hello."

"How did you know my address?"

She shrugged. "Just looked it up in the phone book."

"I might have known. Well, don't just stand there, come in."

She walked to where he stood, both hands at her sides, still wearing the fur coat she had had on before. He took her face in his hands and kissed her on the lips.

"How did you know I was home?"

"I bribed the doorman."

"That's Angelo, all right. He's a soft touch for beautiful women. What happened to that script of yours?"

She held up a folder, which contained the first act of her new play. She longed to share the thrill of her new role with him, but thought the explanation should best wait her return from the Spa. "All seventy-odd pages."

He pointed toward the papers he'd tried to work on. "I didn't get very far with my raincheck. Couldn't concentrate."

"Me neither."

"I kept thinking about someone I was with a little while ago."

"I did, too."

They just stood there, awkwardly gazing at one another. Finally, "Aren't you warm in that coat?"

"A little."

He helped her out of it and hung it in the closet, then he looked at her and shrugged.

"Well," he said, "maybe we can study together."

"Capital idea."

They sat side by side on the sofa, papers spread before them. Each tried his best to concentrate, but inevitably their minds began to wander. He would cast a furtive glance her way, and she his. After ten minutes of the charade, they caught one another looking, not completely by accident. It was pointless.

"Rick?"

"Hmmm?"

"Remember when you said it only takes five minutes?"

"I remember."

"I think I have five minutes now."

Several hours later, physically spent, they lay side by side in his bed. Even then he continued to kiss her neck, her earlobe, the side of her face. Eyes closed, she turned her head toward him and rubbed her cheek against his. He was the most romantic man she had ever met. It was strange how he seemed more interested in kissing her than in doing almost anything else. He kissed her everywhere— her knees, her toes, the small of her back. It was an experience she found incredibly stimulating. What made it all the more wonderful was that she knew he was kissing *her*, something that had happened rarely before other than as foreplay.

Now his lips wandered across her eyebrows, sliding down her face before coming to rest on her upper lip. There were the faintest droplets of perspiration on it, and he wiped them away with the tip of his own nose. Then his lips found hers, a silky touch. They moved like wispy satin across her mouth, a velvety feeling that made her lips grow hot and tingly. The tip of his tongue found its way

137

beneath her top lip. He traced its undersurface, sliding his tongue in the crevice between lip and gum. Then he gently held her lower lip between his teeth. He nibbled, he softly bit, he sucked deeply on her flesh with an intensity that made her want him again.

His mouth strayed to the cleft between her breasts. There his dry lips moved outward, grazing the swell of her bosom. He circled her pink aerolae with his tongue, and she could feel the stiffening of her nipples. His face moved slowly downward, stroking a feathery trail across her abdomen.

"Rick," she whispered. He wasn't going to do it again, was he?

His lips found the crease of her hip, and her legs inched uncontrollably apart. She dug her nails into his hair. Then his mouth slid between her thighs, inching upward to the spot where they joined.

"Oh, God," she moaned, not wanting him to stop, but uncertain if she had the strength to continue. Oh, Rick, she thought, holding him fast. She couldn't. He wouldn't . . .

He did.

Thirty minutes later, Jacqueline was hungry. She put on one of his extra-large shirts and went to the kitchen. The long white shirt came to the middle of her thighs. He heard her rummaging through the kitchen cabinets. Soon she returned with a rather stale wedge of cheese and a box of crackers.

"You don't have much to eat around here," she said, perching on the corner of the bed.

"I don't eat here that often. There's more food for Dart than there is for me."

"I noticed that. Why does the dog chow say 'for experimental use only'?"

"It's a special blend they use in the animal lab. Dart's crazy about it."

"You really love him, don't you?"

"Yeah." While they had been in bed, the dog obediently remained in the living room. Manley whistled toward the door. "C'mere, boy."

The dog was instantly at the bedside. He licked Manley's face before something distracted him. He began to sniff Manley's fingers. Jacqueline reddened.

He looked up at her and smiled.

"He's got a terrific sense of smell, doesn't he?"

They got dressed and went outdoors to walk the dog together. Manley put his arm about her, and they slowly covered the long block between Second and First avenues. Dart rarely strayed from Manley's side unless it was for the purpose of anointing the base of a traffic sign or fire hydrant.

"I thought you had to keep him on a leash."

"You're supposed to. But he heels so well, most people think he's chained to my side."

"What about a pooper scooper?"

"Watch."

At the end of the block was the street grating for a sewer culvert. Dart got down on his haunches and relieved himself, his droppings falling precisely between the metal slats. Jacqueline was amazed.

"Where on earth did he learn to do that?"

"I think his mother was a shopping bag lady."

Going back to his apartment, they returned to bed.

It was midnight before they resumed work in earnest. Jacqueline said she had to leave soon and that she would be away for two weeks, but for the moment she was content to sit beside him on the bed, one of her bare legs draped over his as she casually leafed through her papers. Occasionally her hand dipped into a tin of crackers on the night table.

To Manley, it seemed that she never stopped eating. She wasn't gluttonous; rather, she nibbled away in a dainty yet continuous fashion as she read through her script. He watched her eat, nagged by the illogic of it. From everything he'd seen since he'd first taken her out, she should be gaining weight by now. She clearly consumed more food than anyone else he knew with a similar frame, and yet there wasn't an ounce of excess fat anywhere on her body. And his trained eye could detect no sign of an underlying disease, such as hyperthyroidism, which might enable her to metabolize extra calories.

She rolled away from him, reaching for the snack again. He looked at her smooth skin and let his hand trace the curve of her spine as it rose upward from the small of her back, his fingertips climbing the rounded knobs of her vertebrae. He reached the middle of her torso and instantly jerked his hand away. His jaw went slack, and he stared at his fingertips as if he had touched a hot coal.

The flesh between her shoulder blades was burning.

Chapter Eight

The jetliner taxied to a stop. Moments later the two young women deplaned and entered the mammoth terminal at Los Angeles International Airport. Like Jacqueline, Sheila had brought only one medium-sized satchel of carry-on luggage. As they passed the stream of passengers making its way toward baggage check-in, Sheila was thankful for the one light suitcase she carried, but nonetheless curious about how she would make it through the next two weeks with virtually nothing to wear.

"There he is," said Jacqueline, with a hint of uneasiness, pointing to a powerfully built man who wore a dark suit and black chauffeur's cap. Something about him always seemed to unnerve her.

"Goodness, the Incredible Hulk."

"Ah, Miss Ramsey," said Vincent, nodding perfunctorily to Sheila. "Let me take those," he instructed, lifting their satchels as if they were feathers. "This way, please."

They followed him through the terminal, walking swiftly to keep pace with his stride, soon exiting the building into the bright afternoon sun. The balmy midwinter temperature was in the seventies. He escorted them to a black limousine nearby, opened the door, and asked them to be seated. After locking the trunk, he started the engine and drove off.

"Why is everyone smiling?" asked Sheila.

"That's just the way they are out here."

"Auditions for a toothpaste commercial."

They drove through the endless sprawl of suburbs that

bordered Los Angeles, eventually leaving the freeway and winding through a series of streets that appeared progressively less populated. Moments later, the limousine turned abruptly north onto a little-used dirt road, spewing a trail of dust in its wake. There appeared a distant colonnade of green, arising as if from nowhere, shrubbery which gradually grew into a tall cyprus hedge hundreds of yards wide. The car slowed, and a large iron gate swung open before them.

They entered the Spa at San Sebastian.

To Sheila, it was just as Jacqueline had described it, a small palace within a desert oasis. In its center was a classic white marble building whose smooth, massive pillars and wide porticos were reminiscent of an ancient Greek temple. The grounds surrounding it were landscaped in the style of an elaborate Japanese garden, carpeted fields of green criss-crossed by small brooks and streams, their beds awash with smooth pebbles and their banks girded by large granite borders. Here and there, the stone bridgework of a *Gangyo-bashi* crossed a shimmering pond, like a wedge of flying wild geese. Carved stepping-stones wound among the shrubs and trees in serpentine fashion. It seemed as if a kimono-clad woman might appear at any moment and take dainty steps across the stone surface.

The car swung around a wide circular driveway that led to the building's entrance, where it came to a halt. The chauffeur got out and opened the rear door. Following Jacqueline, Sheila swung her knees into the warm, dry air. They followed the driver along a path of crushed white gravel that ended at a tier of gleaming marble steps.

From the shadows, a man stepped out into the sun and approached the car with a smile. Jacqueline returned his smile, but Sheila could only gape, with the open-mouthed awkwardness of a country dolt.

He was unquestionably the most handsome man she had ever seen. This, she knew, had to be Dr. Hume.

"I think I'm in love," Sheila said.

"Down, girl. Don't smother the poor man."

"If I faint, make sure he gives me mouth to mouth."

Hume greeted Jacqueline first, taking both her hands in his and kissing her on the cheeks. He pronounced her name Jack-leen, with an accent Sheila couldn't place. It was clearly European, but neither French nor Italian; rather, it seemed a mixture of continental tongues. Then he turned to Sheila.

"Welcome, Miss Hastings."

She took his extended hand, noting the cool, firm handshake.

"It is always a pleasure to have Jacqueline as my guest. But never, in all our conversations, did she mention how extraordinarily lovely her friend was."

If that same white lie had been uttered by one of Sheila's acquaintances, it would have sounded ludicrous to her. Now, though, for the first time in her life, she dared to think of herself as pretty. Red faced, all she could manage was an embarrassed, "Thank you."

Continuing to talk in his suave, polished manner, Hume led them both up the steps while the chauffeur followed with the luggage at a discreet distance.

"When you called last week," Hume said to Jacqueline, "it seemed as if we hadn't spoken in ages."

"Time passes so quickly."

"Indeed." He paused at the top step. "I must tell you at the outset, Jacqueline, that I must go back on my word. I regret that I cannot allow you to pay for Miss Hastings."

"But didn't you say that—"

"Please, she is to be my guest. I insist on it." He turned to Sheila. "Such a good friend of Jacqueline Ramsey is always welcome here."

Jacqueline was incredulous. "That's very kind of you, but isn't twenty-five thousand dollars an awfully big welcome?"

Still smiling, he placed his hands on her shoulders and drew her to arms' length, addressing her as a father might speak to a child.

"I have every confidence, Jacqueline, that you will find a way to repay me."

Before she could react, he smiled and pulled away.

"You must both be exhausted. Let me show you to your rooms."

"Is there any chance Sheila and I could room together?"

"Surely you know that each guest has separate accommodations, Jacqueline? I have prepared your usual suite. Miss Hastings will be nearby. Won't you both come this way?"

From the way he stationed himself between them, Sheila had the oddest feeling that he didn't want them to speak to one another. They arrived at her room first. He opened the door and suggested that she take the opportunity to refresh herself. Before she had a chance to reply, he bowed courteously, closed the door, and left.

Sheila sighed and quickly shrugged off the vague feeling of uneasiness. Her bag was already there, having been deposited by the chauffeur. The room was large, bright, and spotlessly clean. Its furnishings were austere. In the center was a double bed, atop which lay a white robe.

She studied the room. Nowhere was the TV she had imagined, nor the standard curtains and garish wool carpet. The marble floor was cool against her feet, and the stark, smooth walls were embellished with a single polished mirror.

So what did you expect? she thought. The Holiday Inn?

Soon she finished unpacking. She used the bathroom, undressed, and put on the robe. She thought it was terry, but it felt satiny smooth against her skin—some sort of synthetic. She had just tied the sash when, after a knock at the door, Hume reappeared. Jacqueline stood at his side, dressed in a similar robe.

"Ah, I see you are ready. Come, my dear, let me show you the grounds."

"How do I look?" Sheila asked Jacqueline. "Do you think—"

"This way," Hume interrupted, drawing Jacqueline away by the arm. "Follow me, please."

As they walked toward the entrance foyer, they were approached by the head nurse. Miss Howell wore an expression of concern.

"I'm sorry to disturb you, Dr. Hume. I would never

interrupt if it weren't urgent. But you asked me to keep you informed about finding a replacement nutritionist."

"Have you?"

"I'm afraid not. I've looked everywhere," she said, clearly exasperated.

Hume remained composed. "How have you been handling the patients thus far?"

"Why, I've been preparing their evening menus myself."

Hume's smile was reassuring. "Of course you have. Which is precisely what you shall keep doing until a replacement is located."

"Dr. Hume, I'm not sure that I'm capable of—"

"Nonsense! You underestimate your ability as a head nurse. Simply continue as you are until a replacement is found."

Miss Howell appeared disconcerted as she stood there in silence. Hume turned away and resumed his walk with the two younger women.

"A pity," he quietly remarked. "She's superb at following instructions, but she has never recognized her full potential."

"Has she been with you long?" Sheila asked.

Hume pursed his lips in reflection. "Oh, within six months of the Spa's opening. She's really far more capable than she believes. Lack of self-confidence, I suppose. But I trust her implicitly."

Outside, an orange sun descended toward the horizon as evening approached. Hume maintained a continual lighthearted banter. He led them across a low wooden footbridge and walked to the edge of a wide lily pond, under whose surface scores of large goldfish swam lazily, sending ripples across the water. Three chairs had been placed by the bank of the pond, and Hume motioned for his guests to sit.

"These gardens are dear to me. They provide comfort and serenity in the midst of this arid wasteland called California. I often come out here alone, to think. But, enough. Tell me, Miss Hastings: what do you know about San Sebastian?"

"Just what Jackie told me."

"Which is?"

From the way he arched his eyebrows, she had the most peculiar feeling of being interrogated.

"That it's the only place where I can be certain of losing weight. At least it worked for her."

"Indeed. Her weight loss was dramatic—was it not, Jacqueline?"

Jacqueline nodded.

"She achieved her goal," Hume continued. "Exceeded it, even. She left looking exquisite, and by returning every six months, she remains that way." He smiled at Jacqueline, then went on with Sheila. "You are also an actress, are you not?"

"I wish all the drama critics realized that. Not on a par with Jackie, though. But who knows what miracle might come from my losing a few pounds?"

"Of course." His smile was benevolent. "And we shall help you do just that. But what else do you know about the Spa—how we work, for example?"

"Not a blessed thing."

"Then I shall tell you." He squinted as he looked toward the brilliant globe of the setting sun. "San Sebastian is a novel environment. It is not some romantic hideaway similar to those resorts which call themselves 'health spas.' To me, those are nothing more than cloistered communities that cater to the affluent, but serve no real purpose. Nor does San Sebastian resemble a medieval spa in Europe, where the sick and infirm take to the waters. Rather, it is a medical facility—unique, I believe—whose sole purpose is to enable individuals I deem suitable to lose weight."

"You mean not everyone can come here, even if they have the money?"

"My goodness, no. I am very selective about whom I choose as patients. There are those who would never be welcome here, regardless of their wealth."

"How do you decide who's eligible?"

"I have certain . . . criteria. But don't trouble yourself about that."

Watching him speak, Jacqueline once again thought she saw a fleeting chill in his expression.

Then Sheila continued. "Aren't there other patients here besides us? I haven't seen anyone else since we arrived."

"Yes, several. They are undergoing their treatments now. I shall explain more about that process later." He arose and held out his arms to them both. "Shall we walk through the gardens? They are lovely at sunset."

They each took the crook of an elbow. Jacqueline glanced at Sheila and could see that she was enchanted with the man. They walked leisurely about the gardens, pausing at a tree-shaded bench here, a small *torii* there. He showed them a magnificent collection of bonsai, beyond which a *Matsa-Jima*, in the middle of a small lake, gave root to a gnarled but beautiful ancient pine. If the object of Hume's garden was to refresh the mind and bring peace to the soul by the contemplation of beautiful surroundings, it succeeded.

They returned to their rooms. Jacqueline washed up and lay down for a short rest. An hour later, Hume arrived to escort her to supper. When they reached the dining room, Jacqueline was mildly surprised to find that Sheila had already been seated.

"But . . . what are you doing here?"

Sheila regarded her blankly, then looked at the place settings around her. "I thought we were supposed to eat, but I imagine we could be auctioning off the silver."

"God—I'm sorry, that sounded terrible. I must have been assuming that . . . you see, Dr. Hume and I always ate alone before."

"Only because you came alone," Hume said, seating her in a high-backed chair. "On this occasion, I wouldn't dream of it."

They dined at the long, handsome table, where they were served by a butler. Hume explained that this was to be their last feast before their treatments began the following day. Even so, the fare was light, the portions small but satisfying, perhaps because they were so pleasingly garnished. During the meal, he engaged both young women in conversation, charming them with his urbane manner.

After dinner, the fatigue of her long day set in. Hume first escorted Sheila back to her room, then returned for

Jacqueline. She held his arm as he led her down the corridor and opened her door. He smiled at her, lifted her hand, and kissed it.

"Good night, Jacqueline. Sleep well."

"Good night."

He started to close the door, then hesitated. "Jacqueline . . ."

"Yes?"

"This play you will be starring in—I have heard wonderful things about it."

"I'm glad."

"I think you have made the right decision. It will enhance your career tremendously."

"Thanks for the vote of confidence."

"I have a great interest in the arts—the theater, in particular." He paused. "I was wondering if you might be able to do something for me."

"Sure, if I can. What did you have in mind?"

"Oh, I'm not certain as yet. But I may prevail upon you to use your considerable influence. It would mean a great deal to me. Can I trust you in this matter?"

What on earth was he talking about? At first, she'd assumed he was alluding to something as innocent as getting choice theater seats. Yet now he was hinting at something more. Surely he realized she was in no position to make decisions of any great significance.

"I'd be happy to help you, Dr. Hume, but anything important would have to go through my agent or my producer. Or both."

"Yet surely they would consider your word significant, would they not?"

She shrugged. "Hard to say. Remember, this Broadway bit is a little new to me."

For an instant, the corners of his lips turned downward, and she thought she saw a flash of annoyance in his eyes. But it was gone as quickly as it appeared, replaced by his typical smile.

"Yes, of course. I understand perfectly. Good night, then."

He turned and walked down the corridor. Jacqueline felt

a peculiar sense of uneasiness as she closed the door. It was not like Dr. Hume to ask for anything. She put on her peignoir, turned off the light, and slid between the bed's cool sheets. As her head sank into the pillow, she waited for the languor to come over her, as it had always done in the past: the sleep that came instantly, the long, dreamless night that followed.

The minutes passed. She opened her eyes in the darkness, astonished that she was still awake. During her previous visits to the Spa, the mere act of climbing into bed had been a soporific, dulling her senses with slumber the moment her lids were shut. She rolled onto her back and stared at the ceiling.

Something was not quite right, a nagging sense of worry that was vaguely disturbing, like an itch under the skin too minor to scratch but too prominent to ignore. She tossed restlessly for an hour. The room felt stifling; she tossed off the covers. She got out of bed and drew the curtains by the far wall. The high tier of windows was just above head level. She searched along their frame for a latch or hand crank with which to open them but found none: the glass was fixed casement. She thought it strange that she'd never noticed that before.

Jacqueline turned on the lamp and dressed in her robe. She quietly opened the door and tiptoed lightly from the room. The corridor was cool and dim. She casually turned the corner and found herself all at once looking blindly up into the black scales of reptilian eyes.

She leaped backwards in fright, her startled breath whistling in her throat. Vincent's stolid expression was fixed like a mask.

"Can I be of service, Miss Ramsey?"

"I . . . You startled me," she said, trembling.

"Were you looking for something?"

"My room," she said, trying to regain her composure. "It was stuffy, and I was hoping to get a little air." She unconsciously fingered the lapels of her robe, drawing them closed over her chest.

"Dr. Hume prefers that his guests remain in bed after retiring, to preserve their strength. Why not return to your room, Miss Ramsey? I'll see that the air conditioning is adjusted."

"Yes . . . Of course."

She turned and quickly retreated, not pausing once to look back. The orderly watched her with brooding deliberation.

Chapter Nine

"There are times when I do wonder about thee."

"Knock it off, Sheila."

Jacqueline put down her script, folded her arms across her chest, and gazed out of the jet's small window. Sheila stared at her friend with a mixture of annoyance and concern. Jacqueline's petulance had grown progressively ever since they had boarded the plane. She snapped at the first-class steward, complained about the food, and was now criticizing the playwright.

"What's with you, anyway? I really don't give two shits if you abhor the man's dialogue. Take it up with him, if you want, but for Christ's sake don't take it out on me."

Jacqueline turned toward Sheila and saw her friend's distress. For the first time in hours the hard cast to Jacqueline's face mellowed, and she reassuringly reached across the armrest to squeeze Sheila's hand.

"I'm sorry, Sheil, I'm just . . . I don't know. Vacation's over, I suppose."

"Some vacation, from the way you talk. Here, I had the time of my life: I can see my toes for the first time in ten years, not to mention touch them; I dined with the world's most charming man for two straight weeks; and I lost twelve pounds in the process. Before we went, you were telling me how wonderful the place was, but now you're whining like it was all some kind of big disappointment, and for the whole damn flight you've been squirming like someone with glass in her tampon. Really, was it all that horrible?"

"No. Just different, I guess."

"You know what I think? You got spoiled, that's what. All those times you had your own trainer instead of being in a class, when you were the only one in the sauna, when you ate alone with Dr. Hume—it went to your head. Maybe you got too accustomed to a good thing."

Distantly, "Maybe."

"But he explained all that. I mean, the man is turning down hundreds of patients each week—thanks in no small part to your appearance on the show. Is it any wonder he had to arrange the Spa's schedule a little differently?"

"No, of course not. You're right."

Her agreeable smile was comforting, and Sheila finally sighed. She picked up the script, searching for the place they had left off, unaware of Jacqueline's affectionate stare.

How could she describe a stinking aroma to a person unable to smell? It wasn't the obvious things that plagued her; why, in many respects, she welcomed the group contact of her recent visit. No, it was the little things—picayune smidgens of insignificance, dust on a lapel: the peculiarly sleepless nights; the hint of an aberration in Dr. Hume's character, which she had by now convinced herself was more imaginary than real; and most of all, the change in herself—her unexplainable edginess, her inappropriate feast of moods.

God, what a crud she had been to Sheila, who certainly didn't deserve it. She couldn't wait to return and discuss it with Rick; perhaps he could make sense out of her irritating behavior. She pictured his masculine, laughing face, and then, strangely beside it in her mind, the dark and handsome features of Dr. Hume.

"Now," said Sheila, leafing through the script, "where the hell was I?"

An unexpected shiver rattled Jacqueline's frame. Yes, she somberly wondered—where was I?

"Never heard of him."

"You don't think he's ever done research in obesity?"

"I didn't say that. Doing research is one thing; getting it

published is another. All I'm saying is that he's never been published in the medical literature—at least not in the field of obesity."

Manley looked away, pensive. He thought that if anyone might be familiar with Hume, it would be Lindstrom. Bjorn Lindstrom, visiting professor from the University of Göteborg, was the world's foremost authority in the laboratory study of obesity; his specialty was the evaluation of adipocytes, the cells constituting fat tissue. He was also an astute clinician, quite familiar with the common manifestations of obesity. Manley was frustrated by Lindstrom's negative reply, for it left him with nowhere to turn.

"If you want my opinion, it sounds like garden variety hyperthyroidism," Lindstrom continued. "Did you measure her thyroid hormone level?"

"I suppose I should. It's just that—well, she just doesn't look hyperthyroid. Her hair texture is normal, there are none of the typical eye changes, things like that."

"But didn't you say that she eats more than average without gaining weight and that her skin is warmer than usual? Those are pretty characteristic symptoms."

Manley's office hours were soon to start. Discouraged, he finished his coffee and pushed himself away from the table just as the waitress brought Lindstrom's fettucini. He thanked Lindstrom and got up, casually glancing at the plate of noodles.

"She eats the same things you do," Manley noted. "Except that's all she eats—night and day."

"Literally?" replied Lindstrom, arching his eyebrows.

"Yes. She says they told her to maintain a high carbohydrate diet. I just might buy her a pasta machine for her birthday."

Tight furrows creased Lindstrom's forehead. "Pasta," he said with contemplation.

"Does that mean anything?"

"Probably not. But there are some people who think a diet rich in pasta stimulates metabolism of brown fat."

Brown fat, Manley reflected. He was familiar with it in a general way, the familiarity of a lecturer who covers all aspects of a topic for the sake of completeness. Yet he was the first to admit that he knew nothing about current research in that specific area. He slowly sat down again and hunched over the table.

"Is that possible?" he asked.

"It might be, but I don't think there's enough data yet to draw conclusions one way or the other. Certainly an interesting area for investigation."

"Bjorn, take sixty seconds and review brown fat with me. Just the basics."

"Come on, you know as much about it as I do."

"I wasn't aware of this pasta theory. Look, just run through it as if I were a first-year med student."

"If you insist," Lindstrom shrugged, drawing himself up in a professorial pose. "Brown fat," he began, "is one of the two major kinds of fat in the body, making up about one percent of the body's fat stores. . . . Rick, isn't this a little elementary?"

"Pretend it isn't. Just go on."

"If you say so," he sighed. "The tissue is brown because of its high pigment content. Ordinary fat is white and comprises the other ninety-nine percent. What's interesting about brown fat is that its cells act like little engines, burning up excess calories."

"And all mammals have it," Manley added, remembering something he had once read about its role in hibernation.

"Right. Primates seem to have the least. In humans it's localized in certain areas—around the kidneys, in the neck, between the shoulder blades. . . ." He halted, wondering at the wide-eyed expression that had abruptly come over Manley. "Is something wrong?"

"Good God, I'd forgotten."

"What?"

"Her skin . . . I told you it was warm."

"So?"

"It wasn't, really—warm, that is . . . I mean, in most places it felt normal. It was only the area between her shoulder blades that was warm. In fact, downright hot."

"Your fingers were probably cold."

"No, I'm certain of it. Could that be significant?"

"Not likely. It probably wasn't as hot as you think.

Why, brown fat would be a magical tissue—the dieter's panacea—if you could increase its amount in the body. Or if its metabolic activity were somehow increased in the few areas where it is found, which I think is what you're suggesting."

"Doesn't increased metabolic activity generate heat?"

Patiently, "It might."

"So if you could increase its activity," said Manley, his mind racing, "a person could eat all he wanted and still stay thin as a rail?"

"Sure, in theory. The problem is that no one has discovered a practical way to accomplish that increase in amount or activity. Not to my knowledge, anyway."

Manley was pensive. "But Bjorn, for all that isn't known about brown fat—aren't there certain factors that do control its activity?"

"You mean increase it?"

"Yes."

"Well, that's getting into a pretty fanciful area. But theoretically, something as simple as ascorbic acid might enhance its metabolism: plain vitamin C. And then, certain brain tumors can alter it."

"Christ, don't even mention that."

"I certainly hope that's not a possibility."

"I doubt it; she has no apparent neurologic symptoms. What else?"

"There are some neurotransmitters—brain peptides—that might have an effect, if present in abnormally high levels. And so might the high-carbohydrate diet you mentioned, though I think its influence would be marginal, at best."

"But if you *were* able to isolate some factor that exerted a profound, continuous effect on brown fat—wouldn't that be reflected in a change in body weight?"

"Yes," he replied. "I suppose it would." Lindstrom narrowed his vision on his colleague. "Look, before you start jumping to outrageous conclusions, I daresay I could settle this for you once and for all."

"How?"

"Get me a little piece of her fat tissue and I'll check it

155

out in my lab. If for some ungodly reason its metabolic activity is ridiculously increased, I'll let you know."

"And if it is?"

"Then, my friend," said Lindstrom, "you and I are on our way to winning the Nobel Prize."

Instead of going home after office hours, Manley went straight to the university library. It wasn't that he didn't trust what Lindstrom had said; he visited the library because he simply had to find out for himself.

He checked the card catalog, dozens of textbooks, and the *Cumulative Index Medicus*, a tabulation of medical articles from journals throughout the world. Hume's name was nowhere to be found. Articles about brown fat, however, were abundant. Research into all aspects of the subject was undergoing a renaissance after having been ignored for over a decade. Manley located some of the more recent publications and began to read.

The library was preparing to close when he finished the last volume, discouraged. Though the articles he'd scanned had increased his general knowledge of the subject, none of them remotely hinted at the sort of breakthrough his mind had envisioned. The university library stored medical journals in bound-volume form, covering the last decade. Manley knew that for the sake of completeness he should review a handful of papers published during the decade prior to that. Before he left, he gave the librarian a list of the most often quoted older articles and asked her to locate their microfilms. He would return for them in several days.

His thoughts strayed. Jacqueline. Ah, Jacqueline. He'd missed her more than he dared admit. She would be home tomorrow, and that prospect brightened his soul. He feared that she was becoming the mainspring of the clock that ticked away his very existence: without her, time slowed. What worried him most, though, was the strange and illogical jealousy that had developed during her absence—a period of time when he had to share her with another man, a strange and powerful man he knew absolutely nothing about.

Chapter Ten

"Like this?"

"Yes. Now don't move."

"Don't try to cop a feel."

"Come on, hold still."

"I can't. It tickles." She flinched. "God, that's cold."

"Only iodine. Good, stay just like that. You'll feel a little stick from the needle."

Jacqueline lay still on the mattress. She was on her stomach, naked, the bed sheet covering the lower half of her body. She couldn't believe she was actually doing this. She thought he was joking when he mentioned the word "biopsy." Her knowledge of medical terminology wasn't that profound, but she knew enough to understand that a biopsy was surgery. And ever since she had had her tonsils removed when she was six, the thought of any surgery, no matter how minor, terrified her. Yet it seemed so important to him that she finally gave in.

They had been together every night since her return from California. Their relationship had become progressively idyllic, and the other aspects of her complicated life were also proceeding smoothly, as rehearsals continued apace.

She had been so delighted to see him upon her return that she had forgotten her misgivings on the plane. She mentioned nothing about what transpired during her absence, and he didn't ask. Their altercation after the talk show was largely forgotten; neither of them wanted to rake over the coals of their discord. And so, by not discussing it, they had tacitly agreed that it would remain on the back burner.

When he had mentioned the word biopsy, she didn't understand what he was talking about. All that sunk in was that it dealt with one of his research projects, and he had said it was so important to him that she couldn't refuse. He assured her that the puncture site wouldn't leave a scar. No one would notice the spot between her shoulder blades. Then he showed her the biopsy needle.

The six-inch wire of sterile steel looked like the dagger in *Othello*. Her knees nearly buckled when she saw it. He caught her and assisted her to the bed. No way, she said. Impossible. But then he was kissing her, his lips on her ear, her cheek, her neck. She closed her eyes and they fell back onto the mattress together.

"This is bribery," she said, as she kissed him back.

He undid the buttons on her blouse.

"It's just part of good medical care."

"Since when?"

"I never do surgery without premedication. It helps the patient relax."

"In that case give me all you've got," she said as she pulled him down on top of her.

He was right. Their lovemaking completed, her tension had lessened significantly, though not entirely. Afterward, when she was ready, he rolled her onto her stomach while explaining everything step by step.

She felt a small pinprick, followed by a little stinging when the local anesthetic went in. Surprisingly, she couldn't feel anything when he did the biopsy, other than the slightest pressure. It was over in seconds. She was even more surprised when she heard herself asking to see the specimen. It was tiny, resembling an ultrathin sliver of vermicelli no more than an eighth of an inch long. He carefully inserted it into a bottle of sterile tissue culture fluid.

"Is that what I made such a fuss about?"

"That's it, Jax," he said, kissing her on the cheek. "You came through it like a champ."

"I bet you say that to all the girls you biopsy."

"Not really," he smiled. "I'm a psychiatrist, remember? This is the first biopsy I've ever done in my life."

"Why, you . . . !" she shouted, her indignation only half feigned. He leaned back out of the reach of her fingernails. Naked, cackling, he quickly danced away as she chased him out of the bedroom.

"I'm going to get you, you bastard!"

She flew after him, but he managed to stay just beyond her grasp. Soon she was laughing along with him, succumbing to the humor of the situation as his path wound through the apartment. The pursuit was short lived. When she finally caught him, he warded off her half-hearted blows until they fell, naked and sweating, onto the carpet. In seconds their struggle ceased, and his lips were upon hers.

Both of their days had been exhausting, and the deep satisfaction of the lovemaking that followed made them all the more sleepy. They lay together on the rug, legs entwined, sharing the warm afterglow of intimacy. Jacqueline's cheek found a spot that seemed made for it in the curve of his shoulder. Minutes later, the slowing and regularity of her inhalations indicated she was asleep.

Manley knew he too would soon drift off. But for the moment, he was awake, staring up at the ceiling without blinking, his mind more alert than his body.

Just a little piece, Lindstrom had said. And now Manley had that piece—ready to be analyzed. Yet what if . . . Don't be absurd, he reassured, not consciously prepared to admit the extent of his worry, worry that was already compounded by Jacqueline's continuing reluctance to discuss her trips to the Spa with him.

In time, he hoped. In time. He rolled even closer to her, circling his arm around her slowly rising breasts. His cheek sought the softness of hers, and he held her like that. He didn't want to lose this woman. Not now . . . not ever.

PART THREE
March

Chapter One

Since agreeing to do the play, Jacqueline had had difficulty adjusting to the increase in her notoriety. Members of the press surrounded her like scavengers ferreting out choice morsels for their columns. She fielded their incessant questions as best she could, leaving them free to speculate about a rumored film offer, her latest love, or friction in the cast. And whereas the sensationalist tabloids plagued her with list after list of sins and achievements, she never took umbrage at their inaccuracies, thankful instead that the columnists might ponder her sex life rather than report that she had no sex life to ponder about.

From all that had been written about her, it was apparent that Jacqueline loved acting, and the public knew she did; in turn, her millions of loyal fans loved her even more. However, she found that between the press and her career, she had little free time. This was all the more true since she'd been seeing Manley, a fact that somehow managed to escape the attention of the majority of the reporters. Prior to going back to San Sebastian, nothing seemed to depress her, despite the pressures. In truth, she didn't have time to get depressed, for her body was occupied and her mind busy with the task at hand: rehearsing for the play. Lately, though, the more astute members of the press had begun to remark that a change was coming over her.

Manley noticed it, too. Ever since her return from California, she seemed to have grown perceptibly edgy. As a trained student of behavior, he was quick to conclude that something profound was bothering her. It wasn't merely the anxiety of the typical psychoneurotic, generated by minor inner struggles or discordant interpersonal relationships; rather, it was a slowly progressive heightening of tension, one which suggested a far more significant conflict.

To complicate matters, he had learned of the Suzanne Fontaine tragedy while he was driving to his early-morning conference at the hospital. Over the radio he heard the same press release that was issued to news services nationwide: Grammy award winner Suzanne Fontaine had died earlier that morning of a heart attack. He acutely recalled Sheila's comments some two months before.

Jackie was eleven, Suzanne ten. . . . They were costars. . . .

When he arrived home, he found Jacqueline white as a sheet, her stare fixed on some invisible horizon. Manley tried to draw her out at once, to get her to verbalize. It didn't work. She was not only reticent, but genuinely loathe to discuss anything.

Her morose attitude made him all the more convinced that he was dealing with a dilemma of major proportions. Tackled separately, either Jacqueline's edginess or the obvious impact of Suzanne Fontaine's death might have been relatively simple matters to confront. Together they could prove far more difficult. He knew that, ideally, he should wait for her to raise each issue of her own accord; yet she remained glum and withdrawn. Thus he broached the subject as any psychiatrist might—in a roundabout manner at first, but then more directly. His queries remained unanswered for two days, until her silent treatment suddenly gave way to verbal retaliation.

"Why didn't you ask that of Rochelle Rothstein?" she finally gibed, clearly irritated.

He couldn't place the name, but he played on nonetheless. "Ask her what?"

She gave an exasperated look.

"When she was potty trained, how often she used to diddle herself, and whether she hated her parents. All the things you're dying to find out from me."

"I'm not very interested in all that."

"Then stop pestering me with your asinine open-ended questions! I'm not one of your goddamn patients."

Her hands made tight little fists. He remained indulgent.

"I don't know a Rochelle Rothstein."

"Of course not, why should you?" she scoffed. "I mean, how many people knew the name Suzanne Fontaine was born with? But in the end she was just another fat slob who wanted to make her mark in the world."

"Did she?" he asked, despite knowing the answer.

"Damn right! Straight to the top! She lost weight and reached for that big brass ring with all she was worth! Made it, too. It was a six-figure payday when Suzanne Fontaine stepped in front of the mike."

"I see."

"Sure you do."

He looked at her bitten underlip.

"Would talking with her have helped me understand what's going on with you?"

She raised her hands in despair and turned her back on him.

"How the hell would I know?"

"Then why did you bring her up?"

She whirled about, livid.

"Why do you insist on provoking me? It's none of your goddamn business, Sigmund!"

He gave a defeated exhalation.

"Jack, all I'm concerned about is that—"

She stormed to him in a towering rage, less speaking than exploding.

"You *bastard!* How dare you tell me what you're concerned about! You have no idea of the agony . . . the *agony* . . . some people go through to get what they want. And if they finally do, it can all be snatched from them in an instant, just like that, and . . ."

A small wetness filled her eyes. Her fury gone, she bit her lip and looked away from him, trying to still the quivering in her chin. Then she wiped her eyes and resolutely stared at him.

"Oh, what's the use. I'm going to sleep."

She walked across the carpet and closed the bedroom door behind her.

* * *

He sat by the phone for an eternity, occasionally taking small sips from the can of beer that had long since grown warm. He was sure he was overlooking something. Jacqueline's ferocious tirade was filled with hidden meanings that he couldn't bring into focus. Baffled, he took to reviewing the basics.

The "neurotic reaction," his professors taught: careful study of the patient's life patterns enabled one to identify the factors that precipitated it. One by one, Manley went over those patterns.

First there were the circumstances that aroused fear that an individual's defense mechanisms were weakening— dangerous desires that once aroused threatened the ego, or unusually traumatic life experiences. He doubted that was a factor. Until recently, Jacqueline's life seemed to have been on an even keel. Then there were those circumstances that necessitated an intensification of defensive processes that ultimately proved too burdensome—failure to achieve unrealistic goals, for example—goals that might lead to a type of neurotic behavior that warded off inadequacy. That, too, Manley couldn't accept: Jacqueline's goals seemed eminently realistic. And lastly there were the circumstances that constituted a reenactment of early childhood experiences that created anxiety. It was this pattern that finally led him to call Sheila.

He briefly related what had happened, keeping his voice to a whisper to avoid waking Jacqueline. When he was done, Sheila immediately drew conclusions.

"I doubt Suzy baby had anything to do with it."

"She must have gone on like that for a reason."

Sheila hesitated.

"You were never fat, were you, Rick?"

"No, never."

"Fat girls identify with one another. We're the original groupies, except that our idols aren't rock singers but guys like Colonel Sanders and Ronald McDonald. Guilt thrives in numbers." She went on to relate secondhand stories about Jacqueline's teenage years with Suzanne, years of misery and wounded pride that followed their earlier flirtation with stardom. "You might say Jackie and Suzanne grew up together," she went on. "A couple of overweight Valley girls. Considering what the papers have been saying about Suzanne, I suppose it's only natural that, well . . ."

"What you're suggesting is that Jacqueline's close identification with Suzanne, followed by Suzanne's death, makes Jacqueline feel threatened."

"I am? Why, how clever of me."

"Don't you think that's what might be upsetting her?"

"It could. But that's overlooking the obvious. Where have you been for the past few days?"

He didn't follow her.

"I've been right here."

"Then you'd better get your eyesight checked. What's going on with Jackie is as plain as the analyst's couch in your office. She's putting on weight, Rick."

He was shocked.

"Are you sure?"

"Positive. Just stop playing kissy face and open your eyes for once. Oh, I know it's not a lot of weight. But she is gaining. And I suspect she knows it."

"Have you talked to her about it?"

"I tried, but she won't listen. You're the doctor: what do you call it when, oh, one of your patients won't admit something that's obvious?"

"Denial?"

"Denial. Right. That's precisely what's happening."

Manley scowled. Jacqueline's weight and figure were the very foundation of her healthy self-image. If what Sheila was saying were true, it would explain much of Jacqueline's anxiety-ridden behavior, redefining it as her personality's last-ditch, desperate attempt to cope with the unacceptable. If it failed . . .

They both heard the click, then the muted sound of a telephone receiver being replaced in its cradle, the undeniable signal that someone had been listening in.

"Oh, Jesus," said Sheila. "Do you think she heard?"

"I don't—" He saw the bedroom doorknob turn. "I'll call you back."

She appeared in the doorway, stoop shouldered and limp, a tattered rag doll. Her spent fury was replaced by a

167

languid melancholia that made her appear forlorn and dejected. He knew she'd heard. Yet she showed no sign of the anger he anticipated. Instead, she wore a grieving, worried, apprehensive look.

Her eyes were puffy and moist. From the way her body trembled, he thought she was going to break down at any moment. He walked over and put his arms around her. Her skin was cold.

"Sheila's wrong," she said in a low voice. "She can't be right. She just can't be . . ."

He pressed her head to his chest and gently stroked her hair. What a crushing blow it would be for her to ever concede it! He understood how horrible such an admission would make her feel, how threatened—and how convinced that everything she now lived for would stand in jeopardy of being irretrievably lost.

"It'll be okay, Jack. I'm sure of it."

"And what if it won't?"

He didn't know what to say. To anyone else, he might have replied, so what? What did a few pounds matter? To Jacqueline, though, they meant everything. Her weight was the cornerstone of her personality. Weaken that cornerstone, and her emotional balance might totter; destroy it, and the pyramid of her ego would come crumbling down.

Chapter Two

On that cold and gray morning, Manley's greatest concern was that Jacqueline might truly be on the verge of losing touch with reality. Her distress about her weight was nothing short of obsessional. It didn't matter that he understood the psychological underpinnings of her compulsion; all that mattered was what he could do about it. And on that score, he felt absolutely powerless.

Long-term psychotherapy might work, but he doubted she would submit to such treatment. Time was a factor, too: she was literally going to pieces before his very eyes. Only two things struck him as potentially useful. The first dealt with restoring her self-image. If, indeed, she *were* gaining weight, he would do his utmost to encourage her to lose it—by any means possible. Failing that, the alternative lay in his gaining an understanding of what had happened to her in the first place: if he could discover how she had so magically shed the pounds so crucial to her, he might get an idea about what he could now do about it.

She seemed so miserable that he debated advising her not to go to work that day. He decided against it; pampering her might prove counterproductive. He bid his most reassuring farewell and departed for work. When the opportunity arose, he would have to talk with Sheila once again, for he was convinced that she was as concerned about Jacqueline as he; perhaps the two of them could work out a satisfactory plan of action. In addition to Sheila, there was that other thing, too—the confrontation he had been avoiding for so long. When he reached his office, he picked up the phone and dialed California directory assistance.

"What do you mean there's no listing?" he asked the operator. "Yes, with an 'H' . . . Then try under physicians and surgeons. I'll hold." He drummed his fingers on the desk. "That's impossible, he's got to be there. . . . Are you certain? Then look under San Sebastian. The Spa at San Sebastian." Again, a prolonged, impatient pause. "Of course I'm sure! Keep looking. . . . Oh, for God's sake!" he snapped and slammed down the phone.

Frustrated though he was, he wondered if his expectations had been realistic. Perhaps he should have expected that such an exclusive clinic might have an unlisted number. It now appeared that he'd have to find out from Jacqueline, if only he could do it in a manner that wouldn't upset her.

He was clearly running out of leads. Until he met with Sheila, all he could do was continue his search in the library: the material he had requested should have come in by now.

As soon as he arrived, he inquired about it at the circulation desk. The librarian checked her file cards and told him that the material had arrived that very morning. Moments later he took the reels to the viewbox, made himself comfortable, and began examining the numerous titles.

He selected the appropriate articles and read each paper carefully, scrutinizing the footnotes and bibliographies. As he anticipated, Hume was mentioned nowhere. That didn't surprise him, nor did the simplistic but useless generalities about brown fat. One article, however, intrigued him.

The fifteen-year-old study dealt with the metabolic activity of fat cells. For some reason, the author had employed brown fat cells rather than white. He alluded to a unique method of making the fat cells divide in tissue culture. It seemed to Manley that the highly sophisticated technique was very perceptive for its day. It involved measuring the rate of incorporation of certain radioactive proteins into the DNA of the cell's nucleus, a rate that reflected both cell division and metabolic activity.

The author had concluded that brown fat cells had a tremendous metabolic reserve. The fine print of the article, though, described further modification of the metabolic activity by addition to the tissue cultures of what, at that time, were rather poorly understood substances—the same family of neurotransmitters Lindstrom had mentioned not long before.

Manley's anxiety heightened as he hunched over the machine and reread the text. He was in the process of trying to evaluate the paper's significance when a hand reached over and switched off the power. He looked up and saw Lindstrom.

"Don't you ever leave word where you're headed?" asked the Swede. "I've been trying to reach you all morning."

"Sorry."

"I finished analyzing that biopsy you gave me."

Manley tried to judge the peculiarly worried look on Lindstrom's face. Ever since he had dropped off the specimen, Manley had tried to maintain an attitude of expectant neutrality: he would accept whatever results the test provided. Subconsciously, though, he wanted the biopsy to prove completely normal—thus letting him off the hook, enabling him to avoid having to grapple with the myriad of bothersome questions unexpected findings would raise. His colleague's expression was grim.

"There's no way I can explain it," said Lindstrom. "The bottom line is this: the radioactive uptake experiments indicate a high degree of metabolic turnover and exchange."

"Meaning what, exactly?"

"Her brown fat metabolism is increased at least tenfold."

Manley was stunned.

"You can't be serious."

"I checked the results twice."

"But how . . . Have you ever run across something like that before?"

"Only in rapidly dividing cancer cells."

"My God, there's no sign of that, is there?"

"No, the cells appear perfectly normal. But it's interesting how the activity started to fall off after I made the first measurements."

Manley was too numbed to follow him.

"How do you account for that?"

"Well, it could be the tissue culture itself: frequently, cells in the lab simply get worn out, away from their natural environments." He hesitated. "Or there could be another factor."

"Such as what?"

"There may be something regulating her brown fat, something within her. Controlling it, as it were. When the cells were removed by biopsy, that control was no longer exerted."

Manley was dazed. He had never wanted to consider that the cells might be abnormal; that was disturbing enough. Yet far, far worse was the possibility that the abnormality might not reside in the tissue itself, but in some other entity that governed it. The idea was frightening: it made Jacqueline's body into something of a freak.

"That is unbelievable," he mouthed. "With that degree of metabolism, it's no wonder her skin was so warm. Would that also keep her thin?"

"I wouldn't doubt it in the least."

"But how? Why would her brown fat be doing that?"

"Precisely what I was hoping you could tell me."

Manley could only shake his head in confusion.

"I don't know. I honestly don't know."

Lindstrom prepared to depart.

"If and when you find out, let me in on it, okay?"

"Yes, of course." As his colleague turned to leave, Manley grasped his arm. "Bjorn, could you take a peek at this before you go?"

"What is it?"

"An ancient article on brown fat."

Lindstrom flicked on the viewbox's power and briefly reviewed the text, shaking his head appreciatively up and down as he neared the end. He seemed every bit as impressed with the work's scholarly insight as Manley.

"Very interesting. Who wrote it?"

"Somebody called Wahlberg. First name Seymour. Heard of him?"

"Yes. We met a few times, socially. Professionally, our paths never crossed. He was a Park Avenue showboat—a high roller in the diet trade."

"What do you mean 'was'?"

"The old boy died—four, maybe five years ago."

"Oh, Christ. I really wanted to talk to him. Did he strike you as the sort of guy who could write a paper of this caliber?"

"Oh, I doubt that he wrote it. He wasn't that kind of intellect."

"Then who did?"

"Reel the film back to the title page."

Manley complied.

"There," said Lindstrom, indicating a name under Wahlberg's. "I bet that's your man."

Manley studied the spot. The words "Robert Emmerich, M.D.," were listed in small print beneath Wahlberg's name. When he had first begun his study, Manley hadn't bothered with the acknowledgments. Examining them now, though, he saw that the source of the work was listed as the departments of Internal Medicine and Neurosurgery at New York's Flower and Fifth Avenue Hospital. He suspected that Flower—now defunct—was one of the places at which Wahlberg had admitting privileges. But Emmerich?

"Does his name ring a bell?"

"Not in the least."

"Could he have been one of Wahlberg's research assistants?"

"Coauthor, more likely. I'd wager he's the one who did the actual writing. If he's still around, he'd be the one to put your questions to."

Manley studied the viewbox. "Neurosurgery," he muttered.

"What?"

"This article came out of internal medicine and neurosurgery. Wahlberg was the internist," he continued slowly, thinking aloud. "But why would someone in neurosurgery be interested in studying fat tissue?"

"Who knows? That was fifteen years ago."

Lindstrom left. Manley returned the microfilm and spent the next hour searching for Emmerich's name. He found no references to the man. However, the university's facilities were limited; he stood a better chance of finding what he wanted at the Academy of Medicine, on upper Fifth Avenue. He took a cab across town and was soon outlining what he wanted with the research librarian.

The woman was similarly unfamiliar with Emmerich. If the man were published, the best chance of locating any of his other works, she explained, would be through a computer search. The academy subscribed to numerous medical indexing systems, some of whose data bases went back as far as the midsixties.

Manley filled out the appropriate requisition, paid the forty-dollar fee, and asked the librarian to put a rush on it. She replied that she couldn't; work was done in the order it was received, though it shouldn't take longer than a week. He walked slowly away, discouraged, his mind still caught up in the article he'd so recently read.

Fifteen years, he thought. Compared to the shortening days of Jacqueline's crisis, fifteen years was a galaxy of moments during which so much could have happened.

Chapter Three

As the days went by, Manley came to conclude that Jacqueline must have found her vague allusion to the fact that she *might* have a weight problem humiliating, for once she had ventured that far, she refused to discuss it any further. Despite his most professional attempts to draw her out into conversation, Jacqueline was steadfastly taciturn, maintaining a jittery aplomb as she continued to ride the seesaw of denial.

She didn't mention the accumulation of disconcerting little incidents at work; she couldn't. With each passing day, it was more and more apparent to Manley that she was slipping away from her former good-natured self. Yet, psychiatric game player that he was, he conceded that there was no way he could force it out of her: it was up to Jacqueline to spell out what was on her mind—on her own terms and in her own good time.

Her mental preoccupation led to noticeable effects in her behavior. She was frequently tired, and she slept more, the somnolence of the depressed. She had also begun to exercise with regularity, at times devoting herself to her aerobics with religious fervor. Her uneasiness had no adverse effect on her appetite. She compulsively adhered to her high-carbohydrate diet. When that didn't work, the amount of food in her diet even appeared to increase. Though she didn't say why she changed, he concluded that her new dietary pattern was—on the one hand—a result of a kind of misguided logic, a deduction that the more pasta she ate, the more weight she'd lose; on the other hand, it might simply be a manifestation of the subconscious, nervous nibbling so common to the fat and once fat.

He was her constant companion. Now, nearly two weeks after her return from California, they took to watching TV together. They played cards and chess. Throughout, Jacqueline kept eating, pressing snacks to her mouth with a neurotic energy. He watched in silence, awed by her behavior. He wasn't so impressed with the amount she ate as he was with the constancy of her consumption. It was nonstop: popcorn, granola, crackers. He was tempted to tell her to slow down, not to eat so much—lest she override her already high carbohydrate tolerance and begin to gain weight coincidentally, by sheer volume. And then, just as he was wondering how on earth she still managed to appear so slender, she abruptly stopped eating, as if she read his thoughts. She stared at her quivering hands and at the fingers that seemed not part of her body. With a scream, she harshly backhanded the bowl of popcorn, sending it across the rug.

"What in the world. . . . ?" he puzzled aloud.

She began to cry.

"My God, look at what I'm doing to myself!"

"It's okay. It's all right."

"It's not all right!" she countered. "How can I sit here and make such a pig of myself!"

At last, he thought. She had finally begun to admit it.

"So that's it," he encouraged.

"So that's what? You don't even know what I'm talking about!"

"It's plain that *something* has been bothering you since you came back. I'm here to listen, Jack. Please tell me about it."

Her expression was the slow and apologetic confessional of a penitent, the long-awaited pain of acknowledgment. Bit by bit, she told him what had been happening, in halting, jerky speech. She related it all: the incident with the costume designer; the deteriorating fit of her clothes; and—most of all—the increasingly frequent and agonizing comments made about her by others at work.

176

No amount of his reasoning seemed to impress her; she was beyond consoling. She was convinced that her fate was preordained, that her weight would start to increase at any moment, no matter what she did. Manley was astonished. She kept talking about it so frantically, so incessantly, that he was afraid she might go off the deep end. He gave up the appeal to logic and instead offered her reassurance and support. She accepted it.

He made love to her slowly, tenderly. Afterward, as she lay beside him in bed, his arms encircled her like a shield. It was well into the night before he drifted off himself. It was a dream-filled sleep that left him with little restful slumber, encumbering his mind with the vivid imagery of apprehension.

He rolled toward her side of the bed and stretched his hand out under the covers, feeling only the satiny quilt atop the warm but empty place in the sheets. She was gone. Curious, but not fully awake, he took a long, deep breath and again began to sleep.

There was a scream.

His eyes flashed open. Jack . . . ? He threw off the covers and leaped out of bed, stumbling toward the hall. She was in the bathroom, her open palms clutching the sides of her face, staring in horror toward the tiled floor.

She was looking at the scale. He slowed, reassured but nonetheless worried.

"What's wrong?"

She was speechless. Her trembling fingers pointed at the scale. He looked at the spot she indicated and saw nothing but the spring-operated Detecto, whose pointer now rested on zero.

"What—the scale?"

She numbly nodded her head.

"What about it?"

Her voice was a whisper.

"I've gained nine pounds."

He began to see what she was talking about.

"Since when?" he replied.

Her hands flew to her temples.

"It's not possible, dammit. I just can't!"

He was sufficiently familiar with her habits to know that she hadn't weighed herself in years.

"Jack, this scale must be ten years old."

"But it's right. I know it is!"

"You can't go by my scale. You have to check your weight on the same scale every time. Mine might be ten pounds different from what yours was the last time you stepped on it."

Panic stricken, she pointed to a twenty-pound dumbbell nearby.

"The scale is perfect! I tested it with one of your weights!"

She was shaking; his arms went around her frightened torso.

"Considering the way you were gorging yourself last night, I'm not the least bit surprised."

"Please don't coddle me. I always eat that way, and you know it!"

"Not as much as yesterday."

It was no use trying to reason with her. He hugged her close and soothingly caressed her back until her trembling ceased. Sniffling, she slipped out of his grasp and stared at her own bleary eyes in the mirror. It would soon be morning.

"I guess you'll just have to eat a little less," he reassured. "Perhaps you should try the kind of diet used by the rest of the civilized world."

"It won't work," she replied, staring dumbly at her reflection. "Nothing will. I'm just going to get fat again."

"Don't be ridiculous."

"But why?" she whispered fearfully. "Why is this happening to me?"

He clearly understood what she was going through: the years of struggle with overweight and obscurity, the miraculous change in her body and in her prestige, and the utter horror that resulted when the former dared threaten the latter. He was about to reply—a logical, reassuring response. But then he decided that the time had finally come to stop playing psychiatrist and to forget the appeal to common sense. Her condition was so fragile now that she had to be handled differently: gently, maybe humorously.

178

He walked up behind her and kissed her neck.

"Did I ever tell you that I'm wild about fat girls? I'd still love you if you were twice as heavy. Gaining a few pounds isn't the worst thing that could happen."

"No, there's something worse."

"Hmmm?"

In the mirror, she gazed at him through hollow eyes.

"The worst will be when my nightmare comes true—when I start to eat and can never stop."

Her tone was so serious, so filled with expectant dread, that even he was touched by the dark grasp of terror that seemed to leave her body as cold and as still as the dead.

Chapter Four

Jacqueline found it difficult to work that day. She tried, making an honest effort to think only about the script, forcing all other thoughts from her mind as she sat in makeup awaiting the call to the stage. When she was summoned, she walked courageously through the corridor, still a frazzle of nerves but too professionally proud to admit it.

Berson, however, took one look at her and told her to forget it. He'd noticed that she'd been on edge for days. Was she ill? There was a puffiness about her, a heaviness to her ankles, the hint of a fold under her chin. Others had noticed it, too; behind her back, they'd openly begun to joke that she was pregnant. If she didn't shape up quickly, he thought, they stood to lose millions.

Yet when he asked with concern how she felt, she tersely replied that she didn't want to discuss it. Berson frowned; he had learned from years of experience that the stage was the wrong place to try to resolve personal problems. If she wanted to talk, he said, he would always be available, but he couldn't possibly let her rehearse in her present condition. He told her to take the day off and relax. By the time she left, he was already hastily reorganizing the day's rehearsal.

Shocked and humiliated, Jacqueline made a subconscious decision to walk home. In the ice of her memory, she recalled the last time she'd walked home: it had been from the tryouts for *Hospice*. Then, she had been nearly delirious with joy at getting the part. Now her mood had come full circle away from joy. Jacqueline stopped and looked at her image in a glassy store window. She was stunned by the reflection that mocked her, that of a leviathan.

Please, no! her mind cried. She stumbled the rest of the way home, filled with worry and disgust. What in the name of heaven was happening to her?

Finally she reached her apartment, breathless. She took the elevator up, her body shuddering with each inhalation. She felt hideously famished, and the sensation sickened her. Her hands were trembling so that it was all she could do to unlock her door.

She knew what she had to do. She raced for the phone directory on her night table. She found the number and dialed it with fingers of marble. And then, mercifully, she heard his voice.

"Dr. Hume, thank God! I thought you would never answer!"

"Is that you, Jacqueline? Whatever is the matter?"

She was frantic, running her fingers through her hair wildly.

"It's so horrible, everything is falling apart. . . . I don't know what's happening to me, I—"

"Calm down, Jacqueline." His voice was all smoothness, softly soothing with its gentle patience. Her tense breathing began to slow. "There, that's better. Tell me, now: what in the world could upset someone as lovely as you?"

"Oh, I can't begin to explain it. I know this sounds silly, but I feel as if something awful is about to happen."

He laughed sympathetically. "I think we must all feel that way sometime."

"No, no, it's true! I . . ." She hesitated, embarrassed by what she was about to admit. More composed, she said, "I've begun to put on some weight."

There was a lengthy pause.

"Are you adhering to your diet?"

"Yes, I swear it! I'm not doing anything different, I—" A single tear rolled down her desperate cheek. "Please, Dr. Hume! I have to come back to San Sebastian."

"But Jacqueline, you so recently left."

"Oh, I know that, I know how ridiculous it sounds," she sniffled. "But you have got to let me return!"

"Dearest Jacqueline, you know I would do anything on earth to help you. Yet what benefit could come from such a hasty return to the Spa?"

"It's just that you're the only one I trust, Dr. Hume. You worked miracles in the past, and I know the same thing will happen if you let me come back!"

Again, his deep, warm laughter, his encouraging tone. "You are so delightfully flattering, and I thank you from the bottom of my heart."

She grew frantic. "But—"

"Just listen for one moment, Jacqueline. You must believe me when I say that I will do everything possible to help you. Yet what you're undergoing is not uncommon. I see this phenomenon at one time or another in up to a third of my patients: we call it rebound. Under stress, such as you are experiencing now, the tissue weakens. You begin to put on weight. Listen carefully, Jacqueline," he said smoothly. "Do you know what you must do?"

Weakly, "What?"

"Simply continue your diet. That is absolutely essential. Do not alter it in any way. Within a week, you will see a dramatic change. That I can guarantee."

The relief that swept over her was immeasurable. She dared to take a deep, shuddering breath.

"Are you sure?"

"I am positive. You must trust me, Jacqueline. Have I ever given you reason to doubt?"

Her tension fled, and she slouched.

"No. Never."

"So you see," he laughed encouragingly, "there is nothing to be gained by returning to the Spa. Trust your diet; it will work. Can you do that, Jacqueline? I must have your promise."

"I promise."

"Good."

His voice was deep and rich as the earth. Its tone was so boundlessly reassuring that she allowed herself a wan smile, and the joyful reflex that followed caused her lids to brim with tears. She was so overwhelmed with salvation that her entire body began to quake. The ferret in her eyes darted about the room—oh, God, where had she placed the damn tissues? Tears of relief wet her cheeks, and she dabbed away their droplets with a trembling hand.

Chapter Five

In the few brief days following her conversation with Dr. Hume, Jacqueline was appalled to find that her relief was short lived. Complying with his instructions, she calculated her carbohydrate consumption down to the milligram. Yet, despite her meticulous obsession with her diet, her weight inexplicably continued to rise.

The dramatic change Dr. Hume had predicted was indeed occurring, but in the wrong direction. When the pattern became obvious, Jacqueline frantically called Dr. Hume back, time and time again; but for some maddening reason, he wasn't available. Every time she phoned, the call terminated with her hanging up in near hysteria.

After several more days of heightening desperation, her condition was such that she felt she had no choice. The carbohydrate diet simply was not working. In a distraught and emotional turnabout, she abandoned it entirely, turning instead to a makeshift menu that soon consisted of virtually nothing at all.

The change in her diet was so abrupt that Manley couldn't fail to notice it; nor did the alteration in her physical activities escape his attention. Jacqueline's sudden cessation of carbohydrate intake went hand in glove with a towering zeal to exercise. The latter had been steadily increasing for days, until there didn't seem to be a spare moment when she wasn't involved in some aspect of body toning. Sweat suits became her second skin. But she still refused to discuss her condition with Manley.

He sat alone in his office, pondering her behavior, when

the call came from the Academy of Medicine. The computer search turned out to be unusually prompt, the librarian said, perhaps because it had located only one pertinent reference. Shortly, Manley returned to the academy, where the bound journal was set aside for him at the reference desk.

He seated himself at one of the long wooden desks, elbows propped up on its fading surface, and opened the volume to the page indicated by a bookmark. The book was the *Annals of Biochemistry*, and this particular edition had been published three years prior to the date of the article he had shown Lindstrom. He underlined the print headings with his finger. The title page clearly acknowledged Dr. Emmerich as the sole contributor. Biochemistry, Manley thought; it was somewhat unusual for a physician to seek publication in a nonmedical field. After he quickly scanned the article, he was even more puzzled by the fact that it had nothing whatsoever to do with brown fat: the confusing technical wording was pure biochemical jargon.

He reviewed the article slowly, more intently. Apparently, Emmerich was reporting on a new chemical base for certain types of injectable drugs. Such medications were customarily injected into muscle in "depot" form—a long-lasting tissue repository that extended drug life over days or weeks. The concept was analogous to that of orally administered sustained-release capsules.

Emmerich was not, however, writing about the drugs themselves; he was reporting instead on a unique new form of depot base, a previously unknown polymer so slowly absorbed that the drug's potential life span could be measured in months rather than weeks.

Or so the paper claimed. Manley wondered what, if anything, it had to do with Emmerich's specialty of neurosurgery; and as for brown fat, there was no obvious relationship at all. Thumbing through the bibliography, he noted that Emmerich's name had one additional credit. Manley scribbled down the reference, closed the book, and returned it to the circulation desk.

It took him a while to locate the final tome—an even earlier, dust-covered log of the *Archives of Neurochemistry*.

Retaking his seat, he leafed through the pages until he found Emmerich's paper. The article was the first the man had ever published, apparently a master's thesis when he had taken a degree at the State University of New York. That explained some of it, Manley understood: Emmerich had been a biochemist before becoming a physician.

The paper summarized the effects of norepinephrine injections in rats. Emmerich had carefully tabulated various behavioral and physical results. Norepinephrine was one of the neurotransmitters Lindstrom had cursorily discussed. Manley read on, only to find the article disappointingly unimaginative. He was about to conclude the study worthless when he caught sight of a table in the footnotes. Captioned, "mean weight loss in grams," it had the semblance of being included haphazardly, almost as an afterthought; but to Manley, it gave the paper new meaning.

He stared at the ceiling. There was an old clock on the wall below, its antique hands clearly weary of consuming seconds. It became his focal point as he tried to judge the significance of what he had read. Neurotransmitters and weight loss . . . animal injections . . . an apparently overlooked depot polymer. It all struck him as obscurely related, perhaps ingeniously so—but in what fashion?

It was getting late. He left the library and returned to his own office and telephone. Everything seemed to revolve around speaking with Emmerich; their communication was essential. His desktop *Directory of Medical Specialists* was several years old, but he quickly flipped through it nonetheless, his face taking on a sullen look when he found that Emmerich's name was not listed. Had the man retired? In the index, Manley found the New Orleans phone number of the American Board of Neurological Surgery. He slowly sat down and dialed.

He hung up, irritated, several minutes later. The long-distance interchange had begun promisingly enough but ended in discouragement. According to the board's public relations officer, Emmerich had been a certified specialist in neurosurgery engaged in active clinical practice in the New York suburbs until seven years ago. At that point, he abruptly stopped paying his dues, and they had no record of his attendance at any board-sponsored educational program thereafter. Nor, the officer concluded, had the board received notice of either death or retirement.

No one simply vanishes, Manley thought.

It was approaching five; Jacqueline would be home shortly. Before returning to her apartment, he paid one last visit to the university library to consult the American Medical Association's Physician Masterfile. Its depressing listing duplicated that of the board in New Orleans; for the past seven years, there was no record of Emmerich whatsoever.

His chin sank to his chest, and he drifted from the library in a blue haze of discouragement. Initially, speaking with Hume had seemed crucial. But Hume was still a question mark, and the only other individual who could possibly help him had, for all intents and purposes, ceased to exist.

Chapter Six

"Good, people—superb!" The director arose from his chair and approached the actors. "Take a short break and then we'll run through it once more."

The cast members dispersed. The director intercepted Jacqueline as she started toward her dressing room. Her lips were drawn in a tight line, and the distress on her face was clear. Yet it continued to amaze him that—whatever was at the core of her problem—she retained her incredible gift as an actress.

"That was wonderful, Jackie. I wish the others had it down as well as you do."

She acknowledged the compliment with a distant nod.

"Do you have a moment?" he continued, jerking his head toward the orchestra seats. "Mr. Berson would like a word with you."

A spasm of twitching indented Jacqueline's chin, and she walked woodenly across the stage and down the steps leading toward the orchestra.

"Sit down, Jackie."

"I'd rather stand, Emil, if you don't mind."

"All right," he began. He stared directly at her as he made a steeple of his fingers. "What am I to do with you, Jackie? What would *you* do in my place?"

"About what?" she asked bravely.

"Don't be coy, Jackie. You're much too bright for that."

She knew what was coming. Oh, God, would she be able to hold back the tears?

"I'm in no position to give you advice." She paused,

wildly contemplating how she could recoup her losses. "All I know is that no one has criticized my performance."

"Not yet. But we both know that's not the issue."

He stared her way, giving her time to reply, but she wouldn't. He sighed.

"If that's all you've got to say," he continued, "I'll have to spell it out for you. We're into final rehearsals and everything's going great—except for one thing. I know it, and you know it, and I'd be lying if I pretended everyone else doesn't know it too. I don't know what your problem is, but you sure as hell have had long enough to do something about it."

His words, however expected, left her near paralysis. Standing there mute and petrified, the tremor that began in her scalp reverberated through her entire body.

"You leave me no choice, Jackie. Either the weight comes off or you do. Much as I'd hate to do it, I'll have to have you replaced."

❧

It was an incredible stroke of luck. Intent on leaving no avenue of inquiry unpursued, Manley had called a psychiatric colleague in Los Angeles, who numbered quite a few celebrities among his patients. Michael Houghton had taken his residency at the same institution as Manley, and although he was two years Manley's senior, their mutual interest in sports had led them into a close friendship, a relationship whose warmth was rekindled on the frequent occasions they spoke on the phone.

After discussing sports in general, and the plight of the Raiders and Rams in particular, Manley focused on the purpose of his call by asking his colleague if he knew of anyone in the Hollywood psychiatric community who might have cared for Suzanne Fontaine.

"Took care of her myself, in fact."

Manley's astonishment was genuine.

"God, I knew I was due for a break. I think you just saved me a small fortune in long-distance charges. Can you discuss her with me?"

"Depends what you want to know. And whether you can keep your mouth shut."

Without going into elaborate detail, Manley revealed Jacqueline's disturbing comments about Fontaine née Rothstein. He went on to summarize his thoughts and observations, briefly sketching the same conclusion he'd previously outlined to Sheila. What he now wanted to know, he said, were the true facts behind all the Fontaine publicity, including her state of mind prior to her death.

Despite the fact that he was Fontaine's analyst, Houghton could add surprisingly little. He replied by painting a psychological profile of a personality essentially similar to Jacqueline's—the lingering anxieties of the once fat that no degree of success could ever fully overcome. To Manley, this was as expected; although as Houghton concluded, Manley discerned a subtle distinction between the two women. Houghton pictured Fontaine as rather vulnerable, somewhat easy to intimidate. Manley guessed that in a similar predicament Jacqueline's fierce will would have resulted in a struggle for survival.

"Much as I hate to admit it," Houghton went on, "I think she lost faith in me. Whatever was going on with her, it was obvious she wasn't comfortable confiding it. She terminated her sessions about a month before she died."

"Unexpectedly?"

"Yes. It was whimsical, not the sort of thing she'd customarily do."

"Did you get any feeling for what caused it? A boyfriend?"

"No, I doubt it was your typical domestic quarrel. I can't be certain, but she gave me the impression that someone was placing . . . well, making a demand on her."

"Any idea who?"

"Haven't the foggiest."

Manley rambled on in circuitous idleness, hoping to stumble onto something that had a possible bearing on Jacqueline. Yet all he wound up with was a plethora of questions, compounded by a sensation of befuddlement that was even greater than when he'd first called. He was about to conclude that he'd reached another dead end when he offhandedly asked if Houghton knew how Fontaine had lost her weight.

"Can't help you with that either, I'm afraid."

"Not even a special diet? Was she an exercise fanatic?"

"Just the opposite. Her vivaciousness was in her personality. Physically, she was downright indolent."

"How did she do it, then?"

"I always suspected she was fantasizing, because I can't find this guy listed anywhere. Yet she swore up and down that she was rather magically helped by a physician she kept referring to as Dr. Hume."

Houghton's reply struck Manley dumb. "Hume . . ."

"You *know* him, Rick?"

"No, I . . . It's just that this whole thing has been such a shock. Jacqueline used to be very close to Suzanne. Naturally Suzanne's heart attack—"

"Did you say heart attack?"

Manley tensed.

"Yes. It was, wasn't it?"

"That might be what they printed in New York, but inside word has it that she freaked out in the hospital. Literally stuffed herself to death. She ruptured her lower esophagus with such force that the food coated her entire heart."

"One more lap—just one!"

"I can't do it," her friend wheezed breathlessly.

"Dammit, Sheil, you promised! Keep up with me!"

Sheila read the anguish in her friend's perspiring face. The look was not one of annoyance but of terror. The desperation of that expression threw spring into her step. With great effort, she tried to follow Jacqueline's last frantic charge around the indoor track.

Finally, Jacqueline pulled up and took slow, measured inhalations. Sheila fell heavily against the wall, gulping air, near collapse.

"Let's go, it's time for aerobics."

"You can't be serious," Sheila rasped.

"We shouldn't keep her waiting."

"For two grand a week, she can afford to wait a few minutes."

"Look, Sheil," Jacqueline snapped, "this was your idea, remember?"

"I must have been out of my head at the time."

"Come on."

Jacqueline walked briskly off the track while Sheila, still out of breath, lumbered behind. They entered a small gymnasium, whose floor was lined with bright exercise mats. Their instructor sipped the last of her coffee as she watched them approach. She yawned, not quite awake, unaccustomed to arising at that ungodly hour. Still, if some people were willing to pay a weekly two-thousand-dollar fee for private, early morning use of all the health club's facilities, she would be happy to accommodate them.

What surprised the instructor more was that an individual with Jacqueline Ramsey's figure was there at all. At least, that was what surprised her until she'd noted the strange puffiness that distended the curves of Miss Ramsey's leotards and the wild and frantic look in the actress' eyes. She looked away and turned on the music, a background tape that throbbed with a rhythmic disco beat.

"How are you today?"

"Just fine," Jacqueline said tersely.

"Are you ready to begin the workout?"

"I'm ready for embalming," Sheila groaned. Nonetheless, she took her place beside Jacqueline, and the two of them awaited the instructor's signal.

"Stand with your legs a little more than hip distance apart, arms loose and relaxed," their private coach began. "Pull your buttocks in, keep your stomach tight, and breathe from your diaphragm," she continued. "Now we'll start with head right, and two, and back, and two; stretch it out, now—left, and two, and . . ."

Jacqueline closely imitated the instructor's sequence, her movements following the music's pulsing punctuations. Sheila was already out of step, though no one corrected her: it was clear that Jacqueline was the object of the exercise. Hands now extended, they progressed to torso bends.

192

"Double time: one, two, three, four; and inhale, pull it out; now to the right—one and, two and; move it down, flat back, straight legs; swing it now, and inhale, one and . . ."

Near the end of the half-hour workout, sweat moistened Jacqueline's brow. Sheila had long since dropped out, unable to keep up. In the flurry of movement nearby, she could not see the grimace that distorted her friend's face, as Jacqueline was finding it uncustomarily difficult to accomplish what had once been so routine.

The music ended, and the instructor turned off the tape. She started to say something encouraging, but Jacqueline had already turned away, heading for the sauna. Sheila shrugged sympathetically and trudged off behind.

Moments later, heads turbaned and skin glistening, they sat in the warm, dry heat. There was no mistaking the cloud of apprehension that hovered behind the film of Jacqueline's eyes.

"What am I doing wrong, Sheil?" she said in desperation. "Why isn't it working?"

"Who says it's not?"

"Don't patronize me!" she fired, inching toward hysteria. "Just look at me."

They both glanced at her waist and hips, at the unmistakable bulges that hadn't been present scant weeks before.

"You should listen to Rick," Sheila ventured.

"Oh, Christ, he's worse than you!" she shot. Shocked by the vehemence of her reply, Jacqueline suddenly couldn't stand the sound of her own voice; her eyes filled with tears of regret. "I'm sorry, Sheila, you didn't deserve that. You've been so good to me through all this. But Rick . . . All he tells me is how great I still look, and how he doesn't care if I gain a few pounds. But I do, dammit, I do!" Her falling tears mixed with the droplets of perspiration that already wet her cheeks.

"Maybe you should have listened to Dr. Hume and stayed on the diet."

"Don't you understand, it wasn't working!" There was a wide-eyed look of lunacy about her. "If I can diet—really diet, eat almost nothing—I *have* to lose weight, don't I?"

Before Sheila could reply, Jacqueline threw off her towel and ran frantically from the sauna. Sheila arose with obvious concern. Jacqueline was literally forcing herself toward starvation while she was exercising toward the point of collapse. She was trying so terribly hard, and yet nothing was working. If only—

The piercing shriek came from the area of the dressing room.

Sheila dashed among the lockers until she found Jacqueline standing by the doctor's scale, whose horizontal bar bobbed slowly up and down. The reading was three pounds heavier than it had been the day before. Jacqueline wailed, seized by panic, holding her sobbing face in her hands.

Chapter Seven

As her mania for diet and exercise increased, the quality of her acting decreased. Jacqueline surmised that it was just a matter of time before Berson dismissed her. Still, the order of her priorities placed her physical self-image above her career. She stubbornly clung to the belief that her salvation lay with Dr. Hume.

She continued to phone him every day, praying that her hopes would be answered, that he might have a change of heart. Surprisingly, when she finally got through to him, it seemed as if their previous conversation had never ended. His voice once again rang with the familiar, resonant sound of his gracious laughter, a sound she found infinitely reassuring. She gathered her wits about her and was preparing to tell him about her failure and desperation, to plead for his support and intervention, when he interrupted her very first words.

"I apologize for not returning your earlier calls, Jacqueline. I have been dreadfully busy. But then I heard the discouraging news about your weight."

"But how did you—"

"It doesn't matter. All that matters is that your career not be compromised. It may even be necessary for you to return once more to San Sebastian."

When she heard him say that, she wanted to weep. Her eyes closed, and her chin quivered with gratitude.

"Oh thank God, Dr. Hume. Whatever you think best."

"Good. Before we discuss it, however, there is something I would like you to do for me."

She felt a wave of uncertainty roll over her. "Anything. What is it?"

He gave a genial laugh. "Merely an impromptu suggestion. It's still rather early in the day where you are, isn't it?"

She glanced at the clock.

"Not quite twelve."

"Good. Do you have a free moment this afternoon?"

She falteringly raised her hand to her jaw.

"Why, yes, I—"

"I understand that Sidney Lambert is in town. Surely you're familiar with his work."

Very much so, she recalled, as an incident bloated in the anguish of her memory.

"I know of him," was all she would admit.

There was a brief hesitation.

"I wonder if you could possibly see him, Jacqueline. As a favor to me. And then we can discuss your return."

"A favor?"

"I would be most grateful. He shan't be in New York long. In fact, I believe he may be expecting you."

Not long afterward, Jacqueline dutifully sat in the rear seat of a cab, heading for the Intercontinental. She contemplated the dull gray afternoon with annoyance, wearing the pout of a schoolgirl summoned by the headmaster. Her hair was drawn back severely, covered with a scarf that knotted under her chin.

Her only encounter with Lambert had come years before, shortly after she had arrived in New York. He was a slimy bastard, her agent had warned; don't get taken in by his promises. Yet Jacqueline was initially so eager for work— any legitimate work—that the prospect of appearing on screen proved irresistible enough for her to dismiss her agent's words of caution.

Had she known what Lambert truly had in mind, she *never* would have responded to the cast call. His interest turned out to be purely financial and basely salacious, and although he glibly described the role offered Jacqueline as nothing more than the mildest of soft-core porn, one look at the other actors was enough to convince her that the production was intended to be the sleaziest sort of gutter cinema.

Several enormously lucrative horror films had nonetheless lent Lambert a modicum of status and considerable financial clout. In a short time he had gained the reputation of a commercially successful producer of generally inferior movies; it was no secret that he preferred films with exploitative themes to more serious or artistic productions. He was the kind of Hollywood mogul that Jacqueline would ordinarily have nothing to do with.

So why am I going to see him? she fretted.

God, it's only a favor, she reasoned; it was the least she could do for Dr. Hume. Yet why in the world would he want her to. . . . She shook her head, dismissing the unanswerable thought as her face turned upward to stare at the impenetrably dull sky.

How little made sense to her anymore. The agony of her changing weight was beyond her comprehension. Then, too, there were the little pauses in her memory, an amnesiac's glimpses of nothingness. And the news of Suzanne—so out of character, so unexpected, so incomprehensible.

The cab pulled up in front of the hotel. Lambert had reserved a suite on the top floor. During the elevator's ascent, all she could think about was whether or not he would remember her—the eager but naive cherub he had once propositioned, in what now seemed to be ages ago.

He did not remember. Once inside his suite she indulgently allowed her lips to trace a prim smile while Lambert launched into a five-minute soliloquy of pretentiousness, a testimonial to his own sense of self-worth; it was verbal bluster that alternated with fawning declarations about Jacqueline's magnificence. Quite unexpectedly, his oratory stopped and he got down to business.

Jacqueline briefly listened to what he had to say. And then she precipitously sat upright in her chair, uncertain that she'd heard him right. She stared at the heavy folds of his eyes.

"Did you say *Pygmalion*?"

"Yeah, you know—that Shaw thing?"

Her fingers interlaced.

"I wasn't aware you were such a patron of the arts."

"It's not exactly my cup of tea. But seeing how the money's right, and with you in the lead—"

She threw him a sharp glance.

"He told you I would do it?"

"I don't know the guy from Adam, honey, but that was the general drift."

She departed moments later, her mood alternating between uneasiness and indignation. Lambert made it plain that Dr. Hume had led him to believe she would most definitely accept the starring role; in fact, he had financially guaranteed it. The producer had just begun to outline his thoughts on the production when Jacqueline went to the door and left.

On the trip back, no matter how tightly she buttoned her coat, she felt chilled. All right, she comforted herself; at least she had satisfied her obligation to Dr. Hume by going to listen. She didn't know why he had even been interested, but she would tell him her thoughts about the producer in no uncertain terms. The doctor was a reasonable man; surely he would respect her opinion. But that Lambert: of all the brazen audacity. Why would that pompous ass even think she would consider. . . . Oh, did it really matter, as long as she could go back to the Spa?

She had barely returned to her apartment when the phone rang. It was most likely Rick, she thought. She smiled warmly when she pictured his face. She knew he thought her unfair for not sharing her problems with him, in keeping her fears to herself; yet she was as determined as ever to avert catastrophe single-handedly. Only when she had succeeded would she admit how deeply she appreciated his concern.

Or, she thought as she headed for the phone, it might be Emil. She had treated him so dreadfully lately. All that would change, of course, once she came back from the Spa.

She picked up the receiver and was surprised that it was Dr. Hume. He made lighthearted banter before revealing that he had just spoken with Lambert. He shocked her by insisting that she take the part.

"Do take it, Jacqueline. It's perfect for you."

She paled. The quivering began in her neck.

"*Pygmalion* is a little out of character for me," she replied, trying to remain diplomatic and to conceal her trembling voice.

"You underestimate your versatility, my dear."

"But my play . . . We're right in the middle of—"

"I believe you are missing the point, Jacqueline. This is a role I would most like you to have. You will make a splendid Galatea. I will see to it that the contract reaches you by the end of the week. Once you return it to me, we shall discuss your next visit to San Sebastian."

She was stunned. Were she not so frightened by his air of certainty, she might have even been annoyed. There was no doubt that she would be eternally grateful if he could help her remain thin, but . . . Why, surely he wasn't going to use this as some sort of bargaining chip. As a rational individual, he *had* to understand that the path of her career was hers alone to chart—hadn't he?

The twitching spread to the muscles of her face. She forced a swallow against an impossibly dry throat.

"I'll have to talk it over with my agent," she said evasively.

"He is not to be involved in this. When the papers arrive, simply sign them and send them off." He sounded so smooth, so confident. "You will do this for me, Jacqueline—won't you?"

The fact that she hesitated—considered what he said even momentarily—was what she later found most repugnant, more revolting than her grossest self-image. She slowly hung up the phone in horror, her skin as pale as the mist round a moonlit tomb.

Chapter Eight

The tumblers clicked like falling dice when he turned the key in the lock of her front door. The rooms beyond were dark. He took off his coat and slowly proceeded into the hall.

"Jack?"

He sensed she was there despite the silence. An antique Waterford lamp was on the desk bordering the living room; he pulled its chain. A yellow mist spilled out and defined the contours of the room. He found her sitting on the sofa, still clad in her outdoor wear.

She was sculpted to the cushions, oblivious to his presence, a study in bereavement. He sat beside her and laid his hand on hers.

"Why were you sitting in the dark?"

Night. Silence.

"Was it something at work?"

Her chin rippled, clefts and crevices that quivered beneath her skin. Little tremors crept up her face. The whispering shadow of her voice rose like a phantom from her throat.

"I'm about to be sacked."

He tried to conceal his incredulity. "Just like that, without warning?"

"Plenty of warning. I must not have been listening."

"Did they say why?"

Her breath was a long, shuddering inhalation. "Isn't it obvious?"

She arose slowly as fog. Her leaden steps plodded across

the carpet toward the front closet. Fatigue punctuated her every move. How much could she take? he wondered. He knew about her frantic dieting, and she had told him, albeit sketchily, about the exercise; it had taken Sheila to fill in the portrait of a fanatic. Jacqueline was on the verge of collapse.

He stared at her from the couch, studying her weary movements. "Didn't you eat anything all day?"

She was abruptly penetrated with animation, and the thickness of her movements vanished in her frenzied pirouette.

"*Eat?*" She spat the word like a hot pepper. "I'm about to lose my job over this, and you have the gall to ask me about eating?"

"Keep going like this and you'll drop in your tracks."

"Everything I worked for is going up in smoke. At this point what difference would it make if I keeled over too!"

He paused, giving a little raise of his eyebrows.

"Would it do any good?"

She looked away, hating the way she could no longer control her temper.

"Only one person could do any good," she said hoarsely. "And he won't help."

"Who won't?"

"Dr. Hume," she said with mournful certainty. "I have got to return to the Spa, and he won't let me."

"What's this, now?"

She looked over to where he still sat on the cushions. It was she who should be on a couch, she thought, not he. She slowly hung her head and closed her eyes, lifting her hand to rub her lids between thumb and forefinger. She took a breath, and in that moment, she decided.

She told him of her conversation, leaving out Hume's quixotic request and her subsequent actions. Manley listened in silence as the puzzle became compounded. He could think of nothing to say. When her brief narration was over, she announced, "I'm going to take a shower."

Jacqueline hung up her coat and went to the bedroom to change. Manley brooded as he followed her. Clearly he had to speak to Hume, a man whose apparent isolation made Manley impatient. Still, he was far more concerned with Jacqueline. From all he had recently observed, she should have been growing thinner rather than heavier, and her fervent desire to return to San Sebastian bordered on the obsessional.

Loose ends by the bushel. Everything was happening so fast; they were living a whirlwind. Jacqueline slipped out of her clothes and walked to the bathroom. Despite the weight she had gained, he still considered her lovely in her nakedness.

In the shower, she rinsed the suds out of her hair. The hot water dissipated her fatigue, lessened her apprehension. The shower curtain slid open, and she felt a cool breeze. Blinking, she wiped the water from her eyes. He entered the shower with her. She looked at his smiling face and felt the last traces of her annoyance vanish.

The sharp needles of spray prickled her shoulders. She looked below his waist and saw his arousal.

"Oh, my," she said. "Is this supposed to cheer me up?"

"Call it therapy."

His arms went around her, and they were under the water together. She spoke with her lips inches from his.

"If I could only lose weight this way."

"Depends how hard you try."

He kissed her lightly then, and the spray rained on their heads and washed down their faces. She pressed her breasts to the damp matted hair of his chest and slid her cheek along his.

Her inner tension was transformed into an overpowering eagerness. The hot water cascading down his body made him feel firm and slippery and sensuous, and when she rubbed her hands along his back his lips were already doing wonderful things to her neck, her ear. She closed her eyes and inched her fingers through his scalp. Their mouths came together, his tongue upon hers, bathed by needles of spray. His palms made little circles on her breasts, and her sigh was a faint undertone of response. He lifted her up by the waist, and her thighs went around his back. She locked his head in her arms as they slid together.

Her breath came faster. She clung to him, moving her

hips and abdomen against his. He threatened to slip away, but she held him fast. Her voice was a steamy whisper.

"Stay up in me," she urged.

In the showering wetness, his hands clenched her buttocks, and as the water ran down their skin, their bodies tensed and moved together until slowly, very slowly, their shuddering ceased.

She felt physically and emotionally drained, yet strangely satisfied. He sensed her weariness and assisted her from the shower, then wrapped her in a thick terry towel. She hadn't the energy to blow her hair dry. Closing her eyes, she leaned against him. They walked together from the steaming bathroom. She crawled into bed and was instantly asleep.

Manley looked at her tranquil face and planted a light kiss on her forehead. He waited until her breath was steady and rhythmic before beginning his search. Quietly, he rummaged through the belongings in her chest of drawers, in her closet, and at the bedside. There—in the shelf of her night table—he found her personal phone directory.

It was listed under the "S," for San Sebastian. He hastily scribbled down the number, neatly folded the scrap of paper, and placed it in his wallet. He would call tomorrow, if he could. He returned to the kitchen and made himself a bite to eat.

Hours later, he stood by the bedroom window, watching the ascent of the bright winter moon. He shed his robe and crawled into bed next to her. In her sleep, Jacqueline rolled onto her side, her back to him.

He lightly stroked the smoothness of her shoulder and let his hand trace the curve of her spine. His fingertips momentarily slowed and then stopped altogether between her shoulder blades, testing the texture of her skin. An unexpected numbness crept up his arm and into his soul.

The middle of her back had grown cold.

White moonlight inched across her quilt and slowly drifted up her cheek to touch her lids. Jacqueline's eyes fluttered open in the pale glow. She sat up trancelike in bed. In her unconsciousness, the sunken galleons of her eyes saw nothing.

She slipped ghostlike from the covers, leaving Manley to sleep undisturbed. She dressed warmly against the outside chill and stole quietly from her apartment. Once in the street, she walked without hesitation to the all-night deli nearby.

Moments later, she left the store carrying a small shopping bag. As she began her return, she first unwrapped an ice cream sandwich and took a large bite. By the time she reached the middle of the block, it was gone. She reached into her package for the Mars Bars and pistachio nuts. She ate the chocolate slabs quickly, one after another, and then started on the nuts, dropping the candy wrappers in the street. She attacked the nuts like a squirrel, nibbling away, hands going quickly from bag to mouth, spitting one shell after another onto the sidewalk; her teeth were working so fast they almost clicked.

The food was vaguely satisfying, but it didn't take the edge off her hunger, a profound, gnawing sensation in her stomach. By the time she reached her building, her shopping bag was empty, and her plastic spoon was well into the last pint of ice cream. Still, it wasn't enough; all she could concentrate on was her appetite. She got on the elevator without so much as nodding to the doorman, leaving him baffled by the wild and staring look on her face.

Inside her apartment, she quickly unbuttoned her coat and let it drop on the floor, walking directly to the refrigerator. She opened the door and eyed the various shelves. She selected several items. Within seconds, she was hastily mixing the ingredients for a large omelette, emptying all twelve eggs into a wide crockery bowl. She turned the stove on to high heat, put on a skillet, and quickly poured the yellow concoction into the pan.

It was ready moments later. Seared by the flame, the eggs were variably cooked, in some places brown and burnt, coagulated, scorched albumin amidst sticky swirls of yolk. She started for the table but couldn't wait any longer. She deposited the pan on the shelf by the sink and opened the silverware drawer nearby. A large salad fork was the first thing that came to hand. She held the pan by its plastic handle, bent over the skillet, and shoveled the eggs into her mouth.

She scalded the roof of her palate, but she didn't care. When she finished the solid parts, she lifted the edge of the pan to her mouth and drank the remaining raw egg. Shortly the skillet was empty. When she returned it to the sink, her mouth was rimmed with yellow flecks of egg within a greasy saffron smear.

She had no concept of how much she had eaten; all she knew was that she was still ravenous. She opened the pantry and looked up and down its shelves. The chocolates were near the top. She sifted among them with her fingers, brushing aside various items she had brought home from a cast party, a diverse selection from the erotic bakery: neatly wrapped phalluses, breasts, and buttocks molded of the finest chocolate. There, at the back of the shelf, Jacqueline found what she wanted—an enormous fudge Easter bunny wrapped in clear cellophane.

She tore off the plastic and devoured the candy hare. Jacqueline strolled into the living room while she ate. En route, she plucked off the chocolate ears and the head and stuffed them into her mouth. Her mouth was filled, her cheeks crammed and bulging with sweet. She lifted the bunny's torso to her mouth, ripping off an enormous chunk with her teeth. Her mouth stuffed nearly to the bursting point, she dumbly gazed around while her jaws ground back and forth. There was a reflection in the mirror.

For a second, Jacqueline stopped chewing and idly studied the image, wondering who it was. The person she saw was standing before the silvered glass, both hands gripping a hunk of unrecognizable brown. Her fingers were coated with it, and it had begun to melt, soft and sticky. Her mouth, swollen with unchewed fudge, was streaked like a child's with stains light and dark, and rivulets of candied saliva ran out of the corners of her mouth in a liquid brown drool.

Momentarily, her awareness returned. Though she saw

205

it darkly, Jacqueline now recognized the reflection as her own. She stopped chewing, aghast.

She couldn't believe what she was doing. As she stared at her reflection, the warm chocolate grew slippery in her fingers. She whipped her hands apart, letting go of the remaining confection as if it were burning her palms. It fell to the rug and rolled in the plush pile. She looked at her hands in disbelief, turning them palm up, their surfaces streaked and coated with stains darker than blood. Her fingers began to shake uncontrollably.

No! her mind shrieked.

Her worst nightmare was now vivid in her mind, bloating there. Jacqueline's heart was galloping, and her legs were weak. She was suffocating in a hot, foul blanket. Her stomach churned, and a wave of nausea swelled in her throat.

She ran to the bathroom an instant before she soiled the room. Sinking to her knees in front of the commode, she spit out what was left of the chocolate just as the first spasm sent food upward into her throat. She gagged continuously, retching for minutes until her stomach had shed its contents into the toilet bowl.

When she was done, she rolled onto her side, gasping. Weak, sickened, she began to cry. It was whimpering, a soft, animal sound that shortly turned to sobbing.

She crawled to her knees as her crying spent itself, the flood of tears largely gone.

She stood cold and trembling before the sink. She turned the faucets with shaking hands and splashed water on her face. She washed the stains from her lips and cheeks, rinsed out her mouth, and patted cold water on her puffy lids. She gazed at her damp face in the mirror. There was fear there, terror in her eyes. She needed help. Rick would know what to do. All at once she remembered that he was there, asleep in her bedroom beyond.

Jacqueline toweled her skin dry. What could she tell him? Deep in thought, she started back to the living room.

Halfway across the room, she saw the partly eaten chunk of fudge lying on the rug. It was still moist and melting, bearing teeth marks and small particles of wool from the carpet. Another tide of revulsion swept over her. Yet as she stared at it, a curious thing happened. Horrified though she was, she was stung by a burst of hunger. It rocketed through her body, tense and electric and jangling. She wanted *that* thing, that remaining handful of soft brown chocolate, that—

"Oh, my God!" she whispered. Her hands went to her temples, and she closed her eyes, silently crying in agony to make the image go away. Don't look at it. Don't!

She stumbled blindly toward the bedroom. Yet all at once her legs were thick and heavy as hunger struck her like an explosion, nearly tearing off the top of her head. Against her will, Jacqueline felt herself beginning to turn around. The drive was overpowering, the ache within beyond her control. In the instant before her mind stopped functioning, fear allowed her one last attempt at salvation.

"Rick! Rick, help me!" she screamed aloud.

Her hands then fell to her side. Glassy-eyed, she finished her slow about face and took one step, then two, toward the thing that lay on the carpet in the center of the room.

Manley rolled over in bed, prying at his half-awake thoughts, tossing fitfully. Then he heard more noises, noises like running footsteps, and he sleepily glanced at the empty sheets beside him. Jacqueline . . . the scale again? He was instantly out of bed. As he hurried toward the sound, blinking his eyes from the hall's bright light, the first thing he saw was Jacqueline, who came streaking out of the kitchen, running frantically toward the bathroom. She seemed oblivious to his presence. Her body was coated with remnants of food. Mayonnaise glazed her upper lip; the pulp and seeds of a hastily eaten tomato ran down her breastbone; and the tips of her fingers and her nose were smeared with ketchup.

"Jack! For God's sake, what's wrong?"

Crying all the while, she kneeled on the bathroom tile and forced her fingers down her throat. Manley stood above her, trying to comprehend what had happened to the bathroom.

Vomitus was everywhere. The rancid splatterings spilled

over the sides of the commode and coated the sink and bathtub beyond. The foul brownish debris had been sprayed with enormous force, anointing the room with chunks of barely digested food.

As he watched, Jacqueline made herself gag. Her upper body heaved when she retched, and the voluminous contents of her stomach spilled into the toilet bowl. Incredulous, he stared dumbstruck at the foul mixture. What in the world had she eaten? He tried to flush the toilet, but it was stopped up. He watched in alarm as the stinking watery soup of bile and foodstuffs welled up and spilled over the toilet's rim.

Jacqueline barely had time to catch her breath; she rocked back, pale and cold, spluttering against the wheeze in her chest. The tide of sewage pooled about her knees. Manley leaned over and took her wrist. With his other hand, he located a face towel and moistened it in the sink.

"It's okay, Jack. It's all over now."

Her face turned his way. It was a tragic mask, lips turned downward in agony, eyes dulled with grief. But there was something else in her expression—terror, accompanied by an animal fear so intense he could almost smell it above the stench in the room.

Abruptly, Jacqueline ripped her hand away and leaped to her feet. In a flash, she was beyond him and into the hall, frantically running back to the kitchen.

"Jack!"

He hurried after her and was soon staring in awe at the sight of Jacqueline rolling on the floor, clutching whatever food she could get her hands on. The kitchen was a mess, a battle zone. Contents of the refrigerator and pantry cluttered the room. Shreds of fruit and vegetables littered the room; raw meats were piled in uneven rows and columns like ghastly marchers in a butcher's parade. In the center of it all, Jacqueline writhed on the floor, rapidly stuffing candy into her mouth without even removing the wrapping.

At first he was too stunned to move. Then he stepped forward and took hold of one of her arms.

From out of nowhere she struck him a vicious punch to the face that sent him sprawling. He rolled to his knees and rubbed his mouth, his pride more wounded than his jaw, and again started toward her.

At the sight of his approach, Jacqueline—on all fours—started to crawl backward into a corner. As she retreated, she stuffed whatever came to hand into her mouth, now swallowing the raw meat without even chewing it. In spite of the sad and tortured look on her face, and the eyes that brimmed over with tears, she sounded as if she were snarling.

And then she was on her feet again, bolting past him in a blur, her cheeks crammed with food. He was instantly after her; yet by the time he reached the bathroom, she was already retching. Manley grabbed her shoulders and steered her toward the sink. She appeared to be helping him lower her face toward it when she collapsed. Her body went limp in his arms. He seized her under the armpits and dragged her out of the foul bathroom, lowering her onto the floor in the hall.

Though her eyes were closed, she was still gagging. Her body convulsed under her chest's effort to expel whatever was in her throat. Manley tilted her head back and tried to pry her mouth open. Her jaws were clenched tight. The more she struggled, the more pale she became; soon her skin had the gray-blue tint of fish flesh. As Manley watched in horror, a pink froth oozed through her lips, bubbles of blood-tinged spittle.

She stopped breathing. Manley kept constant pressure on the angles of her jaw with his fingertips, trying to tilt her chin back and force her airway open. Her throat was in spasm. She was getting no air.

"Come on," he begged frantically.

Seconds later, the spasm broke on its own. The lack of oxygen had so completely benumbed Jacqueline's brain that, as a reflex, her tight muscles relaxed. He quickly opened her mouth and removed the bloody froth and remaining bits of food with his fingers. Still she didn't breathe, and he began to administer mouth-to-mouth resuscitation.

His fingertips sought the pulse in her neck. His own heart was pounding.

A minute passed, then two, though he was unaware of the time. Slowly, perceptibly, color returned to Jacqueline's cheeks. Manley's face was glistening with sweat, but he didn't dare stop. Just when he was beginning to expect the worst, her head miraculously inched to the side, and her contained breath expelled itself in a deep, hacking cough. She started to breathe again.

Her eyes opened. Her vision focused, and she centered it on him. She stared at Manley in confusion. Though still pale, she started to arise.

"Lie still," he cautioned.

Jacqueline disregarded him and got up. She gazed about her apartment in concern. She began to walk, unsteadily at first, but then with deliberation, surveying the devastation that was her residence, shaking her head at what she saw. Manley remained on his knees, still breathing hard from his effort. She paused where he knelt and stopped beside him, encircling his shoulders with her arm, peering into his eyes.

"Rick, what in the world happened to you? Are you okay now? Should I call a doctor?"

It was her expression that tore at his heart more than her words. It was a sleepy look of total innocence, a child's searching soul, as soft and warm as lamb's wool.

Chapter Nine

It being a Wednesday, Manley had no office hours. That was fortunate, for he was so shaken by what had happened to Jacqueline that he was unable to concentrate and would have had to cancel his sessions anyway. The two of them spent the remaining predawn hours cleaning and reorganizing the apartment without once commenting on what had occurred, as if each of them were harboring an unspeakable secret. Then Jacqueline went off to work as if nothing at all had transpired.

Calling Hume was essential; he could delay it no longer. But because of the time difference, he thought it best to postpone the attempt until midmorning, Pacific time. He looked at his watch: he was left with six hours. Rather than spend them in idle impatience, he returned to the university, where he could pursue other obligations.

As a proctor, Manley was continually involved with helping Ph.D. candidates complete their theses. When he arrived at his office, he leafed through several folders before selecting one for review.

It was an esoteric treatise. The candidate was trying to debunk the whole concept of basal metabolism, calling it "a simplistic approach to a complex issue." Most of the student's data was derived from thorough metabolic surveys of the university hospital's inpatients during the year. Manley casually turned the pages, looking for statistical flaws or errors in logic. There were few; the writer had done a commendable job.

Among the numerous columns of information were details of the patients' caloric requirements. Manley's eyes widened in surprise when he noted that a Mrs. Dillon, one of those included in the evaluation, was being given three thousand calories per day, in the form of liquid tube feedings.

Something familiar about the name. . . . He sifted through the ancillary data until he found that Mrs. Dillon was a psychiatric inpatient. Manley looked up in thought; soon, the memory registered. He vividly recalled the patient from ward rounds a month or so previously, when he had peered into her room through the observation mirror. From the few facts he could recall of her case, Mrs. Dillon—an actress—was a catatonic, having become so after she brutally murdered her husband.

As he'd gazed at her, the attractive, middle-aged woman stared passively ahead, mute as a statue, so completely immobile that she might just as well have been made of wax. Yet something had compelled her, Manley knew; some driving force that had pushed her over the brink of sanity into an abyss of unimaginable horror.

As his thoughts returned to the present, he telephoned the head nurse on the psychiatric ward.

"Does Dillon receive any regular visitors?" he asked. "Friends, relatives?"

"Not that I recall," she replied. "I can't say that I blame them. She's not much of a conversationalist. Her butler visited once or twice right after she was admitted. But I haven't seen him lately."

Moments later, Manley was in a cab for the short cross-town trip to the Dillon residence. He preferred a brief personal visit to an anonymous phone call; the former promised better results. Prior to departing, he had simply asked the ward nurse to phone ahead to say that one of the staff physicians was coming over for an informal chat.

The butler was expecting Manley's arrival. He introduced himself as Hadley and escorted Manley to the drawing room, where Manley declined his offer of sherry. Then the manservant inquired about his employer.

"How is Mrs. Dillon, sir?"

"Her condition hasn't changed much."

The butler clasped his hands in solicitude.

"Are you her personal physician there?"

"One of several." He paused. "How long have you worked for the Dillons?"

"Nearly twenty years, sir." He gave a little shake to his head. "This whole chain of events is most distressing. Is there anything I can do?"

"That's what I came to talk with you about."

"I will assist in every way possible."

Manley toyed with the antique bric-a-brac, wondering how to phrase the speculative thought that had suddenly occurred to him.

"Did Mrs. Dillon ever have a weight problem?"

"Are you inquiring if I knew she was fat, sir?"

He smiled. "Yes."

"Mrs. Dillon was somewhat heavy until earlier this year. She consulted one physician after another about it."

"Did they all have practices in this area?"

The butler raised his eyebrows in reflection.

"The great majority."

"Who was the last one she saw?"

Again, the butler was pensive.

"Oh, what *is* his name? He took over Dr. Wahlberg's practice, I believe."

Manley was openly startled by the reply. Wahlberg, he remembered, was the same man whose coauthor Manley was now desperately seeking. He decided to broach the subject obliquely.

"Did Mrs. Dillon follow any sort of diet?"

"Yes, several." The butler allowed himself a discreet chuckle. "None of them worked, I'm afraid. Until recently. Apparently it has something to do with carbohydrates."

Manley was jarred by a shiver. His face grew drawn, his voice hoarse.

"When did that begin?"

"Oh, it was shortly after her last vacation. She spent two weeks at a clinic and returned considerably lighter."

"Do you remember the name of the place?"

"The Spa at San Sebastian. Sir? Are you all right, sir?"

* * *

213

Midmorning arrived.

As he waited for his party to come to the phone, Manley's fingers turned to brittle sticks that scratched the desk dryly. He had already steeled himself for the anticipated hostility of Hume's reply. He was caught off guard by the unexpected warmth of the man's hello.

"This is Dr. Manley in New York," he began. "I'm a friend of Jacqueline Ramsey—"

"Yes, I know," came the cordial reply. "A rather close friend, I understand. Tell me: how is Jacqueline?"

"Not well." He was determined to remain patient. "She's on the brink of physical and mental collapse, she's rapidly gaining weight, and she's got it in her mind that you're the only one who can help her."

The rich basso of Hume's voice rang with deep concern.

"I can't tell you how very sorry I am to hear that. I am terribly fond of Jacqueline. She called not long ago to seek my assistance, but I had no idea she was in such distress."

Manley's bewilderment soared. "She's pushing herself to exhaustion," he continued nonetheless. "Can you suggest anything at all that might help her?"

"I truly wish I could, yet I must confess to being puzzled. Jacqueline was in superb condition when she was last here. Is she adhering to her diet?"

"She's gone off it entirely. When she's not starving herself, she's—" he caught himself, the stark madness of her recent frenzy searing his memory like a fiery brand— "behaving strangely. I was wondering if you could tell me what's so important about the diet you prescribed."

"Since it always worked for her in the past, I saw no reason she shouldn't continue it."

"Why carbohydrates?" Manley persisted. "Are they significant?"

"It's a method I have found particularly effective."

"I understand that—but what's their specific function?"

"They assure the overall well-being of the patient."

Manley was nonplussed. Though Hume's tone was the epitome of geniality, the man seemed to be adroitly refusing to give any concrete answers.

"What do they have to do with brown fat?"

214

"I beg your pardon?"

"Brown fat: does Jacqueline's condition have anything to do with a change in her body's brown fat?"

Hume was betrayed by an instant of hesitation.

"I must regrettably confess that I know nothing of the substance you are referring to."

"Oh, come on, Hume—I've already learned that you discovered a way to increase her brown fat metabolism. I'll be happy to show you the proof once Jacqueline has improved. What I want now is for you to help me get her that way."

There was warmth and atonement in Hume's gentle laughter, as apologetic as unexpected spring rain.

"I am deeply flattered, Dr. Manley. Would that I were the magician you claim."

"Do I take that as a refusal?"

"It's a humble confession that I cannot work miracles."

Manley's irritation mounted.

"You really don't give a damn about her, do you?" he carped.

"On the contrary, I care a great deal."

"The same way you cared for Mrs. Dillon?"

Again, the moment of silent hesitation. Hume's tone grew somber.

"Mrs. George Dillon? Has something happened to her as well?"

"For Christ's sake, Dr. Hume, why don't you stop trying to pretend you don't know that she's currently catatonic, on a mental ward? Thank God she's starting to look a little better."

"I had no idea. . . ." The pitch of his voice grew unexpectedly sharp and determined. "Which hospital?"

Manley lost control. He could no longer tolerate the man's blatant deceit.

"You can damn well find out for yourself!"

He slammed down the phone in a rage of crimson fury.

Chapter Ten

"Something wrong, sir?"

"What?" Dr. Hume turned around, and his distracted expression turned to a smile. "Ah, Vincent. Everything quiet in the special wing?"

"As usual."

"Good, good. We're expecting young Miss Rhodes tomorrow. The actress. She'll be getting our special routine."

"I know."

Hume walked over and clapped Vincent on the shoulder with a grin. "There is little you don't know, my friend—isn't there?"

"Not where you're concerned, doctor. I make it my business."

"So you do. And I'm grateful."

"Never as much as I am, sir. I'd be just another 11B-10 in a wheelchair if you hadn't come to the VA hospital when you did."

"That seems so long ago."

"Nine years, seven months."

Hume's eyebrows arched. "Your memory is remarkable. 11B-10 . . . Special Forces, wasn't it?"

"That's 10S. I was 10R—Rangers."

Hume acknowledged the correction with a nod, although he had been aware of the exact branch of service all along. "Sheer luck, my rotation through the VA."

"Call it what you will, sir. To me it was a miracle."

"I didn't think you believed in miracles."

"Figure of speech." Vincent shrugged. "I generally think

of myself as a practical man. Keep my ears open, you know?"

"That can be helpful."

"I think so. Take just now, for instance. No offense, Dr. Hume, but I happened to overhear your phone conversation."

"Really?" Hume pretended, fully aware the orderly had.

"You're a gentleman, Dr. Hume. Always were. But I can't say the same for the other party. Whoever that might have been."

Hume waved at the air offhandedly. "No one important. Just another boor who thinks he should make San Sebastian his business."

"You don't say?" Vincent frowned. "No relation to one of our patients?"

"Goodness no." Hume paused. "Though the strange part of it—humorous, actually—is that he was a doctor. One might think doctors would have greater understanding."

"Yes . . . humorous," said Vincent, although his expression registered no trace of humor. "Would I recognize the name, Dr. Hume?"

"Oh, I doubt it. Some Dr. Manley in New York."

"Richard Manley," the orderly replied evenly. "Psychiatrist. Goes out with Miss Ramsey."

Hume placed his hands on his hips and gazed at his ex-patient in amazement, shaking his head appreciatively from one side to the other. "You never cease to astound me."

"Nothing to it, doctor. Just a matter of reading the papers. This Manley—he's in all the articles about her. Speaking of which, some reporters hint Miss Ramsey's putting on weight. Think there's any truth to that?"

Hume's smile was beatific. "It's quite possible, Vincent. Quite possible."

"Naturally, if there's anything you want done, Dr. Hume . . . done quietly, that is."

"Thank you, Vincent. You are the very soul of discretion. But as for Miss Ramsey, you needn't worry. I have her case well in hand." He turned to go.

"Doctor—"

Hume drew to a halt. "Yes?"

"I also couldn't help overhearing about Mrs. Dillon."

"Ah, yes, Mrs. Dillon. . . . Such a tragedy. Catatonia."

"So I read."

Hume rubbed his nose in concentration. "I got the distinct impression our Dr. Manley thought there might be an improvement in Mrs. Dillon's condition."

"You mean she might snap out of it?"

"Well, he is a psychiatrist, isn't he? But if she did," he paused, staring at Vincent, "that would prove . . . interesting."

"I can find out the name of that hospital, Dr. Hume."

Hume's eyes blazed, though he gave his head a shake of disgust. "Vincent, Vincent. . . . Depressing matters, these." He looked up blandly. "Well. Whatever you think best."

Vincent's lips deflected infinitesimally upward, the closest he might ever come to a smile. "I spent a lot of time in hospitals. Know their floor plans like the back of my hand."

"No doubt you do."

"You might say I specialize in hospitals. Same, say, as Miss Fontaine specialized in singing."

Hume thought about that. "A fitting comparison," he nodded. "Yet unlike you, Vincent, Miss Fontaine never learned the most important thing about being a specialist."

"Sir?"

Hume was no longer smiling, and his voice was grave. "The ability to follow orders," he said, enunciating each syllable with distinct finality before he turned and walked away.

∾

Rita Goldschmidt was a tough old veteran of medical practice politics. She determinedly served her new employer with the same relentless devotion she had bestowed upon Dr. Wahlberg. She saw to it that no calls went through without her prior screening, that no unnecessary correspondence cluttered the doctor's desk, and that all his bills were paid promptly. Thus she regarded with skepticism the young man who entered the office, assuming that he was a drug company representative or the purveyor of another useless medical service.

She put little credence in Manley's opening remarks about being a doctor at the university who wanted to talk to her about Dr. Wahlberg. Yet as he continued, he slowly won her over with a blend of guile and charm. It was noon, and no patients were scheduled until one; she was flattered when he offered to take her out for a bite to eat. Unfortunately, she had insufficient time to spare, though she could, she conceded, grant him a few moments behind her desk.

Manley sipped a cup of her coffee and approached the topic with circumspection. Rather than focus straightaway on the old reprint, he asked about Wahlberg's medical writing in general. He explained that he was simply reviewing certain fundamental concepts in obesity and wanted to go directly to their sources.

Mrs. Goldschmidt volunteered that Dr. Wahlberg's literary contributions were rather meager. Other than *Forever Slender*, his best-selling diet book, he'd written little. She thought, she said, that she'd saved a folder containing copies of the few articles he'd collaborated on. Manley sat in silent anticipation as she got up to look for it. After a moment's search, she located it in a file cabinet. At the bottom of the compact folder was a reprint of the article Manley had reviewed in the library.

"I remember this one, all right," she said. "I probably would have forgotten it if it weren't for what happened not too many years ago."

He put down the cup.

"I'm afraid you've lost me."

She adjusted her bifocals and indicated a line on the title page.

"See the name here?"

Manley's tongue went powder dry. His lips made a tight line as he stared at the name of Dr. Robert Emmerich.

Offhandedly, "What about him?".

"His wife was a patient of Dr. Wahlberg's. She was an old-timer in the practice. I think she must have come on and off for a dozen years. I never met her husband, though.

And I probably never would have seen him if it weren't for that awful business seven or eight years ago."

"What business?"

"Don't you remember? It made the TV headlines for days."

Manley slowly shook his head in the negative to indicate that he still didn't understand what she was alluding to.

"I remember my first impression when they showed his picture on camera. I kept thinking how unattractive he was," she went on. "He always struck me as rather . . . oily."

He tried to conceal his impatience.

"I still don't get what you're driving at."

Mrs. Goldschmidt threw him a look of astonishment.

"Why, his wife was found murdered."

"*Murdered?*"

She nodded.

"It was a brutal, ghastly job. Some people suspected her husband did it. But there was never enough evidence to implicate him. You honestly don't recall?"

"Regrettably, no."

She shrugged and pulled at a loose thread on her sweater.

"I suppose it's only natural that I should. After all, she *had* been something of a regular. And there was even one time after her death that the police came by to discuss it."

"Why—had she been seeing Dr. Wahlberg just before that?"

"No, she had stopped." Mrs. Goldschmidt looked away, eyes gleaming at the distant memory. "Something miraculous happened to her. None of us could understand how she went from overweight to being thin so quickly. And apparently, she did it all on her own."

Ashen, Manley had to grip the cup tightly to keep it from falling.

"How did she do it?" he managed.

"She didn't say. Oh, she hinted that her husband helped her, but I doubt that. If he had, she would have been far too grateful to do what she did."

"Which was what?"

Mrs. Goldschmidt shuffled some papers on her desk.

"Mrs. Emmerich was one of those women who had to find a new identity to go along with her change in self-image," she explained. "I used to see it all the time when Dr. Wahlberg was alive. Quite a few of his patients were successful—a lot more than we have now. You see, with her new look, Mrs. Emmerich was finally able to do what she wanted. I even heard some say that was why she threw him over."

Manley's face registered confusion.

"For another man?"

"In a way," she replied, and smiled. "I believe it was George Bernard Shaw."

Manley was growing progressively more mystified.

"The dramatist?"

"His play, actually. You see, Mrs. Emmerich was finally able to fulfill her lifelong ambition."

"What are you trying to say?"

Mrs. Goldschmidt turned his way, warming to the memory.

"Mrs. Emmerich once confided that she would have given anything for it. And who knows, perhaps she did." Her eyes pierced his with their stare. "What I'm saying, Dr. Manley, is that the poor woman had always wanted to become an actress."

Chapter Eleven

It was like bits of snowy fluff that whirled in the stormy winter of his thoughts, but he lacked the glue to hold the pieces together. From his own inquiries on the one hand and what Jacqueline alluded to on the other, Manley suspected that what was happening to Jacqueline might, in some as yet unknown way, be related to Suzanne Fontaine—another dieter who had been a patient at the Spa. The truth of what had befallen her was horrifyingly stark in his mind. And then there was the enigma of Mrs. Dillon, although what had happened to her was far less clear.

How he longed to discuss it with Jacqueline! But her moods had become so volatile, her thought processes so irrational, that a reasonable dialogue was no longer possible. His role was becoming that of a caretaker, and it was in this frame of mind that he returned to her that day. Yet, flexible though he thought he was, he was totally unprepared for what she had to say.

Her hands balled into fists as she glared at him.

"Just leave me alone, for God's sake!"

He released her and placed his hands on his hips, exasperated. His reply unintentionally revealed his irritation.

"What do you expect me to do—wait until you pass out, and *then* take you to the hospital?"

"I'm not going, dammit! If you love me, you'll let me be!"

He reached for her again, but she leaned out of his grasp and turned sharply away. Up to that point, they had been standing face to face as he held her firmly by the arms, fighting his own sense of futility while he made one last, desperate attempt to appeal to her logic, her sense of self-preservation. Jacqueline steadfastly refused to listen. She was as determined as ever to pursue her own destiny. This time, however, she implied that she intended to do it completely alone. The instant he'd returned to her apartment, she'd asked him to leave.

"Jax, you're being ridiculous. The fact that I love you has nothing to do with this. Simple English is the only language I know, and I must point out in my native tongue that you are about to sink into a coma. How can I just stand here while your health slips further and further away?"

She was adamant.

"I'm sorry, but you have nothing to do with it. It's *my* life and *my* decision."

"And you want me out that door."

They stared at one another.

In the end, she said quietly, "Yes."

How thick the air seemed to him, how heavy with tension. The incisiveness of their interchange hung like a sword that threatened to sever their closeness. Then, in a sudden turnabout, Jacqueline gazed up at him with a look of affection. She gently took one of his hands, and her cool fingers conveyed a promise, a hint of reassurance. She stroked the hair at the side of his head.

"Richard, don't you see—it'll only be for a few days. Don't make it sound like it's forever. You know I need you. It's just that . . . I *have* to be alone right now. I truly need time for myself. Why," she gave her head a wide-eyed shake, "there are so many things tearing me apart— the pressures at work, this craziness with my weight—that having you constantly hover over me is becoming an unbearable strain." She ran her forefinger across his top lip. "I know you love me—and I love you. But I also know that I can pull myself together, straighten this whole mess out—if you'll just give me a chance to be alone with my thoughts, to work things out in my head." She touched his cheek. "That happens sometimes, doesn't it? That people develop a hunger for moments they needn't share, moments they can call their own?"

Yes, he sadly acknowledged. It does indeed happen.

Manley looked deep into her eyes. She was a chameleon whose physical and mental condition seemed capable of changing in a matter of seconds. At present, she seemed so keen, so logical, so much in control—and so completely recovered from the rambling state of near delirium that had earlier overcome her. He wondered if it were something chemical—an internal, toxic psychosis, perhaps, or some cellular alteration in her tissues that granted her brain intermittent glimpses of reality, little peaks of apparent normality, only to suddenly forbid them and hurl her once more toward dementia.

Whatever its cause, there was no denying the veracity of her observation. Even the most irrational of psychotics needed time for himself. More importantly, however precarious her sanity, he could not in good conscience impose his will upon hers. Wounded though he felt, if it was solitude she demanded, it was solitude she would get. But not—he resolved—without his constant vigilance nearby.

Still staring at her, he breathed a weary exhalation.

"Your mind is made up, then."

"Yes."

He feigned a shrug of nonchalance.

"I guess there's nothing more I can say, is there?"

"No. Not really."

"All right." He slowly turned away and reached for his topcoat. Donning it, he did the buttons and gazed at her once again. "When should I call you?"

He detected something, then—a touch of fear that coaxed the alacrity of her reply. She quickly raised her palm to signal a halt.

"Don't—let me call you."

"I see." He paused. "And I suppose that my check is in the mail."

Her expression seemed genuinely imploring.

"Please, Rick. Don't make it harder than it is."

He looked down and smiled, partially a grin of contrition.

"You know, this is ridiculous. I'm behaving like a condemned man. Next I'll be asking for a last wish."

"Go ahead."

He walked back to her and lifted her chin with his thumb, his voice all Bogart, his smile a pretense of bravado.

"Could you spare an old hockey warrior a good-bye kiss?"

Her head sank against his chest. Her embrace was warm, her hands reassuring as they rubbed his back.

"Not good-bye. Just a little breathing room."

It was a soft and lingering kiss. Then he finally pulled away and walked purposefully to the door, determined not to succumb to sentimentality. He turned the doorknob, hesitated, and looked back one last time, forcing his cheeriest smile.

"I'll be around if you need me. You will call, then?"

"Promise."

"I do love you, Jack."

"And I you—" She dabbed at the sudden wetness in her eye, and she coaxed a little smile. "Go on, get out of here before I do something silly and let you change my mind."

"Right."

He gave a halfhearted nod, closed the door, and was gone. Jacqueline listened to the sound of his footsteps receding, holding her chin all the while to stop its intolerable quivering. She dared not even think about what had just occurred, lest she lapse into a paralysis of unbearable melancholia. She willed the incident from her mind and strode resolutely to the bedroom to resume her packing.

"L'addition, Monsieur."

The restaurant's captain handed Manley the check with a nod and backed away out of earshot. Manley looked at it expressionlessly and then resumed his surveillance of Jacqueline's building, the entrance to which he could distantly see through the tableside window. Sheila picked up the check and slowly raised her eyebrows.

"Isn't twenty bucks a bit steep for two cups of coffee?" She turned in the direction of the captain and gave him a toothy smile. "For that price the least I expect is to get goosed."

Manley turned to look at Sheila. "You're sure you're with me on this—I'm not forcing you?"

She gave him a look of strained patience and held up her binoculars.

"Would I have schlepped these along if you were? If I flash these Nikons once more, I could damn well get picked up like some bleeding peeping Tom. Or whatever the female equivalent is." She looked outward, toward the lights that occasionally flashed in the windows of buildings nearby. "Which is not a bad idea, actually."

The glibness of her reply concealed the deep concern she shared with Manley about what was happening to Jacqueline. Manley had called her the instant he left Jacqueline's apartment, asking Sheila to meet him at La Côte d'Azur, the only restaurant with a vantage point convenient to Jacqueline's building. Over coffee, the situation he painted was depressingly grim. Ultimately, he gave his opinion that, whereas Jacqueline's previous tortured behavior had all the hallmarks of a severe neurosis, her recent loss of touch with reality suggested an ominous deterioration into a far more serious psychosis. Her wild and aberrant activities, accompanied by what appeared to be a total loss of recall, gave him reason to think that Jacqueline was now capable of doing virtually anything, especially the unexpected.

Their meeting at the restaurant was to have been a strategy session of sorts. Yet after reviewing everything at length, they came to share the helpless conclusion that there was precious little they could do except watch Jacqueline's comings and goings and be there to offer their assistance if necessary. Manley conceded that he would grant Jacqueline the few days of solitude she requested. But he indicated that he intended a far more drastic solution to her predicament if her attempt at self-help resulted in failure.

"Are you serious? Is that legal?"

"Perfectly. I've tried not to get professionally involved, but this is a full-scale crisis."

"Sounds like a war game."

"In a way it is. I honestly think her life could depend on it."

They both paused to gaze at the building's faraway entrance.

"How long will you give her?"

"End of the weekend. Tops."

"And if she doesn't call by then?"

"All I have to do is pick up the phone and speak with the right people. If nothing's changed by Monday, Sheil," he continued, turning to look her in the eye, "not a man in hell can stop me from having her committed."

Chapter Twelve

The man with the powerful shoulders eased away from his vantage point on Second Avenue and drifted into the shadows. Although he had arrived at his point of assignation less than twenty-four hours before, it was becoming apparent that the comings and goings of the man he had come to watch were far less predictable than he had anticipated. Far more surveillance was necessary before he could accomplish his task. He looked at his watch. Procrastination was the thief of opportunity; that left only the other, which should prove far simpler. He returned to his motel room to await the deepening of the night.

The man awoke from his nap at one a.m. He sat up alertly, as if accustomed to arising at odd hours, and hefted the autoloader in his hand, tightening his palm around the hard rubber grip. He dressed slowly, methodically, and put everything he would need in an athletic bag. Locking his room, he walked to the motel's lot and slid the bag beside him onto the front seat of the nondescript rental car.

Twenty minutes later, he parked on First Avenue, well away from the nearest street lamp. He removed the white lab coat from the bag, slipped the coat on, and smoothed out the wrinkles, attaching the plastic ID to his left lapel. With one last check of the metal objects hugging his hip and ankle, he stole from the car and walked the several blocks to the hospital. In the darkness, his limp was nearly invisible.

At the hospital entrance, the guard on duty glanced perfunctorily at the ID badge pinned to the coat of the man who approached. He nodded curtly and then turned away as the white-jacketed doctor walked past him into the building.

The university's psychiatric floors, unlike those of most other hospitals, were designed to lock patients out. The questionably liberal philosophy was that the patient was always free to leave; it was far more difficult to get back in. The man in white lifted one of the hospital phones and dialed the floor's extension. In a terse message, he mumbled that he was on his way up to evaluate one of the patients. He hung up without waiting for a reply.

Adrienne Melman looked up from her charts and squinted toward the face that appeared in the small window at the end of the corridor. She wasn't accustomed to visits by unfamiliar doctors in the middle of the night. More often than not, such visitors weren't doctors at all, but street urchins bent on mischief, or a patient returning from a day pass unusually early, unable to cope with the corrosive realities of the outside world. She frowned and walked toward the door.

She looked not so much at the man as she did at the ID on his lapel. The large man's face matched the picture; she was satisfied that he was indeed a physician in the Ear, Nose, and Throat Department. She unlocked the door and allowed Dr. Trotter to enter.

"Can I help you?"

He stepped inside and immediately surveyed the corridor. He had quick eyes, eyes which seemed to take in everything at one glance. His voice was flat.

"I've been asked to do a consult on one of your patients, a . . ." He hesitated as if in forgetfulness and removed a small index card from his breast pocket. "A Mrs. George Dillon."

She looked at his face. It was an animal's countenance with mole's eyes, or perhaps the slinky dark orbs of a ferret.

"At this time of night?"

"I planned to see her in the morning, but I just finished

up in the emergency room. No sense making two trips, is there?"

"Nobody told me she had an ENT problem."

"That's what I'm here to find out, isn't it?" He abruptly moved past her and proceeded down the corridor. "Get me her chart, will you?"

She gave an exasperated sigh.

"All right."

He paused at the nursing station as she extracted the stainless metal folder from the chart rack and handed it to him. The man quickly glanced at the first page, then flipped the chart closed.

"Which room is hers?"

"Third on the left."

"Just give me a few moments alone with her."

He turned and limped away.

"Will you need anything for the exam?" she called after him.

"No," he replied, momentarily turning back and tapping his stethoscope. "Just this."

Seconds later, he closed the door to the patient's room firmly behind him. He paused in the blackness for his eyes to accustom themselves to the dark. The still form of the patient lay quietly on the bed. Whether the woman was awake or asleep, the man did not know. He had been told it didn't matter.

He pulled the pistol from beneath his coat and bent down on one knee. The silencer was in a thin leather case fastened to his ankle with a strap. He removed the metal tube, rose up, and screwed it onto the threads machined on the Luger's muzzle.

Nurse Melman looked up from her paperwork and squinted toward the closed door. Her vague uneasiness surfaced, a delayed realization of what had been bothering her. What kind of decent ENT exam could someone do with only a stethoscope? She knit her brow and pulled open the desk drawer. The otoscope and tongue depressors were in a portable case in the back. She took it out, got up, and started down the hall.

The hulking stranger stopped at the sleeping woman's

bedside. He was in the process of leveling the heavy bull barrel at Mrs. Dillon's head when the door was unexpectedly pushed open.

Adrienne Melman squinted in confusion, unable to distinguish the forms across the darkened room. She felt for the light switch.

"Dr. Trotter?"

The soft plop from the bedside was synchronous with the shattering of plaster on the wall beside her face. She flinched, stung by the masonry fragments, when three more bright flashes winked her way. In that fraction of a second, she had no idea that the parcel she was carrying was her shield; she was only aware that the otoscope's heavy metal case exploded with horrifying suddenness in front of her chest, wrenching the twisted metal from her fingertips. Terrified, she ran from the room just as something else splintered into the doorframe behind her.

At that moment, the thought most prominent in the man's mind was that the nurse must not reach the exit. Calmly but quickly his ungainly stride carried him to the room's entrance. The woman was twenty feet away, bolting for the door. He could hear the sound of her labored breathing. He raised the pistol in a two-hand combat stance, following his target by visual reckoning inasmuch as the silencer's width obscured the gunsight. He aimed with care and squeezed off a round. The shot was high and to the left, but it caught the woman in the shoulder. Its energy spun her to the side wall, but she frantically reeled off and continued her flight with the desperation of a wounded animal.

He fired twice more. Dark spots appeared on her white blouse, powder-rimmed entry wounds that precede the flow of blood. She staggered, and he fired again. She fell face down to the floor.

The man lowered the gun to his side and walked clumsily down the hall. He was barely astride the woman's feet when she squirmed. At first he thought it was a reflex, the disconnected spasms that usher in death, but then she struggled to rise up on her elbows. Without waiting, he

231

fired his last round into the back of her head. This time she slumped forward with terminal stillness.

He put the pistol in his belt and dragged her limp form by the feet. Adrienne Melman's torso bled a red swath along the tile. Inside Mrs. Dillon's room, the man deposited the nurse's body beneath the far window, where she lay in a twisted tangle of limbs.

He walked to the bedside and unscrewed the warm silencer. The Luger's magazine held ten rounds. He had used them all, never anticipating, during his preparations, that he might need more. Taking a firm grip on the barrel, the man raised the autoloader over his head and then violently swung its handle in a downward arc that ended alongside Mrs. Dillon's temple. And then Vincent raised it up and brought it down repeatedly, pounding over and over, until the sleeping woman's skull was crushed under the weight of the blows.

Chapter Thirteen

"And I'll huff and I'll puff and I'll blow your house down."

Berson swiveled in his desk chair toward the familiar sound of her voice. She looks very smart in that suit, he thought. Certainly far better than she's appeared in days.

Jacqueline's taupe jacket sharply defined her waist, flaring lightly over her hips; the matching short skirt spoke with a soft narrowness. The purity of her shape and proportion was evident despite her weight change: accentuated by the slit in her skirt, she seemed all body, all bareness, all leg.

"Hello, Jackie. What was that you were saying?"

Her voice was faint and gray.

"Barber, barber, shave a pig . . ."

His first impression was that she was making some sort of joke he didn't quite catch. But as he looked at her, he began to think otherwise, and he slowly straightened up in his chair, cocking his head to one side, observing her. Her expression was bewildering, inscrutable; her fixed stare unwavering. It was as if she were in some sort of trance.

Softly, "Jackie?"

No reply. Like a mesmerized soldier, she stood at unblinking attention. He snapped his fingers sharply.

Jacqueline jumped. Startled into wakefulness, she closed and reopened her lids just once, very slowly, before gazing quizzically about the room. Then she looked back at him.

"Emil?" she said, puzzled.

He leaned forward, shifting his weight onto his elbows.

"Are you all right, Jackie?"

233

"Why . . ." Her sudden smile was a bit too quick, the trained response of an actress. "Of course."

"If you insist. What is it, then?"

A scramble of thoughts unfolded in her mind.

"You wanted to see me, Emil?"

"No, I did not. I presume you're here to see me."

She seemed to hesitate before waving her hand jokingly.

"Just teasing."

Her smile turned sheepish, a red fathom of embarrassment.

"Honestly, Jacqueline—"

"I've only come for a moment," she quickly continued.

"So I see."

"And I was wondering if . . ."

"Yes?"

". . . if you had come to any conclusion. About my role, that is," she amended.

He leaned back thoughtfully, caught between concern and impatience.

"We've been through this before, Jackie." He crossed his arms, and his body language turned negative. "What happens is fully up to you."

"How much can you give me?"

"How much what?"

"Time. How much time?"

He shrugged.

"That depends. Obviously, I'm not going to wait forever."

"A week? Can you give me a week?"

"Well, I was hoping . . ." He gaped at her. "What on earth are you doing?"

She had shifted her weight to one leg, a graceful flamingo; simultaneously, her impenetrably dull expression returned. She was gazing beyond him with six-year-old eyes.

"Elsie Marlie is grown so fine . . ."

Puzzled beyond mystification, Berson mechanically repeated the next line from memory.

"She won't get up to feed the swine."

Hearing him, she gave an abrupt and sniping look. Didn't he want to play anymore? He seemed to be gazing at her with such strange penetration, his gun-barrel eyes growing darker, closer, the eyes of a piglet. . . . She whirled on her heels and quickly skipped from the room.

Berson sat frowning at the vacant doorway, striving to comprehend what had just happened. Jacqueline had appeared so alluring at first, so much in control, until she had begun to babble those degenerate couplets. And all of them, it suddenly struck him, were nursery rhymes about pigs.

Midway down the hall, Jacqueline stopped. Her stare fixed on a suitcase. So familiar . . . Was it hers? she wondered. The corridor seemed to brighten, and she slowly took stock of her surroundings with an adult's returning consciousness.

I don't want to be late, she thought.

She picked up the valise and nonchalantly sauntered through the theater toward the limousine that was waiting for her at the front entrance.

It was their second evening of surveillance. After hours of sitting in the cramped front seat, Sheila, in her boredom, began to give Manley her unsolicited evaluation of every male in sight. What began as a simple rating system expanded into elaborate speculation about personal habits, sexual preference, and employment status.

"A flasher," she said, lowering her binoculars and nodding in the direction of a man on the corner.

"What makes you think so?"

"The raincoat. It's a giveaway." She watched the man lean against a lamp post. "Don't be shy, darling. Come and give Sheila a little peek."

Manley saw the light go off in Jacqueline's window.

"I bet she's sick."

Sheila shook her head.

"She would have called you. Or me."

"Are you sure she looked all right when she left rehearsal yesterday?"

"Better than ever. She seemed to have decided about something."

He screwed up his forehead.

"So why didn't she show up for work today?"

"How would I know?" She sighed. "You are incurably hopeless. But if you must act so despondent, please don't include me in your dungeon of pessimism."

He tried to relax, reclining against the seat.

"I can't help worrying, that's all."

"Neither can I, but maybe you should take her words at face value. I could swear you admitted that a few days of solitude wouldn't hurt."

"I suppose not. At least, not if she's eating."

"Oh, look at that one."

He glanced in the direction of her stare.

"You were saying?"

"What an extraordinary dark suit. And those gloves. Some frigging Mafia don."

Manley crooked his arms wearily behind his head.

"I still say we should go up."

"And have her tell us to go suck an egg? She's got a will of iron."

He mulled in silence.

"I wonder if she tried to call while we were sitting here."

"Good God, you are impossible. You can't have it both ways. Either we bite our nails by the phone, or we man the battle stations. Honestly, you are intent on turning me into a drooling basket case."

He checked his watch.

"It's still early. Do you think she went to sleep?"

Sheila rolled her eyes skyward and exhaled, her warm breath fogging the windshield. She drew circles and X's on the glass, a game of tic, tac, toe.

"Correct me if I'm wrong, but wasn't it your idea to give her until at least Monday morning?"

His indirect reply was a slow bow of his head. He knit his brow as the light went on again in Jacqueline's apartment. Once more he looked at Sheila.

"Doesn't it strike you as pretty damn peculiar for her to keep turning her light on and off every few moments?"

She patted his shoulder. "Richard, my love, did it even

occur to you that if you keep up this muttering, we will jolly well become a pair of bleeping automatons?"

Silence. Then a thought occurred to him, and he looked over at her and frowned.

"Automatons?"

She mimed a computerized voice.

"Right, R-2. We—"

"Oh, *Christ!*" he interrupted. He flung the door open and pulled her by the arm. "How could we be such idiots!"

He was out of the door in a flash. Sheila hadn't a moment to reply before she was dragged off balance into the street. As she stumbled blindly behind him, her singular thought was that Manley had to be losing his mind. They flew past the baffled doorman. The elevator was well into its ascent before she could catch her breath.

"Stupid of me not to guess," she wheezed, "but what exactly are we doing?"

The doors opened, and he pulled her down the hall, fumbling with his keys.

"The lamp, for Christ's sake!" He turned the key in Jacqueline's lock, shaking his head disgustedly. "I must be a moron! How could I let myself think it was some sort of clockwork magic that kept turning on her lamp so precisely?"

"You're right," she seconded, totally confused. "No question that it's Aladdin."

She took it for granted that once inside, the first thing he would do would be to call out to Jacqueline. But instead, he raced into the living room, whose large window looked out upon the city and whose glass aperture they had been observing from the street below. Sheila watched in befuddlement as Manley first peered under the lamp shade and then knelt to trace the lamp cord to its floor-level socket. Abruptly, his frenzy stopped. He breathed wretchedly, rocking back on his knees, his voice assuming a tone somewhere between self-contempt and stupidity. He lifted a small black box.

"Our automaton."

She regarded it blankly, still not comprehending. She

shot a quick glance toward the bedroom and then stared back at Manley.

"I bet she's sleeping." She started for the bedroom.

"Don't bother," he said wearily. "She's not here."

Sheila craned her neck and gazed into the darkened bedroom, forcing a tone of confidence into her voice.

"Of course she is." She walked inside.

From his vantage point, Manley patiently watched Sheila disappear into the darkness. "Jackie," he heard her whisper. A moment passed, after which Sheila repeated the name more loudly. There was a click, and light spilled from the room. Seconds later, Sheila made a somber exit, her face a pale and brooding expression of fear and confusion.

"Where is she, Rick? How did—"

"Here's your Aladdin," he interrupted. "An automatic timer." He allowed a laugh of grudging admiration. "Crazy like a fox. I should have known."

As she caught on, the sound of self-assurance vanished from Sheila's voice. "That little sneak. . . . But why did she want to trick us?"

"Christ, did she take me in," he went on. "That whole crock about needing time for herself. . . . I ought to have my head examined."

"But—"

"Because she knew we would be watching, that's why," he explained. "She realized we were concerned. And she sensed we'd never let her leave without us."

Sheila slowly shook her head in distress and confusion.

"Leave for where? What is she doing?"

Manley arose mechanically and went to the window. He gazed out across the darkened city.

"I don't know," he said torpidly. "But mark my words— she's up to something."

Sheila joined him and studied the anguish on his face.

"Will she be all right?"

"If she stays lucid." He paused to rub his eyes. When he opened them, they were red. "There's a time bomb inside her," he said. "You've heard its ticking in the way she behaves. She flits from sanity to incoherence like a birdlike mad hatter. I hate to think what will happen the next time she loses control."

Sheila's fingers enlaced as she tried to downplay her concern.

"Is it really that serious?"

"Much more than serious. In Jack's case, it could be deadly." He looked up and observed a mass of dark clouds that moved to slowly blot out the moon. "We have to find her, Sheila. Because if we don't," he said gravely, "God help us all."

Chapter Fourteen

First she would see little flashes, a starlight of twinkling, brightly colored specks. And then, nothingness. It was blankness, an indefinite passage of time of varying lengths, after which she would once again blink and see clearly. She assumed it was merely fatigue, an accumulation of weariness that led her to daydream with more and more frequency. Her mind seemed to wander—though she couldn't recall where or for how long.

Those around her saw it quite differently. What Jacqueline perceived as the forgetful ramblings of a weary soul were in fact the intermittent episodes of a mind losing its hold on reality. Her eyes would become glazed, her expression dull. Most noticeable was her behavior, an abrupt and startling abberration from all that could be considered normal.

The chauffeur was witness to it, her distant stare. On the many previous occasions Jacqueline had requested his services, she had never appeared as she did now. He had been studying her in his rearview mirror from the first moment he had picked her up for the drive to the airport. She had given her usual smile when he greeted her, but she had seemed unexpectedly nervous, an apprehension quite foreign to her. Perhaps it was because of her weight: he'd heard rumors of her problem, rumors he now knew were true. But there was more to it than that. There was a disturbing sloppiness about her, an unkempt appearance totally out of keeping with her public image. And then, midway through the drive, her anxiety gave way to that stare, after which she was somehow . . . *changed*.

"Do you have anything to eat in this car?"

"I'm afraid not, Miss Ramsey."

"What do you do when you get hungry?"

"Stop off at a coffee shop, usually."

"Is there somewhere you can stop around here?"

"Not much on the Van Wyck. Why don't you wait until we get to the airport?"

"Try the next exit."

He shrugged and drove down the ramp, following the service road into Queens. The limousine turned past 188th Street and proceeded down several narrow avenues, passing slowly through traffic until Jacqueline pointed out a supermarket. The driver double parked by the entrance. He waited in silence while Jacqueline put on her dark glasses and shuffled outside.

She returned moments later with several packs of lunch meat, a jar of mustard, and a loaf of Italian bread. The chauffeur remained quiet, watching her in his mirror as he backtracked and resumed the trip to the airport. Jacqueline tore the bread apart and haphazardly arranged slices of ham and salami, shaking the mustard onto it directly from the container. She took several large bites, barely chewing what she ate before she swallowed it and consumed another mouthful.

"You like heroes, Miss Ramsey?"

"Yeah." She bit off another chunk.

"Ever been to Manganero's?"

"Uh-uh."

"Try it some time. They got the best."

She continued to eat, oblivious to his stare. When she was finished, she slouched back for the remainder of the trip.

Shortly, the limousine pulled up in front of the Pan Am terminal. The chauffeur removed her bags and gave them to a porter. He smiled and touched his cap as he wished her a good flight. She didn't hear him. She hopped out of the rear seat and was already yards in front of the porter as she entered the glass doors of the terminal entrance.

She fidgeted at the ticket counter, making a clicking sound with her tapping nails as her bag was marked and checked through. The agent put the ticket in its paper jacket and handed it to her with a smile.

"There you are, Miss Ramsey. Your flight is boarding now."

She looked around quizzically.

"Where is the nearest restaurant?"

"You're on a dinner flight, Miss Ramsey. It's a huge meal in first class."

She spotted an overhead sign whose arrow indicated a nearby lounge. She began walking toward it when the startled agent called after her.

"Your gate's in the other direction, Miss Ramsey. Miss Ramsey?"

Her long strides took her quickly across the terminal. Unexpectedly, she stopped at the entrance to a stationery store. In a whimsical flight of mind, she seemed to decide on something.

She darted inside and paced about confusedly until she saw the confections, arranged in neat tiers beside the cash register. She opened her handbag and had already shoveled a dozen items inside it before the surprised clerk tried to interrupt her.

"Just one goddamn minute—"

She threw a bill his way. He glanced at the fifty-dollar denomination and shook his head.

"I can't break this, lady. You got anything smaller?"

"Keep the change."

Once outside, Jacqueline prepared to unwrap a candy bar when the ticket agent caught up with her and grasped her gently by the shoulder.

"Miss Ramsey? You're going to miss your flight if you don't board now." He paused. "Miss Ramsey?"

Slowly, her eyes focused on the concerned face of a man wearing an airline uniform.

"What?" she stammered.

"Your flight. Here, come with me. I'll get you on board directly."

The loudspeaker overhead was announcing the departure as Jacqueline let herself be led away. The man escorted her among the remaining first-class passengers who walked along the boarding ramp. Moments later, seat belt buckled, Jacqueline gazed idly out the cabin window, still appearing somewhat stupefied, unaware of the sideways glimpses and whispered chatter of the flight attendants about her.

Something caught her eye then, as the plane vibrated and the engines revved for takeoff. She thought it was lint, little flecks of dirt. Yet as she brushed the particles from her coat, she saw that they were breadcrumbs, small morsels of brownish crust that dotted the lowermost periphery of her vision, where her coat rose toward her collar. She had no recollection of how they had gotten there, and it was that sense of ignorance that began to pummel her brain with blows of horror.

With shaking fingers, Jacqueline fumbled with the clasp of her purse to remove her compact and mirror. Her intent was to calm herself down by redoing her face. Yet when she looked inside, she gasped. Her purse was crammed with bars of candy, whose brightly colored wrappers seemed to scream out their presence. In a reflex of terror, she threw her bag onto the empty seat beside her, as if the purse itself were carrion, some grotesquely putrefying animal that was fouling her hands. The mirror's round case was jarred loose and rolled toward her. Trembling, she picked it up.

She opened the compact and studied her reflection. Her cheeks were pale, her eyes dull. And then her vision abruptly halted, frozen at the sight of the streaks of dried mustard which caked her lips and cheek. The compact fell from her numb fingers.

Oh, my dear God, she thought.

She put her face in her cold and trembling hands.

What is *happening* to me?

It wasn't until the flight was on final approach to Los Angeles that Jacqueline's frenzy began to calm down. She had one of the flight attendants clear away the candy, though even when it was removed, she continued to lean away from the adjacent seat as if it were maggot ridden;

and it took a score of visits to the rest room before she granted herself the reassurance that the last vestiges of mustard had been washed free and that all the crumbs had been dusted off.

She was the first person out of the terminal and into one of the cabs waiting nearby. She felt the frightening pangs of hunger begin to tempt her again, making it all the more urgent to reach Dr. Hume as quickly as possible. She had no idea of the Spa's address; she had always been driven there by the chauffeur. Yet she was sufficiently familiar with the route to give the taxi driver satisfactory instructions.

She wondered what Dr. Hume's reaction would be. He had no idea of her decision to visit; in fact, she was fully aware that he had recommended against it. Moreover, during their last conversation, she had flatly refused his request about the Lambert film and hung up on him.

Still, she prayed that he would not take unkindly to her unannounced arrival, for she remained convinced that he and he alone held the key to her salvation.

The cab turned onto the road that was the long driveway to San Sebastian. The vehicle halted at the closed wrought-iron gate. Jacqueline got out, bag in hand. She paid the cabbie, and the taxi sped off.

As the vehicle disappeared, Jacqueline hesitated in uncertainty and trepidation. Before she had further opportunity to dwell on it, there came a click, followed by a mechanical hum, the sound of a motor that slowly swung the iron gates open. Without hesitation, she walked straight ahead.

Beyond the gate was a path of crushed stone that ended at the Spa's white marble steps. Jacqueline was halfway down its length when he appeared, standing motionless in his spotless linen suit, staring at her. At first his features were indistinct, but as she drew closer, she was infinitely relieved to see that Dr. Hume's face bore the same expression with which she was so familiar: the benign and friendly eyes, the gracious and merciful smile. He extended his arms in paternal concern and proceeded down the steps to meet her.

"Jacqueline," he said warmly. "Whatever are you doing here?"

He embraced her, kissing both her cheeks and offering a lingering hug. Then he pulled away and regarded her quizzically, waiting for her to speak.

"You're not angry that I've come?" she said hesitantly.

"Why, of course not. What would make you think that?"

She bit her lip. Her voice was softened with a childlike apology.

"After our last conversation, I thought you might not want to see me anymore."

"Rubbish! I'm as delighted as ever to have you here."

"Will you let me stay, then?" Tears welled in her eyes. "It must be obvious what's happened to me," she said, gesturing toward her body as she contritely shook her head. "And you're the only one who can help."

"Why, certainly you can stay." He regarded her with concern. "You do seem a bit the worse for wear, but I'm sure we can take care of that in no time. I'm here to help you, Jacqueline. After all, isn't that what doctors are for?"

Thank God, she thought, closing her eyes with relief that was immeasurable. Hume reached for her bag and assisted her up the steps. Jacqueline looked about for the solidly built orderly who, during previous visits, had been omnipresent.

"Isn't your butler here?"

"He's away on some personal errands. I expect him back in a day or two." They linked arms and proceeded contentedly inside. "Tell me," Hume continued. "Who knows you are here?"

"No one. I thought it best to keep the trip a secret."

"Good," he said, the sparkle of his pastel blue eyes suddenly etched with frost. "Very good."

Chapter Fifteen

Manley and Sheila had begun a desperate search, a quest that included countless phone calls, frantic personal visits, and exhaustive follow-up. Yet after twenty-four hours of inquiry, he was no closer to discovering where Jacqueline had gone than he was to answering the question why she had gone anywhere at all. Logic told him that, at the very least, she would want to stay close to home, so as not to jeopardize the already slim chance of retaining her job. Yet, he reminded himself, logic played no role in evaluating the illogical.

He tried to imagine where he might go if he were Jacqueline. Clearly, Hume had indicated that he did not want her. That being the case, it was possible that she had consulted another specialist in obesity—but a six-hour excursion through the New York Yellow Pages convinced him that she had not. Finally, Manley telephoned the two-dozen foremost spas in the country, only to learn that Jacqueline was not a guest at any of them.

While Sheila succumbed to a short nap, he spoke with Berson, Hammill, and numerous other acquaintances of Jacqueline's, all of whom were either surprised or annoyed that she could not be located. Ultimately, Manley called the only name underlined in her telephone directory: that of her mother, Maureen Ramsey. The housekeeper informed him that the older actress had left for a weekend in the Caribbean. No, the maid replied, she did not know the precise destination or if the actress' daughter had accompanied her.

Sheila, who had been sleeping on Jacqueline's bed, awoke from her slumber and listened attentively to the conversation's conclusion. While Manley replaced the receiver with a look somewhere between pensiveness and despair, she sat up and rubbed her eyes.

"It's the only possibility," she yawned. "Jackie and her mother were like this," she indicated, crossing her fingers. He continued to stare across the room. "Are you all right?" she prompted.

"Just temporarily speechless." He eyed her with exhaustion. "You really think she'll be back Monday?"

"Tan and rested," Sheila said evenly. "Which is a lot more than I can say for you."

His voice had a rawness in it. "I just can't relax."

"Maybe you should try." She paused. "What would you do if you were *certain* she was okay?"

"Hmm?" He rubbed the fatigue from his eyes. "Oh, go to the cabin, I suppose."

She bounced off the bed and stretched.

"Splendid suggestion. Let's go."

"I'm not leaving, Sheila."

"Nor are you doing any good just sitting by the phone like some heartsick adolescent." She sat in a nearby chair, leaning her elbows on her knees in mannish fashion while she contemplated him. "And by the look of you, you're every bit as ready to collapse as you thought she was. Look—if you're as convinced as I am that she's off with her mother, then you owe yourself some relaxation, too." In his silence, she continued her scrutiny. "Come on," she prompted, "it'll do us both some good. Give a girl a break."

They stared at one another. She folded her hands in her lap, demurely innocent. It was something Jacqueline might have done. In the end, he spoke quietly.

"You honestly think she's all right?"

"I'd wager on it." She gave him a wink and then looked away, reflecting on another thought. "Whatever happened to that dog of yours?"

He abruptly got up and looked at his watch.

"Good God, I haven't walked him in over twelve hours."

"Ah, those pleasant stains on the rug."

"He's a sharp one, Dart. Been known to irrigate the plants in a crisis."

Manley's phone was similar to Jacqueline's in that it had a telephone answering device, affixed with an encoder whereby the owner could periodically call in to review any messages received. After he adjusted Jacqueline's, he returned to his apartment to set his own and walk Dart. En route, he dropped off Sheila to allow her to shower and pack. He planned the briefest of trips, he told her, no more than a day.

Within the hour, the three of them—two weary people and an excited and panting dog—piled into Manley's van. Only the canine member of the trio appeared outwardly enthusiastic about the unexpected trip upstate. Dart greeted the approach of the Tappan Zee Bridge with tail-wagging eagerness. Sheila vacantly surveyed the passing countryside, while Manley, tight-lipped and silent, was content to be alone with his thoughts. He guided the van along the narrow ribbon of highway, never once noticing the nondescript rental car that trailed a safe distance behind.

Throughout their vigil in the city, Manley had purposely avoided discussing his suspicions with Sheila, largely because he was concentrating so intently on surveillance that there was little opportunity for abstract conjecture.

That all changed on the trip upstate. He was reduced to the role of spectator on that bleak gray afternoon, by necessity following the curves in the highway and surveying the drab horizon. Yet although his body was inert—heavy with fatigue—his mind remained quite active.

What did he know, really? Though at first blush it appeared that he had discovered a great deal, the fact that it was all conjectural made it seem frightfully little.

And even when Manley let his imagination soar—when he *assumed* he understood the medical basis for what was happening—it all seemed to pertain to the wrong man: a stranger named Emmerich, an individual who, if Rita Goldschmidt could be believed, bore absolutely no physical resemblance to the Dr. Hume Jacqueline had described to Manley.

When he ultimately confided his suspicions about Dr. Hume to Sheila, she nearly exploded.

"You're out of your mind. That man doesn't have an evil bone in his body."

"Doesn't it strike you as peculiar that he'd be so evasive about brown fat?"

She shook her head resolutely. "Let's say, for the sake of discussion, that he bought the 'process' from this Emmerich character—"

"Bought?"

"Bought, stole, who cares? The point is, if this discovery is as important as you say it is, it's a veritable gold mine. Why would he want to blurt it out over the phone, to share that fact with someone he never met?"

"Because if he's the fine, upright fellow everyone claims, he'd damn well want to help Jack out."

She shrugged.

"I don't think it's fair to assume he appreciates the severity of the situation, no matter *how* accurately you think you described it to him. Remember, the last time he saw her, she was fine. And there's something else," she hinted.

He raised his eyebrows.

"What?"

"This process you talk about—I was a patient at San Sebastian too, if you recall. If the treatments have such an adverse reaction, how come they don't affect me?"

He concentrated on the highway once again.

"I've considered that. It could be that not everyone gets the same treatment."

"Oh, really. You don't think he's selectively choosing certain people, do you? Jacqueline, Rochelle, that Mrs. Dillon you mentioned?"

"Sheila, strange people have been known to have strange motives. It might seem pretty fanciful to you, but it's a little too coincidental for me that they're all actresses."

She clucked and shook her head.

"I think you're grasping at straws. I'd have to see evidence a lot more convincing than that."

"That, dear Sheila, is precisely what I'm looking for myself."

They arrived at the cabin late in the afternoon. Dart was off in an instant, springing through the half foot of snow that still remained on the ground. Manley's somber mood was buoyed by the familiar sight of the cabin, and Sheila was delighted with it. It was a masculine retreat, with carefully hewn logs notched and edged to fit snugly in place. He carried their few belongings inside while she took a stroll around the cabin's exterior. When she came inside, he was already setting fire to the kindling in the hearth.

"Shades of Daniel Boone," she said, inspecting the logs on the walls and ceilings, logs that still retained the smell of freshly cut timber, an aroma that was mixed with the charcoal and hickory scent of dozens of cords of burned wood. "Not bad for a city kid. How long did it take you to build it?"

"A couple of summers."

"By yourself?"

"No. Ben gave me a hand." During the trip he had briefly told her about the recluse. He steered her toward the wide window and indicated a spot a quarter of a mile distant. "That's his place over there."

"Does he know we're here?"

"He knows. These are his woods. Nothing happens here without Ben knowing it."

Sheila glanced at the frozen lake and then at the hockey paraphernalia that hung from the walls.

"This may sound hard to believe, but I actually know how to use those things. I should have brought my own skates."

"Too dangerous. The ice can get pretty thin in places. We'll go out tonight, with Dart. He knows every inch of the terrain. Anyway, he's a moonlight skater."

Manley felt comforted by the cabin. Sheila's suggestion that they come had been a good one. He felt relieved, finally able to relax, at the time he needed it most. He was determined that their brief stay not be interrupted by the wild speculation that had plagued him on the drive up. The isolated cabin was miles from the nearest phone. Here they could rest and regain their strength; they might need it when Jacqueline returned.

He regaled her with tales of Ben and the woods. His rambling conversation was largely therapeutic, an intentional uncluttering of his mind. After sunset, he trimmed the thawed venison steaks he'd removed from the outdoor freezer earlier. He showed her how to cook them over an open fire, using a simple recipe that combined salt and pepper, bread crumbs, venison fat, and elderberry jam. He fried them in a heavy skillet, making enough for Dart and even Ben, in case the woodsman should chance a rare visit.

Dart had been gone for a long time. The sizzling meat was nearly ready when they heard the sound of the dog cavorting in the snow, his bark punctuated by a string of gruff epithets which brought a smile to Manley's lips. The door burst open to the accompaniment of a cold night wind.

"I just might wring his neck one of these days," said Ben as he shut the door. He brushed fresh snowflakes off his coat and lay his rifle against the wall.

"And lose being escorted to dinner?" said Manley.

"Maybe he does have some good points," Ben admitted. He bent down and grabbed Dart by the neck. "Come here, you rascal."

While the dog lapped at his face, he looked in Sheila's direction. His whole face seemed to smile at her, though his lips didn't move. She felt herself automatically smile back his way, comforted and welcomed by his expression.

Manley made the introductions.

"Sheila, Ben." He nodded in the other direction. "Ben, Sheila."

"Hello, Sheila," Ben said. Then he added, "You are a friend of Jacqueline."

It was a statement of simple fact, without a nuance of conjecture. Sheila turned in speechless wonder to Manley, who smiled and slowly shook his head, forever astounded by Ben's almost mystical perceptions of reality. Sheila finally collected her wits and addressed Manley.

"I know we forgot the Tarot cards," she said, "but maybe he can read the tea leaves?"

They had a festive meal. Manley carried the conversation, though Ben's warm and pithy comments made it appear as if he had been surrounded by women all his life, rather than the opposite. Sheila understood why Manley was drawn to him. Ben had a manner that was at one with the earth, a gentle side that was as deep and rich as the ground he walked upon.

A storm front passed overhead, and by nine o'clock the moon rose bright against the cold dark sky. Dart grew restless from confinement and began to prance in front of the door.

"Show time, folks."

Manley pushed himself away from the table and walked toward his hockey gear. Dart whined and scratched at the door with his forepaws. From within one of his skates, Manley removed a yellow tennis ball and palmed it into the air. Dart snared it in his teeth and leaped outside when the door was opened. A gust of chill air blew through the cabin.

"A cold night for hockey fans," Manley said. He put on his parka and slung his skates over his shoulder.

"The myth of your hockey past is soon to be exposed," said Sheila.

"Ah, just wait." He gazed through the front window. "I'd love to have you down there leading the cheers, but it's a little nippy on the rink tonight. Why not stay here?" he said, pulling a tall stool over to the window. "A perfect seat for yonder center ice." He pointed to a nearby spot on the frozen lake.

Sheila perched on the stool and stared lakeward. Elbows on her knees, both hands cupping her round face for support, she felt content—not just for herself, but also for Manley, who had at last been able to put his fears about Jacqueline temporarily aside. Behind her, Ben struck a safety match and lighted his pipe. An aromatic blue smoke soon filled the cabin. Sheila spoke to him while she gazed

252

at the ice, where Manley was lacing up his skates while Dart was already slipping and sliding on the frozen surface.

"Do you skate, Ben?"

"No. Never been closer than snowshoes."

"Is Rick as good as I think he is?"

"I think he'd be good at whatever he set out to do."

Ben got up and stretched, sucking on his pipe. He walked behind her stool and looked over her shoulder through the window.

"I hope you're not saying that just for my benefit."

"No. That young man has a fine head on his shoulders. He's determined, but kind. You can see it in the way he treats the dog."

"He really loves him, doesn't he?"

"He understands him. And I think that says it all."

Wisps of high cloud scudded across the face of the moon. Above the shrill siren of the wind, there came a faint animal sound—a night bird, perhaps an owl. The wood-note passed Sheila by. But Ben heard it; after generations in the forest, nothing escaped his ear. He had been listening for it ever since, hours before, he had spotted the car that trailed Manley's van at a distance, a car that had stopped and parked well down the road. At first, he had assumed it was a wayward hunter, following Manley's vehicle to keep from getting lost. Now, though, he wasn't sure; it was an uncertainty he felt in his bones. He cocked his head and heard the sound again. Through the window, he looked far off to the right, toward dark branches that swayed like witches' brooms, toward heavy boughs that creaked in the wind.

"Go down and watch up close," he said. "Let me help with that stool."

"Looks pretty cold out there."

"Take my coat. Enough sheepskin lining there to poach your bones."

The coat was heavy, a hunter's jerkin with a thick collar that covered her ears. She wrapped her arms about her while Ben carried the stool to the lake's edge. Their puffs of frosted breath were sucked away by the wind that blew in their faces. Ben walked onto the ice and placed the chair

253

on a safe spot fifty feet from shore. Sheila climbed atop it and waved to Manley. He shouted back, and Dart barked in delight.

Ben buttoned his thick Mackinaw and returned to the cabin. He paused at the entrance and grasped the doorknob, looking out into the dark forest. He went into the cabin and retrieved his Winchester. Slowly returning outside, he quietly closed the door and peered into the blackness.

Down on the ice, Sheila clapped her hands and laughed appreciatively at Dart's performance as the dog stopped each of Manley's shots, either blocking them with his paws or clamping them in his teeth. Manley laughed too, amused as always by the dog.

Ben started slowly up the hill behind the cabin, his rifle ready. Mounting the small incline, he paused at the first phalanx of forest pine. He cocked his head and listened.

He heard nothing but the whistling moan of the wind in the tall trees. Yet he knew something was out there, something foreign. He narrowed his eyes, waiting for his night vision to sharpen as the chill breeze settled on his bare neck. He cocked his rifle's lever action, chambering a round. With the wind playing at the strands of his gray beard, he proceeded deeper into the woods.

The chill stung his eyes, making them water. He blinked away the moisture. An old man's eyes, he thought, something he had never felt before. He scanned the clefts between the dark trunks and looked above toward the swaying treetops. He was near it, he knew. His cold fingers tightened stiffly on the rifle's frigid metal as he crept slowly forward. He came to a clearing in the thicket. When he looked down, he saw it.

There were footprints in the snow. A man's footprints, a large man, who had been walking in the direction of the cabin. He followed the tracks' origin, from where they emerged on his left to the point where the footprints met his. And then he stood with granite stillness, as from behind he heard the shifting of weight.

I am old, he suddenly thought. Far too old. It was that, perhaps, or his vision, which had not yet fully adjusted to the dark. Or maybe it was his adversary's skill: after decades of outwitting the creatures of the forest, Ben lowered his rifle, knowing he was powerless. He slowly turned around in the direction of the sound. A gust of wind sent his hair dancing across his forehead as his eyes met those of the man in the overcoat.

The pistol was pointed at his head. He stared into the man's dark, animal eyes. Ben had no fear; it was too late for that anyway. Yet he felt an intense hatred for this man, a feral dislike for the stranger who had come only to do harm. He knew words were futile. But his eyes said it all, blazing with contempt.

The pistol silently flashed three times. The bullets struck Ben in the face. He fell straight backward, his body cushioned by the soft snow. Icy fingers of wind tugged at his Mackinaw, making his collar flutter like raven's wings about his still cheeks. Through half-open lids, Ben's sightless eyes stared up at the star-filled sky that had always been his home.

The big man stood over Ben. He watched for several moments, then put the pistol away. He retrieved his long briefcase and walked to the edge of the woods. The sounds came from far beyond, driven his way by the wind. He could hear them perfectly, though the wind's direction assured his silence. He removed the Nikons from the pocket of his woolen greatcoat and put the binoculars to his eyes.

The nearby inlet of the lake had an irregular shape. Manley and the dog were a hundred yards from shore, ducking in and out of sight as they raced behind a jagged cliff on the right, whose rocky face indented the ice seventy-five yards out. On the inlet's left, a dense copse of huge trees came down to the waterline. The man looked at the girl and then at the space behind her. He would have the most direct line of fire by taking up a position ten yards to her rear.

He kept to the shadows and crept toward the lake. His dark garb shielded him from being seen, as did the gently rising black shoreline that hid his silhouette. Walking in a crouch, he knelt behind a clump of scrub pine and opened his case. The weapon was inside, disassembled into neat components: a modified Krico sniper rifle with a takedown barrel and shortened fiberglass stock, with a flash hider on the muzzle. He screwed on the barrel and undid the straps securing the telescopic scope. The scope was heavy, but it made up in uniqueness what it conceded in weight. It was a Litton night-weapon sight, with an intensifier tube that turned starlight into daylight.

The man fitted the scope to its mount and closed the case. Bending low, he moved stealthily down the bank and stole onto the ice. He stopped ten yards behind Sheila and set up on one knee. A steady wind blew in his face. He lifted the rifle to his cheek and peered cross-ice through the eyepiece.

Sheila clapped in delight at one of Dart's more spectacular saves, a gyrating midair leap that took him seven feet off the ground. The dog landed on the ice and pricked up his ears. He looked in Sheila's direction and let the ball fall to the ice. A low growl rumbled in his throat, and his upper lip retracted over his fangs. Body quivering, he stared toward the cabin in a taut wolflike stance.

Sheila cupped her hands to her lips.

"Overtime!" she shouted. "Is that the best you can do? Come on, the fans want action!"

Behind her, the big man had a perfect view of his target. The scope had a red aiming dot superimposed on the greenish intensified image: the dot rested squarely in the center of Manley's chest. With his eye to the scope, he worked the rifle's big bolt and chambered the first of the magazine's five rounds. He took a breath and applied pressure to the trigger.

Manley, who had been standing still, jerked forward when he saw Dart's alarm. He heard an explosion, and at the same instant a peculiar buzzing passed his face. Dart, who had been snarling, began a heavy canine lope in Sheila's direction. In less than a second, he was streaking across the ice toward something in the distance.

Sheila was nearly deafened by the loud roar. Wincing, she fell forward onto her feet, her hands clamped protectively about her ears. She saw Dart racing furiously toward her and she whirled about. The wind caught her hair and sent it wildly about her round face, where it flailed at her eyes. Behind her a dark form rested on the ice, aiming something that resembled a broom. In that fraction of a second, Sheila knew. She screamed.

The dog streaked in a perfect line. Through the scope, the man centered the red dot on a spot just below the dog's bared teeth. The animal would be on him in an instant. He squeezed the trigger just as the dog's forepaws left the ice in a powerful leap that sent him springing toward the rifle muzzle.

The bullet tore through Dart's throat. The shot struck him in midair, while he was still eight feet from the crouching man. His body sailed harmlessly past the man's shoulder and landed heavily on the ice beyond, where he lay pathetically still and unwhimpering.

Manley had no idea what was happening. He'd lost sight of Dart. Though the steady wind was carrying away from him, he was sure he had heard Sheila scream, and that second booming noise sounded too much like a gunshot. Without realizing it, he had begun skating across the ice after Dart. His heart was pounding as he looked past Sheila toward something dark and indistinct behind her. Bent low, hockey stick rigid in his hands, he streaked her way like a breakaway winger flying toward goal.

The big man had to act quickly. The target was a mere forty yards away and closing fast. He worked the bolt and chambered another round as the spent shell casing skittered across the ice. His target was weaving, a zigzag motion that shifted weight from one skate to the other. The red dot weaved with him. The man fired.

There was another roar, and this time Manley could see the flash. Something whined through the outer layers of his hood. Someone was shooting at him. The very idea made him furious: he crouched lower still, his legs pumping like pistons.

Manley could now see it all clearly. As he flew past Sheila, he had a glimpse of Dart lying motionless behind the dark-coated form. The man held a rifle, and as the moonlight reflected off the scope's front lens, Manley saw that the rifle's barrel was pointing directly at his heart. Without thinking, he jerked his shoulder down.

There was a blinding light, and an explosion shattered the air scant feet in front of his face. His ears were deafened, and something nipped at his scalp. Now nearly even with the rifleman, Manley reacted in a reflex conditioned by years of hockey training. He snapped out of his crouch and whipped his stick straight upward in a vicious highsticking forecheck. His stick caught the rifle's stock, and the scope slammed backwards into the man's face as their two bodies crashed together.

They both went sprawling, knocked yards apart. The man in the greatcoat slid across the ice on his back, still clutching the rifle. Manley was dazed and there was a roaring in his ears. As he struggled to his skates, his stick broken in half, he could see the man clambering to his knees. The big man yanked back the rifle's bolt, ejecting an empty brass casing that flew away like a piece of gold tumbling in the moonlight. When he rammed the bolt forward, Manley sprang.

He crossed the ice like a savage, legs churning in sheer rage. He had no idea what he was doing; all he felt was the fury that boiled inside him. He rocketed across the ice in four quick strides. Just as the man raised the rifle, Manley leaped into the air, horizontally hurling himself skates first toward the man's face. At the very instant that the rifle thundered beneath him, he felt his skate blades slice into the flesh above the man's collar.

Manley fell again. His bare head met the ice with a cracking thud, and his vision blurred. He rolled onto his side, gasping for breath. When his eyes cleared, he saw the other man crawling across the ice on his hands and knees. Then the man slowed. One of his hands clawed at his throat, spasmodically, until his head sagged forward to meet the ice, as if he were about to do a headstand. Then he collapsed.

Manley caught his breath. He arose slowly and skated warily toward the dark, still form. The man lay face down on one cheek, his half-open eyes growing dull and opaque. His lips slowly pursed open and closed. Manley saw a pool of liquid widening under the man's cheek, a pool fed by a weakening pulse in the man's severed throat, a pulse that slowly, slowly ceased to beat.

Manley's heavy legs were like lumber as he skated to Sheila's side. Wide eyed and shaken, she stared at the man's dark torso in a paralysis of disbelief, her fists balled up and bunched about her open mouth. He stepped in front of her to block her view, and he put his arm around her shoulder. Soon they walked slowly to the edge of the lake and sat on the felled log.

They were both too numb to talk. Manley tried to think, but it was impossible. As his adrenalin-charged fury waned, it left him with little mind jolts, electric fragments of thought that sparked through his brain. He kept seeing a man, kept hearing shots and screams. And a barking dog . . .

"You're bleeding," Sheila said.

She touched the crimson rivulet that edged down his cheek from the small crease above his forehead. She wiped the streak away with her fingertips, as if its mere presence were doing immeasurable harm to his skin. She thought it must have gotten in his eyes, for they were filled with tears. As she watched his somber face, he got up and slowly returned to the ice.

"Rick?"

He didn't hear her. All his attention was focused on the huddled pile of fur that lay unmoving on the frozen surface.

He knelt on the ice. Manley reached out his hand and rubbed it the length of the dog's still-warm coat. The tears ran down his nose and fell from his chin.

Oh, Dart, you idiot. You were such a good boy, Dart. God, how I loved you!

He scooped the dog's limp body into his arms and cradled it close. Then, standing up, he walked slowly back across the ice, head held high. His chin was quivering when he reached Sheila, and he blinked his eyes to force away the tears. He hoped she didn't say anything, because right now, he just didn't want to talk.

She didn't. She looped her arm through one of his, and they returned to the cabin. Inside, he lay the dog on the wooden floor in front of the hearth. He took off his skates and slumped wearily into a chair. Sheila paced nervously back and forth.

"Shouldn't we call the police?"

"There's no phone."

"I can drive, if you want."

"It's okay. I'm all right." He paused, staring at the fire. "I just don't understand why . . ." He shook his head, unable to think clearly. He wearily got up and unzipped his parka. "What the hell. Ben can take care of it. I bet any second he'll—"

He stopped, frozen in memory.

His face flashed toward hers. Their eyes locked in urgency, and her fingers rose uncertainly toward her lips. Her voice trailed away in a whisper.

"He was here with me."

"Oh, my God, no."

He bolted for the door and pulled it open. Outside, the wind had risen. It was harsh now, gusting in stinging jets that rode the creases between the cabin's logs. Manley ran ten feet from the cabin, listening to the shrill wind that sailed through the trees.

"Ben!" he hollered. Again, cupping his hands to his lips, "Ben!"

Nothing answered him but the voice of the wind itself.

Chapter Sixteen

Dr. Hume escorted Jacqueline to her room.

From the very first instant of her arrival, the dramatic deterioration of both her physical and mental states had been obvious. There were hesitant pauses in her speech and an undeniable clouding of the thought processes that had once been so sharp. The bags under her eyes were deep and dark, sagging beneath her lids with a looseness that contrasted sharply with the taut quality of the rest of her skin: cheeks puffed and distended, a neck that was growing bulbous.

As Hume appraised Jacqueline, his eyes began to blaze in their sockets, and the corners of his mouth turned downward into a straight line. But whether the change signaled a deepening of the doctor's concern for his patient or the heightening of some entirely different emotion, one could not tell.

He held her overnight case in one hand and encircled the fingers of his other around her puffy wrist. Jacqueline trailed him passively, the shuffle in her gait giving the impression that she was being dragged rather than merely following.

En route, they passed the head nurse, who had been supervising a porter who was cleaning the hall. Dr. Hume's response to her expression of surprise was a curt nod that indicated his full control. Soon they crossed into the familiar separate wing.

Once inside her room, she first gazed numbly about

261

before appearing to brighten, a tone of expectancy creeping into her voice.

"Can I start the treatments now?"

"First you must rest, Jacqueline. I fully understand your eagerness, but an initial period of relaxation is essential."

Her voice cracked into desperate warbling.

"But when? Don't you understand that—"

He stilled her words by grasping both her shoulders firmly and eyeing her at arm's length.

"Soon, Jacqueline. You must be patient. It is imperative that you trust me." His penetrating gaze was a command. "I do have your trust, don't I?"

She looked away and gave a nervous nod.

"Of course I trust you, but . . ." She gave her head a weak and apprehensive shake. "It's just that I don't know what's happening to me anymore. I feel so terribly hungry all the time, and—"

"That no longer matters," he interrupted. "Disregard the changes in your appetite. Once the treatments begin, that will be amply taken care of. Whatever has transpired will become a thing of the past."

A single tear rolled down her cheek and clung to her quivering chin.

"Oh, God—do you really think so?"

"I know so." He kissed her paternally on both cheeks and pulled away, his face a radiant smile of beneficence. "What happened to the trust you promised?"

She managed a weak smile.

"I promise."

"Good." His hands fell to her elbows, which he squeezed reassuringly. Then he released her and walked confidently away before slowing to a halt halfway to the door. He turned back to her with apparent reluctance. "I shan't be able to dine with you tonight, I'm afraid."

The very mention of food made her wince. Her eyes pleaded.

"All I want is to start the treatments," she implored. "I know I said I was hungry, but I really don't want anything to—"

"But you must," he said quickly. "I sympathize with

262

your impatience—but please remember, my dear Jacqueline, the significance of our meals here. They are so very important in your overall therapy. Without proper nourishment, the remainder of the program would be completely ineffective." He paused for emphasis. "You do want to be cured, don't you?"

Her fingers fluttered upward to pick nervously at her bitten underlip. She gazed at his face and tried to grasp the meaning of his enigmatic smile. How could he even ask that? she wondered. She replied with a pathetic nod of her head.

"Consider the next half hour an interlude," he continued. "Wash up and take a few moments to relax. When you are refreshed, simply show yourself to this wing's dining room. You know the way."

Still smiling, he gave a little bow. Then he turned once again, walked out the door, and was gone.

For Jacqueline, the luxury of relaxation was an impossibility. To distract herself, she took a hot shower and tried to succumb to its warmth. However, the usually soothing spray proved debilitating rather than invigorating—the prickly, watery barbs needling her tense muscles into an even greater tightness. She hurriedly toweled dry and put on the familiar white robe, pacing the length of her room as she toyed with the idea of omitting the meal entirely. Yet Dr. Hume had been insistent.

Ultimately, she admitted her helplessness in the matter. In her despondency, she had placed herself entirely in Dr. Hume's hands. She would make an earnest effort to give him the trust he demanded. With a deep sigh, she resigned herself to the inevitable and departed for the dining area.

Jacqueline had barely left her room when she smelled it. It was a sumptuous mixture of scents, the open-hearth aroma of fresh-baked goods that combined with the savory holiday smell of roasting meats. She was already ravenous, and the aroma overwhelmed her; yet it stimulated her curiosity only slightly less than it did her appetite, for such tantalizing scents had always been foreign to the Spa. Growing uncomfortably alert, her gait slowed as she approached the dining room with suspicion.

Inside, the long, slender table occupied its usual position. However, in place of the light and pleasant fare to which Jacqueline was accustomed, the white tablecloth was covered with the makings of a veritable feast: a tureen of steaming soup, a carving board laden with roast beef that oozed its own juices, a platter of the most delectable appetizers and another of desserts. She looked nervously about, expecting to see others; but there was no one. She was alone.

Her sudden desire for everything in sight was stupefying. Driven by hunger and encouraged by Dr. Hume's admonition to eat, she hurried to the table and began to help herself.

Jacqueline ate family style, achieving with one hand what it might require another four to accomplish. Her fingers raced among the bowls and platters as if she intended to pry loose savory bits here and slivers there; instead, she came away with whole handfuls of food, all of which found its way unerringly to her mouth.

Within minutes, she was stuffed. Her perception gradually decreased, in inverse proportion to the filling of her stomach. As she stood there with greasy cheek and paraffin jowl, Jacqueline's appreciation of her surroundings steadily vanished. Her expression turned leaden, and her eyes once more became flat and gloomy. Her hands fell listlessly to her sides, and the remaining foodstuffs tumbled from her grasp, released by fingers of wax. Then she slowly turned, retreated from the dining area, and crept back in the direction of her room.

Though she had no way of knowing it, the physical strain on her system was incalculable. Taxed by days of starvation, and then abruptly shocked by an overabundance of food, her body responded in a reaction of the most extreme stress. Her hormone levels skyrocketed as her glands exhausted themselves of secretions; her blood pressure rose precipitously to dangerous levels, making her already pounding heart race even faster; and her gastrointestinal system, so recently depleted, struggled to equilibrate to the astounding influx of salts and digestive enzymes. By the time she reached her room, her lungs faintly gurgled with fluid, a sign of impending heart failure and eventual circulatory collapse.

An internal alarm of survival commanded her to rest, to be still. Jacqueline slumped onto the bed. She lay there in a motionless daze—unseeing, unknowing—as her body waged a basic fight for self-perpetuation. For the briefest instant, she nearly succumbed in the manner of Suzanne Fontaine. But then, ever so gradually, the forces of survival rallied themselves, and after many minutes of uncertain struggle, her condition finally took a favorable turn. As Jacqueline weathered the storm over the next critical hour, her steady improvement became obvious: the heaving of her lungs slowed, and the rapid pounding of her pulse decreased to an acceptable level. Yet though her condition once again became stable, there could be no doubting the outcome of another such episode.

Then the flickering glimmer resurfaced. Jacqueline's eyes—never really closed—widened in cognition. She sat up in awareness, the dull film gone from her vision, and looked about the dimly lit room.

She had no memory of returning. She vaguely recalled that peculiar meal, and then . . . nothing. It was probably just another daydream, she reasoned, one of those annoying but inconsequential lapses she had fallen prey to so recently. Then she lay back and closed her eyes, thankful that this time, at least, she had been able to fall asleep.

Under the satiny covers, she curled up in fetal position and awaited the return of languor. The vivid memory of her previous sleeplessness loomed prominently in her thoughts. She huddled there motionlessly, frightened that drowsiness might not recur. Her lips felt dry and chapped. She moistened them with her tongue. Their surfaces were parched and withered, shriveled like the skin of one's fingers when submersed too long in water; and they tasted alarmingly salty. Her fingers glided upward to touch her mouth. Her eyes widened in dismay when she noticed that her forefingers seemed frightfully slippery.

She threw back the coverlet and hastened to the bathroom. Inside, she felt for the light switch, found it, and turned it on. Its sudden brightness made her lids momentarily narrow.

But then they widened again in a sharp blaze of fear when she saw her reflection in the mirror.

Her once white robe was covered with stains that crept onto her face. From the waist upward, the entire upper half of her smock was slimy with oily blotches, multicolored splatterings of food sprayed from an artist's palette onto her torso. Her cheek was anointed with a brown splash of gravy, and drying, yellowish pieces of chicken skin clung to the strands of her hair, like larvae wriggling to life. She nervously plucked at them with her coated fingers, but they stuck fast.

Trembling with horror, she turned to the sink—to the liberation of simple soap and water. Something at waist level caught her eye. Jacqueline looked down and gasped.

On a gleaming silver platter, the snout of a suckling pig was pointed in her direction, staring up at her through the gelatinous film of its roasted eyes.

Jacqueline turned white. A terrified cry left her throat, and she slumped backward against the bathroom wall.

Just beyond the two-way mirror, Dr. Hume watched Jacqueline grow faint and fall unconscious to the floor. He stood there unmoving, as silent as a corpse.

Chapter Seventeen

Everything began to fall apart after Manley and Sheila found Ben. For once Sheila's wit abandoned her. She rode the knife edge of terror with Manley, occasionally falling off into the mind bog of profound despair. Then she would pop up again, verbalizing frantically in nearly hysterical banter. Manley tried to act like a stabilizing force, but since he could find no reason for what had happened, his calming influence was negligible. All he could think of was getting out of there and of returning to New York to be ready for Jacqueline.

There would be time for the police later. Much later, when Jacqueline had safely returned to her Manhattan apartment and when he and Sheila had had time to wind down from the nerve-piercing anxiety of living with death. He didn't give any thought to preserving evidence—the tracks in the snow, shell casings, or fingerprints. The idea never even occurred to him. Rather, he busied himself with attending to Dart and Ben. He scooped out a recess in the drifts behind the cabin. He carried Ben to it, laying him side by side with the dog. There was an old tarpaulin atop the wood pile. He used it as a temporary burial shroud, covering it with a mound of snow. Then he went for the man on the lake.

Sheila held on to the sleeve of his jacket.

"Leave him," she suggested.

"I can't."

The more he tried to pull away, the harder she tugged.

"Why don't we just get out of here?"

"Someone might find him."

"So what? Leave him where he is. Can't you just—"

"I have to, Sheila," he interrupted. "It's the only way."

He returned to the wind-driven night, leaving her to stand by the dying fire. The embers' heat lapped at her ankles, but it did nothing to sooth the intense chill inside her. Abject fear was a feeling quite new to her. She was seized by a swell of foreign emotion that swept her to the crest of panic. And yet, as she stood there, she felt compelled to look toward the window, whose crystalline glass panes were bathed in pale moonlight. On the lake far below, she could see Manley lift the man's legs and drag him across the ice. Driven by an impulse, Sheila walked apprehensively to the window.

The dead man's black coat trailed behind him like a magician's cape. Manley lugged him unceremoniously up the bank to the cabin, straining from the effort. Sheila watched through the window with an expression of resignation. The brightness of the clear night sky was accentuated by the snow. In the moonlight, the big man's face was a ghostly gray. Sheila stared at it in mounting curiosity. As she looked, her eyes widened into ovals, and her nails dug into the sill.

Manley was nearly even with the cabin. He dropped the man's legs and straightened up, winded. He could hear the sudden, sharp intake of breath that came through the closed window behind him. He jerked about.

Sheila was staring at the dead man. The web of her fingers loosely covered her mouth, and her expression changed into one of shocked recognition. She stepped backward in fright. Manley hurried into the cabin, presuming the look on her face was the mark of her revulsion at death, her reaction to the deep and jagged laceration that had ripped apart the stranger's throat.

He lightly took her arm and tried to steer her away.

"Don't look. It's not very pretty."

Her face was surprisingly calm and determined.

"It's him," she said softly.

Manley was flabbergasted.

"You *know* him?"

She managed a convincing nod.

"I didn't get a good look at him before," she said, shaking her head. "It all happened so fast. . . . It's Vincent."

"Who is Vincent?"

She looked into his eyes, her forehead furrowing with worry.

"He's the man who picked Jackie and me up at the airport."

For a moment he just stood there, not comprehending. The airport? In California? He averted his eyes to escape her relentless stare. His thoughts spun. Jacqueline's desperation to return to the Spa. . . . His own conversation with Dr. Hume, filled with disconcertingly vague replies. . . . It wasn't possible!

"That's thousands of miles from here," he reasoned. "He's just some nickel and dime hood that—"

"No," she insisted, her face sculpted in furious persistence. "That man is Dr. Hume's chief orderly."

He was surprised by the even tone of conviction in her now steady voice. The concept staggered him; at that moment, it was far too stupefying to give it consideration. Instead, he turned to get her coat.

"We'll talk about it on the way home."

"Rick," she said, firmly, her tone adamant. "I know what I saw. And I know that man."

"All right. You saw what you saw. Now let's get out of here."

She held off the proffered coat.

"You don't believe me?"

"Yes, Sheila, I do believe you. But what I believe isn't important now."

She stood her ground, and as she did so, her calmness curiously increased, in tandem with his mounting impatience. Her tone was urgent, yet composed. She held up her palms, a halting gesture.

"Rick, stop and think for a moment about what I'm saying," she began. "On the trip up here, I considered that what you said about Dr. Hume was ridiculous. After all, the guy was like a saint. But at times I can have a fairly open mind. I told you that I needed more convincing proof. Well," she said, gesturing toward the figure in the snow, "now I have it."

Manley hesitated in contemplation, avoiding her insistent stare. It was a curious reversal of roles, his playing abnegation to her intractability. At first, he had been so intent on keeping her calm that he hadn't honestly thought of what Sheila was implying. Yet as he reflected, the logic of her words began to ring true.

"Proof," he said, eyeing the form in the snow. "That's the extent of the proof, and you're asking me if it fits?"

"Doesn't it?"

"Yes," he concluded. "It may very well."

For Sheila, that left only the obvious.

"Why does Dr. Hume want to kill you, Rick?"

He walked slowly to the window, looking through it downward, fogging the pane with his breath. After a moment of silent thought, he whirled about and swatted the air in irritation, sounding very annoyed with himself.

"Most likely he senses me as a threat. I suppose I was getting too close to something, something he doesn't want revealed—his secret, maybe. Or perhaps public exposure, and ridicule. Whatever it is, it was reason enough to want me out of the way."

"Funny how he simply oozes such a different image."

"That's the face of the psychopath. His outward behavior is a compensation for his insanity." His expression abruptly became agitated. "Christ, I hate to think what that imbalance is doing right now to Jack."

Simple though his statement was, it had never occurred to Sheila; her logic had carried her only so far. She was incredulous.

"You think he's taken Jacqueline?"

"Taken? No, just the opposite: if the mountain won't come to Mohammed . . ."

What he was implying made no sense to her.

"Didn't you say he refused to take her back?"

"True—but that's ignoring the most important factor in the equation: Jack herself." He balled his fists, clenching them emphatically in front of his face. "What the hell was I thinking?" he said, giving his head a disgusted shake.

"You see, Jack was *convinced* that only Hume could help her. His refusal threw me off, sure, but I kept right on ignoring what was much more significant—her own determination. Knowing Jack's compulsion, it should have *occurred* to me that she'd seize the bull by the horns and take her case directly to him!"

"I don't suppose he'd admit as much over the phone, if you called him now?"

He rubbed his cheek.

"I don't need a phone call, Sheila. Jack's not in the Caribbean. I'm certain of it." He hurriedly zipped up his parka. "And the sooner I get out to where she really is, the better," he said, pausing to stare at her for emphasis. "Assuming it's not already too late."

❧

She felt as if she were tumbling, spiraling, doing lazy somersaults in the void of her dreams.

Jacqueline, Jacqueline . . .

Her name came as vibration, the repetitive babble of a thousand lips that reverberated in the subliminal echoes of her mind. She was weightless, a sailplane hovering, floating up in dreamlike currents that lifted her skyward, toward the brightness above. She felt patting, a tapping on her cheeks. So sleepy . . .

"Jacqueline . . . Jacqueline?"

Her leaden lids seemed anchored. She tried to open them but couldn't. She felt her chin fall again, sinking heavily toward her chest, but the swatting annoyance continued on her cheeks, urging her toward wakefulness. She slowly raised her head, and by the greatest of efforts, eased her eyes open.

"Are you all right, Jacqueline?"

It was a voice devoid of form. Something shimmered there, vague and indistinct beyond her vision. She blinked.

"Thank goodness, Jacqueline. Are you awake?"

She was gazing into the face of Dr. Hume. He seemed to be leaning over her. The dryness of her brittle whisper rattled in her throat.

"What?"

271

"You were screaming. I rushed in as soon as possible, but you must have fallen. I hope you haven't injured yourself. Jacqueline?"

She looked dully about. She was sitting on the floor of the bathroom. It was a familiar bathroom, her bathroom, a bathroom where—

Oh, my God . . .

She shuddered into cold and frantic wakefulness, remembering it all now. She felt as if the vivid memory were strangling her, choking off all possibility of words, threatening, even, to keep her from breathing. Yet she managed to lift a trembling finger toward a spot behind him, in the direction of the sink. She held herself rigid, quivering with fright, as he gracefully stepped aside, the slow motion pirouette of a bullfighter.

She thought her lungs would erupt if she saw it. But then she blinked, slowly at first, and then with twitching rapidity, a spasm of butterfly wings. She stared incredulously at the spotless, uncluttered sink and numbly shook her head.

It just couldn't be . . .

Still white with shock, Jacqueline's unwavering gaze was fixed on the basin. Overcome with disbelief, she tried to push herself upward, but her limbs were leaden. Dr. Hume's steady hand rested on her shoulder.

"Don't get up yet, Jacqueline," he said soothingly. "Wait until your head clears."

Her voice was stale and weak.

"The pig . . . what did you do with the pig?"

He scowled in incomprehension. He glanced at the sink and then back at her.

"Pig? Jacqueline, there is no pig."

Her faint voice rose to a shout.

"But I saw it!"

She pushed out of his grasp and staggered forward in suspicion. At the sight of the wash basin, the ovals of her eyes grew wide. The sink was immaculate, Dover white, faintly glistening. Her fingers flew to her quivering lips.

She saw her reflection then, shining her way from the mirror. She looked at it and gasped. Her face and robe were spotless. The obscene stains were gone, the greasy smears vanished, and at the robe's shoulders, the waves of her well-combed hair rested like epaulets, each strand perfectly in place. Her lower lip slowly fell. She turned to Dr. Hume, mouth limp and open.

"It was here, I swear it. . . ." she whispered.

Hume smiled reassuringly. His comforting arm went around her shoulder.

"Dearest Jacqueline, you haven't been well lately," he pointed out. "The only thing in this room has been you. Doubtless the screams I heard were nothing more than the sounds of a bad dream." He paused. "*Have* you been dreaming lately—nightmares, perhaps?"

She turned away from him, wanting to cry. Daydreams and bad dreams, forgetfulness and nightmares. . . . Why, oh why, was this happening to her? Suddenly, she was jolted out of her miserable reverie by remembrance of a feast. Her eyes flashed back at his.

"The dinner," she said distinctly.

His reply was an uncomprehending stare.

"Dinner?"

She lurched away and darted from the bathroom, throwing her bedroom door wide and flying down the corridor. Hume started after her.

"Jacqueline, whatever. . . .? Jacqueline!"

She halted at the entrance to the dining room. As she stared at the long center table, she once again became faint, dizzy with disbelief. On the clean white tablecloth, two small plates contained the tidy remnants of a meager meal. Hume caught up with her just as her sobbing began.

She held her face in shaking hands, and her tears spilled through her fingers. Hume gently took her elbow and eased her back toward her room.

"I asked before for your trust, Jacqueline," he said firmly. "Now I must insist on it."

Moments later, in the darkness of her room, she was again resting in bed, lying between the cool, smooth sheets. Dr. Hume had repeated his assurance that her dreams were temporary, the lapses in her memory part of her illness—all soon to disappear once the treatments began.

She rolled onto her side, her cheek touching the pillow already wet with her tears. She stared fervently into the blackness, praying for the sleep that would not come. She remained like that for the next hour, occasionally blinking in her wakefulness, then closing her eyes for the briefest periods of time.

The rude aroma crept onto her bed, heavy and silent, filthy as gutter fog. Jacqueline's nostrils flared at its touch. It was the unmistakable scent of cooking, redolent of a lavish feast. She bolted upright when she smelled it, eyes locked and frozen in fear. The scent stole into her throat, where it threatened to suck the breath of life itself from her lungs.

Chapter Eighteen

Sheila hurriedly assembled their few belongings while Manley returned outside. He jogged down the bank and retrieved the rifle from the lake's ice. Returning up the snow-covered incline, he knelt beside the body that lay cold and stiffening in the cabin's shadow. He quickly rummaged through the pockets and found a heavy automatic pistol. He slowly examined it in the moonlight, squinting at the polished sparkle that glinted from the heavy barrel. Then he abruptly flung it lakeward with a sharp flick of his wrist and resumed searching the clothes.

Except for the gun, the greatcoat was empty—no wallet, no money or papers. Similarly, the man's trouser pockets and valise contained only several keys on a ring, a box of ammunition, and spare magazines for the weapons.

Inside the cabin, Sheila continued her hurried packing as Manley reentered. He lay the sniper rifle on the floor next to Ben's, tightening his lips in a thin line when a flood of memories swept over him at the sight of the old Winchester Model 94. Thinking about it was painful, a dull ache that consolidated behind his eyes.

"A reason," he muttered.

Sheila looked up.

"What?"

He turned away from her, annoyed at the moisture that filled his eyes.

"Ben always said that everything happened for a reason. I think I'm just beginning to understand that reason."

She continued to pack, folding a robe.

"Maybe you can explain it to me."

He walked slowly across the room and gazed into the dying fire.

"Hume's after something, Sheila. He may want different things from different people, but he has a very concrete motive."

"Which is what?"

"I'm not sure," he shrugged. "But maybe if we can agree on *how* he's doing it, we can better understand why. Are you up to talking it through with me?"

"Right now I'm not exactly up to anything, but go on anyway."

"Give me that."

She handed him the night case, which he carried to the door as she sat down to struggle with her boots.

"Let me go over what I was explaining on the drive up here, in a little more detail," he said. "To begin with, assume that Hume has gotten hold of Emmerich's process and put it into practical use. In fact I wouldn't be surprised if the two of them were working together—a sort of partnership. That might explain why Emmerich seemed to disappear just before Hume emerged on the scene. Are you with me?"

She finished with one boot and tugged at the other.

"So far."

"My understanding of Emmerich's process—let's call it Hume's 'treatment'—is that it works by periodic injections, injections which have to be repeated every six months."

"Why then?" she asked, pulling the leather higher along her calf.

"Because they wear off. You see, Emmerich discovered a way to link chemically a long-lasting depot base with certain neurotransmitters—probably one called norepinephrine, in this case. If you gave a standard dose of that drug to a normal person, you might get a modest increase in brown fat metabolism. It would be temporary, only a matter of hours. But if that same drug level were around for six months, because it's stored in an individual's tissues, the subject's brown fat would be in a state of constant activation. The end result would be that an enormous number of calories could be metabolized, and the person would stay almost magically thin."

She wiggled her toes into the tips of her boots. Satisfied, she reached for her coat.

"And the high-carbohydrate diet—"

"Apparently enhances the way it works," he concluded. "Pasta alone stimulates brown fat. Combine such a diet with an already activated brown fat system, and you've got a surefire cure for overweight."

Sheila finished doing the top buttons of her coat.

"Is that what you meant when you said the biopsy proved it?"

"Yes. The only reason Jack's brown fat had such incredible metabolic activity was because it was being constantly stimulated by something. That 'something' turns out to be the depot neurotransmitter."

She nodded, thinking she understood what he was suggesting.

"So, if she *didn't* get the injection . . ."

"Her brown fat metabolism would plummet. I suppose I could have verified it by another biopsy, but I didn't have to. The clinical proof was obvious when I noticed that her back had gone cold, indicating that her brown fat had stopped functioning. I just wish I was smart enough to have realized it then."

She gave a little nod of her head to indicate that she was ready. Manley opened the door, and they were immediately pummeled by a chill breeze. It was the middle of the night. With the wind gusting about them, he closed the door and quickly led her down the darkened trail to his van.

Sheila was deep in thought as she trudged in his footsteps.

"I'm still not clear how your interpretation explains Jacqueline's behavior."

His breath sailed by her face in frosty puffs.

"Two ways. First, this neurotransmitter stimulated an area of her brain that regulated hunger—or more specifically, satiety. If it's present in sufficient amount, she'd feel reasonably full, so that she would be satisfied just by nibbling. By concentrating on carbohydrates, a little at a time, she stimulated her own brown fat, which merely kept the cycle going.

"Second, she's undergoing a form of withdrawal. Her body must have adjusted to the constant effect of that injection. When it began to wear off, if it weren't replenished, she'd develop symptoms like any other addict—certain cravings, odd changes in behavior."

"Including overeating?"

"Definitely. The reasons I just mentioned would be enough to cause it, but there's something else. In addition to the brain's satiety center, there's also an appetite, or hunger, center. If the satiety center were suddenly turned off, the hunger center would undergo a horrifying sort of rebound and make a person eat insatiably." The image of Jacqueline's mania lingered in his mind. "And as if that weren't enough, the food frenzy itself could alter her behavior even further."

He opened the door to the van. Though they were hurrying, the numbing suddenness of all that had happened made it seem as if they were moving in slow motion. Sheila settled into the front seat while Manley kicked the snow from his overshoes. Then he climbed behind the wheel, started the engine, and slowly backed down the road, without once glancing back at the cabin where he had spent his fondest days.

Sheila overcame her astonishment and continued the conversation.

"You're implying that Jackie didn't get the injection the last time we went to the Spa?"

"Exactly. For some reason, Hume withheld it from her. I wouldn't be surprised if that were related to the sleeplessness she complained about. You see, Jack never recalled getting any injections, so I have to assume they were given while she was asleep. Yet in order to make her that sleepy, she must have been drugged. I bet her bedtime snack was spiked."

"But not mine."

"Precisely—which brings me back to Hume's selectivity.

If my hunch is correct, he focused on actresses. Why *some* actresses and not others, like you, I don't know. Maybe it's a similarity in their body structures or personalities, or God knows what. But once he decided, only those people were drugged, and those same people got the treatment."

Sheila studied his concentration as he drove the van backward, looking through the rear window.

"Does that include your Mrs. Dillon?"

"I think so. At least the timing is right. It's been about six months since she was at the Spa. Her brown fat is probably still fairly active—which explains her high caloric intake—but it's beginning to fluctuate. In her case, the difference is that she's protected by her own psyche: her catatonia is more powerful than her hunger. She would have stuffed herself to death long ago if she hadn't had a mental break. She's saved by her own insanity."

His vision narrowed as he stared down the road. He slowed. "A car."

"Whose is it?"

"I don't know."

He had gone an eighth of a mile down the trail. The car was parked in the middle of the road, blocking further passage. Manley braked and put the van in park, leaving the motor running. Overwhelmed by the frightening chain of events, it had never occurred to him that the stranger must have had a means of transportation. The man had been there, at the lake; for some reason he had assumed that the killer had just *appeared*. He got out of the van and felt for the key ring in his pocket.

He ran to the car, unlocked the door, and swept his eyes over the front and back seats. The upholstery was bare. The vehicle had a fresh, new-car smell of unused leather. He got in and opened the door to the glove compartment, which was illuminated by a small bulb. A packet of papers was on the shelf, inside a vinyl folder. Manley leaned over and inspected them in the dim light.

There were several charge-card receipts, one from an auto rental company, the other from a Manhattan motor inn, both signed by a James Smith. He pocketed them without further thought. The remaining items made his heart skip a beat. One was a parking-lot stub, the other a driver's license and registration, and the third an airline ticket. They had all been printed in California.

His fingers were shaking, his palms cold and moist. Unlike the charge receipts, all the documents bore the name of Vincent Triolo. He leafed through the papers. The driver's license was current; the parking stub—stamped with a date and time several days previously—was from a lot for long-term parking at Los Angeles International Airport; and the airline ticket was for a return flight the day after next. Manley swallowed against a dry throat and momentarily stared into the glow of the small bulb. He couldn't believe it.

He straightened up, put the documents and keys in his pocket, and closed the glove compartment. He started the car and turned on its headlights. By carefully maneuvering the car back and forth, he was able to steer the spinning tires off the narrow road into snow-covered brush between two trees. He locked the car and returned to the van.

"What took you so long?" asked Sheila.

"I couldn't start the damn thing."

In a short while they were on the highway. Manley sped down the interstate, desperate to lessen the distance between him and Jacqueline. Conversation temporarily halted, replaced by an uneasy silence. Sheila couldn't relax. She would occasionally close her eyes, but rest was impossible, and she would open them again, if for nothing more than to stare hypnotically down the passing lines in the roadway. As the speedometer inched toward ninety, Manley tried to concentrate on driving, but his mind was preoccupied.

Why had the stranger tried to kill him? As he had explained to Sheila, the man he knew as Hume obviously wanted him dead—but for what purpose? He'd never even met Hume. There were his calls, of course, and his persistent messages: all unanswered save one. True, he *had* made numerous inquiries about Hume, inquiries which may have become known at San Sebastian. Was that it, he wondered? Did the fact that he was prying—probing here, questioning there—truly make him into the threat he now perceived himself to be?

If so, something Godawful was going on, some sort of colossal secret he had blindly stumbled onto that Hume wanted no one to know. It had to do with Dillon, and Fontaine, and Jacqueline, and Lord knew how many others. And it was something worth killing for.

Sheila's voice came alive.

"What determined whom Dr. Hume selected?"

He shrugged.

"I don't know. That always brings up Hume's motive, which is something I hoped you could help me with."

Her pensiveness gave way to a frown.

"There was one point, when I first met him, that he mentioned certain criteria. . . ."

"Criteria?"

"Yes. I think I'd asked him if the Spa was open to anyone who could pay the tab. There was something oblique about his reply. But he never indicated what criteria he was referring to."

Accelerating past a truck, Manley was absorbed in thought.

"Did he ever indicate how he decided who would be a guest at the Spa—that is, who might be subject to those criteria?"

"Not that I remember. I assumed it was word of mouth."

He eased the van back into its lane.

"I doubt it. He'd probably want a select group of people to begin with, people he could then proceed to be more selective about."

She looked his way. "Could you run that by me again?"

"To begin with," he reiterated, "the Spa's phone number is unlisted, so relying on word of mouth alone is pretty chancy if you have a specific goal in mind. I'm sure there were some cases where it *was* word of mouth—such as yours. But I would also bet that Hume has a feeder. Someone probably directs a certain type of patient to him, and then Hume makes the final selection."

"Emmerich?"

"Possibly. I don't know." He sighed. "Anyway, that still doesn't explain what he wants Jacqueline for, why he selected her. . . . Help me, Sheila. Didn't Jack mention anything unusual to you, in the last week or so?"

"No. Not really."

He exhaled wearily, concentrating on the darkness ahead as he sped toward Manhattan.

"Actresses," he said hoarsely. "Somehow, it deals with actresses. At least I think it does. They seem to be the common denominator. Did Hume ever mention acting? Any comment at all about movies or the stage?"

She shook her head.

"Only in a general way. Somehow, I have the impression he liked Broadway. But I doubt that he's interested in contemporary acting."

"Why do you say that?"

She hesitated.

"Come to think of it, Jackie *did* say something last week, while we were exercising. At the time it just seemed like another nervous, offhand comment."

"Go on."

"She laughed when she said it, then just as quickly changed the subject. I don't remember how we got onto the subject. But she mentioned that Hume would have loved to see her do Shaw's *Pygmalion*."

Manley's jaw dropped. Hadn't Rita Goldschmidt made an allusion to Shaw and Emmerich's wife? It was becoming clearer now, Hume's motive. And the implications were staggering.

Manley tightly gripped the wheel, too astonished to speak. He would know soon enough. With the killer unable to return to California, Hume would shortly realize that something had gone wrong. And whatever Hume had planned for Jacqueline would be accelerated.

Hume held all the trumps. Manley took it as a given that whatever was going to happen to Jacqueline was inevitable; the only hope lay in interfering with its timing. He pressed the gas pedal to the floor and narrowed his eyes on the dark horizon. He thought of the airline ticket and parking-lot stub that rested in his pocket. The barest fragments of a

plan were taking shape in his mind, a plan that had virtually no chance of success. But it was all he had. As the first
glimmer of dawn brightened the eastern sky, he prayed he
had enough time.

The horrifying aroma vanished as quickly as it had
appeared. As Jacqueline sat there, her heart pounding, she
began to wonder if she hadn't imagined the smell—if her
mind weren't once again playing a savage trick on her.

She lay back in bed, staring into the darkness, unable to
sleep. She lay deathly still, her nerves crackling in the
violet cave of her room. There was no medicine to ease her
suffering; her one last hope was the coming of morning,
and with it, the onset of her treatments. As the late-night
hours edged toward dawn, a heavy blue daze descended
upon her, a poultice to soothe her raw consciousness; yet it
was a negligent imposter of sleep, a taunting promise of
rest that abruptly fled at the sound of the harsh knock on
her door.

It was Dr. Hume. He entered without waiting for a
reply. Jacqueline rolled exhaustedly to her side, limbs
weak and trembling. Hume eyed her with ostensible
concern.

"You slept poorly, Jacqueline?"

"I didn't sleep."

"That shall soon change. Come, the treatments are ready
to begin." He helped her struggle to her feet. He looked
into her eyes and noted with satisfaction her dull and
glazed expression. "By this time tomorrow," he said with a
peculiar chill, "you shall be in the midst of the deepest
sleep you have ever known."

He led her from the room. What was it, she wondered,
about the strange acerbity of his tone?

So unlike him . . .

She tried to concentrate, but it was impossible; for in
that instant, she was gripped by an intense and gnawing
hunger, a craving for virtually all that was edible. It dimly
occurred to her that it was breakfast time, and the idea
terrified her.

Don't let him mention food. Please let the treatments start.

They proceeded down the corridor.

"You must be expecting breakfast," he said with precision.

"No!"

It was a shriek. Jacqueline stopped walking and placed her hands over her ears. The expression on her face was a wincing grimace, as if an avalanche of noise roared about her. Hume raised his eyebrows.

"Jacqueline, whatever are you doing?"

He pried her hands from her ears and forced her to look his way. Her face was pathetically twisted with an expression that suggested both insatiability and intense pain.

"I insist you listen to me," Hume snapped. He held her cheeks roughly and glared at her for emphasis. "Ordinarily, as you know, each day begins with adequate nutrition. However, considering the severity of your condition, I have decided to dispense with it and proceed directly to the treatments."

She closed her eyes, weak-kneed with relief.

"Come," he continued, pulling her harshly by the arm. "We shall commence with the exercises."

During her previous visits, each day had begun with a private massage. Apparently Hume had decided to forgo that too; he led her directly to a small but well-equipped gymnasium. As usual, the room was empty, for she'd always had her own personal supervision. But her regular instructor was nowhere in sight. Hume went to a locker and located a leotard. He told Jacqueline to change in the bathroom and return promptly.

She did as she was told. When she reentered the gym, Hume motioned for her to seat herself in a rowing machine. She positioned herself on the sliding seat as he fastened her wrists and ankles tightly. She ignored the chafing.

"No instructor today?" she asked.

"I am your instructor," came his terse reply. "Begin to row."

She looked up at him in curiosity and saw the chill in his eyes. For a moment, she hesitated in uncertainty. It was so very peculiar, she thought, that he should—

"Row!" he commanded.

She flinched at his words, but then recovered and leaned forward to grasp the oars. She braced her feet against the pedals and pulled the oars toward her. Her muscles were pitifully weak. She strained at the initial effort but forced herself to push the wooden poles back into place and continue. As she went on, Hume walked in slow circles around the machine.

"Food was your problem before," he said coldly, "and food may be your problem now."

Her eyes flashed open in a wild paroxysm of fright, causing her to redouble her efforts.

"We shall have to dispense with food until your problem is overcome," he resumed, continuing his steady pacing. "The cakes, the sweets, all the baked dishes to which you have become accustomed—those you shall have to do without, Jacqueline."

She rowed ever faster, fighting the tears and the uncontrollable twitching that contorted her face at the thought of what he was saying. She struggled not to listen, hoping the machine's mechanical sounds would drown out his words. Yet the harder she rowed, the louder he spoke.

"Think of it," he said, in mesmerizing tones. "Everything you crave—the rich sausage, the mouth-watering paté, the luscious fruits, all that your heart desires—"

Jacqueline perspired heavily, shaking her head emphatically from side to side as her heart pounded in agony and exhaustion.

"—shall not be yours, my dear Jacqueline, until you reach a certain point. That is part of your ultimate treatment, and it shall be your ultimate reward." He came to a halt behind her, hands on his hips, towering over her as she continued her frantic pace. "And do you know what that point is?" he said, as his voice rose further still. "Do you *know*"?

His voice was now a violent shout.

"Only when you beg me for it!" he raged. "Then, and only then! All that you want, everything within easy reach—but first you must *beg*!"

285

He turned suddenly and stormed from the room. Jacqueline was oblivious to the sound of his steps. Rowing frantically, she stroked more furiously than ever . . . faster, faster, and faster.

Chapter Nineteen

The plane flight westward was every bit as nerve wracking as the return drive from upstate. Hours before, in the dreary light of first dawn, Manley had torn wildly across the Whitestone Bridge and headed straight for the airport.

It had been a lightning decision. Once he found the airline ticket in the stranger's pocket, there was never any question in his mind as to what he would do. While the van shot southward through the darkness, he hastily outlined his intentions to Sheila. He would confront Hume with what he knew—the obscure medical discoveries, the attempt on his life, and the hint of Hume's complicity—in the hope that the boldness of his unexpected intrusion—underscored by the blatant facts he planned to reveal—would persuade Hume to let Jacqueline go.

His hope was based on the expectation that the weight of evidence alone would be sufficiently persuasive. If it weren't, he anticipated that Hume would find the additional threat of exposure quite compelling. However, the integrity of Hume's thought processes—his logic and sanity—were essential to the plan. If it proved suspect, there was no telling what the man might do. That was the risk Manley had to take.

He hadn't originally intended to take Sheila. Speed was paramount, and he knew that he could move more quickly without her. Still, dropping her off in the city would require an additional hour of precious time. It was an hour he couldn't spare. Then, too, Sheila insisted on accompanying him, arguing that her knowledge of Hume would prove helpful. Anyway, she said, weren't their bags already packed? Grudgingly, Manley agreed to let her come.

Once at the airport, he had Sheila park while he raced into the terminal. He paced apprehensively before the ticket counter, suffering through the ticket agent's observations about how fortunate Manley was to find two last-minute cancelations on an already booked flight. Manley wasn't listening; his state of agitation wouldn't allow it. Finally, after what seemed like an interminable wait, they boarded.

He marveled at Sheila's composure. Much earlier, during their nighttime drive, she had dozed off just outside of Albany. He found it incredible that she could sleep at a time like this. To him, the mental strain was unbearable. Yet despite the unsteadiness of the ride, Sheila had remained asleep until he roused her at the airport. Now, no sooner were they airborne than she nodded off again.

He waved away the flight attendant who brought their meals. He was far too excited to eat, and there was no sense waking Sheila. He fidgeted incessantly in his seat, wishing that the flight were over, rehearsing what he would say to Hume. With an hour left in the flight, high over Utah, the jet began its slow descent.

Sheila awakened when the plane touched down. Manley couldn't remember the last time he'd slept. It didn't matter; his high-strung tension vanquished his fatigue. The aircraft was still taxiing when he leaped into the aisle. He pushed his way through the forward passengers, mumbling apologies, pulling Sheila by the hand. No sooner had they deplaned than he charged through the airport, simply telling Sheila to wait for him at the terminal's exit.

It was early afternoon. Outside, the concrete was hot underfoot in the bright sun. As he dashed toward a uniformed porter, Manley pulled the printed stub from his pocket. The skycap pointed the way toward parking lot C, and Manley raced away, dodging trucks and prancing wildly among taxis. The lot was a long way off. His breath was a wheezing rasp by the time he reached it. He slowed, examining the vehicle registration he'd stored in his wallet.

He quickly scoured the rows of parked cars, searching

for the license plate whose imprint matched that in his hand. The parking lot was vast. His eyes darted among the vehicles, and he cursed under his breath as the minutes passed. Finally, after a seemingly endless search, he came upon it in a middle row. He stopped and slowly ran his eyes the length of the long black limousine.

He fumbled for the orderly's keys, found them, and quickly unlocked the van. The windows were made of a deeply tinted glass that enabled one to gaze outside, though looking inward was impossible. He jumped behind the wheel. Behind him, a partition of firm plexiglass separated the driver from the rear passenger seat. Several unusual plastic devices were affixed to the dashboard. Their appearance puzzled him, but he hadn't time to dwell on their possible functions.

He turned the key. The engine coughed, then spluttered and died. Manley muttered an epithet, pressed the accelerator to the floor, and tried the ignition again. This time the motor roared to life. He engaged the transmission and gunned the auto out of its space and toward the exit, spewing dust and cinders in his wake. He brought the limo to a screeching halt beside the attendant's booth. The seated man yawned and reached for the proffered stub.

"Radar on the ramps, amigo," he warned, reaching for the stub and twenty-dollar bill.

Manley ignored the admonition, examining the registration while the attendant made change. The car was registered to an address on a rural route that meant nothing to him.

"What's the quickest way to Villa Park?"

"Past Anaheim, out near El Modena?"

"I don't know."

"Nothing's quick," the man shrugged, dragging deeply on his joint. Sweetish smoke curled from his nostrils. "But you might try the San Diego Freeway."

Manley left the booth and followed the signs that directed him back to the terminal. He pulled up in front of Sheila moments later, hurriedly waving her inside. She barely had time to close the door before the vehicle leaped forward again.

"San Sebastian should be somewhere near a place called Villa Park," he said. "Beyond Anaheim."

"Disneyland?" she asked, with a sideways glance that preceded a frown of contemplation. "Or is Anaheim baseball?"

He gave her an exasperated look.

"Sheila, just let me know if anything looks familiar."

She eyed the other cars as they coursed through the crowded airport traffic.

"Everyone looks so disgustingly cheerful."

"Just keep your eyes open."

She blinked repeatedly.

"I would if it weren't for this frightful smog. What a squalid city."

"Actresses are supposed to love it here."

"What a loathsome thought."

He sped along the service road, examining the dozens of signs overhead, despairing at their complexity. He grew hopelessly confused; it was becoming apparent that he had no chance of reaching his destination without a map. He spotted a service station and headed for it, veering wildly across two lanes of traffic. Exiting, he skidded to a halt and leaped from the car. He darted into the station's office and was out again before the startled attendant at the pump could ask him what he wanted. Within seconds, they were back on the highway.

He handed Sheila the map of metropolitan Los Angeles. She quickly unfolded it and spread it out on the seat between them, searching for the best route. She underlined the street index with her forefinger, falling back against the upholstery when the car careened forward.

Finally she found it, making a crease in the paper with her thumbnail. She told him it appeared that the area they were looking for was not in Villa Park proper, but rather in an isolated mesa that bordered the distant Santa Ana Mountains. She figured it to be thirty miles away—no more than a speck on the map, but fortunately a rather direct drive. Manley glanced at the area she indicated and floored the accelerator.

He drove southeast, following her instructions. He nervously surveyed both sides of the roadway, beyond which the awesome sprawl called Los Angeles slumbered in a dreamlike aura of smog. He cursed the seemingly boundless acreage as the limousine hurtled forward, finally turning northward along the Newport Freeway.

"There," Sheila pointed out. "Take that exit."

He left the freeway and followed a series of increasingly barren streets that ultimately led to Santiago Canyon Road, a narrower highway that plunged them into a wide expanse of unpopulated terrain. Sheila suddenly leaned forward in animation.

"This is the road," she said. "I remember it."

Manley scanned the horizon of a land part scrub plain, part desert, speckled with the sparse growth of an occasional yucca, chaparral, and coastal sagebrush.

"Do you see it anywhere?"

"I think it's a few miles ahead. On the left."

His throat grew dry. He sped onward, tightly gripping the wheel. Seconds later, a small red light began to blink on and off from its mount beside the ashtray. Sheila leaned back, startled.

"My God, we're beeping."

Manley eyed the plastic box out of the corner of his eye. A faint stencil of lettering was now illuminated in the flickering red glow.

"What does it say underneath the light?"

She bent forward.

"Looks like " 'Main Gate.' "

"What would that be?"

She lifted her eyes, reflecting.

"There *was* a sort of iron grillwork, I think."

She briefly hazarded a description of the Spa's exterior. No sooner had she finished than a plot of green appeared in the distance, in stark contrast to the surrounding wasteland. The sculpted hedgerows grew more distinct, as did the classic marble building in the center of the acreage. Soon he drew abreast of it and momentarily slowed at the turnoff to the Spa's long driveway. Then he drove on, still mindful of the red light's flashing. Sheila was surprised that he continued.

"Where are you going?"

"This is supposed to be a surprise, remember? I'm not going to advertise our arrival—especially in his car. Just keep your eyes peeled."

"For what?"

"A billboard, a wrecked car, whatever. Anyplace to hide this thing."

A quarter mile ahead, Manley suddenly drew to a stop, enveloping the car in a thick swirl of yellow dust. A dense clump of tall cactus huddled just off the road. It wasn't exactly what he had in mind, but it would do. Without hesitation, he drove off the road's shoulder and steered carefully over ruts and stones until the vehicle was nestled in the angular shadows of cacti limbs.

He took a deep breath and looked at Sheila.

"Ready?"

"Yes," she nodded.

He hesitated and lightly touched her hand.

"Sheila, if anything should happen to—"

"I don't want to discuss it," she interrupted. "Everything is going to be fine. We'll be back with Jackie in no time."

"You sound convinced. Did they teach optimism in acting school?"

"Naturally. And they taught self-confidence, too," she said encouragingly.

"All right, then. Let's go."

There was a black plastic button beneath the red light. Manley pressed it, and the blinking ceased. He got out of the car and locked the door. He took Sheila by the hand. Walking arm in arm, they headed back along the highway toward whatever awaited them at San Sebastian.

Hume returned after several minutes. Jacqueline's frantic rowing continued unabated. In her diminished capacity to understand, she had come to believe that her salvation was dependent on the vigor and fury of her exercising—though whether that salvation was to be from the ravages of her appetite or from the increasingly bizarre demands of Dr. Hume she could no longer tell. He walked over and positioned himself by her apparatus as if there had been no outburst at all.

"Wonderful, Jacqueline," he beamed, applauding lightly. "Gradually lessen the pace and we shall move on to the next station."

Her stroking slowed, as much from exhaustion as from his request. Still, the sound of his words was reassuring, for he had used the wonderfully soothing tone to which she was accustomed. Panting, she leaned forward and rested her arms lightly on the oars. With Hume's assistance, she struggled to her feet. He led her stumbling to the next machine, where she collapsed in numbness and fatigue.

The gymnasium housed an elaborate, custom-built group of progressive-resistance exercise machines. As the day wore on, Hume supervised Jacqueline's exercise circuit. Her obvious exhaustion did nothing to deter him. And the more he praised her diligence, the more her self-delusion was perpetuated. By early afternoon she had done thousands of repetitions without a break. From a small room beyond the gymnasium, Hume observed her in satisfaction, returning periodically to offer encouragement.

A buzzer sounded. Hume was expecting no one. He surveyed the video monitors around him and observed that everything in the spa's other wing was proceeding normally. Then he walked down the special wing's corridor, following its bends until he arrived at its junction with the brightly lit main entry foyer. He waited in the shadows of a broad marble pillar and peered down the driveway. The Spa's wide gates had mechanically opened, yet there was no vehicle in sight. Had it been a malfunction? For several minutes he peered suspiciously toward the roadway. He was about to close the gates with one of the controls at his fingertips when the two intruders boldly entered the gates and proceeded down the driveway.

Hume leaned forward, eyeing them intently. At that distance, he could discern only that they were a man and a woman. He scrutinized the man from head to toe but did not recognize him. Then he turned his attention to the woman. As she neared, his eyes opened in surprise. It was Miss Hastings.

Hume hurriedly glanced in the direction of the gymnasium, from which the sounds of exercise continued uninterrupted. Reassured, he returned his attention to the approaching man. Yet after several more seconds of intense examination, the visitor remained a stranger. Hume kept to the shadows and quickly retraced his steps. Reentering the special wing's gymnasium, he interrupted one of Jacqueline's routines with a soft touch and radiant smile.

She looked up at him in dumb insensibility. Hume lifted one of her hands and clasped it in his own.

"You are doing superbly, Jacqueline," he encouraged. "The progress you are making is remarkable. You may not feel it, but my years of experience convince me that the treatments are coming along much faster than I anticipated."

The bags under her sagging lids were deep olive crescents. Yet there was a moonbeam's glimmer of hope in her spent eyes. Faint though it was, Hume saw it and seized the opportunity, squeezing her hand more emphatically than ever.

"You *must* not interrupt the treatments under any circumstances," he gently cautioned. "To do so would be to lose everything. No matter what happens, just continue as you are, and I promise you that you shall soon achieve a state of being the likes of which you have never before known."

Smiling with a godlike beneficence, he gently released her hand before he turned and walked slowly from the room.

❧

They were scant feet from the marble steps when he appeared, clad in a rich damask suit of the purest white linen. Wearing a placid smile, he slowly stepped out from among the pillars and extended his arms their way in a warm, pontifical gesture. Manley halted, growing profoundly uneasy.

"Miss Hastings," Hume intoned. "Your arrival is unexpected—but, as always, more than welcome."

Caught off guard, Manley turned away from the gleaming smile to look at his companion. Sheila opened her mouth to speak but hesitated, unquestionably shaken. Her lips pursed, trembled, and remained silent.

"And who might this gentleman be?" Hume continued, shifting his radiance toward Manley.

Manley gazed at the smiling face. When Hume's azure eyes fixed on his, Manley's initial impulse was one of fear—the impulse of the startled woodland deer that, though momentarily frozen, soon bolts for the cover of the forest. Yet as he returned the man's stare, Manley's instincts gave way to an influence far more persuasive: conscious thought. It was the thought of recognition, of intellectual awareness. He suddenly realized that he *knew* that look. He had seen that same smiling expression, in varying degrees, countless times before, from the very first days of his training in psychiatry. He had seen it in the eyes of the manic, before the lithium enters the bloodstream; in the eyes of the psychotically depressed, before electroshock convulses the brain; and in the eyes of the shrieking murderer, before the straightjacket can be tightened. And in that instant, he knew.

This man belongs in an institution.

That dark moment of understanding completely destroyed Manley's plans. His hoped-for appeal to reason, the threats, the hints of exposure—became so many grains of sand in the surf, washed away in the nightmarish tide of Hume's madness.

Slowly, he cautioned. Go slowly.

"Dr. Hume, I am Dr. Manley."

He delivered the message with precision, in an even tone that didn't vary. He kept his expression calm and unchanging, careful not to look away or to scrutinize too intently. His arms hung loosely at his sides, a body language that said nothing. At that moment, the whole purpose of Manley's being was to project a posture of absolute and unruffled neutrality—a posture from which he might progress, with a little skill and a lot more luck, to a posture of reassurance.

He wondered if Sheila noticed it. He also wondered if she was even watching, for he could hardly afford the luxury of turning to look at her. Yet Manley had seen it:

the instant he mentioned his own name, the muscles around Hume's smiling lips perceptibly tightened, and the finest of lines indented the corners of his eyes. His nostrils faintly flared in warning. And then, just as quickly, the subtle changes vanished. Still wearing his smile, Hume slowly lowered his left arm while keeping his right extended in handshake.

Oh, he is good, Manley thought. *A clever fucking lunatic.*

"A distinct pleasure, Dr. Manley," Hume continued. "I have looked forward to meeting you."

Without taking his eyes from Hume's, Manley reached out. The handshake would be unusual, he knew: most often the grip was overly firm, a pretense of power that didn't exist. Hume's cool fingers encircled his. Surprisingly, the grasp proved remarkably limp. Manley waited for the palm squeeze, but it didn't come; after which he was careful to allow Hume to be the first to terminate the handshake.

"We would like to speak with Miss Ramsey, if you don't mind."

Hume's smiling equanimity didn't waver.

"How unusual," he said slowly. "She led me to believe her visit was something of a secret. I wasn't aware you knew she was here. Did she tell you she was coming?"

"Not exactly. But she spoke about your remarkable work very often, and I know how much she respects you. It stood to reason that she had come here."

"Indeed. . . . I'm afraid, however, that Miss Ramsey is undergoing treatment now. As I'm sure Miss Hastings is aware," he continued, flashing an icy glance her way, "it is the policy at San Sebastian not to allow visitors. I have found that such interruptions have a detrimental effect on the patient's progress. Perhaps I could give her a message?"

Even without looking, Manley felt Sheila staring at him in incredulity. He knew that she didn't understand—that she had been expecting words far, far different.

"Couldn't you make an exception in her case?" Manley went on. "Consider it a request from one professional to another. We promise not to keep her very long."

Hume raised his palms apologetically, and his smile was replaced by an expression of regret.

"I would truly love to, but . . . . Might I inquire what it is that you find so urgent?"

Manley allowed himself an obsequious smile.

"It's simply that Jacqueline hasn't been well lately. We're very worried about her. I'm confident she's in excellent hands, but we'd feel much better if we could just say hello. I'm sure you appreciate our concern."

"Yes, of course. I can well understand your interest. Still, in cases such as this, one must weigh the advantages of the visit against the disadvantages of the interruption, just as if it were a medication that one considered discontinuing." He momentarily paused and looked away, as if in decision, and then turned back, giving his head a polite shake. "I'm afraid I cannot allow it. Could you return at the completion of her treatment, perhaps?"

Sheila, who had been silent up to that point, suddenly spoke out.

"*Two weeks?* You must be out of your—"

"He's right," Manley interrupted, instantly seizing her by the wrist, squeezing it to still her protest. "It might be better if we waited." He gave Hume a deferential look. "Thanks for your time. We appreciate your seeing us."

He tried to pull Sheila away, but she wouldn't budge.

"Have you lost your *mind*?" Sheila blurted at Manley. "Did you forget about the orderly? What about the injections, the—"

"*Sheila*," Manley commanded, insistently glaring at her over his grin. But it was too late. Out of the corner of his eye, he could see Hume flinch, stung by the nettle in her words. The smile left Hume's face, and he straightened up, bristling. His tone was a curious lamination of indignation and concern.

"Orderly?" he said, a cold fire blazing in his eyes. "What orderly?"

Manley laughed submissively, pretending a joke.

"The other day we met a man Sheila thought was your chief orderly." His mind whirled frantically, desperate for the right explanation, yet searching at the same time for

297

some sort of plan. "Naturally, I assured her that she was mistaken. A man of your reputation couldn't possibly be involved in such . . . threats."

"What threats?"

Manley was fawningly apologetic, all mollification.

"It was nothing important, believe me," he shrugged. "I don't know why, but she claimed that you had something to hide," he went on, staring intently at Hume, "and that you wouldn't let us see Jacqueline. Of course, I argued that you did not. And now, after hearing what you have to say, I'm more convinced of it than ever." He paused. "That *is* true, isn't it?"

Hume wore a furtive look. His eyes were snake eyes, a rope of coiled indecision.

"Naturally."

"There," Manley said, turning to Sheila. "Believe me now? Come on—let Jack finish her treatments, and we'll come back for her later. Let's go." He turned back to Hume. "I appreciate your seeing us, Dr. Hume. Sorry to have taken up your time."

"Not at all."

Sheila was numb. Manley pulled her away and began slowly walking down the driveway.

"I'm sure there's a six o'clock flight," he bantered. "I bet if—"

"Dr. Manley," Hume called.

Manley stopped and turned, raising his eyebrows in idle curiosity.

"Yes?"

"For some reason, I have the strangest feeling you are not convinced."

"Don't be ridiculous. Your word is good enough for me."

"Would you truly be persuaded if you saw Miss Ramsey for yourself and observed that she was well?"

Manley's heart nearly stopped; then, quivering though he was, he struggled to remain aloof.

Steady, old boy. Steady.

"That's really not necessary, Dr. Hume. I don't want you to think that—"

"To paraphrase your words, as one colleague to another."

"Well . . ."

"Wait here. I shall return shortly." He abruptly turned and walked into the building.

Once Hume was out of sight, Manley closed his eyes, leaned his head back, and sighed with incalculable relief. Sheila, however—momentarily silent—became incensed. She put her hands on her hips and glowered at him indignantly.

"What the hell are you doing? Wasn't it your idea to—"

Her voice was dangerously loud. Manley looked worriedly at the building and quickly clamped his palm over her mouth.

"Shut up. Don't move; don't make a sound. When I let go, keep your voice to a whisper. Understand?"

She didn't, but she nodded agreement anyway. He slid his hand from her lips, staring at her incessantly. His hushed speech was rapid.

"Just listen, Sheila. There's not much time. That man in there—Hume, or whoever the hell he is—is totally, completely, stark ravingly mad. And not your ordinary mad hatter, either. He's—"

"But how can you say that? I'm starting to think that if anybody's nuts, it's—"

"Goddammit!" he shot. "Didn't I tell you to listen? *Please*, Sheila. You've got to trust me on this. I know what I'm talking about—it's my job. I've seen thousands of lunatics before, but none so completely insane as he. I don't care *what* he looks like. Something happened, and his mind is gone. He's bonkers, totally psycho. Worse than that, he's downright dangerous."

"What on earth are you talking about?"

"Oh, Christ, just listen! This Hume . . ." He looked wildly about, searching for the proper words, "How should I put it? He's . . . unpredictable. He's a time bomb, volatile, ready to explode. For all I know he could have a knife—a gun, even—and start blasting away any second. Don't look at me that way—I'm *telling* you, he could crack at any instant. So please, Sheila. I'm *begging* you. Don't do anything—*anything*—that might provoke him."

"But what about Jackie? How can we help her by just walking away?"

"We're not. Don't you understand, the whole point is to be able to get to see her, and to convince Hume he has nothing to fear from us. We can't do anything until then."

"And when we do?"

"Just follow my lead. Let me work on Hume's ego while you draw Jack into conversation. Once you're talking, see if you can slowly steer her down the driveway. I'll try to keep Hume distracted. I think I can take care of him once you're far enough away. But whatever you do, don't say *anything* that could upset him. Agreed?"

Sheila was overwhelmed. She didn't know what to say.

"Yes, I suppose. But what if—"

She stopped speaking at the sound of approaching footsteps. Manley eased away from her, slowly turning in the direction of the pillars. Yet what they both saw wrenched at the core of their very beings. They silently stood there, open mouthed and gaping, at the image that drew near—at the sight of Jacqueline listlessly shuffling behind Hume like a tethered animal being led to market for slaughter.

"Oh my God in heaven," Manley whispered.

It was worse than he had ever expected. He had anticipated her physical condition—the sallow and swollen cheeks, skin waxy and cadaverous; the recessed eyes, sunken into tunnels of pitch. But he was totally unprepared for her mental state, for the eyes that looked vacuously ahead, numb and unseeing, in an expression of shocked and witless idiocy. Appalled, he and Sheila exchanged pitiful looks of helplessness.

Hume walked closer, his smile now a self-satisfied smirk.

"As you can see," he resumed, "there is no cause for concern. Miss Ramsey is somewhat tired, but otherwise none the worse for wear. I trust this satisfies your curiosity." He paused, eyeing them with a patient grin. Then he turned to Jacqueline. "Come, Jacqueline. We shall resume where we left off."

He prepared to lead her away when Sheila felt compelled to act. Seizing the opportunity, she quickly ascended the steps and took hold of Jacqueline's limp hands, staring plaintively into her deadened eyes. Manley, meanwhile, was immediately at Hume's side, speaking in terms of glowing admiration.

"This is very kind, but not the least bit necessary. I never once doubted you. In fact, from what I've seen, I'm very impressed. Even a little in awe of this place." From out of the corner of his eye, he could see Sheila gently helping Jacqueline down the steps. Everything was timing, now; Sheila *had* to get Jacqueline at least ten yards away. He continued his rapid chatter. "I know this may be an imposition, but I'd be grateful if I could see your facilities. Could you possibly spare a moment to show me around?"

Hume regarded him quizzically. Just out of earshot, Sheila's verbalization with Jacqueline was a frantic whisper.

"Jackie, honey, we're leaving. Smile, darling. Don't say anything, and don't turn around. Just keep . . . on . . . walking."

Though seemingly in a trance, Jacqueline abruptly tensed at Sheila's suggestion. She hesitated and gazed at her friend through blinded eyes. Sheila tugged harder and continued her hushed prodding.

"Not much farther, Jacqueline. Just keep moving and everything will be all right."

Hume finally gave Manley his considered reply.

"I don't think a tour would be appropriate just now. Perhaps in two weeks, when you return."

Manley cajoled, moving his hands in a gesture of supplication.

"Not even the exercise area? I'd really feel privileged. I promise not to take much of your time."

Hume saw them then, inching farther down the driveway. He turned to see what was happening—while Manley, heart racing, struggled to keep one eye on Hume and the other on the women. He braced himself and subtly shifted all his weight to his rear foot.

"Jacqueline?" Hume said, clearly puzzled by her straying.

The two women stopped. Sheila turned in uncertainty, shooting Manley a look of desperation. Manley frowned at her and insistently shook his head up and down, a signal that she should continue. Sheila tightened her grip and immediately pulled Jacqueline away.

Hume glowered darkly and descended the first marble step.

"Jacqueline, I insist that you—"

Manley rocked forward. He transferred his weight and simultaneously threw all his power into his upper arm and shoulder. The looping punch struck Hume flush on the jaw, and the older man went sprawling.

Hume rolled backward among the pillars. Manley leaped down the steps and sprinted furiously toward Sheila.

"Run!" he exhorted.

Far beyond the scuffle, the spearlike open gates beckoned at the driveway's entrance. Hearing Manley's command, Sheila lurched forward, dragging Jacqueline by the wrist, pulling her through the gravel. In seconds Manley drew astride them. He seized Jacqueline's free arm and pulled her forcibly ahead.

In her dazed insensibility, Jacqueline did little to help them; yet Manley knew that as long as she didn't resist, they stood a chance. He and Sheila pulled unrelentingly and were soon halfway there. The entrance loomed up before them, growing more and more distinct in the dust and haze ahead. Manley began to feel confident. If the gates remained open, they would make it.

"Jacqueline!" The roar arose from behind them. "Without the treatments, you are nothing!"

Manley glanced over his shoulder and saw that Hume was struggling to his feet. Astonishingly, at the sound of Hume's words, Jacqueline's legs went rigid. She planted her heels in the gravel, impeding their progress; and pull though they might, they soon slowed to a halt. Manley was beside himself.

"Jack, what are you doing? For God's sake, let's go!"

Behind them, Hume had arisen. This time his shout rippled their way with insidious confidence.

"The treatments, Jacqueline. Only I can give you the treatments. There is no other."

"Don't listen to him! The man's insane. He wants to kill you!"

In her hesitation, a glimmer of awareness flickered in Jacqueline's eyes, and she seemed to recognize her companions. Torn in indecision, she looked at Sheila and then back at Hume, who was slowly beginning to retreat into the shadows of the pillars. Manley watched with apprehension as Hume reached up toward something hidden from view.

Without waiting to see what would happen, Manley bent forward and scooped Jacqueline into his arms. He immediately broke into a run, straining to carry Jacqueline across the uneven bits of fiery gravel.

"The gate!" Sheila screamed.

The double iron grills began to close. Manley watched them in sickening desperation, and his legs pumped like pistons as he charged toward the narrowing entrance. Sheila raced frantically behind, kicking up bits of rock and pebble. Yet fifteen yards from their goal, they realized it was too late. The metal gates slammed closed with a resounding clang.

His lungs were aching, and his breath was a fiery rasp. Sweating heavily, he slowed in a defeated halt and lowered Jacqueline to the ground, still holding her by the wrist. He looked over his shoulder. He could see Hume walking slowly their way. Manley turned giddily toward the twelve-foot fence. Perhaps if he and Sheila could somehow lift Jacqueline over . . . But when he tried to drag her forward, she tensed once again. He breathed an agonizing sigh. Without her cooperation, it was hopeless.

When he neared them, Hume halted, rubbing his jaw slowly.

"An impressive display of bravado," he said. "I enjoyed it immensely."

Manley gazed at him with clenched teeth, wearing a look of naked hate. He started toward Hume, and his hands balled into fists.

"You bastard."

The side of Hume's suit was smudged where he had fallen. As Manley neared, Hume casually reached into his streaked pocket and pulled out a small pistol, which he leveled at Manley's chest. Manley continued nonetheless.

"Rick!"

Sheila grasped his arm with both hands and held him back.

"Do let him go, Miss Hastings. It would be a distinct pleasure to shoot him."

"Your orderly already tried that," Manley snapped.

"Ah, yes. I gathered as much when he did not report back. I must credit your resourcefulness, Dr. Manley. Still, I am unquestionably acting within the law now, protecting myself from a violent intruder who has broken into my property and assaulted me."

Manley tried to control his fury, all the while staring at Hume's rabid eyes. Finally, he yielded to Sheila's insistent tugging. There was no point getting killed at the hands of a maniac.

"More than a dozen people know we're here," he braved. "And half that number have been told your secret. I don't think shooting me would do a hell of a lot for your chances."

"I have no intention of shooting you, Dr. Manley. Both of you are more than free to go. The sooner, I might add, the better."

Manley and Sheila exchanged looks of befuddlement. Insane though Hume might be, he suddenly appeared remarkably more lucid and calculating than Manley thought possible.

"And what about Jacqueline? How long do you think you can keep her here?"

"No longer than she desires. Miss Ramsey came to San Sebastian of her own volition. She is similarly free to leave, whenever she chooses."

"You're joking."

"Am I? Why don't you ask her?"

The reply was one Manley had never anticipated. Although Jacqueline's freedom of choice in making the trip was open to question, he took it as given that she was now a virtual prisoner. Her moribund appearance underscored that belief, but it also made Hume's bold contention all the more astounding. There was no question that Jacqueline would . . . And yet, Manley reminded himself, hadn't he committed a similar blunder moments earlier, when he assumed Jacqueline would cooperate with their plans for escape?

He walked over to her and gently grasped her slouching shoulders. He gazed into her tired eyes and tried by force of thought to inculcate the words that she would answer.

"Jack," he began patiently. "Jack . . . Sheila and I have come to take you home."

There was an innocence to her gray and dismal look, but in it, he also read defeat and submission, an expression of pathos that made him sick with despair. His mind worked frantically, seeking those words of substance and meaning that might get through to her.

"He's trying to trick you, Jack. He's lied to you before, and he's lying to you now. Don't listen to him! You can't lose weight by staying here," he pleaded. "All you can lose is your life."

He saw it, then, the fleeting clearing in the fog of her unconsciousness when he alluded to her weight. Her weight had always been the cornerstone of her existence.

"He is *hurting* your weight," Manley argued. "If you stay here, you'll . . . He can't help you anymore, Jack. *Please* come home with us, with the people who care for you most. It's the only way."

Her willful attempt at concentration was obvious to all, a subtle shifting of nearly frozen mental gears. When Hume grew aware of it, he swiftly interjected in deeply resounding tones.

"The treatments, Jacqueline. Your treatments are the only—"

"Shut up, dammit!" Manley bellowed. "If she has such a choice, let her make it without interrupting!"

The smiling expression that returned to Hume's face was unruffled in explanation.

"I think her choice is quite apparent. Jacqueline fully understands that she must not interrupt her treatments at any cost."

"Damn your vile mouth!"

Hume ignored him. He approached Jacqueline with smiling confidence.

"Isn't that right, Jacqueline? Show these people your decision by returning inside."

She hesitated for the briefest moment, then slowly began to slip from Manley's grasp.

"Jack, don't trust him! For God's sake, *listen* to me!"

Hume continued before she had another opportunity to hesitate.

"The gymnasium, Jacqueline. We shall resume your treatments there shortly."

She completed her wooden pirouette. With her back to them, she resumed her tortured, mechanical shuffle toward the Spa's white facade. With Hume smiling radiantly, Manley and Sheila watched in agonizing silence as Jacqueline ultimately reached the wide marble steps and inched up the veranda.

Manley was overcome with pain. When Jacqueline was nearly out of sight, he screamed her name one last, grief-stricken time, but to no avail. She disappeared into the confines of the building.

"Really, Dr. Manley," Hume said, shaking his head in a smirking rebuke. "Such behavior. Can't you see how upsetting it proves to my patient?"

He gave a disdainful little bow—then turned and began the contemptuous stroll of that most feared of executioners: not he who, shrouded, wields the axe, but he who lops the very hope off his victims, there to leave it rotting in the sun.

306

Chapter Twenty

She was beyond the realm of physical feeling. Her muscles were a lanyard of knots, her sinews so strained that they had long ago passed through the barrier of bodily pain and entered the domain of insensibility. It was evening, and yet still she exercised. Curiously, the once agonizing repetitions were now an anesthetic. Each monotonous cycle was a dram of narcotic that kept alive the frail hallucination of her hopes.

Having to attend to his usual responsibilities in the spa's other wing, Hume had left the gym an hour before with an encouraging admonition to keep exercising. As she did so, the butterfly of her consciousness fluttered between dream-like reverie and senseless stupor. In her dreams, she was thin: prancing onstage, talking with friends, dancing with admirers. It had been hours since someone had come to visit—she could no longer remember who—and an eternity before that when Hume had . . . had . . .

She couldn't remember. Her head rolled loosely on her shoulders, sightless eyes opening and closing like those of a puppet, as her enervated torso rocked to and fro. The only sound was the well-oiled mechanical voice of her apparatus.

It began faintly, a crinkling noise like the distant rustling of cellophane. Jacqueline didn't hear it at first, but as the sound perceptibly loudened, it crept into her mind, working through her subconscious to the higher centers of her brain. Her dull eyes remained open in a tense and growing awareness. She could hear it clearly now. The crackling continued to intensify, bringing with it a return of her fear. Her frightened eyes darted about the room, searching for the source of the noise. It was nowhere, and yet it was everywhere, growing louder with each passing second. As the noise increased, so did her terror, for she now recognized that sound: not crinkling, as she first thought, but the sibilance of sizzling, of roasting, of . . . *frying*.

The room suddenly went dark. On a wall opposite her, a dazzling square of white light appeared. There was a faint mechanical whir and the clicking noise of something being processed, sounds muted by the unmistakable acoustics of cooking. All at once, a bright photographic image illuminated the brilliant white square.

It was a vivid color picture of food at a picnic. Accentuated by the background sizzling, it depicted succulent pieces of chicken roasting on a grill, side by side with browning links of plump sausage growing crisp in its own juices. At any other time, the photographic image would have seemed festive. Now it was positively horrifying.

Jacqueline's eyes widened into terrified ovals, and her sharp intake of breath was a strident spasm of suffocation. She stumbled off her exercise machine, lurching involuntarily forward, torn between the impulse to run and the intoxicating allure of the photo. The decision was not hers to make. In the next instant, all her senses focused on the photographic feast, and the feeling of hunger she had managed to suppress returned with convulsive suddenness.

It was a savage feeling of insatiability. Her gaze riveted on the wall, she shuffled toward it, consumed with a craving that overpowered her. As she proceeded hypnotically forward, the vivid image died, and the wall went blank. There was another click, and a shaft of pale light pierced the darkness, this time coming to shine on the wall behind her. Jacqueline turned in stupefaction while the background sounds of cooking continued. The new picture was of pots simmering on a stove: rich stews, sumptuous casseroles. Compelled beyond thought or reason, Jacqueline abruptly changed direction and was drawn toward the beckoning image.

One by one the color slides vanished, each replaced by a picture of another meal equally delectable. The sequence of their appearance led her in a trail, from the gymnasium into the hall, and from there toward the dining room. Jacqueline's hunger had grown beyond comprehension. Driven by mouth-watering compulsion, her shuffling progressed to an unsteady run, an ambling, drunken gait that sent her reeling through the corridors. As she entered the dining area, the assault on her senses was complete: there, joining the sights and sounds, was the tantalizing aroma she had smelled the night before.

The darkened hall suddenly blazed with shafts of light beamed from overhead tracks. The spotlights converged on the long and narrow table that was once again covered with a cloth like white silk. And as before, the table was festooned with the makings of an elaborate holiday banquet.

A little cry escaped her, a keening whimper of agony. She sank to her knees, fighting the tears no less than she fought her searing hunger. Bit by bit, she crawled forward, knowing as she did that her struggle would soon cease in an orgy of gluttonous consumption.

Scant feet before the table, her progress was impeded by a barrier. It was a partition of sorts, a clear plastic divider. She pawed at it frantically, scratching it with her nails.

Crying openly now, pushing against the partition, she let her forehead sink to the marble floor. Why, oh why, was he making it so difficult?

"Please," she whimpered, no longer caring, beyond the reach of hope.

His voice thundered in condemnation, a roar of indignant wrath that split the white silence of the room.

"But first you must beg!"

He was nowhere, and yet he was everywhere, as the resonant echo of his command reverberated throughout the chamber. A small pool of Jacqueline's tears wet the cold marble that touched her cheek, and she exhaustedly pursed her lips in the act of terminal humiliation.

"I beg you," she faintly pleaded. "I beg you."

There came another soft whir and a cool stirring of air. The partition soared upward, sliding above her fingertips. Jacqueline raised her weary face. Moving slowly at first, and then with a rabid frenzy, she scrambled impatiently forward, mindless of the incessant pealing of laughter all about her.

∾

"Should I boost you up?"

He tugged on the rope, felt it secure.

"Just wait in the car and be ready when I need you."

Helplessly, "Right."

As Sheila retreated to the limousine, Manley pushed through the dense cyprus hedge and planted one of his feet on the vertical fence. He sucked in his breath, pushed off, and slowly began to climb, his shoes walking up the metal as he grasped the stout rope hand over fist. Halfway up, the muscles of his arms and shoulders began to cramp in protest, and he cursed his deplorable physical condition. Fortunately, the fence was not very high. After several more chafing handholds, he reached the upper rampart. Hoisting himself atop it, he steadied his soles on the metal parapet as he clung, crouching, to the spiked rails.

He waited until his labored breathing slowed. The first of his fears was laid to rest the instant he breached the rim of the fence: though he couldn't be certain there was no perimeter alarm system, at least sirens weren't blaring away. He peered through the darkness toward the Spa. At night, San Sebastian was almost completely invisible, with no lamps to illuminate its exterior. In the pale moonlight, the whiteness of its marble walls shone a dim and ghostly gray.

He looked earthward. The carefully tended grass unfolded beneath him like a boundless black carpet. A paratrooper's drop, he told himself; yet inasmuch as he had never bailed out of anything other than high-class entanglements, he found the observation more sobering than reassuring. Before he could dwell on it further, he sprang feet first into the darkness.

He landed off balance and fell heavily onto his shoulder. He winced in discomfort, more stunned than hurt. The grass was dew damp against his cheek. Recovering, he pushed onto elbows and knees and rocked backward into a sprinter's stance. He paused to feel for the two plastic boxes in his pocket. Satisfied that they were in place, he took several calming breaths before springing ahead.

His leather soles were slippery on the damp surface. He tripped several times, but he righted himself before he fell. He ran in a loping jog, leaning forward at the waist, more intent on concealment than on speed. Nearing the circular driveway that bordered the building, he slowed, bent on avoiding the crushed gravel.

Earlier, he and Sheila had tried to determine the building's structural layout. Their conclusions were inferential, based on the little she knew of the interior, Jacqueline's vague description of her separate wing, and what both Manley and Sheila had observed outside. They had no idea where Hume was keeping Jacqueline, though several areas seemed more likely than others. Still, gaining entry was the first order of business.

Keeping to the slick, grassy border, he followed the driveway in its wide and sweeping circle, a curve that eventually led to the rear. When he had discussed strategy with Sheila, he'd pointed out that their limousine was sleek and unblemished, virtually spotless, despite its brief stay at the airport. To Manley, this suggested that it was ordinarily parked indoors, and since there was no such shelter in front of the Spa, he concluded that it had to be somewhere in the rear.

The swath of crushed gravel gradually narrowed when he reached the rear of the structure, merging with blacktop paving that pitched downward under the building. Manley slowed and scrutinized the abutment. Apparently the asphalt ramp led to a concealed underground garage. Satisfied that this was the case, he reached into his pocket and removed the second of the small plastic devices, similar to the one he'd used to open the gate hours before. With a furtive look over his shoulder, he pressed the plastic lever.

Once again he braced himself for alarm sirens, but there were none. The garage's heavy hydraulic door silently rose and disappeared into the contoured roof above. Beyond it, the interior of the garage was unfathomed blackness. Manley crouched lower and stole noiselessly down the ramp into the dark.

Jacqueline lay on her side, unconscious, among half-eaten crusts and toothmarked rinds. Her face was deathly gray, waxen. Every so often her swollen lips pursed and then opened, fishlike, for a pathetically insufficient breath that sounded like a puff. The bulging purplish veins in her neck beat far too slowly to sustain viability. Her sweat-soaked leotard was splattered and stained, a grisly proclamation of self-inflicted horror.

High above the dining room floor, on a narrow circumferential walkway, Hume looked down upon the scene. His thin lips curled into a wry smile. What had befallen Jacqueline was intensely satisfying—even more so, considering her fame and her recognition as an actress; and certainly she was getting what she deserved for refusing to give him his just share of her life. After all, hadn't he created her? Her unexpected visit could have been construed as an omen, had he believed in omens, but he did not: he trusted himself far more than he trusted fate, having grown to respect his nearly divine capabilities ever since that time long ago, when . . . As he gazed downward, his smile turned to a grin, the grin to a leer. How much the woman below resembled that other! His laugh began slowly, a scorning chortle of contempt.

The future promised scores of others, each no less satisfying than this. Indeed, perhaps this might serve as an example to others. Hume's eyes blazed maniacally. Glutted with contented rapture, he slowly looked away and sauntered from his perch.

Chapter Twenty-One

Closed-circuit video monitors were everywhere, hanging darkly from the walls like metallic sentries waiting at attention. As soon as he saw them Manley realized that it was too late to escape their surveillance. If they were in use, he had already been detected. That knowledge freed his movements of indecision, and thus emboldened, he proceeded through the empty garage without hesitation.

A narrow concrete incline angled downward from the room's interior wall. Manley crept up the entry ramp and came upon two doors side by side: one a steel fire door, the other a peculiar platinum-colored entryway. He tried the handle of the second. It was unlocked; turning it, he eased the door ajar. He put his eye to the lintel and peered cautiously past the doorframe. The long, narrow corridor beyond was empty. That was a relief; he began to suspect he'd lucked out and chosen the special wing.

He quietly eased the door closed behind him and made his way into the hall. He walked on the balls of his feet, growing more and more tense with each passing step, his skin chilled, his heart racing. He kept his back to the corridor's interior wall, slinking sideways down the passage. The hallway was illuminated with faint fluorescent lighting. Looking ahead to the end of the corridor, he could dimly make out the outlines of a door. He reached it in quick, deft steps. He doubted Jacqueline was inside; from what Sheila had described, he imagined she was probably at the opposite end of the building. Yet there was absolutely no way of being certain. Nerves taut, he grasped the handle and pushed the door open.

The room was unlit. From the indistinct outlines of the furnishings, Manley gathered it was some sort of office. He swept the walls beside the door with his palm until his fingers found the light switch. He flipped it on, and the room's interior was bathed in pale light. He tiptoed inside.

There was a wide mahogany desk in the center of the room. A handsome leather couch rested before one wall, and a bank of filing cabinets adorned another. The entirety of a third wall was covered with photo enlargements of uniform size. There were at least fifty such pictures, perhaps twice that number. Manley's eyes immediately fixed on a photo of Jacqueline. He walked slowly toward it in mounting curiosity.

The blowup was a view of a theatrical stage, apparently taken from within the audience. The edges of the enlargement were brown with age, and Jacqueline's hairstyle and clothing were oddly out of date. Manley halted in front of the frame and inspected the picture closely. A veil of astonishment slowly blanketed his expression. He suddenly realized that the photo was not a picture of Jacqueline at all, but that of a nearly identical look-alike. Though possessed of a subtle distinction, the woman's features were remarkably similar to Jacqueline's.

Stunned, Manley quickly turned to several photos beside the first. One depicted the same woman, who smiled seductively at the camera as she draped her arm around a male companion. The man was as unattractive as the woman was comely: dark featured, with slick black hair and a conspicuous nose, he had an ineffably sinister look. Still not comprehending, Manley progressed to the third photo in the sequence. Unlike the more glossy blowups, the last was an enlargement of a newspaper clipping. In it, the same man was featured prominently, sitting at a courtroom bench. Manley quickly read the underlying caption. Then the blood drained from his face; ashen, he loosed a spluttering cough and put his hand on the wall for support. Regaining his composure, he hurriedly reread the photo copy—three terse lines which outlined the abortive investigation surrounding a Dr. Robert Emmerich, accused in the murder of his wife.

Mother of God, he thought.

Trembling, he glanced again at the previous photo, for the first time noticing the inscription penned in handwritten scrawl in the lower right hand corner: To Bob and Jean Emmerich. Happy seventeenth anniversary.

Manley felt as if he were suffocating. He quickly looked away, staggered by the discovery, and forced himself to inspect the myriad of other photos. His surprise was gone when he spotted a photo that was unmistakably Jacqueline. Moving on, he thought he recognized a different photo as that of Suzanne Fontaine. Despite the many other enlargements he didn't recognize, it was clear that all the subjects photographed had one thing in common: they were all women. And he felt certain the great bulk of them were actresses.

Though Manley's hurried inspection had consumed less than a minute, it seemed that an eternity had passed. He was about to proceed when his gaze fell on two final pictures, smaller than the rest, mounted in a separate frame. Curious, he inched closer. Each of the pictures depicted two men. One—white coated and balding—struck Manley as hauntingly familiar. He peered at that first enlargement closely, and the instant he spotted the stethoscope protruding from the man's pocket, the realization struck: though he couldn't remember the man's name, he recognized the face as that of a prominent plastic surgeon.

In that same photo, an unsmiling Robert Emmerich was somberly facing the surgeon. Manley quickly examined the other photo, in which the surgeon was shaking hands with yet another man—an individual of height and build identical to Emmerich's.

His mouth went agape. Though the photos bore no inscriptions, they screamed at him with significance. Manley found himself staring in awe at the resculpted face of a smiling Dr. Hume.

Dumbfounded, he turned and walked woodenly across the room. His mind spun. Before and after, he mumbled to himself, repeating the phrase several times as if it were ritualistic liturgy. His body began to shake. All of this, he knew, because of events that went back decades. It was ancient history, buried in the past, the facts dead and forgotten—except in the warped, disjointed mind of one man.

He knew he was procrastinating. By now, Jacqueline could well be dead; at the very best, she was frighteningly near it—and here he was standing like a dolt next to a wall of photographs. He doubted there was anything of further use in the room. Yet, though pressed to leave, his sense of compulsion forced him to sift hurriedly through the file cabinets. It was as he expected: the folders within were patient synopses, each manila jacket bearing a name that matched one of the wall-mounted photos. Studying the folders would be a fascinating evaluation of psychopathology—but damn it to hell, now was not the time!

He left the room and went back into the corridor, rounding the corner where it made a ninety-degree bend. The darkened hall before him was identical to the first. Near its far end, light was emanating from a wide glass window. He crept forward, bent low. Coming even with the window's edge, he held his breath and peered cautiously through the pane.

The twenty-foot chamber glowed with a blue-white light whose glare made him squint. He thought it was produced by unusual fluorescent tubes, but on closer examination, he saw that it streamed from the fixtures of unique ultraviolet sunlamps. While he struggled to comprehend its peculiar meaning, his eyes—now accustomed to the glare—fixed on a most unbelievable spectacle.

He stared in dreamy astonishment toward the center of the radiant glow. A woman was there, a naked woman, whose obese folds rested atop one another like a mound of pleated towels. Manley recognized her at once: an opera singer and sometime actress, she was more renowned for her soprano than her drama. Her eyes were now closed, and she appeared to be asleep, mindless of the dripping intravenous that was firmly taped to one of her arms. Her sightless stupor made him less timorous, and he straightened up in scrutiny.

Her somnolent activity was freakish, that of an un-earthly sleepwalker. Strapped to a machine like an exercise bicycle, her body was in perpetual motion, her limbs moving back and forth in a macabre rowing motion and her pendulous breasts bouncing as her torso rocked to and fro in the sunlamps' brilliant gleam.

He was staggered by the monstrous grotesqueness of the ghostly choreography. He was ready to turn from it when a door opened.

Manley thrust his back to the corridor's wall and stood rigid in the shadows outside the room. Hume entered the room, his eyes shielded by protective goggles. He walked to the side of the exercycle and flipped a toggle switch. The rowing slowed and then halted, freezing the woman's posture.

Hume inverted a vial and inserted the needled tip of a syringe. He aspirated a small amount of the bottle's liquid and replaced the vial in his lab coat pocket. He dabbed the woman's corpulent hip with an alcohol swab and after squirting out residual air bubbles, injected the drug deep into the woman's buttocks. Then he turned on the machine and left the room for one adjacent.

At the sight of the vial, Manley trembled in excitement and apprehension. In that instant, he realized that it had all come down to this. Jacqueline's weight loss, her deterioration, her agony . . . all the result of a bottled cure, a few milliliters of liquid that could either save or destroy, depending on the whims of the madman who controlled it. And it was a bottle that Manley desperately needed to possess.

Hurrying now, he stole past the window's glare. The narrow corridor ended like the first at the perpendicular intersection of yet another hall. Manley quickly rounded its corner and gazed the length of the dark passage. He had proceeded only a few paces when he froze, halting by the glass of another long window. In his haste, he had nearly stumbled right before its floor-to-ceiling pane. Slowly, he quieted himself, remaining just beyond the window's edge.

The blunder was not entirely his fault. Unlike the previous room, this one was dark. Or nearly dark. Slinking against the corridor wall, he crept even with the glass. A faint glow shone from within the room, and its pale beam illuminated the wall by Manley's head. As he inched forward, his eyes were bathed in its dim luminescence. He stopped and peered into the room.

It was some sort of lab. Hume was there, removing the vial and replacing it on the shelf of a refrigerator. Manley watched motionlessly as Hume closed the refrigerator and headed for the corridor exit. Hume opened the door to the hall, stepped into it, and proceeded into the corridor beyond without once looking back in Manley's direction.

Manley stood there, paralyzed, until the sound of Hume's footsteps disappeared. He felt as if a great band were encircling his chest, and as he waited for the tension to lessen, he once again gazed into the room. The flasks and beakers lining the shelves indicated that a complex chemical process was underway. Here and there, the bluish flames of bunsen burners heated a succession of glass containers, all connected with various diameters of rubber tubing.

His eyes flashed toward the refrigerator. His ears sifted the silence for the sound of returning footsteps, but there was none. Then quickly, quietly, he crept to the lab's door. In an instant he was inside, closing the door behind him.

He had to get the drug to Jacqueline. Without hesitation, he opened the refrigerator door and grasped the vial, holding it up to the dim light as he swirled it. The small bottle was nearly empty, containing no more than two cc's of the opaque white liquid.

He hadn't the faintest idea of the proper dose. Was it enough? Frantically, he searched the cooler's remaining shelves, but his vial was the only one of its kind. His gaze flickered to the lab shelf nearby and its trainlike sequence of crystalline containers. The last vessel of the series appeared to be a distillation flask. A heated liquid was bubbling within, and droplets of condensation were beginning to bead on its dispensing funnel. From the volume of distillate, Manley judged that the distillation wouldn't be complete for another half hour. Yet there was no way of being certain, and someone could walk in at any moment. He looked back at his hand-held vial. He couldn't risk it. It had to be enough, dammit; it was all he had!

A standard lab desk adjoined the refrigerator. He hurriedly opened its drawers, searching for Hume's supply of syringes. None was there. His fingers drummed across the desktop while his eyes frantically searched the shelves overhead. Finally, next to a small packet of sterile swabs, he spotted the familiar cardboard cube.

He reached inside and grabbed one of the small packages. His hands shook as he fidgeted with the syringe's protective casing. The clear plastic cap came free, falling to the floor with a clatter as he needled the vial's rubber hub. He withdrew what little liquid remained and sheathed the needle in its scabbard. Then, returning the empty vial to the refrigerator, he placed the syringe in his breast pocket and hurriedly left the lab.

Once in the corridor, he willed himself to pause, to gather his wits about him. He reminded himself he could not endanger everything by blundering clumsily through the rest of the building. He breathed deeply until his heartbeat was under control. Then, ever so cautiously, he continued his search for Jacqueline by proceeding down the hall.

He stopped at the corner around which Hume had disappeared. The series of equidistant passageways gave him the impression that this wing of the Spa was a joining of quadrangles. The one he was in was obviously the work area. If Sheila's recollections were accurate, the Spa's other, more public, wing was in another quadrangle adjoining the first. He cautiously continued down the darkened hallway. At its center, he came to an arch. He clung to its marble portal and peered warily beyond.

Even though it was night, the adjoining atrium was spacious and well lit. At its far end, Manley could see the platinum-bordered archway to the second squarish area that he guessed was his destination. Out of the corner of his eye he saw a nurse skirt the archway as she made her rounds in the other wing. His lips pressed into a thin line of lean determination. If he made a wrong turn in this brightness, he would have a hell of a time continuing unobserved. Yet he had no choice; that was the chance he had to take. With one last look behind him, he sprang into the light.

He moved in a blur. Though he tried to remain silent, the sound of his footfalls resonated. He breached the atrium and jogged into the corridor beyond, looking wildly about for any hint of Jacqueline. The first corridor widened into a broader foyer. He slowed, jerking his head from side to side. Massive pillars like those at the Spa's entrance rose up beside him. He recognized them as counterparts of the exterior columns he had seen earlier that afternoon. He gazed through the vestibule. In the darkness of the distant roadside, Sheila would be awaiting his return.

He raced into the next corridor. The syringe jostled in his pocket. He steadied it with his hand as he searched his surroundings. He reached a door and slowed, peering through its window. It proved to be a well-equipped gym, its stainless-steel paraphernalia standing in the shadows like mechanical scarecrows. Jacqueline was nowhere in sight.

He charged through the hall at a furious gallop now, drunk with concern. The end of the corridor quickly rose up to meet him. He hurtled around it and vaulted into the shimmering brightness beyond.

He found himself in a spacious private dining chamber fit for the most lavish of feasts. Yet he did not see the fine points of its construction—the elegant marble facade, the ornate engravings that embellished the gleaming white walls; for in that same excruciating instant, all of his attention was focused on the leotard-clad form of Jacqueline, who lay cold and unmoving on the alabaster floor.

His flying arms and legs stiffened as he drew to a stop. His voice was hushed, a mourner's lament.

"Jack," he whispered.

He knelt beside her, lifting her wrist. Her pulse was faint and weak. For an instant all he could do was gaze at her in despair. Then he remembered the syringe and berated his hesitation. He pulled off its plastic cap and plunged the needle into the flaccid muscle of her shoulder.

320

He could abide no further delay. Crouching, he scooped her into his arms. The empty syringe fell away and rattled across the stone. Before it had rolled to a stop, he had straightened up and, cradling Jacqueline, leaped across the floor in the direction from which he had come.

There was no hesitancy in his bounding retreat. He ran as fast as his legs would carry him, retracing his steps through the maze of corridors that constituted the special wing—sneaking across the exposed atrium and then flitting from brightness into the ominous gloom of the first quadrangle. His arms cramped, and the whiskey fire of his breath ignited his lungs. At any second, he expected Hume to pop out of nowhere. Yet the darkened corridors were filled with merciful emptiness. His stiffening legs churned, carrying him beyond the lab and past the treatment room's nightmarish glow. In less than a minute, he had reached the rear fire door.

He slowed, his heart drumming in his chest. He shifted all of Jacqueline's weight to one arm, propping her unsteadily between himself and the wall as he fumbled in his pocket for the small plastic box. He found it; holding it firmly in his palm, he turned the doorknob with thumb and forefinger.

The hinges replied with a strident creak. He steadied Jacqueline in his arms and vaulted down the concrete steps, forcing himself through the garage. Its retractable door was still open. He hurtled across the underground entrance and out into the warm night air.

The dark sky welcomed him with beams of pale moonlight. Jacqueline remained unconscious, limp in his arms. Yet the very fact that he had gotten this far charged his wooden legs with newfound vigor.

His breath came in spasms. He plodded heavily up the driveway, then veered onto the damp grass to avoid the crushed gravel. His muscles knotted with ropy tightness as he fled across the moist and slippery surface. His overtaxed body ached in protest, but he didn't dare slow. Staring out across the horizon, he could dimly make out the distant hedgerow and the faint outline of the car that waited just beyond it.

He staggered through the darkness, gasping. The once simple act of inhaling became excruciating, and his lungs were a furnace that incinerated the very air he breathed. Wincing, he shifted the plastic box in his hand and pressed its clicker. He was halfway across the lawn when the heavy iron gates slowly began to open.

Sheila was prowling nervously beside the car. The vermillion of her lips had cracked from being chewed and bitten. She halted in taut anticipation at the sound of the gates' whirring. When she saw Manley charging at her, she hurriedly opened the back door.

Sheila propped her arms under Jacqueline's spine as the two of them lowered her onto the rear seat. Jacqueline's head rolled limply, and even in the darkness Sheila could see the ghastly expression in her friend's half-open eyes, which looked glassily upward. Sheila's chin quivered.

"Is she—"

Manley's chest was heaving as he gasped for breath.

"No time," he spluttered. "Get in the car and get out of here fast."

She gaped at him in bewilderment.

"Aren't you—"

"I can't," he interrupted, shaking his head adamantly, gulping air. "I'm going back."

"For what?"

He hadn't time to elaborate on his uncertainties about the quantity of drug or about the ongoing distillation, a process which might prove invaluable if Jacqueline were to recover. Incensed by Sheila's procrastination, he slammed the rear door and pulled her by the wrist to the front.

"For God's sake get in and drive," he rasped, wiping away the sweat that stung his eyes. "I'll explain later. Now get her to that hospital we passed. Just tell them what we rehearsed and they'll know what to do."

There was urgency in his voice, and he was already peering back at the building when she slid behind the wheel.

"What about you?"

He shook his head vehemently. "Not until you've dropped her off. I'll be waiting right about here."

322

"But—"

"Now!" he bellowed.

Before she could reply, he hurried back through the gates. His moon-washed figure raced through the darkness as the limousine lurched forward and accelerated down the dark and lonely road.

Chapter Twenty-Two

Alerted by the buzzer, Hume pushed out of his armchair. Until it sounded, he had been casually waiting in the master room of the special wing, leafing through a meticulously arranged album of old news clippings. He frowned at the sound of the alarm and put down his book.

The room next to his housed the monitors. Inside, he turned on a series of controls that brought the darkened screens to life. He pressed another button that controlled the perimeter lights. As the exterior of the Spa lit up in brightness, he leaned forward to study the panels.

The first bank of screens comprised the outdoor panorama. Hume knit his brow and slowly walked from one to the next, surveying the deserted ponds and undisturbed gardens. He paused in front of the panel for the monitor that scanned the front driveway. When its slowly moving camera centered on the full length of the gravel, he froze the sweep and telescoped the lens to magnify the image. The open iron gates were clearly seen.

Surprisingly unruffled, Hume continued his scrutiny, moving on to the interior views. The rooms and corridors appeared deserted, the handful of guests safely asleep in their rooms—save two. He shuffled sideways toward the next screen, noting with satisfaction the unconscious woman whose gyrating limbs pedaled in the eerie glow. But at the next panel, his apparent indifference vanished. The muscles of his neck visibly tensed, and an uncontrollable twitch rippled in his cheek. Jacqueline was gone.

His face twisted in rage. He raced from one screen to

the next, finding nothing amiss until he reached the last of the monitors. There he abruptly stopped. Deep lines indented his forehead as he gazed at the figure that crept through the corridor's gray shadows.

Hume switched the monitors off. He grew unexpectedly composed, and the contours of a smile upturned the corners of his mouth. He left the control room and retreated to his own, where a locked cabinet contained everything that he would need.

As the limousine hurtled forward at over eighty miles per hour, Sheila studied the lights that had begun flashing in her rearview mirror. She had been driving only a short while when the dazzling red and white globes had appeared out of nowhere, accompanied by a siren's undulating wail. Her eyes danced between the mirror and the highway unfolding ahead. Jacqueline was in such critical condition that for a moment, Sheila considered trying to outrun the patrol car; but if she did, they might try to ram her, or draw their guns, God knows what. With a defeated sigh, she steered the limousine onto the shoulder of the road.

The two highway patrolmen ambled up behind with maddening slowness, one on either side of her vehicle. She couldn't believe that they were both wearing dark glasses at that time of night. She wanted to yell at them, to scream—to stop this ludicrous parody of police behavior before any more precious seconds ticked away. Yet the moment she lowered the window, the officer nearest her placed his hand on his holster.

"Shoot me later, for God's sake!" she snapped. "I am trying to get someone to a hospital!"

"License and registration, please."

Sheila's eyes rolled helplessly upward.

"I don't *believe* this. Look for yourself if you want," she said, motioning with her head toward the back seat. She watched one of the officers glimpse through the rear window. "Satisfied?"

"OD?"

Sheila stared at him incredulously.

"*What?*"

"What'd she take, and when?"

She turned away from him, dumbfounded. Behind her, the beam of the second patrolman's flashlight wandered over Jacqueline's form, lingering at her face.

"This can't be happening to me," Sheila muttered to herself.

"I'll call it in," said the second patrolman.

"Right."

Sheila turned back to him. "Suppose she was in labor, then what?"

The policeman didn't bat an eyelash.

"Well," Sheila shrugged, "how do you know it's not a very quiet labor? Aren't you supposed to provide a police escort or something?"

"We'll wait for the paramedics, Miss. In the meantime, let me see some sort of identification."

As Jacqueline lay motionless, the high-frequency squawk of the police radio chattered on in the background. The first patrolman stood squarely beside the car door, hands on hips, a posture of infinite patience. Sheila stared straight ahead in helpless frustration, slowly shaking her head from side to side.

"A dream," she mumbled to no one in particular. "This could only be a dream."

❧

Roughly an ounce of the milky liquid pooled in the small beaker below the distillation flask, its volume increasing drop by drop. Manley crept into the lab and silently closed the door. He scoured the lab's granite desktop with his eyes, searching for a suitable container. There were several glass vessels that might do, but none had a lid. His eyes flitted to the box of syringes. Hurriedly, he uncapped two and removed the central plunger of each. With care, he poured half the distillate into each plastic barrel and then reassembled the syringes. Presumably, that would be enough for several more doses, in the event that Jacqueline needed it—and certainly enough to buy time until outside chemists could unravel the chemical formula. He pocketed the syringes and stealthily returned to the hall.

With catpawing steps, he padded down the corridor. Yet he had proceeded no more than a few paces when the hall went dark.

"You are a remarkably persistent man."

Hume's dulcet tones issued from behind him, flowing through the hall like soothing notes. Manley's body froze, congealed. His pulse throbbed chaotically in the back of his neck. But despite his fear, his only thought was of Jacqueline. He wondered if Sheila had yet reached the hospital.

Stall the fucker.

For many seconds, he didn't move. It occurred to him that Hume probably had a weapon. When Manley did finally turn, it was with infinite slowness, a vinelike movement that bore neither threat nor challenge. Hume stood at the end of the corridor, facing him in the dim light.

Hume was pointing a gun. To Manley, it resembled a child's air pistol, though his untrained eye had no way of being certain. Hume's other hand held a plastic device, replete with phonelike buttons; and the outlines of an automatic pistol were clearly visible through his lab coat pocket. He seemed to be waiting for Manley to speak.

"I guess I'm supposed to put my hands up?"

"I'm not the least concerned with what you do with your hands, Dr. Manley. But I would like to know what you have done with Miss Ramsey."

He doesn't know, Manley realized. He wondered if Hume had seen him in the lab, decanting the liquid into the syringes. Ever so slowly, he shifted his weight to his left foot, causing the syringes to tilt sideways in his breast pocket. Concealed by his lapel, the syringes were hidden from view.

"Done? You mean what I *plan* to do once I find her. This time she's coming with me whether she wants to or not."

"I no longer have the patience for your once refreshing impertinence. I noticed that the front gates have opened, indicating how you got in. I'm not quite as certain how you found your way into this special corridor or what your intentions are in this part of the building. But I have no doubt that you will tell me, given time. As for now, I repeat: what have you done with Miss Ramsey?"

He studied Hume's face. The blood began to distend Hume's collar before swelling purplishly throughout his neck in a visible precursor to anger.

"I don't know what you're talking about."

Hume's knuckles whitened around the gun. He made a menacing gesture with the barrel.

"Are you familiar with neurolept anesthetics?"

"My grades in anesthesia were pretty low."

"Not at all surprising. I am beginning to question the intelligence I credited you with. The neurolept dart in this pistol, however, will remove any shred of intelligence you still possess. You will force me to use it if you persist in your refusal to answer my questions."

"What about *your* intelligence?" Manley countered, desperately gambling to buy time. His gaze swept along the corridor. "Are you willing to throw it all away—the genius behind this building, all your fame . . . all your *control?*"

Hume's face grew livid.

"I throw nothing away by destroying you!"

"Sheila's at the police station by now," Manley shrugged. "If I don't return with Jack, they'll be paying you a visit."

"Lies! All lies!"

Manley studied Hume's volatile responses. The man was starting to crack. If somehow he could capitalize on that, play on Hume's weaknesses . . . His voice mellowed with apparent concern.

"I'm not lying, Dr. Hume. I know you've been lied to in the past. All that suffering, all those years of deceit—"

"Deceit? You dare pretend to understand the sin of deceit?"

"It *is* a sin, maybe the greatest sin of all. It's the sort of thing a man can never forgive, something he has to avenge forever." He paused in pained sympathy. "There's not a man in the world who wouldn't have done the same thing you did when Jean deceived you."

Hume's face went white, drained of its color. His eyes grew wild at the memory.

"Jean?"

"Your wife," Manley continued. "Jean Emmerich."

Hume's cheeks pulsated in a spasm. His lips twitched when he tried to mouth the word, but he soon settled into a tremulous silence. His expression had a distant look, and as his gaze fell to the floor, the gun began to waver in his hand.

"You did everything for her, *gave* everything for her," Manley pursued. "And we all know what she did in return. Call it justice, Dr. Emmerich. Jean got what she deserved."

Hume's eyes fluttered.

"What she deserved . . ." he mumbled.

"What they *all* deserved," Manley went on, acting out his hunch. It was a risky gamble, but it was the only chance he had. The moment was approaching; he took a tentative step forward. "All the Jeans that you cared for, that you took in and made thin. All the Jeans that you molded, that you sculpted, that you transformed into ivory perfect Galateas. And all the Jeans, all the *actresses*, that then left you—lied to you, deceived you, in their thirst for the stage.

"The stage," Hume whispered, as bubbles of white spittle formed in the corners of his mouth.

The gun had nearly fallen even with his side. Manley watched it, growing confident that he could now turn and flee and probably make it; yet if he managed to word his phrases precisely, he just might conquer by verbal persuasion alone. Continuing to play the gamble, he continued to inch slowly forward.

"You've won, Dr. Hume. It's over. All those Jeans are gone now. They can never humiliate you again."

"Never . . ."

Manley held out his hand.

"Let me have the gun. You can trust me with it."

He regretted the blunder the instant he made it, inwardly cringing at his own stupidity. Trust was a word one could never mention to Hume, a man who once trusted so deeply. Hume again began to raise the pistol, but unsteadily, his trembling arm coming to rest at the level of Manley's knees. Manley continued forward.

"What are you doing?"

Manley forced a reassuring steadiness into his even strides. He was determined to appear composed, to sound convincing.

"The gun, Dr. Hume. You won't be needing it any more."

"Stop where you are."

Manley halted. He slowly lifted his hands, turning them over in the manner of a supplicant as he lapsed into a smile of faint encouragement.

"Of course. But can I at least make a call? I should let Miss Hastings know."

"A call?"

"On your phone," Manley replied, nodding toward the device in Hume's hand. "It'll only take a second."

The change in Hume was frighteningly dramatic.

"Phone?" he repeated, inching the gun higher. His eyes jerked rapidly between Manley and his hand-held device. "*Phone?*"

Manley stood stock still. He turned his gaze toward the plastic box. The smile left his face; his throat grew dry, and his eyes widened in fear when he realized that it was not a telephone at all.

"You imbecile," Hume ranted. "This is a work of brilliance—a communications device of my own making. For a moment, I truly thought you might understand. But a *phone?* I must be quite mad!"

"Dr. Hume, I merely wanted to point out that—"

Hume cut him short. His voice raised to a shout, and there was lunacy in his eyes.

"Why if I pressed the right button, San Sebastian would cease to exist. Blown sky high, off the face of the earth! Press another and the gates will close; a third, and hidden panels rise," he laughed, jabbing his finger threateningly toward the device. "Press a fourth, and the limousine would—" He abruptly stopped, cocking his head to one side. A distant expression came over him, followed by a

330

frown of recollection. He shot a black glance at Manley. "The *limousine* . . ."

There was pounding in Manley's brain, a sickening sense of helplessness. Manley fought the unbearable tension by trying to feign a smile.

"What limousine?" he joked.

"Oh, I think you know."

He slowly raised the box.

"Dr. Hume, *please* don't—"

"Yes," Hume cackled. "I think you know precisely!"

Hume's finger neared the plastic surface.

Manley was horrified. His arms shot out in beseechment. "No!" he pleaded.

Hume pressed the button.

The ululation of the siren receded in the distance. Sheila closed her weary eyes and momentarily rested her head against the steering wheel. Then she sighed, leaned back, and gazed the length of the highway.

God, she thought. They were so infuriatingly obtuse here. How she longed to leave all this oppressive dreariness behind—the unceasing smiles, the interminable politeness—and to return to the clamorous, rude, frenzied paradise of New York. She stuck out her lower lip and exhaled, ruffling the hair atop her forehead.

She heard a crackle of static, followed by the distorted chatter of a police radio. She turned her head in frustration, looking through the open window on her left toward the police cruiser parked nearby. In the light of its open door, she saw the patrolman standing sideways, leaning against his vehicle as he prepared to write out her summons.

Not the best of conversationalists, she thought, recalling his laconic phrases. But not half bad without those dreadful glasses. She ran her eyes the length of his compact build, which was encased in the tightness of a khaki uniform. For a moment, she considered using her feminine wiles to avoid getting the ticket. Then she turned back and laughed.

Wiles, she thought. Me—wiles? *Lean closer, lover, wiles I show you a real good time.* . . . Suddenly she remembered in anguish that she knew someone who truly possessed wiles. She looked into the rearview mirror and stared at the empty back seat. A feeling of deep sentiment overcame her, and a single tear rolled down her melancholy cheek.

Jackie's going to be okay. I know it.

She had to bite her lip to stop its intolerable quivering. She wiped her eyes on her sleeve, sniffled, and then wiped her runny nose. She stared at the dampened fabric.

"Class," she said. "A class act."

She looked up once more, peering intently ahead into the darkness, now barely able to discern the faint, twinkling lights of the distant van. Growing impatient, she turned toward the police car again. The officer now had his back to her, and he bent over to retrieve something on the front seat.

My, my. A quality tush, she said to herself.

Sheila deliberated. Then she gave a little smile and decided to chance it.

"What the hell," she reasoned. "You only live once."

With a last, hopeful glance at the paramedic van that sped Jacqueline away, she reached for the door handle. Just as she pulled it, a deafening blast dismembered the car, hurling her lifeless body into the night sky.

Chapter Twenty-Three

"You maniac!"

Hume fired just as Manley leaped. Manley felt a needle-like stinging in his chest—not terribly painful, but startling enough to throw off his lunge. His hands clawed at Hume's throat. They missed by inches, but a pawing swipe batted away the pistol and bowled Hume over. Momentum sent Manley tumbling to the floor.

His vision began to blur. He thought it was sweat. Crawling onto all fours, he frantically blinked his eyes, but the film remained. He looked down at his chest, expecting it to be covered with blood. He stared in dumb fascination at the hypodermic flechette. Its needle had penetrated his skin and was protruding from his flesh like a dart-board projectile in a back-alley pub.

Several yards away, Hume rolled lightheadedly to his side. Manley plucked the dart from his chest and drew back his hand to throw it at Hume, but his arm felt impossibly heavy, and the flechette sailed harmlessly past Hume's face.

Hume was in a daze, clumsily fumbling for the automatic in his lab coat pocket. Manley struggled to one knee. The drug-filled syringes had fallen from his shirt. He hurriedly scooped them up, thinking confusedly about Jacqueline. It was just possible that Sheila had reached the hospital before the limousine had been destroyed. If he could somehow escape . . .

Hume tugged on the automatic, but its hammer snagged on the cloth of his pocket. Manley struggled unsteadily to his feet. The medication that raced through his bloodstream was continuing to take effect. His mind whirled, and his vision fogged; yet all he could think about was his woman, and what little time she might have left.

"Jack . . ." he slurred.

Hume freed the gun and thumbed at its safety. Manley sobered. He turned and frantically lurched away, vaguely recalling the direction from which he had come. His legs were wobbly, and his mind was spewing gibberish.

Maybe outside, he thought . . . a car . . . *Jack* . . .

The gunshot roared as he stumbled around the corner. Marble fragments exploded from the wall beside his neck, stabbing his face with shards. His mind was in an ivory stupor. He moved forward, a pinball that veered from side to side. He reached the atrium exit door. Grasping its handle, he turned it and wielded his shoulder against the metal frame. The door burst open. Off balance, Manley tripped on the concrete steps and tumbled to the garage floor.

Hume's self-assurance was total now. He rose to his feet and gave an insane little chuckle as he lifted the plastic box. With a congratulatory nod to himself, he pressed another of the buttons.

From the floor of the garage, Manley heard a liquid humming, and he raised himself to one knee. Through glassy eyes, he watched as the garage door began to lower. He stumbled forward, bent over, arms swinging like an ape. But before he was halfway there, the door met the concrete pavement.

He reeled to his right, dizzily scanning the walls. He no longer thought of escape or of Jacqueline; the little that remained of his consciousness concentrated on revenge. He blinked his eyes frantically and stumbled sideways, examining the dark objects that hung from the nearest wall.

They were automotive tools, each neatly hanging from a separate hook. A tire iron flanked a jack. Manley grasped it and pulled, nearly falling backward when it came free with unexpected ease. It seemed absurdly heavy. Panting, he steadied it in two hands and staggered back up the steps.

He fought with the door handle until he was inside, plunging blindly ahead.

He was a sailor swaying on a storm-tossed deck. Everything was weaving, and he could barely focus. Driven by blind instinct, he made it through the first corridor and careened into the second. He squinted; he thought he could make out Hume, who stood there leering, pointing something his way. With the last vestige of his strength, Manley raised the crowbar overhead and charged forward.

Hume aimed casually, contemptuously. Manley approached from twenty feet away, staggering between the wall and the glassed-in lab. Like a battered fighter, he telegraphed each uncoordinated movement. Yet despite his physical stagnation, his mind was infused with a feeling of the most intense hatred. As he prepared to swing the bar, a cry of animal rage erupted from his lungs.

He split the air with the heavy iron rod, slashing away like a besotted gladiator. Just before the pistol roared, it had been pointing toward his heart, but Manley's clumsy last-second gyrations threw off Hume's aim. The bullet flew high and wide, ripping through Manley's shoulder. Instead of stopping him, the heavy slug's impact accentuated the twist in his movements. The tire iron corkscrewed from his fingers and crashed through the lab's huge glass window.

Manley's momentum propelled him behind it, and he spun through the jagged shards like a top. Both the lab and the corridor were showered with glistening fragments of the broken pane. Yet he still stood, struggling to raise the bar again, coming dangerously near the distillation apparatus.

"You idiot!" Hume shouted.

Hume's eyes widened, inflamed with fury. He looked apprehensively at the glassware. The very implements of his greatness were being imperiled by this menace. He aimed again, trying to align the gunsight on the drugged and stumbling man. He fired just as Manley sagged to one knee. The bullet punctured what was left of the glass, whining scant millimeters above Manley's scalp.

A new sound was heard, rising above the tinkling of falling glass. It was pure sibilance, the hissing of a coiled snake. Hume recognized the sound as the sudden rush of gas escaping under intense pressure. He searched in alarm for the source of the emission. His eyes came to rest on a stainless steel tank against the lab's far wall, from which a maze of tubing fed the bunsen burners.

He didn't dare fire now. He was riveted in place, his eyes white and staring, his gaze fixed upon the neat round hole in the tank's silvery skin. Stenciled just below it, in large black letters, was the word PROPANE.

Manley was unaware of what had happened. Having fallen to both knees, his ears rang with the high-pitched hiss. The room grew dark, and he felt himself slowly sinking away. In the twilight of his awareness, he called upon the meager residue of his sapped strength. He seized the bar in both hands, and in a final moment of desperation, he flung it savagely across the lab.

Hume began to back up as the massive steel rod somersaulted through the air. Its tapered tip flew toward a block wall, where a length of insulated conduit joined an electrical junction box. The bar's heavy metal point landed flush, slicing easily through the mass of protruding wires. For the briefest fraction of a second, there was a bright spark. And then the quiet desert night was shattered. The Spa's sturdy walls exploded, and chunks of marble flew skyward in a blinding orange detonation.

Restraints of rolled gauze bound Jacqueline's wrists and ankles to the emergency-room stretcher. Caught in the throes of a convulsion, her body had gone rigid, and every muscle twitched with a shuddering violent enough to shatter bone. Two padded tongue depressors were in place, holding her jaws open to keep her teeth from shearing off her tongue. Foamy white sputum bubbled at her lips, and her eyes rolled back in their sockets.

Status epilepticus.

The term hung like a sword over the emergency medical care group. It was one of the most feared complications in medicine. Those who treated such patients felt an overwhelming sense of futility, as the seizures recurred over

336

the course of minutes and hours and the victim's existence slowly ebbed away.

Jacqueline had suffered her first seizure while the paramedics were wheeling her into the emergency room. In the brief time since then, she had grown incontinent, and her severely disturbed breathing mirrored her high pulse rate. She perspired profusely, and her blood pressure was dangerously elevated. It seemed as if her body were mocking the very efforts to treat her, as every so often her weakened limbs would flail like those of a scarecrow tossed about by a storm.

The two emergency-room physicians looked down on their unconscious patient. They had absolutely no idea what was causing her seizures, and their ability to treat her was hampered by lack of a proper history. They sifted through and eliminated various possible diagnoses as they awaited the preliminary lab reports. After a seemingly endless delay, a nurse interrupted their vigil and somberly showed them the initial lab data.

"Good God."

"How bad are the 'lytes?" asked his assistant.

The first physician handed him the paper slip and then turned to the nurse.

"Ask the page operator to locate any internist in the house."

She nodded and hurried away.

"Think it's a lab error?"

"Christ, that would let us off the hook. Sure as hell more than we can handle if it's not." He looked up at the clock. "I wonder if Schein's still around."

Isadore Schein was an astute diagnostician of internal medicine as well as one of its more conscientious practitioners, often remaining in the hospital long after others had departed. That evening, as the hour approached midnight, he was preparing to go home when he was summoned to the ER.

After extensively examining the patient and rechecking the lab data, he met with the others in a small room at the end of the hall. He gave his head a worried shake while those about him exchanged puzzled stares. Uncharacteristically, he was stumped.

"The picture just doesn't fit," he concluded.

"Why can't it be straightforward hyperosmolar coma?"

"A couple of reasons. First, those cases are usually in diabetics, and her blood sugar proves that she isn't. Second, you don't usually find this degree of hypernatremia—the elevated sodium—unless the patient's on tube feedings. Which she obviously is not."

"But doesn't she appear hyperosmolar? Clinically speaking?"

"Well, yes and no. If you mean the neurological symptoms, sure. She's in a stupor and she has convulsions."

"Doesn't that verify the diagnosis?"

"If the diagnosis were correct, doctor, she'd be getting better, wouldn't she?"

Those about him were clearly confused.

"Maybe we're just not treating it right."

"Look," Schein reassured. "This is a damn peculiar case, so don't be so quick to criticize yourselves. It's not easy to make sense of anything without a decent history, so we're left with guesswork. We're postulating that this is probably a psychiatric case—a patient who, for some ungodly reason, ate an enormous amount of salty food, after which she began vomiting to the point of dehydration. The lab studies bear that out and confirm the hypernatremia. She went on to develop an encephalopathy, the mental confusion. What probably began as simple lethargy progressed to deep coma. She then deteriorated to the point of full-blown renal insufficiency, lactic acidosis, and seizures." He looked around and saw their eyes intent on his. "What I'm driving at is that we can ordinarily handle all those things, simply by juggling her IV fluids. But in her case, it isn't working."

The ER physicians exchanged baffled looks.

"Then if it isn't hyperosmolar coma, what *does* she have?"

"I don't know," Schein admitted. "But be prepared for the worst. This could be one of those instances where you do your damnedest and fail anyway."

"Meaning she might not improve?"

338

"No," Schein said gravely. "I mean that within the next hour, she may be dead."

A nurse interrupted their discussion with news of yet another seizure. They quickly returned to the bedside, where a different nurse was preparing an injection.

"What if the Valium won't hold her? We already gave the Dilantin."

"Where's the Amytal?" asked Schein.

"On its way from the pharmacy."

"Then we'll have to try that."

Arms folded, Schein stepped back and anguished over the patient's deteriorating condition. He'd used every trick in the book, plus a few he'd ad-libbed on the spot. He was aware that the others were relying on him, and that sense of bestowed responsibility made him feel even more powerless and alone.

During the next half hour, fully aware of the dangers confronting him, he directed all therapeutic efforts toward stopping the seizures. At any moment, the patient's exhausting, sinew-tearing convulsions could interrupt the vital flow of oxygen, shutting it off like a valve. Her brain might become hopelessly damaged, and her kidneys would fail, if her heart did not stop before that. The Amytal seemed to work at first, but only briefly. Administration of even higher doses was a double-edged sword: give too little, and the seizures wouldn't stop; give too much and her breathing would.

He had long since placed her on a respirator. It was beginning to appear that the only chance to save her would be to take her to the operating room, where she could be anesthetized with enormous doses of deep barbiturate or general anesthesia. Yet even if that worked, he knew, they couldn't keep her under anesthesia forever. It would be a temporary solution at best. Unless something miraculous happened soon, the unknown young woman would surely slip away into oblivion.

The OR called; they would be ready for the patient in five minutes. As the flock of attendants prepared her for transport, she was seized by yet another fierce convulsion. Her teeth clamped down on the tube that went into her windpipe, threatening to bite the plastic contrivance in half. Schein watched her pathetically contorted body, counting off the seconds in the seizure, wondering how soon the precious stream of oxygen would cease and leave her mind a useless brain-dead organ.

Chapter Twenty-Four

The two sounds were discordant, without harmony or likeness. One was a distant crackle, the continuous wrinkling of cellophane; the other, a steady roar like surf in a tunnel. But what temporarily wakened Manley was the pain. In his drug-induced stupor, he didn't realize that there had been an explosion mere seconds before. As he was jolted into consciousness, all he knew was that his arm hurt. Lying on his back, barely able to see, he somehow managed to roll onto his side and peer at a spot below his left elbow.

Oh, that's all it is, he thought. My skin is on fire.

The middle of his forearm was ablaze. He numbly watched the curly hairs on his skin flicker and wilt in the flames. The flesh itself was red and oozing, starting to char in places. He watched in detached curiosity for several more seconds—strangely fascinated that part of his body was actually burning—before it occurred to him that perhaps he should put the fire out. With the apathy of the nearly unconscious, he smothered the flames with his free hand, burning its palm in the process.

He tried to sit up, wondering where the train was that was making that incredible roar. And what is that thing pinning my feet down, he thought, unaware that the slab of sheet metal had torn free, acted as a shield, and saved his life. His face felt hot, and he squinted. There, perhaps fifty feet away, was an immense blossom of pure orange flame. The heat-shimmered image of a middle-aged man ran through the inferno, his hair ablaze. Manley narrowed his eyes but could see no more.

Someone should call the fire department, he thought, before the combined weight of the drug and his injuries became too heavy and he fell back unconscious.

Schein walked out of the doctors' dressing room with the self-consciousness of a man wearing beachwear to a formal dinner. His scrub suit was several sizes too large, and his scrub pants were hopelessly baggy.

The patient's stretcher was being wheeled down the corridor by three attendants and the anesthesiologist. Every few seconds, the anesthesiologist would squeeze a bag that forced oxygen through Jacqueline's endotracheal tube. Schein trailed close behind. His disposable shoe covers felt awkward, and he had inadvertently draped his head with a bouffant nurse's bonnet rather than a tight surgeon's cap. Still, his skittishness disappeared as he reviewed the principles of managing the comatose.

What concerned him most was the need to maintain circulation. He stared at the color of the patient's skin. As they were transferring her from the stretcher to the OR table, it had suddenly become shockingly pale, the grayish white of old marble. Curiously, he was the only one who seemed to have noticed it. The anesthesiologist was casually taping the cardiac monitor leads to the woman's chest before plugging their terminals into the cardioscope. Schein had his stethoscope in hand at once. He inserted the earpieces and placed the flat end beside the patient's bosom, while everyone else seemed to stare uninterestedly at the cardioscope's flat line.

Schein looked up and made a terse announcement.

"She has arrested."

"The machine takes a few seconds to warm up," the anesthesiologist glibly countered.

Schein—who knew the sound of a heartbeat every bit as well as its absence—immediately began to give external cardiac massage. The flabbergasted anesthesiologist seized him by the arm.

"What the hell are you doing? I told you, the machine—"

Schein wrenched his arm away and quickly resumed pumping.

"Listen for yourself, you idiot."

By now, everyone was growing concerned about the monitor's persistently flat line, whose only squiggle coincided with the external compression. The anesthesiologist frantically grabbed his own stethoscope and pressed it to the patient's ribs. Then he quickly tore it from his ears and shouted to the nurses.

"Get the crash cart!"

The operating room became instant chaos. While everyone scurried about, the bewildered anesthesiologist looked to the perspiration-studded Schein for advice.

"Should I put her under?"

"*Under?* She might already be dead," Schein calmly replied. "Just keep bagging her."

Even when he has no cases of his own, it is not uncommon to find a surgeon accustomed to making late rounds come strolling through the OR at the oddest of hours, curious to see where the action is. At that moment, the chief of thoracic surgery—fresh from visiting a postoperative patient in the nearby recovery room—came sauntering down the hall. Hearing the commotion, he paused and assessed the situation. Seconds later, flanked by two surgical residents, he entered the room, his manner all business. He barked at a nurse to get him a scalpel handle and knife blade. Then, knife in hand, he assumed a commanding position beside Schein and flung off what little remained of the patient's gown.

"How long?" he asked.

Schein glanced up at the clock.

"About two minutes."

"Move aside and I'll crack her chest."

Schein continued pumping. "What are you talking about?"

"I'll get right down to her heart."

Never one to stand on protocol, Schein continued his massage more vigorously than ever. "Get the fuck out of here."

No one had ever spoken to the head of thoracic surgery

343

in that tone of voice. Speechless, he backed away from the table, while one of his residents instantly began to feel for the femoral pulse in the patient's hip. Other medical personnel filtered into the room.

"Someone give her an amp of bicarb," Schein said calmly. "Draw up some calcium and bring over the defibrillator. Is there any intracardiac epinephrine in here?"

Nurses scattered in all directions as he continued to pump.

"How's my compression?" he asked the resident.

"Good. A good pulse."

Now two and a half minutes into the arrest, Schein paused for the first time and stared at the cardioscope. Miraculously, small blips of cardiac activity appeared on the monitor. Schein watched it in astonishment, astounded that the beating continued on its own.

There was a restrained though audible communal sigh of relief. Tension ebbed, and the initially frantic format of resuscitation grew more orderly. Now satisfied that the woman's heart was indeed functioning, Schein could not resist making an observation.

"It looks like the machine has warmed up."

The anesthesiologist was silent. He inserted an esophageal temperature probe and pumped up the blood pressure cuff. Both instruments gave digital readouts. Schein, peering at the numbers, was amazed at the results.

The patient's pulse and blood pressure had completely returned to normal.

The anesthesiologist was aware that the woman had been severly hypertensive in the emergency room. Anticipating Schein's query, he immediately called for another machine to verify the readings. Within a minute, it became apparent that both values were correct, as were the patient's other vital signs.

Schein was now utterly baffled. Here was a woman who had been a heartbeat away from death, in as critical a condition as anyone could imagine. Yet moments later— barely recovered from the arrest—her eyes began to flutter open, and she started to breathe on her own.

"Can someone please draw some stat electrolytes?"

One of the residents applied a tourniquet and drew several tubes of blood.

"If it's okay with you," said the anesthesiologist, "I'll hold off on extubating her until she's in recovery."

Schein was not accustomed to such deferential treatment. "Certainly."

The patient was now fully awake, fighting her tube. As they wheeled her from the operating room, one of the nurses spoke to her soothingly. The thoracic surgeon brushed by and wordlessly clapped Schein on the back. Schein permitted himself a smile; the surgeon hadn't said a kind word to him in years. Yet his sudden recognition did nothing to solve his diagnostic dilemma. He was more perplexed than ever.

The processional wound its way to the recovery room. There the anesthesiologist deflated the tube's cuffed end and gently eased the apparatus from the patient's lungs. She spluttered and then relaxed, breathing easily, eyes wide open. Moments later, when it was beginning to appear as if nothing had ever happened, the resident returned with the lab results. Schein studied the values in mounting disbelief. Not only was the woman's sodium level normal, but her other lab tests made her out to be the healthiest person under his care.

The recovery room was growing crowded. A whispering began among the nurses; eyebrows were raised, and there was a good deal of insistent pointing and nodding. Jacqueline Ramsey? someone scoffed. Seeking to resolve the dispute, the head nurse disengaged herself from the others and approached the stretcher, where she diplomatically queried the woman. The patient's hoarse reply of acknowledgment created an uproar that made the excitement preceding it seem tame.

Word of Jacqueline's identity immediately leaked out, and within minutes, reporters were descending upon the hospital. The administrator sent Schein a message, asking him to hold an impromptu news conference. Though the frenzy was mounting about him, Schein remained with his patient for the next half hour. Finally convinced that she was indeed normal, he shook his head and slowly returned to the doctors' lounge to change.

It seemed impossible that a patient with such deep coma, violent convulsions, and absolutely bizarre laboratory values could return to normal so quickly, and yet she had. He was even starting to think that there might be no lasting aftereffects whatsoever. It was the closest thing to medical magic he had ever seen—a sort of unexplainable witchcraft, as if someone had simply flipped a switch or given a potion.

In the lounge, he tossed his disposable cap into the trash, wondering if anyone had noticed the floral print on his hat. No matter. What mattered was how to explain this to the press.

He wasn't sure he could.

The two figures shimmered just out of focus, clad in gray, beckoning like ghosts of the departed. They seemed to be gesturing, to be talking to him, and the sound that filled his ears was the echo of his own name reverberating across a deep canyon: DOCTOR MANLEY, Doctor Manley, doctor . . .

He felt as though he were floating, an aerial hovering he found quite pleasant. He slowly blinked his eyes, but the blurriness would not lessen. He had the impression of being in a strangely familiar room, lying on a bed. He tried to move, but the effort made his whole body ache; so he lay still. He was no longer sure there were two of them, for they appeared to do everything in unison. They thrust their wallets his way, as if expecting him to render acknowledgment, and then they returned the identification to their pockets in identical crisp movements.

"Are you awake, Dr. Manley?"

How did they know his name? He certainly didn't know theirs. And then their distorted faces peered closer, scrutinizing him, as if he were a bug under a magnifying glass.

"Tell us about Hume, Dr. Manley."

Hume? What were they talking about? And then a dim memory began to surface, bobbing in the still-shifting sands of his mind, a mind now starting to recall flickering images of nightmarish horror.

"Jacqueline . . ."

"Is safe, Dr. Manley."

They were still speaking, but he no longer heard the words. Eyes closed, he relaxed on the pillow, a serene smile on his lips. He knew he was drifting off again, but it didn't matter. Nothing mattered anymore now that she was safe.

Chapter Twenty-Five

"Are you up? How do you feel?"

His lids fluttered open. He could see clearly now, and his gaze fixed on the nurse. She was taking his pulse. He looked about the room, recognizing the familiar features.

"This is a hospital."

"Indeed. Seventy-eight," she said, announcing his pulse. She took his blood pressure. "One sixteen over seventy. Pretty good for someone just off the critical list."

"How long have I been here?"

She gave a little smile, looking at him askance.

"You really don't remember, do you? The accident, your surgery three days ago?"

"Three days!"

"It's two in the morning, Dr. Manley," she concluded, preparing to leave the room. "It might be better if you saved your questions for doctor's rounds."

"But—"

"Incidentally, a gentleman has been waiting all day to see you."

She turned and was gone, leaving Manley in confusion. He noted the bandages on his arms, and he became aware of the pain in his upper chest and shoulder. Everything was clearer now, at least as he was beginning to remember it: the Spa, Hume, the explosion. After that . . . nothing.

A man entered. He wore a gray suit and had a vaguely familiar look that Manley couldn't quite place.

"John Reilly, Dr. Manley," he said, extending his hand.

"I was here yesterday morning with my partner, but you weren't quite awake."

"You said something about Jack . . ."

"Word has it that Miss Ramsey plans a visit later this morning. Right now, it's essential that we—"

"How is she?"

"Damn good, from what I under—"

"Thank God," he said, closing his eyes.

The man paused, frowning slightly.

"Dr. Manley, it's important that we talk. This investigation is already seventy-two hours behind schedule."

"First I want to know where Jack is."

"Staying with friends. In fact," he said, looking at his watch, "until she was discharged eight hours ago, she was a patient right here in this hospital."

"*What?*"

"Closest medical facility to San Sebastian. Or what's left of it. Now how about it, Doc? Can we get down to business?"

"Only if you get me Jack's phone number."

"You're going to call at this time of night?"

"Well . . . first thing in the morning."

"Be better to wait until she gets here. She might not be there when you call."

"Why not?"

"They were planning on a sunrise service."

"A what?"

"Memorial service. For Miss Hastings."

He told the man everything he knew. Sobered by the stunning news about Sheila, he spoke in a melancholy tone, occasionally pausing to dab the wetness from his eyes. Reilly scribbled notes throughout the interrogation, not once altering his stolid expression during the astounding recitation about secret injections and arcane psychopathology. When Manley finished, the man quietly closed his pad and rose to leave.

"That's about it for now, Dr. Manley. I think we could both use some rest."

Manley studied him.

"Do you believe me?"

Reilly shrugged.

"A lot of it tallies with what Miss Ramsey had to say. Of course we'll have to go into more detail later."

"That doesn't answer my question."

"I'm a detective, Dr. Manley. I save the believing for churchgoers."

Manley looked away, momentarily pensive. Then he turned back.

"You're sure about the syringes?"

"Locked in the hospital lab," Reilly nodded.

"They're important, you know."

"Don't worry. They're safe." He walked to the doorway and turned. "I'll bring Dr. Schein when I return this afternoon. I'm pretty anxious to sit in on your chitchat. And Doc—"

"Hmmm?"

"Sorry to break that news about Miss Hastings."

In the moment when night changes to day, during the intensely soothing span of time known as daybreak, that which was equivocal becomes clear and the vague images obscured by night grow distinct in the white, still light of morning.

Everything fell into place for Manley as the magpies and wrens sailed through the purple sky outside his window, and what had been slumbering mysteries at midnight vanished with the dawn. He had been wrestling with his thoughts for the remainder of the night. His confusion was now gone, replaced by the obvious explanation for all that had happened.

Few knew. There was the police officer, but his interest seemed to revolve more around the details of the explosion—a blast that had claimed Hume, four patients, and three of the Spa's staff among its victims—than around the principles underlying the Spa's cure. Though Reilly hadn't said as much, Manley had the impression that the detective considered the more bizarre elements of the tale to be a sort of postoperative window dressing, farfetched embellishments to which the ill were entitled. And then there was Schein: he would have to be told the truth about Jacqueline's recovery, the details of which Manley had only partially learned from fragmented discussions with the nurses. Schein's understanding and assistance, especially where the drug-filled syringes were concerned, would be invaluable. Finally, there was Jacqueline herself. More than anyone else, she had a right to know.

Explaining what had happened to her would be far easier than guessing what the future held in store. For the next six months, while the drug was still effective, she would be in a kind of holding pattern. What happened after that would largely depend on the astuteness of Schein and the chemists who tried to duplicate the drug. Even if they weren't cooperative, however, Manley was confident that he was sufficiently familiar with the underlying details to direct his own drug investigation. Of course, this all presumed Jacqueline would *need* the drug; it was equally possible that he could wean her off it, to the point where sensible diet alone could keep her thin.

If she pressed him, he would reveal the reason for it all. Hume saw those he rendered thin and beautiful as his creations, creations who owed him a price for their glory. But that alone was not enough. Driven by hatred and jealousy, one man's twisted mind had schemed to gain unending retribution for what had been stolen from him: the woman he most adored. It was not sufficient that she had been destroyed; Emmerich's insanity compelled him to perpetrate the act of revenge over and over again. His more submissive victims had yielded to his humiliating, extravagant demands and his unceasing control; the more defiant victims, of which Jacqueline was the embodiment, were condemned from the outset by their reluctance.

Enactment of the psychodrama had required many years, during which Emmerich had perfected the biochemical techniques that gave him mastery over others. Manley thought he understood it, from a psychiatric point of view. A man so profoundly rejected—in part because of his physical appearance—might seek to surround himself with a world of beauty. He could cast off his own yoke of ugliness through plastic surgery, but building a private garden of elegance would reinforce his new image. The crowning achievement of his psychopathology would be to control the bodies of others, to make them thinner or fatter at will, to make those selfsame symbols of the woman he once adored beholden to him—and ultimately, to make them beg him for mercy.

Manley's doctor, one of the staff surgeons, arrived shortly after eight. He revealed the extent of Manley's injuries: a fractured clavicle and scarred upper lung from the bullet wound, and third-degree burns of the arm and leg, already skin grafted. If Manley's condition continued to improve, he would be discharged in a week.

Midmorning came and went. He thought of Sheila several times, largely wistfully, but not without a sense of guilt. Still, he managed to make peace with himself, for he had said his good-bye hours earlier, when he lay there staring out into the slow, rosy stillness of dawn. Now all he wanted to do was to see Jacqueline.

He had the nurse bring him soap, a wash basin, a shaving mirror, and a razor. He hadn't shaved in nearly a week, and the heavy stubble on his face was the coarsest of short beards. He wet his cheeks with his uninjured hand and lathered his whiskers. He stared at the reflection of his eyes in the mirror, mentally jousting with himself, for there remained one item of unfinished business, without which the puzzle was incomplete.

He made short strokes with the blade while he ruminated. All along, he had assumed that Hume had a feeder, someone who directed a specific type of patient to San Sebastian. Sheila ventured it might be Emmerich, and he'd concurred, but now that he knew Hume and Emmerich were one and the same, Hume's feeder remained a mystery. Unless, of course, Hume had been able to contact his own patients without a feeder, in which case—

"Where the hell's my puck?"

The grumbling phrase came from the doorway. As he looked that way in surprise, she popped into the room like a jack-in-the-box, holding a hockey stick in her upraised arms, a beaming smile on her face. She looked more gorgeous than he thought possible. He dropped the razor into the basin, grinning from ear to ear, while Jacqueline's smiling eyes darted about the room in lighthearted mimicry.

"Where's your what?"

"Puck, my love, as in—"

"Oh, *puck*. I thought you said something else."

She lowered the hockey stick and stood arms akimbo, now all seduction in her smile, tones of Mae West in her voice.

"If you weren't laid up, big boy, a girl might trade in this stick for the real thing." She raised her eyebrows suggestively, paused, and then let her arms fall to her sides as the pantomime faded. Then, somewhat embarrassedly, "How'm I doing?"

Half shaved, with soapy water dripping from his chin, he gazed at her fondly, in silence. She looked back at him longingly, still wearing the trim navy suit she'd put on for the service. They both knew her bravado was a front, a charade of humor intended to defuse the tension of their long separation and to reduce the unspoken heartache of Sheila's death. Jacqueline's smile slowly disappeared. She bit her lip, feeling the long-suppressed anguish beginning to surface. Her eyes brimmed with tears.

"And here I swore that I wouldn't cry, because I've cried enough already. I promised myself that I was going to be good, that I was going to cheer you up . . ." Her chin quivered. "I'm not very good at this, am I?"

He held out his arms.

"Come here, you."

She flew across the room and was instantly in his embrace. They kissed slowly, tenderly, not wanting to let go. Finally he pulled away. He smiled at her lovingly, wiping bubbles of soapy lather from her upper lip.

"Just seeing you is enough to cheer me up."

"Me, too."

She touched his cheek and looked at his bandages, tracing them lightly with her forefinger as she searched for the words.

"They told me how you came back for me at the Spa, and about the fire. I've thought about the whole, horrible thing dozens of times, but I knew I could never believe it until I asked you." She looked up at him for reassurance. "Is it really over, Rick?"

He took her hand and looked deep into her eyes.

"Forever," he said, kissing her fingertips.

She closed her eyes, tight-lipped, and her body began to shake, silently quaking with grief.

The doctor in him said to let her get on with her grieving. Yet he fretted at the enormity of her inner pain, and therefore the man in him cried out for it to end: she'd been through enough already. He looked about for something to distract her. He reached for the hockey paraphernalia.

"Where'd you get the stick?"

She opened her eyes, sniffled, and put on a cheerful face.

"The women I'm staying with—one has a boyfriend who plays for the Kings." She glanced at his bandaged arm. "I thought it might help you take your mind off these boring injuries. God, they have you wrapped up like a mummy."

"Ah, yes. The finest in medical care."

She suddenly became effervescent, bubbling with enthusiasm.

"I almost forgot to tell you. I spoke with Emil last night."

"Really?"

"He heard about what happened, and he said he wants me back." She looked away and pretended a nonchalant yawn. "I told him I'd think about it."

"You didn't!"

"Silly boy—of course not. Believe me," she said, running her finger across his lips as she gave a little wink, "this time I'm gonna knock 'em dead."

He did believe her. The conviction and determination blazed in her eyes. Suddenly, she straightened up in animation.

"I brought you a present." She hopped off the bed. "It's just outside. I'll get it."

She returned in a moment, carrying a basket covered with a small blanket. She placed it on the bed. He appraised it from a distance, moving his head professorially from side to side.

"Now, what might we have here?"

"Go on, take a look."

"Cookies for Grandma, by the shape of it."

"Just one eensy peek."

"You don't want me to guess?"

She grew cheerfully exasperated.

"For God's sake—it's a gift, not a contest."

He lifted the coverlet. Inside, a tiny German shorthair puppy began to wag its tail furiously as soon as the blanket was gone. He spilled out of the basket, walking unsteadily on his oversized paws. Manley was overcome. The puppy resembled Dart so much. He reached over and rubbed the dog's long, floppy ears.

Jacqueline sat motionless beside the basket, observing his reaction. Her words were subdued. "The policeman told me about Dart." As she watched Rick, an expectant smile lit her face. "Do you like him?"

"Yes," he confessed.

The puppy waddled toward his burned arm and flopped playfully on his bandages.

"Oh, no!" she said.

The little dog tugged at the tape of his dressing, nipping it with his teeth. Manley felt immensely happy, and yet sad at the same time. Warm tears trickled from his eyes. Jacqueline tried to lift the animal by the scruff of its neck, but it wouldn't budge.

"He's a disaster. Are you okay?"

"I'm fine," he smiled, as the puppy lightly bit his forefinger. "I'm just fine."

Moments later, there was a knock at the door. Manley looked up in time to see a balding, cherubic man hesitate and then enter. The stranger wore the white cotton coat of an attending physician. Curious, Jacqueline cocked her head to look over her shoulder.

"Dr. Schein?" she asked.

That seemed sufficient introduction. Schein nodded to

her and smiled; then he extended his arm and approached Manley. Manley returned the handshake.

"Just came by to say hello." He looked at Jacqueline and then at the puppy. "Hope I'm not intruding."

"Not at all. Just one big happy family," said Manley.

"I'm on my way to a conference, but I understand you wanted to speak with me."

"Yes, very much."

Schein consulted his watch.

"How about after lunch? Say one-thirty?"

"I'll be here."

"Fine. Until later, then." He retreated toward the hall, slowed in the doorway, and turned. "About those syringes the police officer mentioned . . ."

"Yes?"

"Shouldn't they be refrigerated?"

"I presume they are."

"You gave them to the floor nurse for refrigeration?"

A bell of distant warning tolled in Manley's brain. He apprehensively pushed himself up in bed. His throaty words were hoarse with concern.

"No, they should be locked in the lab's refrigerator."

Schein opened his mouth as if to speak but didn't. He frowned, peered out of the corner of his eye, and lightly shook his head in confusion.

"Then I'm at a loss, Dr. Manley. I had assumed it was you," he continued, fixing Manley with his stare. "You see, I've just come from the lab."

Manley's heart beat wildly.

"And?"

"The syringes are gone."

Chapter Twenty-Six

Inside the Pasadena recording studio, work continued well into the evening. Under the bright stage lights, the young female singer held the last high note until her musical accompaniment faded. After receiving a nod from the sound man, she removed her headphones and walked off mike. In the unlit rear of the studio, two individuals intently watched her departure.

"Is she as good as I said or not?"

"Definitely. Better than I expected."

"So we have a deal?"

A pause. "At your price, no. My offer is firm at twenty percent less."

"But her potential . . . She's a gold mine!"

"Entirely up to you. Take it or leave it."

There was a sigh. "All right." They exchanged handshakes. "She's yours."

"Excellent. Tell her I'll meet her in her dressing room in five minutes. And, oh—mention that I brought the surprise I promised."

"She'll understand what that means?"

"She'll know."

The man walked down the aisle in the direction of the sound stage. Several moments later, the woman who had been seated beside him got up and left the studio, strolling out into the warm night air. Above, the sky was a dome of unparalleled beauty. The woman gazed up into the darkened night; a profusion of stars glinted like mica, endless flecks of glistening silicate.

She stood there, reminiscing. It was on one such night that it had begun, long ago. Eight years . . . nine? She had been a struggling actress, then. For nearly twenty years her career had proved uniformly unsuccessful, but unlike many of her acting peers, she had been astute enough to recognize her shortcomings. She had awaited only the right opportunity to go back to her former profession. Her introduction to Hume, not long after he'd opened the Spa, had occurred by chance, backstage, after one of her last roles—was it Shaw? It was one of her most dismal performances, but one which seemed to please him nonetheless. They talked for a long time. She told him about her past and her current displeasure. When he casually mentioned the opportunity at the Spa, she seized it.

She never questioned his genius. However, he'd more than once made it clear that he considered her potential limited. But deep inside, she had never doubted her own ability, her own inner strength.

He had been particularly fascinated with theater, drawing her into lengthy conversations about it. The demands of her new career were many, but she'd still managed to maintain the slender thread of her theatrical connections. He'd even encouraged her in that. And although he had his own supply of patients at the start, he'd increasingly relied on her acting contacts to attract the proper clientele. Yet he never once acknowledged the debt he owed her.

She'd resented the way he'd looked down at her—so sure of himself, so smug. Increasingly, she'd found herself tempted to tell him to piss off, to forget the whole thing. He'd been so certain she was incapable that he hadn't realized what a keen observer she really was. But over the years, she'd figured out what he was doing. Not everything of course—yet enough. Incompetent? What a laugh!

The most marvelous thing about what had happened at the Spa, therefore, was its timing. It couldn't have occurred at a more auspicious moment. For quite a while she'd been wrestling with the dilemma of precisely what to say to him, mulling over how to proceed.

She gave a self-satisfied grin. It was so considerate of all the entanglements to unravel themselves so favorably. She would start again, rebuilding the Spa at a future time, in a different place. Oh, she'd make mistakes in the beginning. But there was plenty of time. Still, there were certain concessions that had to be made to a changing era. Actresses wouldn't do—no, not any longer.

A generation of TV babies had come of age, bringing with them different expectations and a hunger for new forms of the video medium. The dramatic growth of video music was having its impact on the entire entertainment industry.

She had been quick to perceive the implications. A singer's video exposure would be crucial to a successful career. Thus she had begun to purchase young singers' contracts whenever opportune, realizing that proper guidance was far more important than artistic talent. Competition for control was keen, but she possessed something her competitors lacked. Something that was . . . *unique*.

She returned inside and made her way through the darkened corridors to the vocalist's dressing room. Rounding a corner, she let out a sniff of amusement. Gaining access to the hospital had proved far easier than she had anticipated. It was remarkable how old skills could be remembered so quickly. But then, hadn't she been a successful nurse long before she'd become an actress? And now that she had the syringes, everything else should prove rather simple.

She knocked on the singer's door. It opened quickly, revealing a young woman whose plumpish face bore an eager expression. The singer hugged her visitor tightly and then pulled away, beaming.

"I was so afraid he wouldn't sell—thank God!" Still radiant, she clasped her hands together. She seemed hesitant. "Did you bring . . ."

The older woman laughed. "Of course, my dear."

"Are you sure it will work?"

"Absolutely certain." She opened her handbag and withdrew the syringe, holding it upright to squeeze out the bubbles of air.

"There's no catch? Nothing special I have to do?"

"The first thing you have to do," said Miss Howell, slowly turning to eye the young woman with a penetrating stare, "is simply roll up your sleeve."

ABOUT THE AUTHOR

DAVID SHOBIN is an obstetrician and gynecologist who teaches and practices in Long Island, New York. He is the author of two previous novels, the bestselling THE UNBORN and THE SEEDING.

From the bestselling author of *THE SISTERHOOD*

Michael Palmer

The world's best-kept medical secret is also the most deadly . . .

SIDE EFFECTS

· · · · · ·

Dr. Kate Bennett seems to have it all: loving husband, promising career, an offer of promotion to chief of pathology at Boston Memorial. Then she makes a shattering discovery that may cost her not only her career and marriage—but her very life. For Kate is up against a project that important people will stop at nothing to protect, a terrifying medical breakthrough rooted in one of mankind's greatest evils.

Read SIDE EFFECTS, available March 20, 1985, wherever Bantam Books are sold, or use the handy coupon below for ordering:

Coming soon in paperback . . .

THE AQUITAINE PROGRESSION

by
ROBERT LUDLUM

The modern master of the superthriller returns—with his most gripping adventure yet. THE AQUITAINE PROGRESSION is the story of Joel Converse, a man who stumbles onto a shocking international conspiracy involving the world's most renowned military leaders, a conspiracy bent on creating Aquitaine— Charlemagne's dream of an Empire engulfing all of Europe, and the lands across the Atlantic as well. Isolated, running for his life, Converse is the only man alive who can prove that Aquitaine exists . . . that the day of the generals is at hand.

Don't miss Robert Ludlum's THE AQUITAINE PROGRESSION, coming in March 1985, from Bantam Books.